The Bombshell

The Bombshell

DARROW FARR

PAMELA DORMAN BOOKS • VIKING

VIKING
An imprint of Penguin Random House LLC
1745 Broadway, New York, NY 10019

Copyright © 2025 by Darrow Farr

A Pamela Dorman Book/Viking

The PGD colophon is a registered trademark of Penguin Random House LLC.

VIKING is a registered trademark of Penguin Random House LLC.

DESIGNED BY MEIGHAN CAVANAUGH

ISBN 9780593833247

Printed in the United States of America

"A woman lays claim to as many native lands
as she has had happy loves."

—Colette, *Break of Day*

Ajaccio

1993

1. Enlèvement

In the hours before her kidnapping, Séverine Guimard claimed Antoine Carsenti's virginity in a grotto overlooking the Mediterranean Sea. She'd felt his eyes on her since she transferred to the Lycée Laetitia Bonaparte the year before. She knew she wasn't beautiful in the dark-haired, olive-skinned way of the Corsicans around her, but Séverine was something to look at, with her sharp cheekbones and gold-washed hair and huge nose. It was a nose that belonged on the marble bust of a Roman senator, not a seventeen-year-old girl. Her mother always told her she'd look common without it, but Séverine had convinced Papa to pay for a nose job as a combination graduation-birthday gift so long as she passed the baccalauréat next week.

It was perhaps this one flaw that endowed her with a keen awareness of her body, how it moved beneath clothes, how to angle her face in overhead lighting, how to make people watch her. Admittedly, she also possessed a certain magnetism based on her father's position as prefect of Corsica. She'd been to the Élysée for dinner, and President Schneider had kissed her hello; she'd vacationed in Greece with the head of the IMF and his family; she'd even played pétanque with a mid-succession-line Grimaldi on the beach in Monaco one time. But she did not feel like Papa's position and influence eclipsed her infant star; in fact, she was confident that she'd eventually burn brighter than him. She would be an actress, a very famous one whose poster teen boys would tack to their ceilings. Once she had her nose fixed.

Séverine loved how Antoine Carsenti already gawked at her like she was *somebody*; she'd ask to borrow a pen and he'd hand it to her while thanking her for asking him. Last year, he was all baby fat and a bad crew cut, but he'd since shot up and slimmed down, let his hair grow out and parted it down the middle like Leonardo DiCaprio on *Quoi de neuf, docteur?* He wasn't hot yet, but in another year or two, he would be. It was the ideal moment for Séverine to initiate him, before he was corrupted by his new status, when he was still sweet and grateful for her attention.

Seeking a break from all the frantic, last-minute test prep, she had invited Antoine for a beer at the paillote by her house. He was incapable of playing it cool, twisting his cocktail napkin into shreds and asking her dull questions.

"Do you like it better here or in Paris?"

"Paris, obviously. I mean, the beach is nice but otherwise it's so boring. Anyway, I'm going back—well, as long as I pass the bac, I'm starting at Paris III this fall. God, I hope drama school is less of a drag than lycée." She took an anxious drink thinking about the impending exam, which determined whether they'd be going to university or held back for another year of terminale. Although she'd argued in favor of skipping university and going straight to LA (a hard no from her parents), the thought of failing the bac, of her parents' disappointment and embarrassment, of confirming she was a total bimbo airhead, made her want to bury herself alive in the sand.

"My parents think I should 'get a good education' first," Séverine continued with a sigh. "It's annoying, but I guess Hollywood *is* impressed by Shakespeare in the Park types." She didn't expect Antoine to know what Shakespeare in the Park was, and that was the point of name-dropping it. Séverine was worldly, with a French politician father and American poet mother.

"What about you, where are you headed?" she asked.

"I guess l'Université de Corse."

"Are you going to become radicalized there?" she teased. "Join I Fratelli? Write nasty things about my father in the student paper and start thinking of me as a dirty colonizing pinzutu?"

Antoine let out a soft laugh. "All that pro-independence stuff is pretty lame. Besides, I'm not that into politics."

"All Corsicans are into politics," she said. "You can be honest, what do you think of my dad?"

Hesitating, he said, "My parents say it's good he's pushing for autonomy, but it's probably a way to pretend he's fighting for us without changing much." He winced, afraid he'd blown it by telling the truth.

"I get it," Séverine said diplomatically, although Antoine's parents were clearly idiots. "But it's only been a year. He's got a lot of ideas. He really wanted the job; believe me, my mom and I did everything possible to make him turn it down." For a moment, she felt silly articulating this resentment while chewing on a mint leaf fished from her mojito, feet sunk into fine sand that led to the tourmaline-blue sea. Corsica was dead half the year, but now, at the beginning of summer, the island came alive—droves of people traveled from the continent on vacation, the sun emitted powerful golden light well into the evening, and nights were warm as bathwater, made for drinking cold wine. It finally blossomed into the île de beauté the postcards promised, where something exciting might happen for once.

"I guess I'll miss some things about this place," she added with affected wistfulness, gazing towards the water. Then she turned, locking eyes with him. "I'll miss you, for one."

They got a little drunk and walked along the beach as the sun extinguished itself in the ocean. When they reached a tiny cove between the cliffs, Séverine leaned against the rock and pushed her hair out of her face.

"Come here," she said.

"What?" Antoine asked, like a dunce. Séverine placed his hand on her face and took his thumb in her mouth, biting gently. As she closed the distance between them, he leaned away, but once she touched her lips to his, he returned her kiss frantically. She did her best to control the inept speed and pressure of his tongue. It wasn't that pleasant, but this was the deal; she had to be patient as she trained him to do exactly what she liked.

After a few minutes, he pulled back, flushed and shuddery, and said, "You're the most beautiful girl I've ever seen." Séverine knew this was objectively untrue but understood the gist: he felt both blessed and bewildered, unsure how to express or even identify this chaos of emotion. Séverine found it cute; she had chosen him for this gentle, simple nature. She wanted a guy who'd be properly appreciative. His dumb disbelief that she was in his arms, the trembly panic—that's what turned her on. She'd been with boys who were good-looking and knew it, or worse, mediocre boys with an overabundance of confidence, and she'd learned her lesson. These entitled types abounded in Paris, while the Corsican guys in school harassed her out of some insecurity that she thought she was better than them, which was absolutely correct: she *knew* she was better than them.

Now she only kissed boys like Antoine—quiet, decent, and boring, but on the cusp of a change.

She'd guided him onto his back in the sand. "Is this your first time?" she asked, hovering over him. Disoriented, open-mouthed, he nodded. So far, she'd taken the virginities of four boys. Antoine made five. She liked the idea of being never-forgotten, a landmark. She liked the feverish tremors they emitted when she ignored them in the hallway afterwards. Funny enough, her virgins never told people at school what transpired. They had their own private experience of Séverine—what they considered the *real* her, she guessed—and protected it with a touching, misguided loyalty. In reality, they weren't closer to knowing her than anyone else.

She pulled her red dress over her head and untied her bikini bottom, watching Antoine watch her with suspicious anticipation, like she might be pranking him. Once he was inside her, though, his demeanor turned solemn, verging on spiritual.

Sex itself wasn't yet so satisfying for Séverine. She'd read in her mother's American *Cosmo* that women don't reach their sexual peaks until their forties and internalized this fact with patient expectation. Pleasure wasn't the point here; the pleasure of the boys' devotion was. Besides, she had her trusty electric toothbrush she pressed between her legs when she couldn't fall asleep.

She was on the pill, so it didn't concern her when Antoine came without warning, his eyes wide, witnessing some miracle invisible to her. Afterwards, she rolled off him and crouched in the surf to rinse off. It was a relief to be alone in the water. That was the only thing about the virgins; they were like mortals, and she was a god condescending to them. If pleasure wasn't the point, neither was mutual connection, but there was still a small part of her that thought of this ritual as a search for her diamond in the rough: a good guy who contained something interesting that she could excavate and shape, who might inspire her to be at least partially as devoted as he was.

Antoine approached, his feet sloshing annoyingly in the waves; she felt him lift her hair out of the water, twirling it around his hand. The gesture was overly intimate and Séverine's throat burned with embarrassment for him. She jerked her head, and he let go. His adoration, although the objective, was also off-putting. He slid his hands in his pockets, as if he were content to stand staring at her until she instructed otherwise. Sex: such a simple but effective power!

Séverine refused Antoine's offer to walk her home and left him on the beach, watching the waves and taking stock of his new manhood. The bike ride home was uphill and brutal, and Séverine arrived at the neighborhood gate sweaty and breathing through her mouth.

"A vision of poise and class," J.F., the night guard, teased. He sat inside the guardhouse with the door open and a small fan whirring directly on his face.

"If you tried riding up that hill, you'd drop dead," she panted, casting her eyes at his gut.

By the time she arrived at the villa—modeled after a Corsican bergerie where they traditionally kept sheep, with chunky sand-colored stones and a red clay tile roof—it was dark enough that she could see her parents through the living room window. They sat in matching oxblood leather armchairs, reading by the light of a large arc lamp. Her mother flipped through one of her women's magazines imported from the States, a guilty pleasure; her father, some hefty book about World War II. At fifty-two, he was still so handsome, at once boyish and important-looking with silver-streaked hair worn a tad long.

Unthreateningly confident, a generous winker and master of re-assurance, Paul Guimard had entered politics because what else could he possibly do with a personality, a smile, eyes as blue as that? Be a movie star, but he was unfortunately civic-minded. He continued to believe reasonable progress could be made by showing people that what they wanted—big picture—was more or less what their opponents wanted, too. This optimism, plus his ability and willingness to gab with anyone, earned him the prefecture appointment. Séverine resented him for dragging them to this backwater, but it was a resentment tempered by enormous pride. He was destined for greatness, and that meant greatness was Séverine's inheritance, too.

Through the window, Séverine watched her father reach over and rub her mother's earlobe between his fingers while they both continued reading. Every innocuous gesture was imbued with affection. Because of her parents, Séverine understood love to be the harmony of small pleasures and large ambitions. They were formidable figures in their respective fields of politics and literature and viewed each other's successes as a boon to their own careers. So far, that had proven to be correct.

Sometimes this made Séverine feel like the third wheel in their marriage—they were so synced, so alike, and parts of her personality were alien to them. They couldn't fathom how she was so hopeless at school or where these frivolous interests of hers—celebrities, TV, clothes, clubbing—came from. At best, her parents were entertained by her, marveling at how they'd created this person who was charming and outgoing like them but also vastly different. Lately, however, she exasperated them, and they exasperated her with their infuriating contention that they knew what was best for her future.

She ditched her bike on the front lawn and crept to the big picture window, leaping up and smacking her hands against the glass. Both parents jumped at its violent rattling, and her mother yelled in English, "You better get a rag and wipe those handprints! Maria just cleaned!"

Ignoring her, Séverine went to the L-shaped pool behind the house. All the garden lamps had been turned off except those within the pool, and a nimbus of turquoise light hovered over the wobbling water. She pulled the sandy dress over her head and eased down two steps before gliding into the shallow end like a seal. The salt of her sweat, and Antoine's, dissolved away.

Her mother slid open the glass door that led from the kitchen to the back patio, and Séverine could feel the air-conditioning emanating out.

"I'm serious," her mother said.

"I'll do it tomorrow," Séverine replied, spinning to float on her back. The two of them always spoke English, French when her father was present, a mixture of both if she was fighting with them. Her mother was wearing her wire-frame reading glasses and blue-striped pajama shirt. Perhaps not the ideal politician's wife—not the lacquered, ever-smiling, inoffensive beauties she was so often seated beside at dinners—but Bonnie Guimard possessed her own austere allure. She exuded a kind of severe intellectualism informed by the esoteric prose-poems she published in anglophone literary magazines, underscored by a healthfulness that verged on sensuality. More handsome than beautiful, she was straight-backed and immovable-looking. She shared button-down shirts with her husband, swam every morning, and ate black bread standing at the kitchen counter as her wet hair stiffened in the air-conditioning. Séverine admired her mother, but wanted to be nothing like her in these regards.

"What about studying?"

"Done."

"Are you sure? The tutor says you're still shaky on the philosophy questions."

"Maybe you can read Tocqueville for thirteen hours a day, but I'm done," Séverine snapped.

"You're the one who's desperate to leave Corsica," her mother said. "Passing the bac is your ticket out, remember that." She closed the sliding glass door before Séverine could have the last word.

Séverine swam two laps fuming, fantasizing about hitchhiking to the airport and getting on the next plane to Paris. Then she hoisted herself out of the deep end, pausing with her arms taut, examining her breasts and imagining herself on the cover of a men's magazine. If by some miracle she did pass the bac, four more years of school would be such a waste of time—she wished her mom could see that. Alas, she'd be mortified to tell her well-credentialed friends that Séverine was skipping university. Nothing was more important to her than these symbols of academic success; in her mind, that's what made a woman worthy of attention. But Séverine knew better. If you were pretty and magnetic, you didn't need to be brilliant. Bonnie had worked with what she was given, and Séverine would do the same.

After wringing her hair out onto the cement, she dashed through the frigid kitchen and down the hall to her bedroom. Although they'd lived in Corsica for a year, Séverine's room still looked semi-occupied: white walls except for an R.E.M. poster and the print of Van Gogh's *The Bedroom* that had hung in her nursery. Her old bedroom in Paris had been plastered in photographs of her friends and layers of posters that thickened with each new celebrity crush. She'd assumed she'd make new friends to take Polaroids with, collect new totems of her new life in this new room.

But the girls in Ajaccio were wary of outsiders, like everyone in

Corsica, and Séverine's social tactics didn't help. She figured that as the new girl, her best bet was to cultivate mystery through aloofness. She expected them to find her intriguing and exotic, to shyly seek her friendship, and she'd open herself to them little by little until they couldn't remember what days at Laetitia Bonaparte had been like without her. What actually happened is they pegged the girl from Paris with the huge nose as an equally huge bitch. When the girls failed to approach Séverine, she reasoned that they were too provincial to recognize her appeal and told herself that she was better off alone.

After showering in her en suite bathroom and changing into a dry dress, Séverine made to once again slip out the kitchen door.

"Where are you off to now?" her father called from the living room.

"Bike ride," she replied in French.

"Shouldn't you be studying?" he asked, appearing at the kitchen entrance with his big book tucked under one arm.

"Exercise helps blood flow to the brain." Séverine flashed her best smile, knowing how to work him.

Her father moved towards her, placing a heavy hand on her head and caressing the hair along the side of her face. "Take your helmet, and don't be too late," he said, and angled his cheek for a kiss, which she obliged. She would, however, leave the helmet on its hook. Feeling the wind whip her hair back was the best part.

Since spring, Séverine had been riding her bike in circles around the neighborhood, listening to tapes on her Walkman and smoking cigarettes. Her mother, being more American than she'd cop to, found cigarettes revolting and forbade her from smoking. Séverine had been caught only once, shortly after they'd moved to Ajaccio. She'd taken to smoking crouched among the foliage behind the house, looking at the sea, until she accidentally set some of the dry scrub on fire, which she, her screaming mother, and their house-keeper Maria put out with saucepans of pool water. Naturally, a rumor spread around the neighborhood that it had been an I Fratelli plot against her father.

So now, under the guise of a healthy nightly bike ride, she cruised around to Tracy Chapman or R.E.M., imagining herself in a music video, and smoked one thin Vogue Lilas. When the cassette ended, she'd return the bike to the shed, dizzy from nicotine and wind. It was quaint compared to how she got her kicks in Paris: drinking vodka–orange juice at Pilar's or Hélène's (more likely Pilar's because her parents were always traveling and didn't notice when a bottle of Absolut mysteriously disappeared), applying makeup in front of Pilar's full-length mirror before trying and failing to get into Les Bains Douches, then ending up dancing with all the other lycéens at Le Vinyl.

The night was balmy and the insects shrill. Séverine rode through the neighborhood and past J.F., who was watching a football match on a handheld TV and eating a kebab, too occupied to notice her leave.

She turned onto the road that led down to the beach, the moon-light glinting knifelike along the waves. She stopped to extract the cigarettes and matches from her pocket. A car crept past as she lit up. Its ruby taillights floated down the pitch-dark street towards the beach, then stopped a few blocks away. Undoubtedly it was a couple taking a moment to kiss in front of the view, she thought wistfully.

She'd chosen the "What Is Love" cassette single as her sound-track tonight. There was something both urgent and melancholy about the synths that gave her a fluttery longing feeling. She imag-ined a stranger approaching from across a smoky dance floor, his motion slashed by strobe lights, pressing a pill onto her tongue. She balanced the cigarette between her lips, pressed play, and pushed off, gaining speed as she coasted down the hill, feeling like a bird flying towards the water.

In the instant she reached the idling car, the passenger door flew open and a man jumped out, grabbing the back of Séverine's dress and tearing her from her bike.

It felt like being swallowed backwards into a black hole—overpowering, confusing, terrifying. The bike continued a few meters, like it was running for help, before careening on its side and skidding into the bushes. Séverine's head knocked against the man's, that unmistakable shock of bone on bone. In this moment, everything that had seemed so slow and accidental became chilling and real: a man's body pressed against hers, his arms coiled around her rib cage. She began to scream, the sound scorching her throat. She bucked her legs and beat her fists against the man's thighs; she felt possessed by some savage, essential force, a fear that had its own intelligence.

A second man wearing a ski mask appeared in the faint red glow of the taillights with a roll of duct tape. With shaking hands, he forced a rag into her mouth, his fingernails grazing her palate. Reflexively, she gagged and bit down; the man cursed and slapped her full on the cheek. She had never been hit in her life. The shock of it was so intense that at first she felt nothing, then a fiery stinging spread across her face.

"Relax, man," the person holding her reprimanded. There was a disconcerted note in his voice, like he didn't expect that kind of behavior from the guy who was now stuffing the rag back into her mouth and sealing it with tape. This time, she was too stupefied to resist. As he wound more tape around her wrists, he avoided her stare, as if ashamed. Then he tied the blindfold over her eyes. Where the fuck was J.F.? Hadn't he heard her screaming?

She felt herself pulled upright by a formidable strength. The second man took her by the ankles, and they hauled her up like a trussed pig. The terror was paralyzing, yet at the same time, a part of her was able to see what was happening as if watching a movie: the ski masks, the duct tape, how they were opening the trunk and dropping her inside, slamming the door, pulling away with a conspicuous squealing of wheels. It was exactly like some clichéd action movie, the kind she considered too dumb to watch.

Since her kidnapper had bound her hands in front of her, Séverine managed to peel the tape away from her mouth and remove the gag and blindfold. A strip of tape was stuck to her hair; on top of everything, she'd probably have to cut it out. At first, she cried and shouted and kicked at the door with her one red espadrille—she must have lost its mate in the struggle—but as the car jostled along, stopping and starting and turning without warning, nausea roiled from gut to throat, and she vomited mojito. She lay tucked all the way back in the trunk, skin chafing on the coarse carpet, left cheekbone throbbing, avoiding the mess of bilious rum, trying and failing to dispel her claustrophobia.

Over the next hour or so, Séverine managed to calm down and think more objectively. First, she determined this was an I Fratelli job, not the mafia. If she knew one thing about the Corsican mafia, it was the best-functioning bureaucracy on the island. To kidnap the daughter of the most powerful politician on the island, they'd hire Sardinian professionals, but these guys were amateurs, Séverine thought as she bit at the silver tape around her wrists. Not even tying them behind her back.

That said, I Fratelli had plenty of experience with kidnappings: only six months ago, they'd taken the son of the owner of AC Ajaccio.

Everyone knew the football club laundered money for I Fratelli, but rumors began to circulate that the owner was skimming off the top. He paid three hundred thousand francs and his son was returned the next day, after a night spent eating chips and playing Nintendo with his masked captors. But he wasn't a girl, Séverine considered with a chill.

Maybe it was that new group, Novi Patriotti, who'd announced their defection from I Fratelli on New Year's Day. But according to her dad, Novi Patriotti was busier messing with I Fratelli than the French government. He said most of these "militants" were less concerned with independence than lining their pockets with extorted money they framed as a "revolutionary tax" and acting like big shots.

Surely, Séverine's captors would hold her in some literal pigsty for the night, call her father demanding—in their eyes—an ungodly sum of money that her family wouldn't bat an eye withdrawing, and she'd be returned by morning. Maybe she'd even get a postponement on the bac! Papa would see that the police apprehended these assholes mere hours after her release. It was possible the police were already trailing them, waiting for the car to pull over so they could avoid a chase on these dark, dangerously narrow roads. Messing with the island's moneyed class was one thing, but kidnapping the prefect's daughter was another. They'd be made an example of.

After what could have been one hour or three, the car stopped and the engine turned off. Once they took her out of the trunk, she'd make a run for it, she decided. Heart pounding, she put the tape back over her mouth, sans gag, and retied the blindfold, positioning it so she could just see over it with one eye. The trunk leapt open with a hollow click.

"Oh, beurk," a man said, recoiling from the stench of her vomit, which mortified her.

He took her by the wrists and guided her out. "Swing your legs around. That's it," he said, pulling her upright. The ends of her hair were pasted to the skin of her back; it was puke, she realized, nause- ated. She tentatively lowered her feet—one bare, one still wearing the red espadrille—until they touched the ground.

He led her towards an idling vehicle just ahead; its headlights scarcely penetrated the thick blackness of the night. It was so dark she had no sense of which direction she should run with her one shoe. The air smelled of eucalyptus and thyme, no trace of salt, and it was cooler and less humid than by the coast. They must be up in the ma- quis, the precipitous interior of the island, where boars ran wild.

Séverine hadn't spent any time up here; it was craggy and sparsely populated, the land of the treacherous snowcapped mountains you saw from the beach. She was not an outdoorsy person, and the ex- tremities of nature held no fascination for her. Every year, hikers were seriously injured or even died trekking the GR20 through these inhospitable mountains, and those were people who'd trained for their expedition. It was also wildfire season. If she ran off into this opaque darkness, she was as good as dead, she rationalized as she reluctantly let herself be guided into the trunk of the second car.

"All good?" a third person asked from the front seat, his voice thinner and younger. The trunk was not closed off from the main cab, so they must have switched from a sedan to a 4x4, she realized. After only a few minutes, the car turned and began shuddering back and forth, metal jangling violently. They had veered off paved roads and were traveling farther up into the maquis. The men were too edgy to speak, and in any case, the 4x4's rattling was deafening. The fear she'd managed to diminish in the first car returned thicker and heavier. She was so far from her parents, and she had no idea who these men were or what they would do with her.

After maybe another twenty minutes, the car stopped again. She heard the doors creak open and shut and gravel crunch underfoot. The trunk groaned as someone lifted it open, and unseasonably crisp night air rushed in.

"Come on," the man who'd hit her said. Already, she recognized his voice as different from the other two, his diction more precise and accent less Italianate. It was the voice of someone who hadn't spent his entire life on the island.

He led her towards a cottage, dark save a slab of stone illuminated by a dingy light beside the front door; around the house, shadowy patches of scrub and scraggly trees silhouetted black against the plum-colored sky. Entering the cottage meant resigning herself to their unknowable schemes; it meant having to wait for someone to save her.

"Do I have to go inside?" she asked in a small voice, pressing her heels into the gravel. But the man only pulled her more forcefully. There was no other choice; the screen door whined open, and she was over the threshold.

"She's covered in puke," said the third man, if you could call him that; he sounded like a teenage boy.

"I'd actually love a shower," Séverine piped up.

"Let's get something clear right now: you are not a guest, you are a prisoner of war," the man who'd hit her snapped.

A prisoner of war. The pompousness, the delusion! These bored little boys ran around blowing up construction sites and shooting at each other and had the audacity to call it "war." And now, Séverine was caught in the cross fire of one of their stupid games.

"She's gonna stink up the whole place," argued the man who'd first grabbed her.

The man who'd hit her hesitated. "Make it quick, and straight to the closet afterwards."

With a tentative hand hovering over her shoulder, the boy led her down a short hallway and through a door to her left. He flicked on the switch and dim orange light filtered through her blindfold.

"No one's watching me shower, prisoner of war or not," she spat. "Out."

"What if you lock yourself inside? No, no, Bruno would lose it—"

"Bruno—" she interrupted him. "He's the one in charge?"

The boy said nothing, just helped her step over the ledge of the tub and closed the shower door. Séverine took off her blindfold and draped her foul clothing over the door. The frosted glass distorted the boy's features, but she could tell he was tall, easily 1.9 meters, with a bleached buzz cut and protruding ears. It was as if a child's head rested atop an ungainly man's body. He was leaning against the sink but unable to keep still, a nervous wreck. As for the room, it was tiny, covered in outdated peach tile. To her left was the closed door, to her right a pebble glass window the size of a pizza box; small, but not so small she couldn't squeeze through.

When she turned the taps, she noticed her hands shaking. She peed in the shower—appalling, but preferable to being monitored on the toilet. As she dragged a bar of streaked yellow soap across her sore skin, she thought how strange it was to perform such a quotidian act in this hostile place. She carefully recalled what had just happened to her. It was as if she'd somehow slipped into a parallel dimension; a part of her was certain she was simultaneously at home in her bedroom, listening to the new Cranberries tape on her boom box and combing her hair, getting ready for bed.

"We won't touch you, if you're scared about that," the boy said above the torrent of water.

"But you did touch me. Your boss there—Bruno, is it?—hit me in the face."

"He did?" the boy asked, surprised. "Well, I meant . . . you know."

"I see," she said. This boy could not hurt her, she realized. He might help her, even, if she played it right. "What *did* you agree to do with me?"

Someone rapped loudly at the door. "That's long enough," a man said from the other side; not Bruno, but the one who'd grabbed her off her bike.

Obediently, she shut off the water, and the boy tossed her a thin, stiff towel.

"What am I supposed to wear?" she asked.

He called for someone to bring her a dress or something; the bathroom door opened and closed, and the boy handed her a wash-faded navy cotton dress. It was an enormous, shapeless smock, sleeveless with gaping armholes that exposed the sides of her breasts. He had not provided any underwear.

"Can you help me with something?" she asked.

"What?"

"I can't get this duct tape out of my hair."

"Um. Okay. But you have to put the blindfold back on."

"Not that one, it's all nasty," she said. "The tape's kind of on the back of my head, so you can stay behind me and I won't see you."

Facing the peach tile wall, she heard the shower door clatter open and felt his fingers lift the tape, gently picking at each strand of hair.

"You should have said something before you washed your hair," he admonished. "I might have to cut it out now."

"How old are you?" she asked.

"Eighteen," he replied.

"I'll be eighteen in a month," Séverine said, and they both seemed to wonder at sharing even one thing in common.

The bathroom door opened, and Séverine instinctively whirled around: in the doorframe stood a hulking man in a black leather racing jacket, his dark hair buzzed like the boy's, with a thick mouth and sunken eyes and the shadow of a unibrow. She saw the boy, too: long, blond eyelashes, a crooked nose, and his bottom lip full and wet, a baby's pout. As soon as the man saw Séverine see him, he slammed the door shut.

"Why the fuck is her blindfold off?" he barked.

"She was in the shower," the boy stammered. He swung around, frantically looking for the damp strip of fabric that Séverine had dropped to the floor. She crouched to pick it up and retied it herself.

"It's on. I didn't see anything," she lied.

The door burst open and the man's rough hand grabbed Séverine's wrist, pulled her from the humid bathroom, and pinned her against the hallway wall. A cold and heavy metal object pressed against her chest. Without ever having been in such proximity to a gun, she recognized it immediately. Its heaviness seemed more than a material property; its awful potential burdened it with weight like a body. For the first time in her short life, she realized how delicate and uninsured her existence was. It was stupid, absurd how impermanent she was, how this little machine could extinguish her with a twitch of a finger. What a colossal waste it would be for her exceptional future to vanish at the hand of this troll.

"This is not a game," he told her with an edge of desperation, a plea. The direction of his voice turned back towards the bathroom. "*You* might be interested to know what prison's like, but I'm not going back because of this bullshit."

"What the hell are you doing?" She heard the man who hit her—Bruno—charge down the hallway.

"She saw us," the other man said.

"Put the gun down! Jesus," Bruno spat. "You think we have any leverage if she's dead?"

The man removed the gun from her breastbone, and she massaged the spot as if she'd been wounded just by its touch.

"She's been here ten minutes, and already you're pointing a gun at her?" Bruno yelled. "Both of you need to pull it together. They're expecting a call in twenty minutes."

"My parents?" Séverine asked. "You've spoken to them?"

Bruno ignored her questions. "Are you hungry? Do you need to use the toilet?"

"No," she said, frustrated. "Have you spoken to my parents? Do they know what happened?"

"Then you'll be brought to your cell."

The man in the leather jacket placed his hand between her shoulder blades, but she planted her feet. "When am I going home?" Séverine asked, steadying her voice, using the tone of the inconvenienced wealthy.

"That depends on the cooperation of the occupation regime," Bruno said. "And your parents."

Without further discussion, the other man led her a short way down the hallway, opened a door, and thrust her inside. Her back thumped against a wall, and the door was shut before she could object. She pulled down the blindfold and found herself surrounded by a dense blackness, much darker than inside the trunk. Before her arms fully extended, her fingers touched wood. They had stuck her in a closet, no wider than one and a half meters. She ran her hands down the wood until they met a doorknob. It wouldn't budge.

It was sweltering inside the closet, and she felt like she was in a coffin, buried underground, overwhelmed again with claustrophobia. To top it all off, the fucking tape was still tangled in her hair. The last vigilant part of her told her to cry quietly, that she should keep up this charade of strength and defiance for her dignity, but

Séverine no longer cared. She wailed low, a sound that made her ears ring, and the crevices of her face and neck filled with tears.

A knuckle rapped against the door. "Quiet down," the boy pleaded.

"I'm suffocating in here," she wailed.

"There's a fan to the right of the door. Turn the knob at the base."

Whatever antiquated contraption they'd placed in the closet whirred to life like a jet engine, sweeping staid air along her face. The closet was too small for her to stretch her legs all the way, so she propped her ankles against the wall and stared at the darkness above her.

Beyond, she heard the murmurings of men. How was any of this real? How did any powers, earthly or otherwise, allow her of all people to find herself in this situation? How could her parents have let this happen? She couldn't help but start crying again, quietly. She folded her legs against her chest, and the moments before she'd left the house flashed before her with the haziness of last night's dream as it dissipates from memory: the safe glow from the windows, her mother's glossy magazine draped over her knee, her father's hand on her cheek.

2. *Negotiations*

At first, Séverine assumed the knocking at the door was her mother, waking her at an ungodly hour of morning. But then she smelled the stale cedar air and saw the crack below the door so close to her nose, and she remembered.

The lock clicked. "Your blindfold better be on." The voice belonged to the man in the leather jacket, deeper than the others, and the way he rolled his *r*'s was more discernibly Corsican.

Séverine felt around for the rag, then tied it around her head. "It's on."

"Breakfast," he said, and she sensed him set a plate on the blankets beside her.

"Haven't you gotten a hold of my parents?"

He hesitated. "Yes."

"So when am I going home?" she asked.

He closed the door without replying, which was an answer of sorts. The men's demands must be obscene, something more problematic than money. But her father would make a more realistic counteroffer, in a manner that made them think this was what they actually wanted all along. That's what he did—made everyone think they were walking away triumphant, like they'd pulled one over on Paul Guimard or the Parti socialiste. Only later would they realize they'd been finessed into compromising.

On the plate were three biscottes, each smeared with a layer of butter and raspberry jam, and a liter bottle of water, which she unscrewed and drank a third of in one go. When she finished eating, she pushed the plate into the corner with her foot and leaned against the back of the closet, hugging the water bottle the way she used to hold her stuffed bunny, Milou. If she closed her eyes, she could imagine herself back in her Paris bedroom with Milou, under the canopy of her antique Chinese wedding bed. It was a strange piece for a child's room, but she'd loved its intricate carvings of temples and ginkgo trees and emperors and courtesans.

But her parents had sold her beloved bed to some collector when they moved, and Séverine now wept at the thought of it. They never should have left Paris; she hated her father for evicting her from that lovely life where she had cool girlfriends and partied every weekend and was popular at school. It had been the worst year of Séverine's life, and this kidnapping was the cherry on top.

All of a sudden, her intestines knotted. She retied the blindfold and pounded on the door, crying, "I have to use the bathroom!"

The door opened, and the big, rough hand of the man in the leather jacket pulled her from the floor and marched her half a meter down the hall. He nudged her into the toilet and closed the door, leaning his weight against the pliant wood.

Trembling, Séverine pushed the blindfold up over her forehead and sat on the toilet seat. The room was even smaller than the closet, and she felt too aware that she was separated from the man by only a few centimeters of wood and plaster. However, she couldn't hold it. She tried to go quietly, but her insides were so irritated. It didn't take long for the man to walk away; he didn't want to hear this either. The indignity of the situation brought fresh tears. When she finished, she was returned to the closet without a word. She could tell the man was just as embarrassed as she was.

The bergerie was strangely quiet. What she did hear was the constant smacking of a screen door in the back of the house. It didn't sound like purposeful coming and going, rather restless pacing, the men's attempts to busy themselves while they waited. It was only morning; no need to despair. At any moment, the telephone might ring; minutes later, they'd fling open the closet door and drive her to some obscure spot in the maquis. Before scurrying off, they'd instruct her to count to one hundred, and at ninety-nine, she'd untie her blindfold to find the police crashing through the trees with her parents close behind.

Instead, the rest of the morning passed in a fog of shallow sleep during which she floated on the surface of strange, tense, thirsty dreams where someone was standing in the doorway of the closet watching her sleep, and she couldn't tell if she was being rescued or in danger.

In the afternoon, the man in the leather jacket came with lunch.

"What's happening?" Séverine asked.

"You'll know when you're going home," he replied. "It's not like we're gonna keep you around for fun once we've reached an agreement with Jonnart."

"Jonnart?" She was not expecting him to invoke the minister of the interior. There was the familiar burning she always felt upon hearing his name, the irrational dread that whoever had brought him up knew about the party two Christmases ago. "What about my father?"

"This is beyond his pay grade," he said, closing her in.

He'd brought a sandwich on a fresh baguette, cut on the diagonal; it looked like the ones sold at her old bakery on Rue des Tournelles and tasted just as good, too, with a light smear of butter and mustard, lean ham, and sharp Gruyère. It revived her enough so she could begin the tedious work of picking the duct tape from her hair.

The rest of the day passed at an agonizingly slow tick. She was uncomfortable and anxious; the isolation and lack of light were unspooling her senses. Never in her life had she been so full of nervous anticipation and so bored—no TV, no magazines, not even a clock to watch. All she had were her tormenting thoughts: questions she had no answers to, memories that only intensified her discomfort. She cried out of self-pity, but also because there was nothing else to do.

Please, God, please, get me out of here, I promise I'll study really hard for the bac, I'll be a better person, and when I'm famous I'll donate ten percent of my income to charity and, and . . . Screw that. No, once she got out of here, she'd tell her parents what they could do with the bac. She'd ask her American grandparents to release a portion of her trust fund, and she'd go off to LA and be in movies, like she was born to do. No more wasting time.

Séverine spent the rest of the day wiping her tears with the hem of her enormous dress and standing very slowly to stretch her legs and reach her arms up to the ceiling, feeling drugged by the rush of blood. She could only wait for the next event to occur and hope it was in her favor. It enraged and flustered her that she was now a person who things happened to, when all her life, she'd felt like the force happening unto others.

As the day dragged on, the slit of sun beneath the door faded until someone flicked on a watery light in the hallway. Shortly there-

after, the front door opened and closed. She knew it was Bruno—
she could sense an attention directed towards him; not only hers,
but that of the men inside the house.

"So?" the other man asked.

Bruno said nothing as his boots stomped in the direction of the
closet. Séverine quickly retied her blindfold, and the door swung
open.

"Am I going home?" Séverine asked.

"They're not capitulating to our demands."

"Who, my family?" Séverine exclaimed, scandalized. "I don't believe you."

"No, your parents have held up their end of the deal. I mean the
state," Bruno clarified.

She paused, processing what that meant. "How much did you get
from my parents?"

He hesitated. "Five million francs."

Séverine let out a laugh like a bark. Five million francs! It was a
ridiculous sum, a Hollywood amount of money. There was no way
her parents had five million francs in cash, ready for withdrawal.
They must have had to ask all their rich friends for help, or her
American grandparents, or secured some kind of government loan.
The nerve of these men, who understood nothing about how things
like money or politics worked. To be so ignorant, and so vindi-
cated!

"Five million francs," she repeated coldly. "That's not enough?"

"No," Bruno said. "It's not. Honestly, it's not an unreasonable ask."

"Then why am I still here?" Séverine asked, jaw clenched.

"The government doesn't give a shit about us, but I thought it
would give a shit about you. I guess I was wrong," he said with a bitter, exhausted laugh and shut the door.

Séverine didn't move, frozen in disbelief. Five minutes later, the man in the leather jacket delivered a bowl of beef stew and a bottle of water. The meat was tender, but she dropped the spoon in the full bowl and pushed it into the corner. Twenty-four hours had passed, and with each hour that slipped away, the chance of some rescuer kicking through the door seemed less and less likely. The disbelief began to curdle into unease. Someone—Jonnart—was fucking this up, and she was paying the price.

It was not good to think that way; she must trust her parents. Surely, her panicked mother was at the commissariat, refusing to sit, making rude demands in her heavily accented French to the overwhelmed police; her father in his office at the prefecture, on the phone, speaking calmly although his nostrils flared with each breath, a sign he was on the brink of a rare eruption.

Although she knew some version of this scene must be transpiring, sitting in the darkness, hearing her captors' clinking utensils as they silently ate, it was much easier to imagine her parents as they were when she left the house—forever suspended in that moment, unaware their daughter was missing.

This irrational thought made Séverine irrationally angry. She couldn't believe they'd let this happen to her. *It's above his pay grade*, the man had said. Séverine had never considered that anything might be out of her papa's domain; this realization embarrassed her, made her see her father, for the first time, as ineffectual and inept, a small fry. She felt afraid and alone, lost in a world that had previously seemed safe and familiar, where danger was merely tantalizing, not so terrible and real.

⁓

The next morning, Séverine was woken again by a knuckle rapping at the door.

"Breakfast." It was Bruno. The door opened, and she flinched when he placed the plate directly on her lap. It was a hot, silky omelette—thugs though they were, these guys could really cook.

She sensed him standing there watching her eat. "Is there something I can help you with?" she sneered.

"Yes, actually," he replied. "Your parents want a message from you, to know you're unharmed."

"Am I?" she asked, pointing to her tender cheek.

"I'm sorry, but you *bit* me," Bruno replied.

"What, you thought you'd grab me off my bike and place me in the trunk just so, like a little doll?" Séverine acted this out with mincing hand gestures. "And that I'd be ever so pleased about the whole thing?"

"I expected you'd know your life depends on your compliance," Bruno said.

This shut her up. Was he sorry he hit her, or was he capable of doing worse? The fact that she didn't know, that the answer seemed to switch erratically, further calcified the fear that had begun to grow like a new bone inside her.

"If you want to go home, you have to do what I say," he told her more gently.

"And what's that?"

"Just a quick recording. Move over. To your right."

Bruno entered the closet, and she heard a click. Then he shut the door behind him.

"What are you doing?" Séverine asked, panicked.

"Nothing, relax." He seemed astonished by her alarm. "I just don't want the recorder to pick up ambient noise. You can take off your blindfold. See?"

After she removed it, Séverine noticed a piece of cotton twine above her head, connected to a bare bulb in the ceiling. So there'd been a light in here this whole time. By this dreary yellow light, she took in Bruno: knees tucked to his chest, a ski mask covering his face, his eyes, visible through the mask, a deep brown. He wore light jeans with big holes in the knees, black Doc Martens crusted in dried mud, and a white T-shirt with the Jordache horse head logo. She hadn't expected her kidnapper to look so . . . urbane.

"All right?" he asked.

She nodded and tugged up the neckline of her dress.

He dug in his back pocket for a sheet of yellow lined paper. "I prepared your statement."

She scanned the text while he clicked a new tape into a handheld recorder. The handwriting was small and slanted, all caps, the product of a hurried hand and mind.

"Hi, Maman and Papa, this is your daughter, Séverine." She stopped. "She's American, I call her 'Mom.' This doesn't sound anything like me."

"It doesn't have to—they just need to know you're alive."

"Now 'alive' is good enough? We can forget about 'unharmed'?"

"Yes, I think 'alive' will suffice for your parents." He pressed record and nodded, signaling her to begin.

"Hi, Mom and Papa, this is Séverine. I just wanted to let you know that I'm safe and unharmed." She narrowed her eyes at Bruno. "Soffiu di Libertà is feeding me, they have given me adequate shelter and are treating me in accordance with the Geneva Conventions relative to the treatment of prisoners of war." It was ridiculous, this script. Maybe it proved she was alive, but it wouldn't comfort them; if anything, these force-fed words would frighten them more.

"Really, I can't spend one more day here. I'm sweating to death in this tiny closet, and they're feeding me pretty well, but I'm *so* bored. Please, please, just do whatever they ask," she spat out in English. Bruno clicked off the recorder.

"What did you just say?" he snapped.

"You don't know English?" she asked disdainfully.

"Stick to the script," Bruno muttered. He rewound the tape and pressed record.

"Hi, Mommy and Papa, this is Séverine! I just wanted to let you know that I'm safe and unharmed!" It was as if she had sprinted through the front door, breathlessly relating some juicy gossip to her mother.

Bruno shut off the recorder a second time. "Do I need to explain why you should take this seriously?"

"I don't want to sound stiff," she said.

"Séverine, it doesn't matter. It's not one of your school plays."

It was the first time he or any of the other men had said her name, and his casualness was appalling. Also, how did he know she acted? Particularly as she'd resigned from theater club in protest after the part of Hélène in *La guerre de Troie n'aura pas lieu* was given to Chantal Cipriani, a wooden performer who didn't personally comprehend the burden of beauty.

Like a newscaster, she read the statement precisely. "Hi, Mom and Papa, this is Séverine. I just wanted to let you know that I'm safe and unharmed. Soffiu di Libertà is feeding me, they have given me adequate shelter and are treating me in accordance with the Geneva Conventions relative to the treatment of prisoners of war. They've received your donation and thank you. However, it is essential that you convince Monsieur Jonnart to release the political prisoner Matteu Casanova right away." She paused to look questioningly at Bruno—this was the reason she was still here? Jonnart wouldn't agree to a straightforward prisoner swap?—but he rolled his wrist impatiently, and she continued. "This point is nonnegotiable. Failing to concede will endanger my life."

Bruno clicked off the recorder, the last words of the statement weighing down the air like an additional layer of heat.

"We have to play hardball here. Or at least give that impression," Bruno said, but she was not reassured by the words of this faceless person with such intense, calculating eyes. The Paris-appropriate outfit, his pretension, his vacillation between threats and overfamiliarity— Séverine couldn't figure out how it added up, what kind of person this guy truly was.

"Ah!" he said, pushing himself to his feet. "I forgot." In the few moments between his opening and closing the door, Séverine found herself tilting like a plant towards the light coming from outside. Then she was again surrounded by the weak artificial yellow of the lightbulb. She was so close to the front door, only four or five paces between the closet and the outside. But outside was a different kind of trap.

Bruno returned with a rolled-up newspaper in his hand.

"I'm sure you'll like this," he said, and although his mouth was covered, Séverine sensed a wry smile beneath the cagoule. He unfurled the paper, and she recognized her school portrait, enlarged and in color, on the front page of *Le Monde*. She'd blow-dried her hair, and it shone more gold, less brown in the overhead lighting. She was smiling closemouthed, lips painted a light shade of raisin. The first two buttons of her tight black cardigan opened to reveal a tasteful hint of cleavage, and her hazel eyes gleamed naughtily.

Séverine had been so delighted with how it turned out. Her photo lacked the stiffness of her classmates' and looked much more like a famous actress's headshot. She'd hoped to communicate her specialness, her vivacity, and a sense of destiny via these school photos. Now seeing her portrait on the front page of the newspaper, she confirmed she'd been successful.

"I need you to read the date and headline," Bruno said, clicking on the recorder.

"June 8, 1993. 'The Search for Séverine Continues,'" she read, her voice a bit dreamy. "'Soffiu di Libertà Demands Release of Convicted Terrorist.'"

He turned off the recorder. "That's fine."

"This is you? Soffiu di Libertà?" she asked.

"That's us," Bruno said with pride.

"I've never heard of you," she sniffed. "I thought maybe you were the new one. Novi Patriotti."

Bruno screwed up his face. "No way. I mean, sure, José Kadiri—he's the head guy—is less compromised than I Fratelli, but he's a lot of talk. They've only pulled off one attack since the scission."

"What do they call it when they plant a bunch of trees and flowers on like, golf courses and rich people's lawns?" Séverine asked.

"Re-maquisation," Bruno mumbled.

"Yeah! That's pretty cool."

"It's more of an art installation than actual resistance." He seemed to like the sound of this. "Novi Patriotti's a performance art troupe, and I Fratelli's a bunch of mafiosos. With Fanfan as the godfather."

Séverine had heard this name before—Fanfan Bartoli—her father spoke of him with exasperation. It was an open secret that he was the head of I Fratelli. On the record, however, he was an esteemed small-business owner.

"What's so different about you guys?" she asked sarcastically.

"Everything," he said. He took the newspaper from her, opened it up, and carefully tore out a narrow section from the front page. "It's all here," he said, letting the scrap of paper fall to her lap before he left.

She skimmed the florid manifesto in which Soffiu di Libertà stated their objective: to win independence from the French colonizers through a people's revolution, install a true socialist democracy, encourage self-sufficiency by supporting the island's agricultural sectors, halt the wanton development of the coast, and ensure that the future of Corsica was decided by Corsicans alone. There was also some stuff directed to Corsican youth, exhorting them to decolonize their minds and dedicate themselves to a greater cause.

As if! Cars, clothes, girls—that's what the guys in her high school cared about, not independence. Not to say they weren't proud Corsicans, with the gold pendants in the shape of the island they wore around their necks and the specifically Corsican machismo they aspired to. But militants were impractical dreamers and therefore unmanly, despite their guns. Her papa was an idealist, but even he said every hooded radical squawking about *Corsica libera* and *A Francia fora* lacked the brains and discipline necessary to run their own organization, let alone a country. She was sure Soffiu di Libertà was no different.

Her third night in the closet passed restlessly, unease moving through her system like poison. She didn't get why Jonnart wouldn't just release that prisoner. What did he care? This rankled Séverine on a personal level; he *knew* her. Ostensibly, she even enticed him, gross as it was to think about. Or, she thought with alarm, did he resent her for pushing him away that night? Was he punishing her?

She dared to consider what the men would do with her if Jonnart refused to release that prisoner. They couldn't lose face by returning her without receiving their full ransom, but they also couldn't keep her in this closet forever. *Failing to concede will endanger me.* She had a powerful sense of all she was meant to do and become in this life; surely no one would be endowed with that clairvoyance if they were fated to die before it was realized. At the same time, a small part of her was beginning to think nothing was under her control, and nothing was predetermined either—what happened to you was total chaos. This frightened her most of all.

On her fourth day, the door opened and closed only four times; once for lunch and dinner, twice so she could relieve herself.

"I'd like to take another shower," Séverine said when the man in the leather jacket brought her dinner. "I'm soaked in my own sweat."

"After what you pulled last time? Not a chance," he responded, shutting her in. The boy came shortly after with a cold, moistened washcloth, which was insufficient but not unappreciated.

By the fifth day, Séverine suspected she might truly be losing her mind. She felt like a caged animal, her muscles atrophied as veal. Whenever one of the men escorted her to the bathroom, her legs trembled. She'd doze in a semiconscious state during the day's long, silent stretches. Then all of a sudden, a car door would slam, the house would be full of the men's clomping, and a radio would be turned to its highest setting, blasting "Alison" by Jordy. His five-year-old soprano sliced right through the walls, rattling around Séverine's skull as the men talked below the earsplitting music.

They were hesitant to speak to her. They seemed tired, and worse, nervous. It made them harder to read and less predictable.

In turn, she felt her spirit—the flame inside her she'd always been so proud to possess, the element that made her more special and more capable—flickering in and out. She was shocked and disappointed by her sniveling demureness, her failure to remain the brassy heroine, to charm the men into returning her without their full ransom, her willingness to lie supine in the closet and waste away. Her sense that this was now her life was beginning to overtake any certainty that she'd get out and go back to normal. Her fear solidified into something dull and inanimate, a numbness and resignation that made her days both bearable and bleak.

On the sixth day, Bruno knocked at the door. Wearily, she tied her now-grimy blindfold.

"I need your help again," he said.

She shrugged and began to cry. She'd wanted to avoid crying any more in front of these men, but she'd lost all resolve.

"Fuck!" In a burst of rage, Bruno kicked the door, and that scared Séverine's tears away.

"I'm sorry. It's not you—Jonnart is fucking it up for everyone. This should have been over days ago. It was supposed to be straight-forward! Fuck!" Bruno roared.

Séverine said nothing. He was framing the situation like it wasn't his fault she was here, but Jonnart's. Like he and Séverine were on the same side, against the minister of the interior. Truth be told, she had no love for Jonnart. Again, she remembered the Christmas party in the sumptuous apartment of some politician or other: her black velvet dress, how it slunk around her hips, the low cowl neck, how womanly she felt wearing it along with a pair of her mother's stilet-tos; passing Jonnart in the narrow hallway on her way to the bath-room, the palpable brush of his eyes along her body.

"Screw it," Bruno said. "Do you want to go outside? We can re-cord outside." As if he were doing her a favor by offering to take her outside after almost a week in a closet.

"Just don't try to make a run for it. We're in the middle of no-where, and it's super dangerous to wander around if you don't know where you're going. I'm not saying that to scare you, it's true."

"What's the point of the closet then?" Séverine grumbled.

He helped her to her feet, then guided her by the shoulders down the hall and to the left. Séverine felt the sun warm her face even be-fore Bruno opened the screen door. She stepped over the threshold, from linoleum to cement. The morning air trembled with the threat of impending heat, but there was a weak, welcome breeze. The herbal scent of the maquis, the movement of the air, the birds calling to each other struck her with a sharp, exaggerated force. She remembered she was a human being with a body that experienced sensations, including pleasant ones.

Bruno led her onto grass and pressed down on her shoulders, encouraging her to sit. The gentle wind lifted a strand of hair from her face.

"We need you to record a statement addressed directly to Jonnart," Bruno said.

"It won't make a difference," she said flatly.

"You're underselling yourself. Here." He placed a sheet of paper in her lap. "Take off the blindfold."

She found herself sitting on a modest lawn, looking towards the edge of the maquis, short, dense pines surrounding them on all sides. To the left was a vegetable garden, and the wholesome domesticity of it struck her as perverse.

"Eyes here." Bruno sat cross-legged before her with his mask on. It was strange to spend all this time with someone without seeing their face. She'd at least caught glimpses of the boy and the man in the leather jacket, but Bruno was still a mystery. She sensed he was good-looking and knew it; something about the way he carried himself and the self-assured way he spoke.

"Ready?" Bruno asked. She nodded and he turned on the recorder.

"Monsieur Jonnart, this is Séverine Guimard. It is Friday, June 11. Cissokho has been elected president of the Senegalese National Assembly." Séverine paused, amazed at how the world continued without her.

"I beg you to release the political prisoner Matteu Casanova on my behalf. He harmed no one, yet he's been condemned to nearly fifteen years in prison—at twenty-five, he's barely lived as long as his sentence. To you, his release may not seem like a politically expedient move; however, which is the greater publicity nightmare: the release of a nonviolent prisoner, or my continued imprisonment? Or the fact that the Gendarmerie nationale has failed to locate me?" Séverine swallowed hard, but the tears flowed involuntarily and her teeth began to chatter. "Monsieur Jonnart, you must do what these men say; otherwise, you put my life in danger. Please, for my sake, expunge Casanova's record and arrange his safe return to Corsica."

Bruno clicked off the recorder. "That was perfect," he said a bit sheepishly as she wiped her eyes with the collar of her dress.

"I'm telling you, it's useless." Séverine shrugged and folded the paper into smaller and smaller squares. "Jonnart's probably delighted this happened to me."

"What do you mean?" Bruno asked. "You know him?"

"Sort of. I don't know, forget it." Finally, the tears dried up. She shuffled her bare feet through the still-dewy grass. "What are you gonna do with my ransom?"

Bruno slipped a finger beneath his mask and scratched the back of his neck. "Every political movement needs funding: for supplies, dissemination of a free noncorporate press, lawyers' fees, supporting our political prisoners and their families—I could go on. You know about Matteu's case, right?"

"Not really."

"He was arrested last spring for allegedly—allegedly—bombing and stealing arms from the gendarmerie in Borgo. They tried and sentenced him in a Parisian court and sent him to live out his sentence in Villepinte, which, from Ajaccio, is a two-hour plane ride to Orly, plus another hour and a half by train, then a cab to get to the prison. How often do you think his family is able to visit? And how much do you think transportation and hotels cost, all for thirty minutes of face time?"

"All right, I get the picture," Séverine interrupted. "But why can't you just ask Jonnart to transfer your friend to the prison here in Corsica? Why does he have to be released?"

"We thought with our bargaining chip, we could make a big ask."

Séverine flung the little square of paper at Bruno, and he swatted it away, making it look like the impotent, girlish tantrum it was.

"You've already hit the jackpot robbing my family!" she yelled. "Consider it a victory and move on! Let me go home!"

"Relax," Bruno said, agitated.

"And what about you? Don't you have a life? A job, a girlfriend, a family? Don't you have *something* to get back to?"

"This was a mistake," he said to himself, plucking her blindfold from the grass. He grabbed her wrist, and she wrenched it away.

"What, you want me to go back in the closet? Have I abused my privileges?" she hissed.

He grabbed her wrist again, more forcefully this time, and yanked her towards him so he could tie the blindfold around her head. His strength, intensified by his anger, cowed her, and once again, her little flame was extinguished.

~

The night passed, another day began. A week in the closet. Time had become this sticky sap that she was trapped in, like a wasp in amber. The house was quiet again today; God only knew what the men were doing.

A knock on the closet woke her.

"What time is it?" she asked groggily.

"Late. Put your blindfold on," Bruno said. He helped her to her feet, much more gently than he'd handled her yesterday.

"What's going on?" she asked.

"Put these on, too," he replied.

She heard the plastic slap the floor as he dropped a pair of thongs to the ground. He guided her feet into them as if she were Cinderella.

"Am I going home?" she asked, her hope like a flint that couldn't quite spark.

"Yeah," he said, but his voice was strange—somber and distant.

As he led her to the 4x4 and helped her climb into the trunk, Séverine felt disconcertingly nonplussed. The car pulled off. A rustling in the back seat indicated that the boy was there, too, although none of them spoke. Someone shut off the radio.

Finally free from the closet: that was most important, she told herself. But the road got bumpier and bumpier, and the car seemed to be climbing when it should have been moving down towards the ocean.

"Where are we going?" she asked.

For a few seconds, no one responded. Then Bruno said, "Not far." His tone was noncommittal, and it watered the seed of anxiety growing inside Séverine. Another part of her maintained that there was nothing to worry about; for the hell these men had put her through, they'd never lied to her. They had principles, they were the kind of men for whom principles were everything.

After about a half hour, the car made one last turn. They all sat motionless for a few moments.

"This is where my parents are meeting me?" she asked. The sound of her voice surprised her; it was so girlish and eager to please, eager to be told yes.

"Let's go," Bruno murmured, and the men opened the car doors. The boy helped her out of the back, his touch on her forearm so light and timid.

They walked a few meters across rough and dusty ground. This part was like she'd imagined, but the atmosphere was off—the men did not seem in a hurry to leave. She could sense their grimness. In the most important way, this was not at all as she'd imagined it.

"Sit here," Bruno said, guiding her onto a low, flat rock.

"I'm sorry about yesterday," Séverine said spontaneously. "I know I can be a pain in the ass, it's just . . . I don't feel in control of myself right now, with everything that's happened. I mean, I know you're doing your best, but—" She was rambling. As soon as she shut up, she clocked how still everything was. The men weren't going back to the car; they were just standing there, silent.

She tensed like a rabbit with its nose to the wind, waiting for the shift, for some movement that would indicate the last week was done with and she was free. What she heard was a click, slow and sickening. Here was the change in pressure she'd been waiting for: the leadenness of a gun hovering beside her head.

Without thinking, she lifted her blindfold.

Directly in front of her there was only scrub, nothing around them except silver grass lolling in the wind and the moon hanging high and icy white.

She turned her head, and there was the hole of the barrel gaping vulgarly. She felt more disgusted than scared. The person holding the gun was Bruno, maskless, breathing heavily. It was the first time she was seeing his face, and yet it was as if she already knew it. He was handsome, as she'd expected, with the same haircut as the other two, full dark eyebrows, and a generous mouth. He looked like the hero in an old Cinecittà film, a slave turned gladiator. He feigned steeliness, but sweat streamed down his temples, milky in the moonlight, and both his lip and the hand holding the gun trembled. The other two stood stock-still behind him. The boy looked like he might vomit, and the other man's expression was so blank it was as if he'd gone somewhere else, a place where he could pretend he wasn't part of this.

Had she made a miscalculation? She hadn't considered Bruno capable of making good on the threats he'd assured her were only for show, pulling this trigger after talking to her, touching her, feeling her name in his mouth. Maybe she'd been wrong about him and everything else, the whole trajectory of her life. But it didn't make sense—it was against nature for him to end her big, dazzling, important life in service of his doomed plan for this stupid island. The brightness of her own spectacular future lit Séverine from within, and she stared up at Bruno with a loathing so sublime his gaze wavered. She would not submit. Her time was not up.

"Get that thing away from me," she sneered, smacking his hand aside, and it was like she'd dropped a boulder in a pond: everything fluctuated violently.

Bruno fumbled to hold on to the gun while the other man caught Séverine's wrists as she screamed and writhed. The boy rushed to help him, but she kicked him in the stomach, and he keeled over. The other man wrestled her to the ground and pressed a knee into her back. With her face in the dirt, she tried to wriggle out of his grip, but he was too strong. Bruno approached, pointed the gun at her head. He ran the sleeve of his jacket over his face with the twitchiness of a junkie. Then he held the gun out to the other man.

"Petru, you do it," he said.

Séverine felt the other man's—Petru's—grip loosen. "This was your idea," he replied angrily. "You're doing it."

"This—this?" Bruno's voice cracked as he gestured towards Séverine with the gun. "Was not my idea. You were the one who suggested we—"

"Hold on," the boy cut in. "We were discussing options, and Petru only said this was one of them."

"Stay out of it, Tittu," Bruno snapped.

Petru's knee came off Séverine's back. "It wasn't a suggestion, I was stating a fact," he said, his voice low. "But kidnapping her in the first place—that was all you."

"Are you kidding me?"

"Look, you want to act all tough, like you're the generalissimo, you have to take on shitty responsibilities."

"Sorry I'm not *tough* like you, beating some poor guy half to death—"

At this, Petru let go of her wrists. Shakily, she pushed herself to her knees and watched him walk right up to Bruno, chest to chest, towering over him, the tendons in their necks taut. Something hot and long-contested was simmering between them.

"You got in over your head, and you don't have the balls to get yourself out. Admit it," Petru growled. "Matteu didn't want this! This isn't even about him anymore, it's about your fucking ego."

Bruno's grip tightened around the gun.

"Stop!" Tittu screamed, getting between the two men and pushing them apart. "We're not doing it! We're not doing it, okay?"

Bruno did not resist as Tittu took the gun, engaged the safety, and stuffed it in his waistband.

Séverine oddly felt like she had no part in the drama before her. Whatever was happening over there began to mute out. She'd never seen so many stars, didn't know they were in fact iridescent and pulsing. This maquis pulsed, too—not only with the activity of animals and insects but with the wind, lapping and retreating like a wave, sweeping dust across the ground, shaping and reshaping the granite island. Everything in motion. Everything forever changing.

3. Acquaintance

Séverine spent one last night in the closet, the first in which she truly slept—though it was less sleep than deactivation, a total blackout. When she finally woke, she was drenched in afternoon sweat and felt something akin to a hangover. From outside came hammering and the occasional buzz of a drill. She pounded on the door so someone would escort her to the bathroom, but no one came.

She sat passively, concentrating on the throbbing of her bladder, unable to muster any anger over last night's events. It was just another thing that had happened to her; she was too tired to process it as different, worse, more extraordinary than anything else that had occurred this last week. And yet she had swatted away the gun—she possessed a savage will to survive after all.

Five minutes later came a knock on the door.

"There's no point wearing the blindfold," she said. "Let's not pretend I don't know what you all look like."

Without a word to the contrary, Tittu opened the door and helped Séverine to her feet. Once in the toilet, she sat taking in the sunshine like a wilted plant. When she came out, Tittu was leaning against the wall opposite, head bowed.

Something had changed; Séverine and the boy had the same standing in the house now. This was no longer the men's territory alone. Without asking permission, she explored her surroundings. The front door was beside the bathroom, and past that a living room with walls of large misshapen stones, gloomy with the curtains drawn. This was a real bergerie—the living room appeared to be the original sheep pen, constructed a hundred years ago or more, the nucleus of the cottage that had been expanded upon over generations. As she made her way back down the hall, she noticed a bedroom across from the bathroom; maybe she could finagle her way into an actual bed. But first, a shower.

As she rinsed the dust out of her hair, generous amounts of natural light hit her eyes for the first time in days. The rosy-peach tile, the milkiness of the tub's porcelain, the sun glowing on the pebbled glass was a relief to Séverine, who'd seen nothing but brown walls, gray blankets, and jaundiced light since being thrown in the closet. It felt like a sign, a reassurance that the worst part was over. She called for Tittu to bring her something to wear, and through the cracked door he handed her an oversized blouse that, to a boy, might look like a dress. These clothes were someone's mother's, summer clothes for the country house. The bergerie inevitably belonged to the family of one of these men, which seemed stupid, easily traceable. But then, they hadn't anticipated staying so long.

When she came out of the bathroom, Tittu was hanging around sheepishly with a sleeve of biscottes in hand. She snatched them from him and leaned against the doorjamb.

"We're moving you out of the closet," he said. "We all feel really bad about what happened."

She crunched on a stale biscotte. "Uh-huh."

Tittu's whole head flushed red. "I'll show you."

She followed him past a second bedroom and through the kitchen, another relic from the past: powder-blue curtains, matching wallpaper, peeling linoleum tile, a round table with a lace-edged tablecloth, and four wooden chairs. Yet there was a sweet quality to the reverence inherent in its cleanliness, that the decorative plates on the walls had been recently dusted.

They went through the back door and into the yard, where Bruno and Petru were attaching a door to a small shed at the edge of the woods. It looked like a tiny cottage, the plywood pre-painted in tasteful neutrals, the roof sloped. The gardener in Séverine's gated community kept his tools in the exact same model. When Petru, cigarette between his teeth, finished drilling the last screw, he stepped back to appraise his work. Bruno opened and closed the door, and they both nodded.

"I'm moving into a shed from the Würth store? Is this a joke?" Séverine asked contemptuously.

With his tongue curled over his top lip, Bruno walked over, arms crossed. "Look, I don't know what to say," he said.

She kept her expression blank.

"It wasn't supposed to go down this way. We had to improvise, and we didn't always make the best decisions. I'm sorry about that."

Séverine nodded, neither an official pardon nor censure.

"Come see," he said. "You'll be more comfortable here. It has windows; we got a futon for you."

"And we'll run an extension cord from the kitchen for a fan and a lamp," Tittu added.

She silently followed Bruno into the shed, noticing that an open padlock had been slipped through the latch hole of the door. It was about twice as big as the closet. As a temporary fix, it was better, but maybe "temporary" was delusional. She felt like she was in purgatory—it was both unthinkable that her captivity would end and that it would go on this way forever.

They joined the other two outside. "Okay," Séverine shrugged. "Now what."

"What, now what? Now you spend your days here," Bruno replied testily. "Or would you rather go back in the closet?"

"I'm not only talking about myself. What about you?" Séverine asked. "Obviously Tittu's a student. But don't you two have jobs? Lives to get back to? Or will you leave me locked up all day and come feed and walk me at night like a dog?" She lifted and dropped the padlock, letting it clunk against the shed.

"I don't know," Bruno said. "But I promise we'll figure out something that works for you, too." Finally, he was dropping the cold-blooded act, and for the first time, she sensed he was being honest with her.

"What about my parents? When can I talk to them?" she asked.

"We're in a media blackout," Bruno replied, less kindly. "We can't let you do that."

"Did you tell them you were going to kill me?" she asked.

"Not expressly."

"They have to know I'm okay, they'll go completely insane," Séverine said.

"We have to stick to our terms," Petru said. "No clemency for Matteu, so we go dark."

"So there's still a chance they'll let him go?"

"It's more like . . . a punishment for not cooperating," Tittu explained.

Turning angry, Bruno blustered, "Jonnart is already preparing his presidential bid. He wants to say he's got a track record of total commitment to the unity of the republic. No concessions. What a farce!"

"Oh," Séverine said, now understanding why Jonnart wouldn't agree to let the prisoner go. His party had won the majority in the parliamentary elections earlier that year, resulting in a center-left incumbent president and a new right-leaning prime minister, who then filled his cabinet with other conservative ministers, including Jonnart. This was only the second time an executive split had ever happened, and the extraordinariness of it emboldened the right.

"How long does the blackout last?" Séverine asked.

"Till we pull off our next action," Bruno said.

"When's that?"

"In three weeks."

"*Three weeks?*" she cried. "What am I supposed to do for the next *three weeks?*"

"What do you normally do?" Petru asked.

"I'm seventeen, I go to school," she snapped.

"That's not a bad idea, actually," Bruno said. "We could include her in collective study."

"What's that?"

"We read texts and discuss them together."

Séverine threw her head back and moaned, then narrowed her eyes. "I just realized, today's the first day of the bac. I thought being kidnapped would at least mean I'd be spared philo, but apparently not. Ha, ha." Dejected, she pointed to Petru's cigarette. "Can I have one?"

"They're hand rolled," Petru said.

"Beurk, forget it. Will you get me a pack of Vogue Lilas?"

"We're not your errand boys," Petru said.

"We can get the cigarettes," Bruno conceded.

"Thank you," she huffed. "So I'm supposed to go into this shed? And you lock me in?"

"That's the idea," Bruno said.

Séverine shook her head, pushed past Bruno, and plopped gracelessly on the futon, like the sack of meat they treated her as. Inwardly, however, she began to earnestly think about escape. The picture they'd painted was a total drag—as if she was going to spend the summer sitting around in this dump when Hélène and Pilar were supposed to visit in July for her birthday, when Corsica would become glamorous as it only did during the summer.

She still felt hesitant to strike out into the maquis, but it occurred to her that she could ingratiate herself with the men. It was hard to win someone over when you couldn't look them in the face, but now the masks were off. She could see them, and they could see her; that had always worked in her favor.

Twenty minutes later, Petru returned with a croque madame and a book. Someone was trying to apologize with this sandwich: thick-cut pain de mie and lots of melted, browned Gruyère and a perfect fried egg, golden around the edges with an orange yolk that oozed when Séverine pierced it with her knife.

"Are you the one making my meals?" Séverine asked as he was leaving.

He half turned, caught off guard. "Yeah."

"You're actually a good cook."

"Okay," he said suspiciously.

"Did your mom teach you?"

"No," he said, like Séverine was stupid for even suggesting it.

"Where then?"

"Restaurants. Working. Regular people have jobs," he said, and shut the door behind him.

Only after she ate did she pick up the book with butter-greased fingers. It was a livre de poche with a glossy cover that had gone pulpy at the edges. The title read *Les damnés de la terre*, written by a guy called Frantz Fanon, whose likeness took up two thirds of the cover. His expression was reproachful and defiant. And he was a Black man. If Séverine had seen this book in a store, she would have passed it over; the cover was too stark, too serious, too accusatory. But there wasn't much else to do in the shed. She skipped Sartre's preface and flipped to the first page, blank except for three bold words smack in the middle: "DE LA VIOLENCE."

She skimmed the first lines until she came across a clause that had been twice underlined with a blue ballpoint pen: "<u>Decolonization is always a violent event.</u>"

Séverine flipped through the other pages; the whole book had been marked up, sentences underlined, bracketed, notes scribbled in the margins and between lines, all in the same small, racing hand as the scripts Bruno had given her to record.

Appalled and fascinated, Séverine read on. She didn't understand everything—much of it was abstract, or overly academic, or assumed the reader should already be familiar with concepts she'd never heard of, like "Aristotelian logic" or "Manichaeanism"—but she was getting the gist: kill your colonizers.

She was essentially reading two superimposed texts: Fanon's and Bruno's. Beside a passage that purported colonized subjects feuded with each other in order to feel control over their own lives, he'd written *clanisme*. Fanon's explanation, flanked by Bruno's one-word note, cracked the shell of an assumption she'd always held about Corsicans: that murder was a genetic predisposition, a fundamental aspect of their national character.

That was basically what everyone in France thought. Even in the Asterix comics, ancient Corsicans threatened to kill each other over pointless, generations-long blood feuds. Now she felt kind of bad for thinking that; Fanon was saying it was a coping mechanism, a way to feel independent and human in the face of degradation.

Funny, she'd never felt inspired to think about the things written inside books, nor had a book ever changed her mind. Or rather, the book as interpreted by Bruno. She felt—dare she say it?—a little smarter. Séverine had always thought pleasure was purely physical, but in this moment of understanding, she felt a similar electricity as when she emerged from Le Vinyl's runway-like tunnel onto the pulsing dance floor. It was the anticipation of new experience, and of life expanding to accommodate it.

She turned to the back of the book and read the author bio: born in Martinique, member of the Algerian National Liberation Front. Séverine had traveled throughout the French West Indies and Northern Africa on vacation with her family, but her experience of those places was never this mutual hostility and resentment between white Europeans and Black locals. The resort staff always acted friendly towards the Guimards, like they were grateful for their support of tourism and, by extension, their jobs.

Even more confusing was Fanon's way of talking about socialism, as if it were different from the Socialist Party of which Séverine's father was a member. He classified Europe as "capitalist," but Séverine didn't understand how that was incompatible with "socialist."

There was a knock on the door.

"Come in," Séverine called. Tittu unlocked the padlock and entered with a small red plastic gooseneck lamp in one hand, a drill, and the end of a long orange extension cord dragging from the other.

"Have you read this?" She lifted the book to show Tittu, who was rigging up the lamp.

"I'm reading it for the first time now, like you," he said.

"Wild stuff," Séverine said, tossing the book behind her. "Hey, will you bring me a pencil so I can take notes?"

"Sure," Tittu said. He was drilling a hole in the door, through which he threaded the extension cord; there was a deliberateness and ease to his actions that he rarely demonstrated.

"What are you studying?" she asked.

"Um, organismal biology and ecology."

"Really," Séverine said, a bit surprised. "You want to be a scientist?"

"No, my family has a farm," he said.

"You want to be a farmer?" Séverine asked in disbelief.

"What's wrong with that?" Tittu challenged, turning back to the lamp.

"Nothing," Séverine said, although she did not think it was a career you should strive for; it was something you had to do because you had no education, no other recourse.

"I just don't know any farmers," she backtracked. "What do you like about it?"

"I like the idea of feeding people, of growing good food that's part of our heritage. I like the process, that you do all this work, then you have something to show for it. And I like tending to our animals," he replied.

"I never thought about it that way," Séverine said, regretting her snobbery.

"Land is freedom. To be self-sufficient, we need to feed our own people," he said. "We're slaves to importation, and that's how the state wants it. You know it costs more to buy clementines grown an hour away than ones shipped in from Spain? And our patrimony is agriculture: our honey, cheese, chestnuts, wine."

Séverine had never heard him talk so passionately and unselfconsciously—she wondered if he didn't normally get the chance. Bruno was always the one talking; he was serious, the "idea man," and Tittu the apprentice. If Tittu needed someone to talk to, she could be that person.

He seemed to catch himself and stopped, embarrassed. Without another word, he pushed the button on the back of the lamp, and there was light.

⁓

That night, Séverine read with a pencil in hand. Both the author's text and Bruno's notes were so self-important. Bruno had bracketed a section where Fanon said violence rid the colonized of their inferiority complex, that it restored self-confidence. Is that what this was all about? The men of Soffiu di Libertà needed a confidence boost? Pathetic. She doodled a picture of a stick man with a sad face and tiny penis. Elsewhere, another double underline for "Violence is a cleansing force." Bruno was visibly obsessed with the idea, but what did he know about violence? Thinking of the other night, she was grateful the answer was *nothing.*

At times, she was actually entertained by how dogmatic and crazy the text could get, especially when she thought about this being Bruno's bible. Where Fanon claimed that every militant must commit an irreversible act, she wrote, *Like kidnapping Séverine.* Next to his assertion that the colonized are owed reparations, she wrote, *My ransom* ☺. And beside a paragraph where he described the revolutionary potential of the ignored and wayward lumpenproletariat—"the pimps, the hooligans, the unemployed, and the petty criminals"— Séverine added *lycéens.* It felt good to make fun of Bruno, if indirectly.

That said, there was something alluring and potent about Fanon's description of revenge, how it flung your body into a zone of turbulence, plunged you into a dreamlike state, how the sight of the other induced vertigo. As she read, these sensations arose humid and pulsating in her own body. The encounter between victim and enemy bordered on erotic, she realized. It made sense; a million rom-coms followed this logic. *Sounds like love*, she wrote. Or what she'd heard of it; she'd never been in love.

Occasionally, Fanon would allow that colonizers, particularly the "European masses," could turn coat and ally with the colonized in their fight for freedom. Duh! Even she'd heard of the network of French activists who'd aided the National Liberation Front during the Algerian War. Next to "European masses," Bruno had written: *laborers, immigrants, banlieusards, the unemployed*. Séverine added with self-satisfaction: *anyone who wants to help*. Like her papa, for example. She liked to think that, if the occasion called for it, she, too, would find herself on the right side of history.

After spending the whole book being told all the ways she was nasty and terrible, the possibility of redemption was a real relief. Then she felt annoyed for being emotionally manipulated this way; it was ridiculous to feel guilty for events that had nothing to do with her, as if she should atone for the past crimes of her birthplace. She wondered if that was the point of Bruno giving her this book, to make her feel guilty, a first step in persuading her to sympathize with his crazy crusade.

Séverine circled the last sentence, which urged comrades to change the world and "set afoot a new man." With a smirk, she wrote, *Me after you brainwash me.*

In the morning, Tittu came to wake her up and escort her to the bathroom. On her way back to the shed, as they passed through the kitchen, Petru handed her a plate of eggs and toast.

"You ran out of biscottes," she said as she accepted it. "I'm so glad."

"You'll work out with us every morning from now on," Bruno explained. He was sitting at the round table with its white lace-edged tablecloth, eating his own eggs, dressed in black soccer shorts.

"Great," she deadpanned. Gym was her least favorite subject. She didn't see the point of working out if you were already skinny.

"Petru, we have something else she can wear, yeah?" Bruno asked.

Petru sighed and left his place at the stove; Séverine followed, eating her eggs as she went. He entered the bedroom across from the bathroom but closed the door halfway, blocking her view.

"Is this your mom's stuff?" Séverine asked.

He expelled a short, bitter laugh. "No."

"But it's your family's house?"

"What makes you think that?" he asked, handing her a T-shirt, elastic-waisted shorts, and white socks rolled at the ankles.

"The way Bruno asked *you*," Séverine responded. That was part of it, but the house also fit Petru. It couldn't possibly belong to Bruno's family; he radiated the same middle-class self-consciousness that many of her schoolmates did—Corsican families with a modest amount of wealth who were nevertheless Not Posh. Petru and Tittu were undoubtedly country people, but there was no sense of comfort or familiarity between Tittu and the rooms. Petru, however, looked like this place—overgrown and unrefined.

He tossed out one sneaker, then another. "Well, is it?" she asked, pushing back the tongue—38, a size too large.

Petru swung open the door, and they found themselves chest to belly. He hesitated, unsure how to get around her, embarrassed by their proximity. Interesting: maybe he was less immune to her than she'd thought. Maybe this susceptibility existed in all men. Maybe she'd exploit it against all three of her kidnappers so she could get the fuck out of this place.

"None of your business," he said, and slid past her.

‎———

The men were doing sit-ups on the patio, Bruno panting out the count. She felt a wave of embarrassment watching them perform so seriously, like a fake army platoon.

"Thirty-three . . . Jump in, come on," Bruno wheezed.

After about eight, she gave up. Next, it was push-ups, mountain climbers, knee touches. It was so stupid. They did a hundred reps; she did about ten.

"Séverine, keep up," Bruno called out.

An inspired idea came to her. "Can I talk to you over there?" she asked.

Bruno stood, and they walked around to the other side of the house.

"I'm supposed to get my period this week," she said matter-of-factly.

"Oh," Bruno said, as if this were a marvel.

"I'm going to need . . . stuff. And I think I should take it slow today."

"Absolutely," he said, conciliatory.

As the men ran around the perimeter of the property again and again, Séverine walked, leisurely taking in a 360-degree view of the bergerie, which seemed to be as secluded as a witch's cottage. The entire house was encircled by the maquis; the only way in or out appeared to be a packed-dirt path that only a 4x4 could navigate. Indeed, there was the dark green 4x4 whose trunk she was well acquainted with, plus a motorcycle she hadn't noticed before. The front of the house was more or less how Séverine had pictured it: the traditional Corsican bergerie, made of sand-colored stone and terra-cotta roofing, shaped like a house a kid would draw. Continuing around, here was her shed, the stone patio, and then to the right of the house, the garden. Steep hills peaked above the trees, bearing down upon the bergerie.

After they finished, the men sat on the patio flagstones chugging water. Séverine settled into a patio chair and looked out towards the forest, soaking in a little morning sun.

"No, no," Bruno said. "Back to the shed."

"Who's here? You're expecting company?" she cried, arms outstretched.

"You're not a guest," Petru said. "You're a liability."

She was loath to go back, especially since she'd finished the Fanon book. It would be a better use of her time to hang out with Tittu.

"That garden on the side of the house; you take care of it, Tittu?" she asked.

"Yeah," he said cautiously.

"Let me help you," she offered. "I want to learn how to grow stuff. What you were saying last night was really interesting."

"What were you saying last night?" Petru asked Tittu, teasing, making Tittu blush.

"I guess she could stand to get some dirt under her fingernails, no?" Bruno directed the question to Petru, not Tittu. Séverine related to Tittu in this regard—they were young, and no one took them seriously.

"Isn't it Tittu's decision?" Séverine asked, then turned to him. "Would you mind?"

Startled, Tittu looked to the others for approval, and Bruno nodded once. "Um, sure," he replied. "Just let me shower and I'll come get you."

A half hour later, Tittu collected Séverine from the shed, two plastic laundry baskets in hand.

"The fruit trees need picking," he explained. "When they ripen on the branch, they attract pests, so we have to stay on top of it."

She hadn't noticed before, but beside the garden a path was trodden into the grass. They walked along this path until they came upon a small grove of fruit trees laden with apricots, plums, and nectarines.

"Why haven't I been eating these for breakfast?" Séverine wondered, reaching up to press a plum between her fingers.

"You have," Tittu said. "The jam."

Séverine laughed in surprise. "Who makes the jam?"

"Petru."

She shook her head, amused. "What's his deal?"

"What do you mean?" Tittu asked, hoisting himself up into the crook of a nectarine tree, resting his belly along a bough like a panther. He plucked a fruit and handed it to Séverine.

"He does all the girl jobs in the house: makes jam, cooks. It doesn't really match his tough guy thing." As she spoke, she put the nectarine to her nose, then placed it in the laundry basket.

"That's his job, he's a cook," Tittu said. "And he *is* tough. He's only been out of the Foreign Legion for a year, and he was in prison before that."

Séverine was surprised. Corsicans despised the Foreign Legion regiment that was stationed in Calvi. They saw it as an occupation army that harassed their women, picked fights with their men, and, when they deserted, snuck around the island committing crimes.

"What'd he do?" she asked, remembering Bruno's comment when he and Petru were arguing in the maquis.

"He beat up a security guard pretty bad while he was trying to rob an electronics store."

"Ah-ha," she said. "So he's a criminal. And a loose cannon."

"I wouldn't say that," he said. "Deep down, he's a good guy. He had a messed-up childhood and ended up in a bad place."

"What, did his mommy spank him?" Séverine asked sarcastically.

"I think spanking was the least of it," Tittu replied, which made Séverine feel like a jerk. "He lived with his aunt for a while, but she died."

"This is his aunt's place," Séverine realized.

Tittu dragged the basket to the next tree, unwilling to confirm. "You can pick from the lower branches," he said, doing the same. "This part should be getting soft." He showed Séverine the divide in the fruit, running a finger along its cleft.

Séverine placed her index finger on the nectarine and glided it along the crack from the bottom up, till it reached the underside of Tittu's wrist. She felt him tense and smiled like a child who knows she's being naughty. Just as quickly, she neutralized her expression and pried the fruit from his hand, as if he were the one messing around.

"What about Bruno?" she asked.

"What about him?" Tittu asked.

"How old is he?"

"Twenty-six."

"So he's the oldest," Séverine said, more to herself than Tittu. "But it's not just that. He acts like the leader."

"There's no leader," Tittu replied testily.

"Whatever you say." She leaned against a tree and closed her eyes; how lovely to take in sun after all those days in the closet. "Don't you want to know anything about me? Girls like it when guys ask them questions about themselves."

Tittu didn't respond for a moment, but she could sense him processing this. "I already know a lot about you, actually."

"What do you mean?" Séverine asked.

"We surveilled you before we—" He loosely flicked his wrist to indicate their present circumstance.

Séverine opened her eyes. "As in, you spied on me?"

"It was reconnaissance," Tittu said. "How else would we know you'd be riding your bike on that street at that hour?"

Séverine flipped through a random assortment of banal memories from the weeks before her kidnapping: leaving school, stopping at the tabac for cigarettes and a Coca-Cola, shopping for new bras with her mom on the Cours Napoléon. To think, she may have been watched that entire time. The idea of being watched when she could be purposeful about the way she held herself, when she could control her smile and the timbre of her laugh, that was fine and good. But that she may have blown her nose and wiped it too vigorously, or slouched in a way that made her back look scoliotic—it was unnerving. Another thought crossed her mind, that they'd seen her with Antoine in the cove.

"You guys are fucking creeps," Séverine said.

"It's not like we watched you undress or anything," Tittu explained, flustered. "Just to figure out your schedule, the places you went."

She stared blindly into the dense maquis, burning with anger and embarrassment.

"So I already know you get the pain au chocolat at Pantalacci and that you read fashion magazines and drink Cocas at the tabac. You're alone a lot." Tittu said this last part cautiously.

"I choose to be," Séverine said haughtily.

"Me too," Tittu said. "Well, until I started hanging out with Petru and Bruno."

"How'd you end up with the two of them anyway? You're kind of an odd trio."

"Through Matteu. He's my cousin."

"Matteu's your cousin?" she asked, impressed; he'd taken on a kind of celebrity status for Séverine.

"Yeah. Petru and Matteu grew up together, and Bruno met Matteu in—" He stopped himself. "Maybe I shouldn't be telling you this."

"Who am I gonna tell?" Séverine said. "But you didn't want to join one of the pro-independence student groups? Bruno and Petru are so old."

"The student groups aren't serious," Tittu said scornfully. "And I get along better with *adults* anyway."

Séverine could read between the lines: shy, unconfident Tittu who was happiest with his plants, not crass or callous enough to fit in with the boys, yet too boy-like for the girls to take him in. Someone who wanted an excuse to be told what to do. He was the perfect candidate for a terrorist group; he sought a fraternity, friends who became family. After the year she had, she could understand that part perfectly.

4. *Discourse*

Séverine was flipping through *Les damnés de la terre*, looking again at Bruno's notes, envisioning him as a university student scribbling away in his bed, enflamed, this book altering his brain like a fever. As if she'd summoned him, Bruno appeared with dinner and a pack of Vogues.

"How's it going? I know it can be dense reading," he said, passing her a plate of salade Niçoise and a plum wrapped in a cloth napkin.

"I'm done." She speared a roasted potato with her fork.

"What do you mean?"

"I mean I read the book. I'm done," she said, her mouth full.

"And you understood it?" he asked, taken aback; suspicious, even.

"I'm not an idiot."

"It's just more advanced than the type of thing you read in terminale," he said.

Séverine handed back the plum. "I don't really like plums."

He took a bite.

"He talks a lot about Europe being the bad guy," Séverine said, tapping the book with the handle of her fork. "But you're European." She wanted to catch him in an inconsistency.

"And Fanon also talks about how the European underclass should ally itself with the Third World."

"And how does Soffiu di Libertà do that?"

"Corsica *is* the Third World," he said. "One in five Corsicans live below the poverty line. We're the poorest region in France with the highest cost of living: food, petrol, clothing, housing, it's all more expensive here than on the continent. You never noticed that?"

"Our housekeeper does the grocery shopping," Séverine admitted.

"Of course." He laughed cynically. "What else? We have the highest unemployment level in the nation during a historic unemployment crisis but the lowest share of public housing because our slimy politicians get better kickbacks when the land goes to luxury developers and wealthy foreigners." As he ticked off these points, Séverine felt bombarded. Whenever anyone talked about the Corsican Problem, they talked about how complex it was. But Bruno made the issues sound so straightforward.

"Okay, but do you know anybody this kind of stuff has happened to?" Séverine flipped to the end of the book, trying to regain her footing. "Torture by electricity, intravenous injection of Pentothal, an enema of soapy water at high pressure, which apparently *killed* people?"

"I know the government pays barbouzes to attack us."

"That's not real," Séverine said.

"It's very real," Bruno said.

"But he's talking about racism," Séverine tried again. She flipped to the beginning of the book. "'This explosive population growth, those hysterical masses, those blank faces' . . . 'the black, brown, and yellow hordes that will soon invade our shores . . .'" It felt very satisfying to have these smart, sophisticated words in her mouth as if they were her own.

"The French don't say the exact same thing about us?" Bruno countered. "I mean, a former minister of the interior literally said we have a 'criminal chromosome.'"

Séverine felt a familiar frustration coming on. He had a quick response for everything; it was like he wasn't really listening, like he thought he could dismiss her outright.

"I think Fanon breaks down the path to revolution for all colonized people, whether they're Black, white, whatever," Bruno said.

"But like, Corsicans can be racist, too," she said. "What about the *Arabi fora!* graffiti all over Ajaccio?"

"Soffiu di Libertà does not condone that," he said simply.

She didn't understand how Bruno didn't feel at least some of the same culpability she did; it was weird that he felt like Fanon was speaking directly to him. She knew from high school that the chain of oppressed and oppressors was always in flux, that sometimes the roles swapped, or, more often than not, you were both simultaneously.

"What else?" Bruno asked. There was a twinkle in his eye—he was actually enjoying their argument. So *this* was intellectual sparring! Her parents did it all the time, about everything, and Séverine had always found it so tedious and annoying, but again she felt this new rush of pleasure. She hadn't considered Bruno might be challenging her opinions to get a sense of who she was, what she was made of. She was flattered. What's more, she could do the same.

Loosening up, she asked, "So you think change only happens with violence? What about Gandhi and Martin Luther King Jr.?"

"I don't know a ton about the American civil rights movement.

But I do know about the race riots that happened in Los Angeles last year. So it doesn't seem like nonviolence solved everything."

"Okay, fine. But everyone knows about Martin Luther King, and I've never heard of this Fanon guy before," Séverine said. "Clearly, this strategy doesn't make you very popular."

"It's not a popularity contest," Bruno said a little more vehemently. "We're trying to change society."

"You know what else doesn't make you popular? Kidnapping innocent girls," Séverine said with exaggerated solemnity, although she was partly teasing.

Bruno didn't roll with the joke; instead, he looked browbeaten, like they were at the beginning of an old argument he was sick of having.

"My dad always says the people who are most fed up with the militants are Corsicans themselves," she continued self-righteously.

"Not exactly," Bruno said. "They're just uncomfortable about what it'll take to get us to a place where we can self-govern."

"I don't get why it has to be independence," Séverine said. "What's wrong with autonomy?"

"Autonomy says, 'You're a little different from the rest of France, maybe it's okay to do a little self-governing.' But we wouldn't have control over the police, the army, the justice system—the organizations that most repress us. We couldn't truly govern our people and manage our own land. Only independence will grant us that power."

There was something intoxicating about this little rant, which ended with all the polish of a campaign speech. His passion and eloquence had an elevating effect, as if she rose to his level just by listening.

"What do you do? As a job?" she asked. "Can I guess? I think you're a teacher."

"What makes you think that?"

"Well, for one, you'd have summers off, which explains how you can be here all day. But mostly the way you talk, like you get off on telling me everything I don't know."

He laughed despite himself. "I get *off* on helping people open their minds. If anything."

"What subject? History?"

Bruno raised an eyebrow, which she took for confirmation.

"Are your students the same age as me?" she asked, thinking of the girls who hung around after class to get the attention of the young, good-looking teachers.

"No, I teach collège," he said, folding his legs to the side like a picnicking lady in an Impressionist painting.

"So you like them young," Séverine joked as she opened the pack of cigarettes and struck a match. He rolled his eyes and plucked an olive from her mostly finished salad. The intimacy of it stopped the flame midway on its journey to her cigarette; she felt simultaneously indignant and perversely thrilled. Collecting herself, she met the match to the cigarette and extinguished it with a practiced flick of her wrist.

"Anyway, did you like the book?" Bruno asked.

"I don't think it's the kind of book where you can say you liked it or didn't like it," Séverine said, exhaling. "He's trying to rile you up. Like saying enlightenment and beauty are worthless—come on. I mean, he calls them 'Mediterranean values,' so they're your values too, no?"

"Give me one of those?" Bruno asked, hand outstretched.

Séverine obliged. He didn't look silly with the long, feminine cigarette in his mouth; he looked like he didn't give a shit how he looked, which was cool.

"First of all, the Enlightenment was used to justify hundreds of years of imperialism, and as far as beauty, I think he's talking about European conceptions of it. No man is actually opposed to beauty." He tapped the ash, grown long while he talked, against the side of the plate.

"Not even you?" Séverine asked. She never felt quick unless it was in a situation like this—flirtation.

Bruno laughed. "Even me," he agreed. He knew he was being flirted with, but he didn't take the bait. It must happen all the time with his students, she thought—she'd have to be subtler.

"Anyway, what I'm saying is that we go through the French school system and are taught certain 'truths,' a certain morality. Before going to fac, I never considered independence was worth thinking about, let alone fighting for. But once I started learning about things that supposedly had nothing to do with Corsica, I realized they had everything to do with Corsica. And as I read Fanon, Debord, Lenin, Marcuse, Mao, Zola, Lefebvre, Chomsky, I felt my brain rearranging itself; I felt myself becoming a different person. You know the Allegory of the Cave? It was like that, realizing the shadows were only shadows and facing the light for the first time."

Séverine laughed; he was so pretentious. Then it struck her: a similar awakening would win him over more than flirting would. If she led Bruno to believe his books were affecting her the way they'd affected him, that he was molding some new consciousness, he'd be more liable to trust her, and she could make him do what she wanted.

Séverine reclined on her side and rested her cheekbone against the heel of the hand that held the smoldering cigarette. "Are you trying to indoctrinate me?" she asked with a crooked smile.

"Look, the world is very small when you're seventeen. I remember. Stuff happens to you—life—and you change your mind about things," Bruno said. He took the book from her and thumbed the pages absentmindedly.

"You wrote in it," he said.

"Sorry, was I not supposed to?"

"It's fine," he said. "It goes without saying I'm a notetaker, too." He took a pen from his back pocket and scribbled something in the margins there and then.

"Interesting," he said cryptically. "I'm going to bring you something else, hold on."

He left the shed, not bothering to close the door. The night outside was relatively cool and seemed so wide and wild framed by the doorway. She dared herself to stand and step through, but didn't. She wanted to know what Bruno found interesting about her. It was disorienting how much their conversation made her feel like herself again, a better version, even.

He came back and handed her a slim book with Che Guevara's handsome face on the cover, smoking a cigar and wearing a jaunty scarf—it seemed that all important men got their faces on the covers of their books. It was called *Guerrilla Warfare*.

"I think you'll find it thought-provoking."

"We'll see," Séverine said.

Bruno stood and gathered her plate. "I have to say, you've surprised me."

"Just you wait," Séverine said, watching him as he went. This time, he locked the door behind him.

⁓

Séverine began to fall into a routine: exercise in the morning, read, lunch, read some more, help Tittu tend to the plants, then Bruno would bring her dinner and they'd discuss what she'd read that day.

After a week of exercise and good food and manual labor, she could already feel herself getting stronger. What the men did while she was locked in the shed, she hadn't the faintest idea, but whatever it was, she didn't care as long as it meant she'd get to talk to her parents soon.

She heard their vehicles regularly come and go, and it was strange to think they were having dinner with their families or seeing movies with friends or going on dates while she'd been hidden up here for nearly two weeks. It made her stir-crazy, but it probably wasn't much different from what she'd be doing if she hadn't been kidnapped: sitting alone on the beach, counting down the days till Pilar and Hélène arrived, sick of hanging out with her parents. Preferable to this, but not so fabulous either.

Over the next week, Bruno followed up Guevara with Mao, then Marx's *Capital,* which was so dense and monotonous.

"I'm struggling with this one," she admitted. "Can you bring me something else?"

"It's not easy," Bruno agreed, "but it's important. We can go chapter by chapter. Write your questions in the margins, and we'll talk it through."

Bruno started bringing his own dinner to the shed, and they ate together by the light of the gooseneck lamp. She liked the way he unraveled knotty passages and how it felt to comprehend some concept that had eluded her—that was a new, exhilarating pleasure. Even more, she liked when her questions illuminated parts of the text Bruno had never considered, or when he silently contemplated her opinion.

They did clash at times: if they disagreed too vehemently, or if he made her feel stupid, she'd get sullen and reply in monosyllables, then he'd leave. But Bruno always returned the following evening. It seemed he was getting something out of these meetings beyond "educating" Séverine; she had a hunch he'd been missing these types of conversations since Matteu Casanova got shipped off to prison.

"What's Matteu like?" Séverine asked Tittu one day in the orchard.

"He's a really good militant—the best," Tittu gushed. "He makes you feel like it's totally possible to win independence—like our generation's Pasquale Paoli, I swear. And he's the one who got Bruno into the fight."

"How do they know each other?" she asked. Over the last couple weeks, the fraught friendship she groomed in her virgins had begun to develop between her and Tittu. He should be ready to share with her now.

"From Paris. Matteu was going to Nanterre and Bruno was at Sciences Po."

"Wait, wait—Bruno went to Sciences Po?" Séverine asked, flabbergasted.

"Just for a year. Then he moved back and finished in Corte."

Imagining Bruno in Paris was completely disorienting yet explained so much: his more continental accent, the fact that he was the tiniest bit cool. She wondered why he hadn't mentioned this to her. Sciences Po was the most prestigious university in France, where the sons of her father's colleagues applied, and even they didn't always get in—but Bruno did, then defected. He could have become a politician instead of a middle school history teacher and part-time terrorist. She thought of a line from *Les damnés de la terre*: "In order to secure his salvation . . . the colonized intellectual feels the need to return to his unknown roots and lose himself, come what may, among his barbaric people."

On the Friday that brought her close to three weeks kidnapped, Bruno came with a new request.

"Come inside the house for dinner tonight," he said. "The guys don't like that I'm skipping meals with them."

"Yeah?" Séverine asked. She felt giddy, like she'd been granted some lavish privilege. To sit at a table and eat with others, even miserable Petru, would be a welcome change.

"We've all been working hard, you included," Bruno said. Hands in his jean pockets, he seemed in good spirits. Whatever *he* was working on must be going well. They were ten days away from their next attack; she'd been counting.

He escorted Séverine into the kitchen, where Tittu was setting the round table for four, and Petru was placing a chard omelette beside a plate of charcuterie and cheese, basket of sliced baguette, and bowl of cherry tomatoes Séverine and Tittu had picked earlier, still warm from the sun. Petru looked at her with suppressed animosity; this had not been his idea.

"This is one of Petru's signature dishes," Tittu said excitedly. If this dinner had been anyone's idea, it was Tittu's; maybe he was jealous of her evenings with Bruno, she considered.

They sat down as Bruno opened a bottle of red wine and filled everyone's glasses. Séverine spread the linen napkin, embroidered with small white flowers, over her lap. The early evening sun streamed through the open door and spilled across the kitchen floor.

"It's so weird for you to be here like this," Tittu said.

"What, like a fellow human being?" Séverine asked.

"That's not what I meant," Tittu said, and took a mouthful of wine.

They spent the first part of the meal in uncertain silence, but once a second and third bottle were opened, conversation did, too.

"What is this wine? It's good," Séverine said.

"Niellucciu," Petru said with a proper Corsu accent, a stark difference from his thickly provincial French.

"You speak the dialect?" Séverine asked him.

"Corsu is a language, not a dialect," Petru corrected.

"Petru is one of those Corsican mountain men you hear about who never really learned French," Bruno joked as Petru began rolling a cigarette, expressionless. There was a strange note of pride in Bruno's voice, as if Petru's *cursichezza*, as the locals called it, made Bruno more authentically Corsican by extension. The comment brought an awkwardness to the table that Séverine didn't totally understand but wanted to dispel.

"The omelette's delicious," Séverine said, changing the subject. "All I can make is toast. Maria, our housekeeper, cooks everything. She makes the best Bolognese in the world." She could practically conjure the taste. When Séverine was little and her parents abandoned her to attend some dinner party or other, Maria would always cook enough pasta to feed a family, and the two of them would eat it all in front of the TV, a normally forbidden activity. Shamefully, she realized this was the first time in weeks she'd thought of her beloved Maria. Meanwhile, Maria was probably lighting a candle at this very moment, begging in Portuguese for some saint's intercession on Séverine's behalf.

"Petru's a sous chef at the best bistro in Bastia," Tittu proudly told her.

"*Was*," Petru clarified.

"What happened, they sacked you?" Séverine asked.

"I quit," Petru said, shooting a resentful glance at Bruno.

"We needed him when things went haywire," Bruno explained to Séverine, but it was directed at Petru. "And now we're full-time militants."

"Thanks to the Guimard scholarship," she said pointedly.

She thought for a moment. Petru was the only one she hadn't yet developed a rapport with, and proximity was clearly key. "Maybe you can teach me to cook?" she asked him. "That way you wouldn't be doing it all by yourself. I could help."

He released a booming, derisive laugh along with a cloud of smoke. "What's the point? You'll always have some housekeeper."

"Exactly!" Bruno exclaimed. "Her whole life, she's been alienated from the work that keeps her alive."

"She'll just get in the way," Petru said.

"No, I won't," she huffed. "I've been really helpful in the garden, right, Tittu?"

Tittu slowly finished chewing a tomato, and Séverine narrowed her eyes at him. "She's been really helpful," he repeated mechanically.

"And I've been helping Bruno understand Marx better, too," she joked.

"Speaking of, did you get through Section Four yet?" Bruno asked.

"Yes, but I have to reread it. I literally fell asleep twice."

"What are you struggling with?"

"For one, I don't get what he means by 'commodity fetishism.' I thought a fetish was a sex thing."

"If you had to guess?"

She groaned. "Maybe like, being more interested in the money you get for something than the fact that it was made by a person."

"That's more or less it," he said with pride, which in turn made her proud.

"But how would *you* put it?"

Tittu slumped in his seat and lit a cigarette, which he held the way collégiens did: pointed down, pinched between his thumb and index finger.

"So the word 'fetish' refers to an object with religious significance, like a saint's bones," Bruno explained. "The bones are special because they were a holy person's, not because of their bodily function. With commodity fetishism, you have something like a chair, and people understand its worth only in relation to how much it costs. Not because a furniture maker, a skilled laborer, made the chair, and it took him so many hours. You understand?"

"Yes," Séverine said hesitantly. "But doesn't the chair get priced based on how hard it was for someone to make it?"

Petru began whistling.

"Sure, but Marx's whole thing is that the labor element—"

Tittu interrupted. "We're not supposed to discuss *Capital* until next week."

"Are we bothering you?" Bruno asked testily.

"Yeah, it's boring," Petru said.

"You say that about everything we discuss in collective study," Bruno sulked, standing from the table. "Come on," he said to Séverine.

"Wait, sit. Can't we just talk about something else?" Tittu asked, but Bruno ignored him, grabbing the bottle of wine and their two glasses and striding out the open door. Séverine shrugged apologetically at Tittu before following Bruno outside.

Night had just about fallen, and the sky glowed deep blue. Bruno entered the shed, turned on the light, sat with his back against the doorframe, and splashed some more wine in each glass. Séverine sat opposite him, carefully arranging her legs so they might touch his if he shifted.

"He can be such an asshole," Bruno said, to her surprise. She knew they were the ones who'd been rude, not Petru and Tittu, but kept this to herself.

"Usually to me," Séverine said.

"He's just unhappy about our present situation."

"How is 'the present situation' my fault?" Séverine asked with indignation.

"He had some hesitations from the beginning," Bruno admitted. She remembered the words exchanged that night in the maquis, how Petru made it seem like the whole hackneyed plan was Bruno's attempt to prove himself. She didn't like to think Petru might have been onto something.

"Don't sweat it," Bruno said. "Petru will come to like you once he spends some time with you."

Séverine laughed, discomfited, flattered, and curious. "So now that you've spent some time with me, you like me?" she asked, daring herself to look right at him. She was a bit drunk.

"You're not bad conversation for a seventeen-year-old." He smiled patronizingly—another small humiliation.

"I'm basically eighteen. July 29." Wiping an errant drop of wine from the bottle, Séverine asked tentatively, "Where will I be celebrating?"

"One thing at a time," Bruno said. "Let's just get through this next action first."

"But what if they still don't release your friend?"

"Then you're sticking around a bit longer."

Her frustration surged, and she chucked the empty bottle. It landed in the grass with a neutered thump. "I'm supposed to do karaoke with my friends for my birthday, I'm supposed to start drama school in the fall and be an actress! What about all my plans for my life?"

Bruno ran his hand over his face, his shoulders slumped. "I don't know, Séverine."

She felt her eyes well up with tears and turned away so he wouldn't see. She no longer felt like playing the game tonight. The man sitting across from her was the same villain who'd grabbed her off her bike three weeks ago. Whatever he'd given her, this feeling of competence, it wasn't enough to forgive what he'd done.

"Do you still want to talk about 'The Fetishism of Commodities and the Secret Thereof'?" Bruno asked, anticipating rejection.

"I don't," she said, standing and handing him her empty glass. "Good night." For the first time, she shut herself inside the shed.

5. *Affinity*

The next evening, Séverine met Petru in the kitchen, hot from the sun baking the back of the house and the oven preheating.

"What's for dinner?" she asked with exaggerated friendliness.

Petru removed a whole chicken from the fridge and thunked it on the counter in front of her. "First, you need to remove the giblets."

"Do what?" she asked.

"Put your hand in the cavity and pull everything out."

Séverine looked at him pleadingly, nevertheless knowing it was a punishment and test. He was unsympathetic. Grimacing, she stuck her hand in the chicken and pulled out squishing chunks of cold, maroon-colored meat. She held out her fist questioningly, and Petru grabbed the trash can. It was the first time she'd seen him smile.

Petru spoke only to give directions—how to properly score an onion, which knives to use for each task—and Séverine spoke only to ask clarifying questions. She sensed the best way to ingratiate herself was to be as unobtrusive as possible. He had her chop carrots, onions, and fennel into neat cubes, which they tossed in olive oil with baby potatoes and arranged in the roasting pan around the chicken. It was almost pleasant.

They stuck the chicken in the oven and Petru set the timer for an hour and a half. He uncorked a bottle of red, poured himself a small glass, and looked begrudgingly at Séverine before filling a second glass from the drying rack.

"You can go back to the shed now," Petru said.

"I'd rather not," Séverine replied, sitting at the table and tapping out a cigarette from its pack. "Do you want to open your own restaurant someday?"

"I'm not gonna be your little pal," Petru said.

"So you're gonna be a prick instead?"

Petru's face took on a sulky pallor, and he sipped his wine slowly. Séverine smoked her cigarette and stared at the wall, where she noticed a boom box in the built-in shelves. She popped open the cassette deck and examined the tape inside: *The Chronic* by Dr. Dre.

"Whose is this?" Séverine asked.

"Mine."

"French people don't listen to this stuff," she said as she clicked the tape back into the deck and pressed play.

"This *Corsican* does," Petru said.

"As a *Corsican*, I figured you only listened to polyphonic chanting and Tino Rossi," she teased. "Do you understand what they're saying?"

"I know '*Fuck tha police*,' N.W.A," Petru said in heavily accented English, pointing his fingers like a gun.

Séverine burst out laughing. "The whole point is the words! Do you have the liner notes? I can translate them for you."

"I don't know where the case is," Petru said.

"I could listen and write down the lyrics," she offered. "I do it all the time for my friends. They're obsessed with English music and understand like two words."

So Petru brought her a notebook, rolled himself a cigarette, and they restarted the tape. For the next hour while the chicken roasted, Séverine scribbled down everything she understood, stopping and rewinding over and over again. There were many words Séverine couldn't parse or had to first dissect phonetically ("put these bizzalls in your jizzaws" was replayed multiple times, and she still didn't get it).

With ten minutes left on the timer, Bruno came through the front door, and his face fell like a disappointed parent's.

"Oh no, you listen to this crap, too?"

―――

Once Séverine started helping in the kitchen, she joined the men for every meal—it was only right. Cooking together turned out to be quite pleasant for both Séverine and Petru. His rap music grew on her, mostly for the comfort of hearing the language she shared with her mother. Séverine counted down the days until she'd get to talk to her and her papa. She missed them. She missed how her mom set a cup of coffee on the nightstand in the morning before school, and hearing her dad go over a speech in his home office, and the satisfaction of making them laugh.

At the same time, she was strangely settling into a groove at the bergerie. Séverine's cooperation encouraged the men to loosen up. They finally allowed her to read outdoors, so she began lying in the grass with whatever book Bruno had assigned. From this vantage point, she got a clearer picture of what they actually did all day. After they exercised and ate breakfast with Séverine, they disappeared into the maquis perpendicular to the orchards, snatches of gunfire and shouted commands traveling through the thicket. Next, the four of them ate lunch. After that, Petru returned to the maquis, where he stayed until it was time to make dinner. When she asked what he was up to back there, he became curt and evasive, but it was so obvious he was building a bomb.

Bruno and Tittu didn't hang around in the afternoon; they came and went, Bruno in the 4x4 and Tittu on the motorcycle, never wearing a helmet. The first time Séverine saw him riding it, he'd torn behind the house as she was reading in the grass, a flash of white, red, and black in a wavering cloud of gas. The scream of the engine made her fumble her smoldering cigarette onto the pages of her book.

"Sorry," Tittu called as he cut the engine. His long legs straddled the motorcycle with casual mastery and a confidence he rarely exuded. He looked nearly like a man. If she could consciously cultivate a crush on him, that would make the job she set out for herself much easier.

As they grew closer, however, it started to feel less like a manipulation. Séverine talked to him about the fabulous life she'd left behind in Paris and how depressing her year in Corsica had been, their trips to visit family in the States (for some reason, Tittu was desperate to see the Grand Canyon), and her dreams of becoming an actress. Tittu told her about his own family, whom he saw every Sunday for dinner, leaving the bergerie after training and returning with Tupperware containers full of leftovers for his "dormmates." His mother suffered from multiple sclerosis, his dad was hapless, his older sister had a bum boyfriend she'd probably marry, and his younger sister just wanted to get the hell out of Corsica. He talked about his family's citrus orchard, which had stood in Linguizzetta for seventy years, and how his parents wanted to sell and rid themselves of this generational burden—yet he fought for them to keep it.

"What do they think you're doing this summer?" Séverine asked as she sprayed the tomato plants with a homemade pepper concoction.

"Interning at the National Research Institute for Agriculture. Living at the dorm there." Tittu paused. "I did get the internship. Things just turned out differently," he said with a hint of regret.

"Maybe you should have settled for the ransom then," Séverine replied frostily.

They both talked about how they didn't always feel like their families understood them, and these were the times Séverine forgot she was working an angle and found herself confiding in Tittu.

"God, it's nice having a normal conversation with someone," Séverine said. "Petru doesn't speak, and Bruno only wants to talk about revolution or capitalism or whatever."

"Well, Bruno likes talking to *you*," Tittu said, which gave her a nervous flutter.

"What do you mean?"

"That's not really our thing, Petru and me. But you can get on his level. You're basically doing us a favor."

"What about his girlfriend?" Séverine asked, fishing. "Can she get on his level?"

Tittu snorted, as if sharing an inside joke with himself. "Christine? No."

She felt like she'd fallen off a curb. "That's his girlfriend: Christine?"

"More like an ongoing rebound, some chick who works at the Bastia Airport Hertz," Tittu said. "He did have this long-distance girlfriend who went to the Sorbonne. She was smart and cool, but they broke up last year."

She could see the two of them sitting outside a café in the Latin Quarter in the fall, passing a cigarette back and forth and reading aloud passages from *Surveiller et punir*. A total cliché.

"What about Christine? Is she smart and cool?"

Tittu laughed to himself. "Christine doesn't have to be smart *or* cool, she's an absolute bombasse. But that's the main thing you look for in a rebound."

Séverine pursed her lips and turned her attention back to spraying the plants. It was unspeakably offensive for Tittu to acknowledge another girl's hotness in front of her.

"What about you, got a girlfriend?" She knew the answer before he confirmed it.

"I don't have time," he said unconvincingly.

"Have you *ever* had a girlfriend?"

"I'm not a virgin, if that's what you're getting at," Tittu retorted.

"When did you lose it?" she asked, dropping the spray bottle and lighting a cigarette. She was smoking more than ever, and the possibility she might now have a real nicotine addiction felt so adult.

"The summer before I started university. So a year ago."

"What was it like?"

"I mean, good," Tittu said, his ears reddening. "It's honestly kind of fuzzy, we were both drunk."

"Yeah, same," Séverine said, thinking back to that ill-fated night last year with Julien Laporte, the months—no, years—of buildup and how it all soured in the space of half an hour.

"Things didn't work out with that girl?" she asked.

"It was a one-time thing," Tittu said quietly.

She leaned back on her elbows and let her right knee splay open. "I bet you're one of those late bloomers. Not physically; it's an energy. You're still a little bit 'boy.' But girls will start paying attention to you soon. And you won't even realize you've changed. That's not an insult, by the way," Séverine said.

Tittu stared at her like she was divulging some secret of the universe. "I don't think it's an insult," he said. It was almost too easy.

⁓

As muscle developed in her arms and legs that she'd lacked even pre-kidnapping, Séverine felt not only more herself, but like an advanced version. There were things she could do now that she couldn't before: run five kilometers and do thirty push-ups. It would be insane to say she was happy, but she could submerge her general distress beneath petty pleasures: a sun-warm nectarine, a mouthful of cold water after sunning outside, being told her contribution to a meal was delicious. She found no joy, however, in Lenin.

"Aren't there any other books besides all this dry stuff?" Séverine asked Bruno after a particularly brain-sapping afternoon with *Imperialism, the Highest Stage of Capitalism.*

"What, you want to be *entertained*?" he asked teasingly.

He led her to the living room. It was probably cozy at some point but now felt musty and abandoned. There was a rust-colored shag rug, a nubby green couch below the front window, and an enormous curio cabinet filled with porcelain figurines. And in front of the couch sat a TV, the kind without a remote.

"Does it work?" Séverine asked.

"No," Bruno said quickly.

To the right of the TV was a small bookcase; among the thrillers, romances, and family photos, Séverine noticed a book called *Citizen Jane.* She pulled it out, and there was Jane Fonda on the cover with her big blond perm. It was like running into an acquaintance at a party full of strangers.

"This could be interesting," Séverine said with feigned nonchalance.

"Barbarella?" Bruno scoffed. "Fake revolutionary."

"What do you mean?"

"She traveled to North Vietnam during the Vietnam War, advocating for peace. Needless to say, the Americans freaked out and called her a traitor, and she went on this whole apology tour instead of standing up for the guerrillas," Bruno explained. "If you're looking for drivel, you found it."

It could not be said that the biography was a work of great writing, but the accompanying photos were captivating: Jane, pouty and gorgeous in a suede trench coat and shag haircut, handcuffed, radiating a sensuality unsuitable for the occasion of arrest; Jane in a combat helmet with eyes turned upward and lips parted like she was witnessing something momentous, even transcendent. By contrast, she looked half-bored in the photo of her Oscar acceptance. The superficial smile said this was a secondary thrill.

The respite of Jane enabled Séverine to finish Lenin five days before Soffiu di Libertà was supposed to execute their mysterious second action. No question, Lenin was right to condemn the global superpowers for extorting labor and goods from developing countries and gaining status through exploitation and brutality. Yes, France was one of those superpowers, and yes, her father was part of that machine, but Séverine knew he'd gotten into politics to break that cycle.

"Did he, though?" Bruno asked. "He facilitated construction of that Italian-owned golf resort despite the Corsican Assembly's recommendation against it. Two thirds of our population have left the island because there isn't enough economic opportunity, and something like forty percent of property owners aren't Corsican."

"He's trying," Séverine maintained. "He had all these plans to give Corsica more autonomy, but Jonnart's making it impossible."

"But there are politicians who are up-front about being scumbags, like Jonnart, and there are those who say all the right things but never change anything. It's not in your dad's interest to make Corsica more autonomous or economically stable because he works for the state, and the state needs us dependent to control our land and labor force."

The way Bruno was talking about her dad was uninformed and, frankly, disrespectful. But Séverine didn't want to get into another spat with him; there were other ways to poke back.

"So Monday's the big day, huh?" she asked. "What's Soffiu di Libertà's next act in the glorious fight for independence?"

"No comment."

"I would just like to know if I'm getting a roommate," she said.

He blew a raspberry. "You're enough of a hassle."

Séverine squinted at him. "Are you assassinating someone?" she asked.

Bruno's face screwed up like she'd said something derogatory and nonsensical. "Of course not."

"What happens if you get caught?"

"You'd like that, wouldn't you?"

"No," Séverine said, a little too quickly and genuinely. "Not if I'm stuck up here and no one knows how to find me," she added.

Then she had a real question: "How am I supposed to go to the bathroom while you're gone?"

Bruno evidently hadn't thought this part through. "I guess . . . we'll have to leave your door unlocked."

Séverine felt a delicious jolt, like when her parents first left her home alone.

"You're not scared I'll run away?" she asked.

"You wouldn't make it very far," Bruno said casually. So casually, she knew he wasn't bluffing.

⁓

Over the next few days, the three men became increasingly twitchy. She and Bruno paused their discussions, and dinner became a more modest affair of pasta with jarred sauce.

"You can tell me the plan," Séverine goaded Tittu as she swung from a branch. It was Sunday evening. "I won't say anything."

"Stop asking," Tittu said, annoyed.

"Are you scared?" she asked, pulling up her knees and flipping backwards through her arms, casually flashing her underwear.

He didn't respond.

"If you go to prison, I promise I'll write," she said.

"That's not cute," Tittu said.

"Oh, come on. I'm just saying I'd miss doing this with you."

Tittu gave her a strange, irritated look and dragged the basket of nectarines towards the bergerie. She burned with embarrassment at this rejection and because she'd kind of meant what she'd said. Would she remember the men from that first harrowing week, or from the last three with the companionship they'd established? She felt a premature pang of regret.

She ran after him and grabbed his wrist. He looked down at her dejectedly, a look that said he wanted something he knew he couldn't have. She couldn't help but indulge him; standing on her tiptoes, she placed one hand on his shoulder and the other on his lower jaw, and kissed him. It wasn't passionate, but affectionate. Initially, he seemed bewildered, then he let go of the basket, wrapped his arm around her, and pulled her close.

She'd missed this sensation of a man's hand on her waist making her feel small! Tittu's lips were fuller than hers, like kissing a girl (naturally, she'd made out with Pilar on multiple occasions when they were high from dancing and rum and no worthwhile boys were at their disposal, plus a few times with Hélène when she was especially pathetic). This coexistence of her desire, which was free-standing and ever-present, and her platonic feelings for Tittu didn't present a contradiction or obstacle. She was used to indulging her whims as the mood struck her. So far, she'd avoided weighty, anchored desire but would reconsider it as a grown-up; for now, she wanted to have fun. And kissing Tittu was fun. Surprisingly, he wasn't a bad kisser: not too much tongue, not too many tricks, and he kept his hands respectfully, or apprehensively, around her waist. After a few minutes, the heat and anxiety that had propelled her into his arms faded, and she pulled away. He blinked at her like a mouse paralyzed by snake venom, anticipating the moment of devouring.

"Here, I'll help you," she said airily, and lifted one handle of the basket.

Reality settled in. Tittu cleared his throat and averted his eyes, silently picking up the other handle. He wouldn't tell the others, she knew.

———

The men left the bergerie Monday evening before the sun went down. Petru had prepared her côte de boeuf and vinaigrette for a green salad, all wrapped in plastic and waiting in the fridge.

"Don't dawdle outside once it gets dark," Bruno said. "There are boars."

"And mazzeri," Petru added.

"Mazzeri don't actually roam the maquis, they just dream about it," Bruno said.

"Some do," Petru said.

"What's a mazzeri?" Séverine asked.

"A mazzer*u*," Bruno said, stressing the singular, "is a dream-hunter. They dream about killing an animal with the face of someone in their village, then that person dies."

"You make it sound like it's their fault," Tittu piped up from the corner of the kitchen, where he was thoughtfully smoking. "The death is already decided. The mazzeru just gets the message." He had been silent and preoccupied since yesterday's kiss. Séverine had to admit, she felt a little strange around the other men now, like she'd done something to betray them. She'd accomplished her objective but felt unsettled, like she'd done the wrong thing or chosen the wrong one—like maybe she valued Tittu's friendship too much for her own good.

"The point is, don't hang around outside," Bruno said. "See you tomorrow night." He squeezed her shoulder; it was the first time he'd touched her since hitting her the night of her kidnapping, and she felt a weird thrill.

"And when you get back, you'll arrange for me to talk to my parents," she reminded him.

"Yes," he sighed, annoyed.

Tittu lingered after the other two left the room, just to the side of the doorway, where he couldn't be seen from the front of the house. He clearly felt like he should say or do something but needed a sign from Séverine. She turned to face him.

He finally found the nerve to look at her. "Bye," he murmured.

"Bye, Tittu," she said in a neutral voice, waiting.

He hesitated, then dared to pull her into another kiss. She allowed it: if he was about to be arrested or shot or blown up, he deserved this final luxury. It only lasted a few seconds before Tittu pulled away, whispered one more goodbye, and left.

From the front door, she watched Bruno and Tittu pile into the

4x4 while Petru hefted a lumpy duffle into the trunk; with a thrill, she thought, *The bomb*. Then the car rumbled down the dirt path and out of sight. She was alone.

———

The first thing she did was lift the receiver from the phone on the wall, but the line had been disconnected—of course it wouldn't be so easy. Next, she poured herself a glass of rosé. Not quite knowing what she was looking for, she opened all the drawers in the kitchen—ones that held utensils, scissors, grocery lists, and an address book filled with feminine, old-fashioned handwriting. She flipped through a Rolodex with annotated recipes for brocciu-stuffed sardines (*use mild cheese*), veal with olives (*tomato soup* crossed out and revised to *tomato purée*), chestnut flour cake (*2 eggs for Pierre*). There were no clues. Nothing but a richer picture of the woman who'd lived here first.

Séverine found herself back in front of the living room bookcase, free to examine the photos more carefully. There was one of a pudgy boy holding a duckling and smiling with pride; a woman crouched behind him with her chin on his shoulder. Séverine removed the photo from the frame and saw written on the back, *Pierre and Marie-Laure, Easter 1975*. She laughed: so Petru was really Pierre; he'd changed his name to the Corsican version. And this woman with curly hair and a round, kind face must be his aunt. She imagined Petru's arrest had devastated his aunt, and that losing his aunt had crushed Petru.

Séverine's own mother was not one of these women who collected recipes or wrote the dates on the backs of photos; Bonnie Guimard believed in a mother's right to demand time for her own pursuits, to refuse the tethers of an outdated, oppressive family system. Séverine had never wondered what it would be like to have a "normal" mom—she'd always thought her mother's exceptionality meant she was predisposed to be exceptional, too—but as she replaced the photo on the shelf, it touched her that somebody had once cared that Petru preferred the texture of his cake with two eggs instead of three. Maybe it would have been nice to have a mom, and not only a housekeeper, who paid attention like that.

As she wandered towards the bedrooms, she stopped in front of the closet and opened it. She expected it to look like the crime scene it was, but it had miraculously transformed back into a normal closet filled with nondescript coats, hiking boots, some souvenir baseball caps from the annual honey festival in Murzu, and a stack of puzzles. The ordinariness unsettled her. It was like she'd never been kidnapped at all.

The first bedroom was apparently shared by the men: there were three futons, identical to hers, rolled up on the untouched twin bed. Séverine figured they must sleep on the floor together, probably to avoid the hierarchical problem of two beds. The image was brotherly and sweet. As an only child, Séverine had never experienced that kind of intimacy with another person. Perhaps when she married a brilliant director who'd been pegged as a forever bachelor until he fell in love with her, she might.

Beside the door stood a tall dresser, atop which sat a collection of deodorants and a bottle of Cerruti 1881. She uncapped and spritzed it, leaning towards the mist. She'd never detected this particular scent—piney and dense, but also floral, like grass after a summer shower—on any of the men. It was so evocative of universal masculinity, it was as if the cloud of cologne had arranged itself into the shape of a man, even as the space before her remained achingly empty.

She opened each of the drawers. The first belonged to Tittu, the clothes thrown in haphazardly; the second, everything orderly and uniformly folded, was Petru's. The third drawer was Bruno's, who was so much vainer and more self-curated than the others. He owned a lot of band tees: U2, Dire Straits, Red Hot Chili Peppers. She recognized the three pairs of jeans he cycled through but was surprised to discover they were all Levi's, which were ridiculously expensive in France. Even Séverine's mother waited to buy jeans until they visited the States. Piled against the wall were three stacks of books, a quarter of which Bruno had already given Séverine to read. There was nothing frivolous in the pile. She wondered what he did for fun, or if whatever he was doing at this very moment was his fun.

After returning to the kitchen to refill her wineglass, Séverine moseyed back down the hallway to the last room on the right, where Petru procured her clothes. Inside was a pristinely made bed with white blankets and pillows and an intricately carved headboard. The bedroom had an air of preservation, like the queen's chambers at Versailles, and she proceeded to snoop with due respect.

She noticed a corner of the white bed skirt nudged forward ever so slightly and lifted it to find the edge of a black plastic trunk. Inch by inch, she tugged the long, heavy case out from under the bed. She flipped open the latches and lifted the lid—it was filled with her ransom money and guns. The sight of the cash in its neat bundles nauseated her, but the guns were terrifying. There were—she counted—seven, all different sizes, piled carelessly. Two, which required the length of the case, looked exactly like Rambo's.

"Violence is a cleansing force," Bruno had underlined in the Fanon book. They'd been telling her from day one that they were preparing for a revolution, but it had seemed theoretical, something

Bruno just enjoyed talking about. Then again, there was nothing theoretical about her kidnapping. They'd already proved their capacity for violence, and she was the proof. So why was she shocked? Because she'd grown to like them?

Apprehensively, she picked up a black pistol by its handle; it was heavy for its size, a bit longer than her hand. It looked like the one Bruno had pointed at her; but now, she was the one holding it. She was its master.

It didn't seem overly complicated. Here was the safety, here was the trigger. If she wanted to use this thing, she probably could—she'd seen enough movies. With her finger resting on the trigger guard, she lifted the gun towards the vanity and stared into her own eyes. Her reflection was shadowy in the early evening gloom. In her oversized collared shirt worn like a minidress, she looked like a child, unsure. She took one hand off the handle and tucked her hair behind her ear, relaxing her jaw.

She imagined she was watching herself on-screen. She saw the actress Séverine Guimard, perhaps playing a teenage black widow, a girl who seduced wealthy pedophiles and then murdered them while they lay spent in their beds. An excited chill ran through her as she stared at her own image, pointing the gun at her own mirrored heart. She slackened and let out a soft, satisfied snort. Nailed it.

She reconsidered the gun in her hands and briefly entertained the thought of taking it back to the shed but replaced it in the trunk. It was too late for that kind of threat. She was just as incapable of following through on it as the men had been; her methods were more artful.

She lit a candle and ate dinner while reading about how Jane Fonda's activism had only briefly affected her career; by the late seventies, she was being nominated for Oscars. Funny how the public could hate you then root for you again; they loved a comeback even more than a fall from grace.

The twilight was rich and blue, and it was cozy in this cottage with her candlelight and book and perfectly cooked steak. But once she finished and washed her plate, Séverine found herself feeling useless and bored. Thinking of the boars, known to attack, even kill people with their long tusks—and maybe a little of the mazzeri— she had no desire to explore outside in the dark. The clock read 23:00; depressingly, it was more or less bedtime. She turned off the lights except the one in the kitchen and raced on her tippy-toes back to the shed.

On her way to the bathroom the next morning, Séverine noticed the men's boots by the front door and their rucksacks propped against the wall. They hadn't been due back until late that afternoon.

By the time she'd showered and dressed, they'd woken; Bruno and Tittu sat groggily at the kitchen table while Petru brewed coffee on the stovetop.

"What happened?" Séverine asked, leaning in the doorway.

"Nothing," Bruno said without looking at her. His fingers grazed the back of his fresh buzz cut, maybe self-soothingly.

"Technical difficulties. It was my fault," Petru said, his back to them as he took four cups from the cabinet.

"It wasn't one person's fault," Bruno said with effort. "At least we made it out."

"That sucks," she said. "What about talking to my parents?"

"Give me a fucking minute, Séverine!" Bruno exploded.

"Don't take it out on me!" she yelled back, and stormed off to the shed.

The day passed with depressed indolence. Séverine read with one eye on the men as they puttered around the bergerie, pretending to be busy. Finally, at the normal hour, Tittu waved Séverine over to the orchard.

"It was a car bombing," he admitted once they were out of ear-shot. "Or limo bombing, technically. Jonnart's."

"He's in Corsica?" Séverine felt so disconnected; it had been a month since she'd so much as laid eyes on a newspaper.

"Was. He's back in France now."

"What happened?" Séverine asked breathlessly; the thought of Jonnart being blown up held some appeal for her, admittedly.

"The idea was for it to explode at night, when he was in his hotel. It was supposed to go off at 02:00 in the morning, but then it was 02:30, then 03:00, then 04:00, and Jonnart got up to fly back to Paris. At that point, we thought the bomb was gonna go off while they were driving. It's one thing to blow up his limo as a warning, it's another to actually blow him up. So we just sat in our safe house totally wired, waiting to hear an explosion or sirens or something, but nothing happened. We were actually relieved, but then we were like: Why? We fucked up. And we couldn't sleep anyway, so we just came back."

Séverine nodded with disappointment. If she didn't wish Jonnart dead, she at least wished him terror upon hearing his limo explode, understanding on a carnal level that he was not invincible, that he was not master of this world.

"Don't tell Bruno or Petru I told you. Don't even bring it up," Tittu said.

"He takes everything so personally," Séverine complained. There was no need to specify she was talking about Bruno.

"I think he doesn't feel as confident without Matteu," Tittu said. "He was kind of the glue that held us all together."

Séverine mulled this over. Bruno wasn't a born leader, but he'd assumed the role in Matteu's absence—or maybe he just wanted to be someone he wasn't.

She realized Tittu was looking at her, and in his silence hung expectation. He leaned in, and although her thoughts were elsewhere, she let him kiss her. He'd shed his uncertainty; his hands found their way under her shirt. He kissed her more intently—he was ready to go further, but she wasn't. The danger of their attack had passed, and her interest with it. With a little laugh, she pulled away and tucked her shirt back into her skirt. They shared a conspiratorial smile and went back to work. As Séverine pulled fruit from the tree, she wondered how she was going to get herself out of her own brilliant scheme.

Dinner was quiet and somber. Their sulking was annoying, particularly Bruno's. He was in his head, disengaged from everyone at the table. While everyone else was picking at their frozen pizza, he rose from the table and declared, "I'm going out."

"Where?" Petru asked.

"I don't know. In town," he said. "I just need to blow off some steam." He grabbed the keys to the 4x4 and was out the door.

"That's kind of rude," Séverine said, offended on their behalf.

They shrugged and went back to their mediocre dinner.

Séverine had trouble sleeping. It was 03:30 and she hadn't heard the 4x4 return. She wondered with a strange sick feeling if "blowing off steam" meant seeing—what was her name? Something trashy— Christine. Did he go to the rental office under the pretense of reserving a car, then after inspecting it for dents and noting the petrol level, did she wordlessly get in the front seat and drive to an unfrequented part of the airport, behind some cargo warehouse? Did he turn off the ignition and recline his seat, and did she climb on top of him? Did her long, dark hair fall over her face as she hiked up her skirt? Did he sigh with relief as she pulled her cheap lace underwear aside and guided him inside her? Did they even kiss? Was he the type of man whose face closed in monstrous pleasure, or whose face opened, who watched you in wonder at what your body could do to his?

Séverine threw off her blanket, slipped on her thongs, and crept across the lawn into the house. No one had thought to lock her in the shed tonight; hopefully that had become the new de facto policy. From the bathroom, she heard the roar of the 4x4 accelerating up the last hill of the dirt road. Quickly, she finished peeing and flushed. Bruno's boots clomped as he kicked them off, and his footsteps were heavy, irregular. He was drunk, the idiot! Séverine flung open the bathroom door and practically ran into him.

"Where have you been?" she demanded in an angry whisper.

He looked down at her, oblivious as only a drunk person can be. "Out," he said, and angled himself to slip past her and into the bathroom.

"Doing what?" she asked, blocking him.

"I have to pee like a motherfucker," he said, putting his hands on her shoulders and moving her out of his way. As he passed, the scent of Cerruti 1881 pierced her like a knife.

She waited with arms crossed until he emerged with the whooshing of the plumbing.

"We've been really worried," she said.

"Yeah, it seems like the other two are losing sleep," he said, teasing.

Séverine remained stern.

"I went to see some friends, that's all," Bruno said.

Friends. Séverine felt a hot brand within her, an unfamiliar, inflamed emotion.

"Actually, I brought you something. In the bag by the door."

Her irritation vanished—he'd gotten her a gift! She saw nothing besides a wrinkled plastic Carrefour bag, which she brought back into the light of the bathroom. It was filled with clothes. Not new clothes, but ones that had been laundered and folded; they still gave off the artificial floral scent of detergent. From the top of the pile, she pulled a daisy-printed halter dress in thin, stretchy fabric. She checked the tag: Pimkie. This dress belonged to some other girl. Chest burning, she dug through the rest of the bag: plaid miniskirts and floral-printed jeans with elastic waists and stretched-out rib-knit T-shirts and one wrinkled black vest. She could see her perfectly, this girl. She got up early to do her hair and makeup, claimed to be into fashion because she bought *Vogue* once a year, and was saving up for a resort vacation in Tunisia—the type of girl Séverine dismissed outright. There was no question that these clothes belonged to that Christine—*hot* Christine.

"I can't wear this stuff, it's heinous," she spat. She examined the tag of the dress in her hand, which had an *M* for medium. "I'll be swimming in it anyway, it's enormous."

"Um, okay," Bruno said, confused.

"You want to do something nice for me? Get me on the phone with my parents like you promised."

"Séverine," he began, dragging his hand over his face. She knew he was far too drunk to talk about this, but he deserved the exasperation. "The idea behind the car bombing was to reiterate our demand for Matteu's release, see if it would get reconsidered.

But the bomb didn't go off. So you're gonna have to wait till next time."

Séverine trembled with anger. "You promised," she said, willing herself not to cry.

"I promised you could speak to them after our next action. And there was no action," he said, not without compassion.

"That's not my problem," she replied through her teeth.

"I'm sorry, but we have a strategy in place."

"You promised," Séverine repeated, humiliated by her hot tears.

"I'm sorry," Bruno said, then turned and went to his room.

Séverine stood there for a few minutes, her mouth slack, tears running down her neck. She let herself cry; it had been weeks since she'd cried, she realized. She'd only stopped because she'd grown to trust these men and had been foolish enough to believe they cared for her, that they saw her as a person and not just a bargaining chip. She'd meant to gain their trust for her ends, but she was the one who'd been played. It was stupid to think they'd eventually release her without getting what they wanted. They wouldn't even let her talk to her parents after an entire month.

As Séverine returned to the shed in a state of dazed indignation, the fact of her freedom dawned on her. She was alone outside; all locks had been unfastened and all doors thrown open. Her plan to escape by winning their affection had worked; she just hadn't registered it. She could walk down that dirt road and no one would notice for hours, at which time she could have already come across a village, knocked on the first door, been ushered in by a kindly mammona who let her use an old-fashioned rotary phone to call her parents and fed her cheesecake as she waited to finally be saved. It seemed silly that she'd been so nervous to ven-

ture out. So long as she stayed on a road, she was as good as rescued.

There was nothing inside the shed except her half-empty water
bottle, which she gave a swift, petulant kick across the room. *Sorry,*
Bruno had repeated. Well, he would be. She walked around the side
of the house and took her first steps down the road.

6. *In the Maquis*

At first, Séverine did not feel afraid. The night was at its ripest point before morning; the crescent moon had begun its descent and hung below the trees. With each step, she felt a meditative calm, doing the impossible and doing it steadily.

After forty-five minutes or so, Séverine was still walking along the dirt path; she'd expected to reach the paved road by now. The sky turned early morning gray; animals awakened and chattered to each other. She was sick of the sound of her thongs smacking against her feet, and she was getting a blister between her toes. Also, she was hungry. She hadn't thought to raid the kitchen before setting off. It had felt like she had to leave at that very moment if she was ever going to leave at all.

The path narrowed and the maquis, a moist green, closed in from all sides. No way the 4x4 could fit through here. She considered turning around, but it was about the time Petru and Tittu would be getting up; perhaps they were just now realizing she wasn't in the shed; perhaps they'd already woken hungover Bruno and were running to the car, about to fly down the road looking for her—or flying down the road to a new safe house, in anticipation of Séverine's betrayal. She scolded herself for thinking "betrayal." It wouldn't be betrayal; it would be justice.

It was probably safest to stay on this path, wherever it was taking her, so on she walked. She tried to re-access her zen state, acknowledging the beauty of the morning, the gentle sun that refracted through the film of humidity in the air, the dainty yellow and violet wildflowers that sprung up among the long grass, the smell of damp earth and rosemary. The sun rose directly in front of her—east almost certainly meant going deeper into the interior of the island. She might very well be all the way up north, where she could walk in the wrong direction for days and not pass a soul. South was the way she wanted to go, no matter what. Séverine stared up at the sun, but there was nothing else it could communicate that she'd understand. She was a city girl; she'd never even gone camping.

No use worrying, she told herself. She didn't quite believe in God, but she believed in that Hollywood vision of herself like a prophecy—reading scripts poolside at her mansion, her director-husband bringing her a piña colada and asking if she'd let Gianni (Versace) know which dress she'd decided on for the Oscars ceremony. The clarity of this vision meant she would inevitably stumble onto a paved road, then a village, then go home and get to making it real.

Soon the path was completely overtaken by the maquis, but retracing her steps was not an option. Séverine knew what was back there, and she was done with that. She turned to the right—south, hopefully—and forged through the forest without hesitation.

Flip-flopping through the wild grasses in thong sandals was not the same as following a trail, and her place slowed. The heat was alleviated by the trees, but anytime she walked through a rocky bald patch, the sun burned like she was an ant under a magnifying glass. Pretty soon, she drank the last of her water. Gnats flitted around her, taunting, sticking to her tacky skin. She felt utterly alone and victimized by the natural world. She hated this place, resented and cursed the whole island.

If only they had never left Paris, and she was still in the big, beautiful Marais apartment, growing up sleek and savvy, as all her old friends surely were. She hoped her parents were happy. If it weren't for her father's outsized ambition, she would never have found herself in this situation: kidnapped, nearly murdered, accessing the part of herself marked "For Emergency Use Only." Most people never had to pull that lever, and doing so had fundamentally altered her, in a way she didn't know if she liked and certainly didn't feel ready for. She hated her parents, she hated Bruno and Petru and Tittu, she hated Corsica, she hated herself for not knowing how to survive better.

Amid all these vicious thoughts, Séverine found herself sitting on the ground, leaning against a pine. She hadn't been aware that she'd stopped moving. The sun seemed to hover right over her head—it must be noon. She'd been walking for six or seven hours, which seemed impossible, laughable. The maquis here looked the same as the maquis she'd trekked through: remote, nowhere near a road. She was exhausted but feared what would happen if she stopped to nap, if she woke up and it was dark out. First, she needed to find water, but she was unsure if it was safe to drink from some random stream. As the thirst crept up, she knew it wouldn't matter soon.

Walking through the mazelike forest with no true sense of where she was headed was uncanny. Multiple times, she found herself at the side of a steep ridge she had no hope of scaling, which forced her to make a hard turn—east or west, north or south, she was never entirely sure. She encountered no one except animals: a small herd of deer that eyed her suspiciously as they high-stepped through the grass, little birds in trees cocking their heads at her, like they'd never seen a girl before. The thirstier and hungrier she became, the harder it was to carry on, the more she wanted to lie down in the pine needles. Somehow, she continued to walk and walk. Her body felt brittle, her mind untethered like an anchor cut loose from a ship, sinking down and down to darker depths.

Finally, she lay down under a tree and closed her eyes. At least sleep would neutralize her thirst, the cramp in her belly, her throbbing feet.

Waking felt like being pulled from a lake she was happily drowning in. The sun had plunged below the horizon, but it wasn't yet night. The effect on the maquis was eerie: the sun glazed the edges of the trees, making everything untouched by the light appear much darker. It was as if she'd woken in a different place than she'd fallen asleep. Her hunger and thirst returned. There was no hope of eating before morning; water, however, was imperative, no matter how frightening the thought of navigating the maquis in the dark. She stood slowly, black dots blooming across her field of vision, limbs trembling, a hot wave of nausea roiling through her. She had no choice but to walk.

Séverine had never been in a situation that called for bravery, and so she'd never considered the physicality of summoning it. With each careful step, she assured herself that the maquis at night was the same as in daylight; if she could tap into that same sense of peace, she'd manage just fine. Then she remembered the wild boars. Nighttime was their time, and Séverine was intruding. With an earnest shudder, she also remembered the mazzeri.

She looked up at the stars, which now seemed a smattering of heartless light. Their arrangement meant nothing to her, left her directionless. So much was beyond her understanding.

All of a sudden, a great black figure loomed from the shadows just beside her. Séverine's throat closed with fear, and she let out a small, sharp cry, but the thing didn't flinch; it was still as stone. She reached towards it, hand trembling—it was, in fact, stone, and curiously warm to the touch, like a body. It was shaped like a body, too, broadening at the shoulders, although it was much taller than an average person: it was a menhir. They existed in France as well, but she'd never seen one until moving to Corsica, when her history class had gone on a field trip to the most famous menhir site in Filitosa. Some had serious, masklike faces with blank eyes staring into the middle distance, while others were faceless and shapeless, prehuman.

Séverine's exhaustion had caught up with her, and she sat in the grass, her back against the menhir. The world was so, so old—this maquis, this dumb little country, this menhir and the rock it was made from; its impenetrable granite might be as old as earth itself. And Séverine was just another beating heart in a crowded forest.

Then she heard it, unmistakable: water. She pulled herself to her feet and went towards the sound. Only a few meters away, down a slight slope, flowed a wide stream, moonlight winking white against the water. When she reached its banks, she lay on her belly and opened her mouth, letting the cold and silty water rush in. It definitely wasn't some pure, crystalline spring, but it quenched her thirst.

Full to the throat with water, she rolled onto her back. From this position, she noticed a black branch dangling dark little spheres right overhead. She must have torn past it, oblivious to everything but the stream, but now she sat up and plucked off one small globe. It was—a plum. She laughed, the butt of some universal joke—then devoured ten of them.

Exhausted, she made her way back to the menhir. When she lay down to get some sleep, it hit her just how chilly the mountain air was at night. Shivering, she tucked her arms through the holes of her sleeveless linen dress, wrapped them against her chest, and folded her knees into the skirt, sidling up to the menhir for warmth it could not provide.

Séverine gave up on sleep at first light, making her way to the stream to soak up what morning warmth she could. The pile of plum pits was strewn about, like some creature had rummaged through. She choked down her breakfast of plums and decided to cross the stream; there seemed something symbolic about it, that on one side was her captivity and on the other, her freedom.

She gathered her dress around her waist and took off her thongs. The stream must have been about as wide as a four-lane highway— nothing insurmountable, but the current intensified as she waded towards the center. Whitecaps fringed the waves as they slammed against her; she slipped, her free arm plunging into the water to catch her fall, almost losing her thongs in the commotion. *Screw it*, she thought, and turned around. She wasn't going to drown just to indulge a metaphor.

There was nothing to do but gather a few plums in her skirt for later and choose a direction. Turning right, with the current, felt correct.

For the first part of the day, Séverine's spirits remained high. She followed faithfully as the stream meandered this way and that. Now that she'd found it, she was never letting it out of her sight. With each turn, she anticipated a road appearing, a house with a defunct mill attached, a gang of children splashing in the water. She imagined reuniting with her parents, how they'd embrace her, their tears dampening her hair. And eventually, she could talk to her dad about everything she'd learned, help him do right by this deranged little island so something good would come out of this cursed experience.

It dawned on her that she would never see the men of Soffiu di Libertà again. Or actually, she might: at their trial. What they did to her was wrong, but she didn't know if she could rat them out. The idea of sending Tittu to prison horrified her; Petru even more so. After what he'd been through, it seemed gratuitous. Bruno might actually do well; he'd be the type to teach workshops to the inmates. It was more the thought of excising him from her life entirely that caused a pang in her chest. Whether she turned them in or not, she'd never see them again; it's not like they could organize a monthly coffee date. But she'd remember eating peaches off the tree with Tittu, his hands on her waist, how he'd leap in and out of the branches like a panther. She'd remember quietly preparing dinner beside Petru, his American rap, the smell of fried onions. She'd remember sitting very close to Bruno, how his hand would graze hers when pointing to a passage in an open book she was holding; she'd remember the feeling of her brain working, how they'd talk over each other trying to articulate everything the other had illuminated within them.

Séverine began to cry as she continued along the bank of the stream. She knew it was twisted to shed tears for her kidnappers, but look, she'd made the best of her situation, and that required forming some attachments. People would only be able to wrap their minds around some soapy narrative in which the men had been heartless and bad, and she was a plucky heroine who'd used her wits to escape. She'd never try to explain the truth to anyone.

She wondered how she'd seem different to her parents, and in what ways her old life would seem different to her. She'd never found

it strange that everyone at the resort in Sperone—where she and her
mom liked to lunch while her father played golf with the club
owners—was French, German, Swiss. She didn't think she'd still
be able to enjoy the scallop salad so innocently knowing this huge
chunk of virgin land had been razed and fenced for the exclusive use
of wealthy foreigners. It was so weird that this didn't bother her
parents.

She wondered how much they paid Maria. *A lot!* a voice inside
piped up, scandalized. Her parents loved Maria, and she them. They'd
brought Maria on all sorts of exotic vacations, places she'd never in
her life have visited without the Guimards paying her way. Did that
justify Maria's life being more or less subsumed by theirs?

Séverine had been accommodated in so many ways by so many
people, some she knew by name and others she'd never laid eyes on,
whose existence she'd never even thought about. There was a food
chain, and Séverine topped it. She'd always known abstractly that
people starved, that girls were mutilated, that people were being
slaughtered in places like Bosnia, but it never occurred to her that
that world overlapped in any way with hers. She'd never realized
that she lived amid injustice, that she might even be contributing to
it. For some reason, she was being forced to connect herself more
literally to the pain of the world.

Maybe her plan to influence her father was stupid. Paul Guimard
had no experience with hardship; he was the son of the most prom-
inent cardiologist in Gascony. He had attended the best schools,
learned English at Cambridge, been escorted up the professional
ladder by dozens of rheumy old-timers who deludedly saw something of their younger selves in him. He was compassionate and
motivated, but he genuinely thought his moderate solutions were the
correct ones, which made him a token for the Parti socialiste, enjoying

all the benefits of status while claiming some trumped-up moral high ground. She stopped in her tracks—that thought hadn't come from Bruno; she'd produced it herself, she realized queasily. She felt infected by him.

Was this the light Bruno had told her about? It wasn't soft and lovely, but harsh, and it burned. She cried—for herself, for all she hadn't known and now knew, for her parents, and for Bruno and Tittu and Petru, with tenderness towards their noble, insane, impossible undertaking.

Soon enough, the sun plummeted below the tree line. She'd been walking all day, and her feet were blistered, aching. She decided to try and push through until the sky blackened, then find some tree to curl up under and start all over in the morning. There was no other choice.

Then a pinpoint of light twinkled through the trees on her right, so small she initially mistook it for a firefly. Abandoning the stream, she hurried towards the light, its aureole growing as she neared. She emerged from the trees onto a gravel driveway, and it was the 4x4 she first recognized. The house loomed dark like a witch's den, and she was permeated with nausea. No, it wasn't possible—all this walking, all this misery, to end up back where she started. She would not give in to them again.

She turned to creep back into the woods when the door to the bergerie opened, and a shaft of light struck Séverine head-on. Bruno was silhouetted in the doorway; one hand gripped the doorknob and the other was plunged in the back pocket of his jeans, about to remove his car keys when he caught sight of her. He blanched, frightened, as if she were an apparition.

She told herself to run back into the maquis, but no part of her would cooperate. Instead, she found herself walking towards Bruno, drawn back to him by an instinctual force, the same force on which she'd staked the whole idea of her destiny. Then she was standing just before him, head tilted up so their noses practically touched. She could kiss him if she wanted, or she could stick a knife in him if she'd had one. But he pulled her into a hug, her neck in the crook of his elbow, and kissed the top of her head three times. He released her and smoothed her hair, examining her with a happy, ironic expression.

"We thought we'd lost you for good," he said.

"That was the idea," Séverine replied sullenly, which made him laugh, so she couldn't help but laugh, too, then sob—relief, devastation, relief. Bruno clucked like a grandmother and wrapped his arms around her; she relented, letting him bear her entire weight, and allowed herself to cry on his T-shirt, to be comforted by the scent of him.

~

Tittu and Petru rushed from the kitchen, asking questions that Bruno disregarded as he steered Séverine to the bathroom. He stopped up the tub, turned on the water, and said, "I'll be right back." Water thundered from the faucet, a soothing white noise that dulled her mind. When she sank into the hot tub, the muscles from the arches of her feet up to her jaw unclenched, and she made her first full exhale in forty-eight hours.

There was a knock at the door, and Bruno said, "Room service."

Séverine cracked opened the shower door, and he placed a plate of cheese, thick slices of saucisson sec, and marinated olives on the ledge of the tub. She forced herself to eat at a normal pace even though she felt like she could swallow the plate whole.

Bruno sat on the bath mat while Séverine washed herself. She closed her eyes, listening to the faucet drip languidly. There was no pretending she wasn't glad to be back. Funny how there was always something worse than your initial worst-case scenario.

When the water began to cool off, Séverine cleared her throat. "Will you hand me a towel?"

Bruno rose to his feet, pulled a towel from the rack, and held it out for her.

When she opened the frosted glass door, he was leaning against the sink and staring at his beat-up Reeboks, crossed at the ankle. She couldn't interpret his silence.

"You had us really freaked out," he said.

"Why, because you thought I was going to rat you out?" Séverine asked, tightening the towel around her chest to give her breasts a little lift. She didn't know why her first instinct was to act bitchy.

"Because we thought for sure we'd never find you out there."

She looked at him skeptically.

"We've been frantic, driving all around and hiking into the maquis. We each did like fifteen kilometers a day, going in separate directions. We weren't bullshitting when we said it's remote."

"Okay, yes, I get it now." She stepped out of the tub onto the bath mat, forcing Bruno to move aside, and began combing her hair with her fingers in front of the mirror.

"Why would you do something so stupid?" he asked.

Her fingers tore from her hair as she swung around. "You *kid-napped* me! I haven't spoken to my family in a month!"

"Okay, okay." He raised his hands in surrender. "I'll get you in touch with them."

"Tomorrow," she demanded.

"It might be a couple days, but I promise I'll make it happen as soon as possible, for real this time," Bruno said. He was looking at her with concern, a small vertical wrinkle beside his eyebrow. "I'm sorry, I'll let you get dressed."

The house smelled like fish fried with lemon. Séverine entered the kitchen to find the guys seated around a table carefully set, waiting nervously.

"Sit, eat," Bruno said, pulling out her chair.

The taste of the food didn't register to Séverine, just the sensation of a hole in her gut slowly being filled. No one tried to make conversation till her plate was clean. Finally, Petru spoke.

"Where the hell have you been wandering around?"

"I swear I just went down the path, but I must have gotten turned around at some point because I never made it to the road," Séverine replied.

Petru frowned and considered this. "I wonder if you somehow ended up on the old hunting trail."

"I don't know," Séverine shrugged. "I did pass a menhir."

"What menhir?" Petru asked.

"If you follow the stream over there for like, a day, there's a menhir just off the banks."

Petru got up from the table and rummaged through one of the kitchen drawers, pulling out an old map Séverine had somehow missed in her snooping, which he placed on the table.

"We're here," he said, reaching over her shoulder to point to an *X* marked in blue pen towards the bottom of the map, surrounded by a large swath of green. In fact, this entire portion was green. In the lower right, one town was identified: Terraperta. She'd never heard of it.

"It's not on the map, but this river here branches out into the stream that runs beside the bergerie. I think you somehow got onto the old hunting trail"—he dragged his finger eastward—"then went south and west into the maquis." Now, the thick finger traced down towards the town of Terraperta. "You must have been right on the other side of the T20."

"So you're saying if I'd crossed the stream, there was a highway on the other side?" Séverine asked numbly.

"Yeah."

Séverine stared at all that green on the map, the threadlike blue and white lines running through this small corner of civilization, until her eyes unfocused.

"You must have covered sixty, sixty-five kilometers."

Séverine nodded, detached. She had been so close but hadn't *felt* like she was only a few meters from civilization. If anything, she'd felt pushed away by the furious water. She had felt pulled not to the town, not to her parents, but back to the bergerie.

"What would you have done if you'd made it to Terraperta?" Tittu asked.

Séverine gave a soft snort and shrugged. "I don't know. Gone home. Slept. Took the bac and started fac in the fall?" This was no way to lead a life; it was a waste of the zenith of her youth, that brief intersection when she was still young enough to be universally desirable and old enough to capitalize on it. She didn't want to go to fac, she didn't want to study drama for four years then go to Hollywood and claw her way up the ladder. She didn't want to rot up in the bergerie either. She wanted stardom, her future, now. She wanted to change something fundamental about her life and her role in the world, and she wanted to change the world itself. It didn't seem that hard. There was some destiny to fulfill, she knew, and it was up to her to make the first move. There were people who never did, and greatness, which always required a risk, eluded them. Séverine would never be one of those people.

"I want to help you," she announced. Had she actually said it aloud? She felt possessed.

"What do you mean?" Tittu asked.

"Maybe I'm supposed to be here."

"Say what you *mean*, Séverine," Bruno said. His voice was strangely antagonizing.

"I don't want to be your hostage anymore. I want to join Soffiu di Libertà."

She looked at Bruno. He was staring at her fixedly, as if he were trying to see straight into her brain, examine this most extreme thought and judge its intention.

Petru laughed. "You just tried to escape, and now you're saying you want to join us?"

"Why?" Bruno asked her.

"What do you mean, *why*? Why'd you have me read all those books?" Séverine answered heatedly.

"What do you think it means, joining us?" he asked.

"Is it that different from what I've been doing? Training, reading," she replied.

"We do a lot more than that," Bruno said.

"Do you?" Séverine pushed back. "Because by my count, you've kidnapped me and failed to blow up Jonnart's car. Do you even have a new plan?"

"Just because we haven't shared our plans with you doesn't mean they don't exist," Bruno said, haughty and unconvincing.

"I think it's a great idea," Tittu declared. "It solves all our problems."

"Hardly," Petru said. "This is a military organization, and she's not a soldier."

Bruno clucked. "What about Celia Sánchez? Ulrike Meinhof?"

"She's not like that," Petru said.

"I can prove myself," Séverine insisted.

She flipped through her mental Rolodex. She knew so many people who could stand to be chastened, but it had to be someone who messed with Corsica specifically. Then it hit her: the Laportes. A family who, for decades, had enriched themselves through war profiteering, and who'd used that money to build a hideous villa in Corsica. If she also had her own grievance against Julien Laporte, no one needed to know. Making him suffer would be the cherry on top.

"The Laporte villa," she proposed. "What if I help you blow it up?"

"As in the Laporte Group? Military aircrafts?" Tittu asked.

"I remember reading Pierre Laporte's obituary in *l'Humanité*," Bruno said. "Basically every modern war that involved a national power squashing an insurgency involved Laporte fighter planes: Algeria, Palestine, El Salvador, the list goes on."

"They have a vacation home in Calvi," Séverine added.

"You know them?" Tittu asked.

"I know them," she said darkly.

"So why do you want to blow up their house?" Petru asked.

"What do you mean? You heard what Bruno just said. And their big ugly villa sits empty ten months out of the year."

Petru narrowed his eyes, arms crossed. "No. It's personal. Why do you hate them?"

Séverine laughed breathily. "What, it's not good enough for Soffiu di Libertà?"

"We don't want any action to come across as vendetta," Petru said.

"He's a defense contractor, not some random guy she has a grudge against," Tittu countered.

As they argued, Bruno stared out the window over the sink, deep in thought.

"What are your options?" Séverine ranted. "Kill me? You couldn't. Send me home to my parents? You don't seem to want to do that. So what's left?"

"She's right," Bruno finally said, resolute. "Séverine will join Sof- fiu di Libertà. She'll record a statement saying she's enlisted in the fight for independence, and we'll send it to the press." He turned to Petru. "If we can convert the prefect's daughter, we can convert anyone."

"So you want to use me as a propaganda tool," Séverine said.

"Look, Petru's right: you're not a soldier. But that doesn't mean you can't be useful." Bruno turned to Petru. "What do you think?"

"Does it matter what I think?" Petru muttered, arms crossed.

"Petru, what do I have to do for you to take me seriously?" Séver- ine asked sincerely.

"If she's going to join us, she needs to join us one hundred per- cent," Petru said to Bruno. Then he looked at Séverine. "You get what that means? No special treatment. And you have to follow our rules."

"Sure, whatever. But I have a couple conditions, too," Séverine said. "One, I stay inside the house from now on."

"There's no room for you," Petru said.

"What about your aunt's room?" Bruno asked.

"Girls need their own space," Tittu said.

Petru exhaled hard through his nose. "Her own room, that's not special treatment?" Séverine could tell his irritation was less about the special treatment and more about the room's enshrinement.

"Two, I need proper clothes," Séverine continued, shooting a pointed look at Bruno.

"Tell us what you need," Bruno said.

Séverine grabbed a notepad by the phone and wrote out a shop- ping list. When she finished, she spun it to face Bruno and tapped the pen at each bullet point. "Three pairs of Levi's 512, light, me- dium, and black wash, size 7 Regular. Seven black T-shirts, extra- small, and boots like yours, size 37. Bras, 85B, and underwear, small.

What else do guerrillas wear? Camouflage? Oh, and black eyeliner, the pencil kind."

Bruno laughed and said, "It's not going to look normal buying all this women's clothing plus tactical gear."

"Then send your girlfriend in," Séverine retorted.

Bruno looked at her with genuine curiosity. "Who?" he asked.

"The girl you see. From the rental agency. The one you got the clothes from," she mumbled, looking at Tittu in accusation.

"Funny how few people it takes for gossip," Bruno said. "And the clothes are my sister's."

Séverine felt herself blush. She stood, trying to regain her composure. "Those are my conditions," she said. "I'm going to bed. Don't forget what you promised me, Bruno."

He nodded.

On her way out of the kitchen, Petru, still seated, grabbed her wrist.

"I'm very happy you're safe. I want it to stay that way," he said, looking at her with red-rimmed eyes. He was unshaven and his skin hung like a middle-aged man's, not a twenty-four-year-old's. He looked like he hadn't slept in days. Touched, Séverine leaned down and kissed his bristly cheek.

When she entered the bedroom, she opened its one window. No screens meant mosquitoes, but she was done with enclosure.

There was a tentative knock—Tittu, she knew. She did not have the energy for this but didn't put up a fight when he stepped inside the room and closed the door.

"I know you must be tired, but I just wanted to say—when I realized you'd run away, it hurt my feelings at first. No, wait—" He put a hand out, stopping Séverine as she opened her mouth to tell him off. "But then I realized how selfish that was. And I got nervous that—that maybe I'd taken advantage of the situation in some way."

He looked at the floor, and the tops of his ears were scarlet. Séverine's anger melted, and she placed her hand on his cheek. Instead of explaining that it was her who'd tried to take advantage, she said, "You didn't."

He smiled with relief and took her hand from his face and kissed it.

"But I need some time to like, process all this," she said, taking back her hand.

He nodded with genuine understanding, then left, closing the door behind him. The matter of his infatuation, this solution that was now poised to become a problem, would have to be addressed sooner rather than later.

Séverine removed her dress and slipped naked between the tightly tucked covers; the cold sheets on her sunburnt skin felt medicinal. As she drifted off to sleep, she dreamed she was in her bed in Ajaccio, and the millisecond of total comfort she felt startled her awake. How would she tell her parents she wasn't coming home?

7. Grudges

For the first time in a month, Séverine was woken by nothing—no banging at the door—she merely opened her eyes to a gray afternoon and white eyelet curtains tenting with the breeze. For a moment, she forgot where she was and how she came to be in a bed again; when she remembered, it wasn't with panic but a sense of satisfaction and purpose.

She made her way into the kitchen, where Petru was washing dishes and Tittu was flipping through a brittle-paged detective novel, a cigarette balanced between his elegant fingers.

"You never played piano?" Séverine asked, pulling out a chair.

He looked up, startled. "Yeah, actually. I suck now, though. I haven't played much since I started fac."

"Don't listen to him. He'll bring a tear to your eye," Petru said over his shoulder, and Tittu blushed.

"I wanna hear you play one day," Séverine said. She surprised herself; she was no longer trying to manipulate. She meant it.

The screen door slapped against the frame, and Bruno came into the kitchen laden with shopping bags.

"Merry Christmas," he said, placing them at her feet.

As she removed the clothes from the bag, Séverine did feel the euphoria of Christmas morning: here was everything she asked for, crisp and new, professionally folded, still smelling like the store. The store! The clothes were like an artifact from another world. She was desperate to get back to that world; she just needed her new comrades to trust her enough.

Séverine assumed Bruno would have pre-written a carefully curated statement, but when they sat at the kitchen table with the tape recorder, he placed an outline before her.

"I would like your input," he explained. "This communiqué can't sound forced; it has to sound like you came up with it. Now . . ." He tapped a pen against the legal pad and gave her a bulleted list of talking points.

"Now you have me writing a dissertation?" she whined.

"Think of it as monologuing. Here, you talk, I'll write."

As they invented, performed, and revised each sentence, Séverine found herself engrossed. Anytime Bruno would nod, hand racing across the legal pad, and say, "Yeah, that's good," she felt a jolt of pride she'd never felt at school. She felt capable, clever even—she imagined her mom listening to the final product and feeling perversely proud.

There was a certain language used in all the literature Bruno made Séverine read: "late capitalism," "material," "kleptocratic," "manufacturing consent." At first, she'd thought it was how smart people talked, but now she realized it was the way people talked to sound smart. As long as she knew the vocabulary and sentence structure, she could reproduce it with ease. And by sounding smarter, she felt smarter. After about an hour, they had not only a script on their hands but a new slogan: *U futuru avà,* "the future now"—the promise Séverine had made to herself the night before.

"Be animated, not rigid," Bruno directed, stealing one of her *Vogues.* "Like it's all clicking for the first time and you want the world to get on your level. Proselytize."

Séverine nodded, and Bruno pressed the red button on the tape recorder.

"This is Séverine Guimard. I was taken by Soffiu di Libertà thirty-three days ago, but it honestly feels like a year. Not because I'm lonely and miserable and everything's terrible, but the opposite—because I've found real friendship and purpose here, and I've grown so much. For the last seventeen (almost eighteen) years, I never questioned why I had so much and most people had so little. Because of my family's wealth and status, I never met anyone who was struggling, or if they were, I wasn't aware of it. I knew injustice existed, but it seemed so far away, like it all happened in a different world, and it sucked, but what could I do? And I didn't have half that compassion for the Corsican people. I thought the reason for the protests and bombings and referendums was Corsicans being Corsicans: violent and vengeful.

"But since I've been with Soffiu di Libertà, I've learned the real reasons for all the unrest: the abuse of the island's land and bodies of water, the suppression of its culture and language, and the government's subjugation of Corsican citizens when all they're asking for is the right to make their own decisions about how their land and people are taken care of." As Séverine found her rhythm, she also found herself getting more swept up in the words.

"Now that I know how Corsicans are really suffering, I can't turn a blind eye. Returning to my former life seems immoral now. The incremental politics of the Parti socialiste are not going to change anything. All politics is compromise, and the idea of compromising on people's freedom is so fucked up. I want to bring about real transformation, the kind that will change people's lives for the better—not later, now. That's Soffiu di Libertà's whole mission, and that's why I've officially joined their cell." She took a breath, steadying herself; this part was the real performance, addressed to her parents, but meant for everyone else.

"Mom and Papa, I know you don't believe I mean it, but I do. I'm not being manipulated, I haven't been brainwashed. You taught me right and wrong: Isn't it the right thing to try and make up for all the wrongs I've committed, even unknowingly? Papa, I hate that you're an arm of the colonial state. It goes without saying that I love you and always will—but I wish you'd use your influence to break the status quo and actually help us. Please do everything in your power to bring Matteu Casanova home—not for my sake, but because it's right.

"Liberating Corsica from colonial rule is only the first step; it's our mission to secure freedom, dignity, safety, and prosperity for oppressed people everywhere. If I can see the light, if I can dedicate myself to making the world a fairer and more beautiful place, anyone can. We don't like to admit it, but as much as we're a nation of intellectual and cultural achievement, we're a nation of violence, bringing death and destruction to Africa, Asia, the Caribbean, and home to our own people. Why would we want to perpetuate such an awful history? To hoard resources that could just be shared? Wouldn't it be better to usher in a new era, where France is a force for reconciliation and restitution?

"I call upon Corsicans, all France's second-class citizens, and exploited people worldwide to join me in this fight for the freedom of all, starting right here in Corsica. U futuru avà!"

Séverine clicked off the recorder and sat back in her seat. She was surprised by the extent to which she actually believed what she'd said.

Bruno stared at her intensely, reevaluating her. A knuckle's length of ash fell from his smoldering cigarette onto the table.

"That was good," he said eventually, crushing the cigarette in an ashtray and removing the cassette from the recorder. He paused again to frown at her, then wrote *Communiqué 9 luglio* on the label. "So, you *are* an actress."

"Yes," Séverine said haughtily.

"But you also believe what you're saying, yeah?"

"I do," she replied adamantly, as if confirming her love to an insecure boyfriend.

He nodded and tapped the cassette thoughtfully against the table. "You'd kill on television. Just at this table, there was an energy about you."

She thought of her school photo in the paper, how she'd been able to communicate exactly what she'd meant to; the communiqué was good, but the visual was her realm. "We should send a picture with the statement," she said.

"What kind of picture?"

"Of me, dressed all in black with the big boots. People should see that I'm a militant now, not just hear about it."

Bruno nodded. "I saw a Polaroid around here somewhere."

Séverine went into the bathroom and examined herself in the mirror. What did a revolutionary look like? She could never be the makeup-less kind with Coke-bottle glasses—she was more of a Jane Fonda. She found *Citizen Jane* on her nightstand and flipped through the photo inserts. Jane had dressed simply in T-shirts and jeans, but her shag hairdo and false lashes were pure A-list glamour. The key was to seem like you didn't care about looking good while still looking good, exuding both femininity and toughness.

Back in the bathroom, Séverine traced a thick wedge of black liner over her eyes that came to a graceless, aggressive wing. It looked appropriately punk. She tousled her sun-lightened hair, which was getting a little scraggly, but it accentuated the unpolished, belligerent look she was going for, like Debbie Harry.

"Very rock star," Petru said when she went back to the kitchen.

"You look like you're in costume," Bruno remarked as he loaded film into the camera.

"It'll come across better in pictures," she claimed, a little hurt that he didn't say she looked cool.

Séverine followed Bruno and Petru into the hot, still afternoon, where Tittu was digging in the garden, his white T-shirt tied around his head like a turban. They entered the maquis, and she caught the honey scent even before they came upon a small clearing filled with yellow flowers whose fuzzy heads fanned out like tentacles of coral.

"Ah, the immortelles are still blooming," Petru said.

"Here is perfect," Séverine murmured, grazing the flowers with outstretched palms. "So pretty."

"Too pretty," Bruno said. "It's not a perfume commercial."

"But it has to look a little appealing," Séverine said. "Like something people want to be a part of."

"Aspirational, you mean," Bruno mused. "Weaponizing the visual language of luxury against itself. Hm." He took a photo of her standing in the field with her arms crossed, but it didn't look *real* enough. Something was missing—a symbol.

Before she could say it, Petru did. "If she's supposed to be a soldier, she needs a firearm."

"The Kalashnikov," Bruno agreed.

Petru went back to the bergerie and returned carrying an enormous military rifle—sharklike, sleek and steely, with dead-eyed power. Séverine recognized it from the case under the bed and felt the same trepidation she did the night she'd first laid eyes on it.

Petru stared down at Séverine with a serious expression. "This is loaded because without the magazine, it'd look totally fake. The safety is on. However, you won't so much as place your finger on the trigger. Understood?"

Séverine nodded.

"Left hand gripping the handguard, right hand on the pistol grip. I will say it again: do not touch the trigger. Don't even slip your finger in the loop."

He handed her the rifle like a father handing over his new baby, and she accepted it uneasily. The little pistol she'd played with in front of the mirror had been one thing, but this was another. It was heavy. There was no mistaking it for a toy. It radiated awful authority, which in turn permeated her. Holding this weapon, her back straightened and arm muscles tensed in a way that proved her new strength.

"Where do you even get something like this?" she asked as he lifted the strap over her head.

"Your buddy robs the gendarmerie in Borgo," Petru said, and Bruno shot him a look. "Allegedly," he added.

"Focus," Bruno reprimanded, then said to Séverine, "Angle yourself a little more towards the right. Your right."

She did as she was told, and Bruno snapped several shots.

"Let me see," Séverine said, and he handed her the photos, still developing and bleached out. They looked like Nazi-era propaganda paintings. "They're stiff," she said. She reclined in the grass and lay the rifle across her lap, holding it like she would a baby tiger, or any other conditionally tame animal.

"Full perfume commercial," Bruno complained, but he crouched and began snapping pictures, tossing them to the ground to develop.

Séverine stared at the lens of the camera, positioned like a giant eye in front of Bruno's slightly scrunched face, and tried to convince this eye of her commitment. She hadn't even noticed Tittu wander in, watching with his arms crossed in front of his bare chest, as Petru collected the photos.

"This will always be the face of Soffiu di Libertà. Whenever anyone mentions us, they'll think of this photo—you know that, right?" Petru said, passing a Polaroid to Bruno.

Séverine watched Bruno examine it. He nodded, first while deliberating, then with conviction.

"It's not about us," he said.

"That's what I mean," Petru said. "It's gonna be all about her." The three of them stared at Séverine abstractly, like she was merely another photo. She placed the rifle on the grass and walked towards them, hand extended, and Bruno passed her the photo. Polaroids always had a flatness about them, a blown-out quality, but it was the perfect format for this picture—gritty yet dreamy. The precise contours of her face became hazy, so the eye gravitated to the hair made golden by all the light absorbed and reflected by the sun-colored immortelles, her sensual gaze, her litheness, the dark slash of a gun, the black severity of her clothing and boots and eyeliner against so much soft and glowing nature. She sensed Petru would be right: this photo, along with her communiqué, would make her a star. For the first time in a long time, she felt like she was doing what she was meant to do.

"People need to look at something. They need an image in their minds. So far you've only given them big blocks of text. No one reads all that," Séverine said.

"They already have Séverine as the image in their minds when they think of Soffiu di Libertà anyway," Tittu added.

"Okay, but are we gonna be seen as a serious militant organization if we're associated with this Calvin Klein ad?" Petru asked, holding up the stack of photos.

"We'll be seen as a serious militant organization if we act like one," Séverine said. "On that subject: the Laporte villa. We should do it so it's part of my coming out; I was thinking Bastille Day. The whole family will be at Paul Dorbon's big party like they are every year."

"That's in five days; it took weeks to plan the limo bombing," Petru said.

"It takes weeks to build a bomb?" Séverine asked.

"To scout, to work out the details, and then, yes, to build the bomb."

"You don't have to worry about scouting," Séverine said. "I know that house, I've been there."

"A bombing isn't the type of thing you dash off," Petru said.

"I can draw up a map of the property for you," Séverine offered. "Maybe you go once to see for yourselves, but I'm handing this to you on a silver platter. It'll be way easier than kidnapping me or blowing up Jonnart's car."

"Petru, you don't think you could turn it around in five days?" Bruno asked. "It would be really effective if we could do this in tandem with Séverine's announcement."

"It makes sense for Bastille Day, too," Tittu ventured. "The cops will be busy with crowd control for the fireworks."

"You can do it, old pro," Bruno said, grasping Petru's forearm and giving it a little shake of encouragement.

"You come up with a risky plan, I warn you against it, you disregard me," Petru grumbled. "I should be used to it by now."

"Will you show me how you do it?" Séverine asked Petru. "I want to say I made the bomb that destroyed that asshole's house."

Petru raised an eyebrow. "Which asshole?"

"Claude Laporte, obviously," Séverine spluttered.

Petru shook his head. "Bullshit."

She rolled her eyes. "I know the whole family, and I can tell you, the dad is an asshole, the mom is an asshole, and the kids are assholes."

"I'm going to go out on a limb and guess you have history with one of the asshole kids," Petru said. "Did she steal your boyfriend? Or maybe he *was* the boyfriend."

"Definitely not a boyfriend," Séverine muttered, glancing guiltily at both Bruno and Tittu.

"Ah-ha," Petru said like a detective cracking a case. "He dumped you and you want revenge."

"Dumped *me*? I don't get dumped. That's not even close to what happened," Séverine replied.

"We don't do vendettas," Petru said firmly.

"At least half the people you'd want to target, I know personally," Séverine pointed out.

Petru sighed. "You can watch me build the bomb, but you touch nothing. If you speak when I tell you to be quiet, if you breathe wrong—you're out. Got it?"

"Naturally," Séverine said, flashing a smile.

———

They packed the photo and communiqué, which Bruno additionally transcribed via typewriter, and they secured one Polaroid to the corner of each statement with a paper clip. In neat block letters, Séverine wrote *Communiqué—Soffiu di Libertà—9 lugliu 1993* on the face of each cassette. Then she slid the contents into padded envelopes addressed to *Le Monde*, *Libération*, *Le Figaro*, and *Corse Matin*.

Bruno would drop the envelopes in two separate mailboxes served by different post offices, then busy himself with arranging Séverine's phone call with her parents so she could tell them about joining Sof-fiu di Libertà before it hit the presses Monday. As Séverine watched the 4x4 rumble out of sight, kicking up yellow dust behind it, she felt like a butterfly watching a ripple of wind from its beating wings float off to become a hurricane on the other side of the world.

Petru had been working from an old shack, decrepit with age and exposure, a little way into the maquis. But since Séverine had been evacuated from the shed, it was repurposed as Petru's workshop. There weren't too many elements actually required to make a bomb, as it turned out: a five-hundred-kilogram Tyvek bag of fertilizer, a red petrol canister, a plastic bathroom scale, and a box of what looked like slim silver tampons with wires for strings.

"Detonators," Petru explained. "For the thousandth time, do not touch. It was a huge pain in the ass to get a hold of them."

"What do they do?" Séverine asked, desperately wanting to touch them.

"The explosion that sets off the explosion," Petru said. "The bomb is a mixture of ammonium nitrate"—he pointed to the fertilizer—"and fuel oil." His finger singled out the petrol canister. "ANFO for short. But the ANFO won't detonate just by igniting it. You need an initial explosion: a smaller wave of heat and pressure that sets off the big bang. That's the detonator's job."

"So all those little tubes are explosives?" Séverine asked.

"Exactly. Which is why I handle them very carefully, and you stay away from them."

"What'd you have to do to get them?" Séverine asked.

"Steal them from the quarry in Pie-d'Orezza."

"When?" Séverine asked, a little shocked.

"Tittu and I drove over one night when you and Bruno were yakking it up. He detained the night guard, I grabbed what they had, and we ran off."

She'd had no idea; but then again, how would she, when for weeks she'd seen nothing but the inside of a closet, then this shed. "You make it sound easy."

"It was and it wasn't. It's easy enough to walk into a building, pick up a box, and walk out. The hard part is the human factor: your nerves, the nerves of everyone else involved. If a security guard is protecting something we want, he knows we're coming for it sooner or later, and most of them aren't interested in being a hero. But you never know if you're gonna get that one new guy who thinks he's the star of his own movie."

"But don't you have to believe you're the star of your own movie to be a revolutionary?" Séverine asked.

"Just the opposite," Petru said, like a warning. "Anyway." He kicked a large plastic bucket into the center of the shed. "First things first: mix up the ANFO."

When he'd finished, the gasoline and fertilizer had formed a thick sludge.

"That should do it. Grab the plastic wrap."

The mixture, which had the texture of stiff dough, splatted onto the plastic wrap, and Petru proceeded to form it with his hands so he had three neat, white bricks.

"Good. We can get into the electrical stuff tomorrow," Petru said.

"But what *is* this?" Séverine asked.

"What do you mean? It's the bomb!" Petru said.

Séverine looked at it with disappointment.

"What were you expecting, a black thing with a fuse coming out of it like in a cartoon?" He placed the packet inside a clean drywall bucket and screwed on the lid. "It doesn't have to look dangerous to be dangerous."

"Like me?" she teased, sticking out her tongue.

"No, you definitely look dangerous," Petru said.

As she went to leave the shed, Petru added, "Don't bank on feeling better about what the Laporte kid did to you."

She swiveled around. "I don't know what you're talking about."

"Sometimes, the worse whatever they did, the less satisfying revenge is," Petru said, busy putting the materials back in their place. "'Cause you still have to live with what they did, plus what you did to them."

"That's not very Corsican of you." Séverine laughed. He needn't worry; she had thought up a million different scenarios in which Julien Laporte got what was coming to him, and she had no doubts she could stomach it.

—

Julien had always been top dog in their class since he was a good soccer player and had honed the delicate balance between bullying and charming his classmates. His mother came from a Réunionnais rum family, and although Bonnie Guimard found Madame Laporte's desperate striving to be tiresome, she indulged her out of some misguided expat solidarity. Despite their mothers' provisional friendship, Julien had rudely called Séverine "Le Pif" in maternelle, and it had followed her ever since. Then in première English class, Julien, who sat behind Séverine, began *psst*-ing her constantly, demanding her help.

"*Hey, American Girl*," he said in heavily accented English, leaning over his desk. "What's the answer to number six?"

"She literally just went through irregular conjugations," Séverine replied without turning around.

"Okay, but I missed what she said about 'dream.' 'I dreamed of you' or 'I dreamt of you'?"

"You're so stupid," she said, unable to control a smile, a grave mistake.

He began to materialize with his friend Gaetan at the tabac where Séverine, Hélène, and Pilar always stopped after school for a Coca and clope and to browse the magazines. One day, he tapped Séverine on the shoulder and said, "Come sit at our table; we're not kids anymore, you don't have to act like we have cooties."

The girls looked at one another, silently consulting. Julien was brash and exasperating, but that he wanted Séverine to sit with him made her feel chosen, special.

"All right," she said, and without further discussion, the girls moved from the bar to the table. A month later, Pilar was nestled under Gaetan's arm, to Hélène's quiet devastation, while Séverine and Julien bickered affectedly.

Not long after that, Gaetan threw a party while his parents were out of town.

Séverine and Pilar got ready at Hélène's. Séverine remembered distinctly the white and yellow floral baby doll dress with buttons down the front and white platform sandals she wore; she remembered the pink lip gloss she slicked on, how the wand dragged across her lower lip like a thumb might. The three of them applied the same frosty white eye shadow sitting cross-legged in front of the sliding mirror doors of Hélène's closet.

"Are you going to fuck Gaetan tonight?" Hélène asked meanly, wiggling a mascara wand back and forth in her lashes.

"I think so," Pilar said, focusing just as intently on her hair spraying.

Both Hélène and Séverine stopped what they were doing to stare at their friend in the mirror. Pilar continued combing up sections of her hair and blasting them with puffs of hair spray, nonchalant. At the moment, the girls were more or less equally sexually experienced. That Pilar might soon be the most worldly and mature would shift the carefully balanced hierarchy of the group. As of now, there was no clear "leader," but that would surely change once one of them lost her *virginity*.

They walked over to the Fourniers' large Haussmannian apartment, laughing at the older men who fluttered around them like moths. The party included about thirty classmates and half as many bottles of vodka and orange juice. Julien greeted Séverine by kissing her on each cheek and handing her a strong drink. Someone put on music and turned out the lights, and Séverine found herself dancing with Julien. His hands appraised her new contours, he was drawing her closer, and then they were kissing. He really wanted her! She felt she could be persuaded. His previous aloofness made her want to exert her new power.

Hélène, on the verge of tears, suddenly wrenched her away.

"They just went to his room," she said.

"Who?" Séverine asked, airy-headed.

"Pilar and Gaetan!" Through her tears, Hélène cast a disappointed look between Séverine and Julien, only now registering who she was kissing.

"What do you want to do, call the pompiers to break down the door?" Séverine asked.

Hélène turned on her heel and grabbed Nathalie Moreau, a satellite friend for when it was necessary to complain about the other two.

"I have an idea," Julien said, taking Séverine's hand and leading her down the hallway towards the bedrooms. Julien tried the handles of the double doors at the end, but they were locked.

"You pervert, doing it in your parents' room!" he yelled.

"Get lost," Gaetan yelled back.

They ran back down the hallway, absolutely dying with laughter. Julien grabbed Séverine's wrist and pulled her towards him, kissing her, maneuvering her into Gaetan's room, shutting the door, and locking it.

"What are you up to?" she asked, playing it cool.

"Nothing," Julien said, pulling her to the bed. Her ears buzzed; she became aware of how drunk she was.

Julien unbuttoned her dress to the waist. "Take this off," he said.

"You take it off." She was acting like she wanted something she wasn't sure she actually wanted. That didn't mean she was afraid or incapable of saying no to him, but one rejection and the whole long flirtation would be over. She wasn't sure she wanted to be Julien's girlfriend, but she definitely wanted to sustain his interest. Having sex with him would secure that.

More important, Pilar was doing it just down the hall, and Séverine did not want to be left behind. Here was a convenient opportunity to get rid of her virginity, which had begun to feel like a hideous appendage. She had no preexisting fantasy of how her first time might go down and harbored no illusions that it would be great and wonderful. Conventional wisdom said to save it for someone you loved and who loved you back, but wasn't there something special enough about losing it to a guy you'd known your whole life, even if he'd spent most of it annoying you?

Julien reached the last button of Séverine's dress and lazily tossed it open. He looked down on her with a soft, druggy expression as he undressed himself—and there it was, pushing ridiculously against his boxers.

He slid his hand under her neck and pulled her towards him, towards his erection. She found herself opening her mouth, and then here she was, blowing him. Fine. It was a necessary feminine skill, and although she'd never done it before, intuitive enough. Suddenly, he twitched and his stomach creased; just as Séverine realized what was happening, his semen was already in her mouth.

They stared at each other: she waited for him to get her something to spit into, he waited to see if she'd swallow. The nightstand held only a lamp and a library copy of *Society of the Spectacle*. Burning with anger, she swallowed.

She had two options: One, recover Hélène from Nathalie Moreau and leave the same person as she'd arrived. Two, she could spend another twenty minutes with this idiot, do what she'd already decided she'd do, and leave the party with some experiential foundation she could then improve upon.

"You could have given me some warning," Séverine said.

"You're so hot, I couldn't help myself," Julien replied. It was a ridiculous etiquette they were participating in.

He put his arms around her waist and kissed her neck. She willed herself to be turned on by his touch, and it began to work; but when she tried to kiss him on the mouth, he jerked his chin away and maneuvered her onto her back. He grabbed his jeans and fished a condom out of the pocket. Séverine wondered if he'd planned on this happening, if he'd gauged her better than she had herself.

No further discussion, no attempt at foreplay; Julien wrangled on the condom and directed himself inside her. There was an initial sensation of discomfort that felt unbecomingly gynecological—a familiar but unwelcome pressure—but then it stabilized, and she could think. *It's happening*, is what she thought. Again, she sensed an exchange between them, different from what she'd been told to expect (love, warmth, pleasure); instead, they were providing a mutual sense of release for all the confused longing they'd cultivated within each other over the entirety of their short lives.

Then Julien announced, "I'm gonna come," and loudly did, or so Séverine assumed.

He rolled off and caught his breath. His sweat cooled on her skin, and she pulled up Gaetan's navy comforter.

"Well done," Julien said, finally rolling to face her.

She leaned in to kiss him, but again, he jerked back.

"What?" she demanded.

"You have come-mouth," he said with the same kind of laugh as when he called her "Le Pif."

In that instant, the possibility, all the speculation and daydreaming of the last couple months was destroyed, and here was the same acned moron as before.

"Well, you suck in bed," Séverine said, throwing off the comforter and pulling on her clothes.

For a moment, he wore an expression of hurt and humiliation, and she almost felt bad for being so harsh. Then he composed himself and said, "Sorry, I didn't realize you were so *experienced*."

"Fuck you," she said weakly, and hurried out the door before he could hit her with another zinger.

The three girls found each other and walked home in silence, feeling bedraggled, knowing apologies must be made but lacking the energy. In the morning, Séverine and Pilar shared war stories while Hélène quietly suffered.

"It was just weird," Pilar had said. "It seemed so much better for him than for me."

"Do you feel different?" Séverine asked.

"Yeah," Pilar sighed.

Séverine felt different, too. A small part of it was regret—ideally, her first time would have been nicer—but mostly she felt the lightness and freedom of adulthood. She'd found something she was good at: the process of seduction, from the initial attraction to the culmination of sex. *Well done,* Julien had said.

Monday came around, and Séverine's classmates were giving her sideways glances. She just knew, even before Séb Thomas crouched behind her chair in chemistry and whispered, "Come to the bathroom and let me bust in your mouth like Julien."

She whipped around and shoved him, but it only made him laugh. The most immature boys harassed her for about a week, and Séverine endured it stonily. Inwardly, though, her feelings were wounded because despite everything, the experience *meant* something to her. For Julien to tell the whole school about it in such vulgar terms, he must not feel the same way.

To make matters worse, he started seeing some girl from l'École normale catholique, a blonde with limp hair and gigantic boobs she compressed under navy sweaters. And although Séverine acted like she couldn't care less, she obsessed over the question of what this girl offered that she didn't. Again, she had the impression that Julien had seen through her the whole time, that he'd known she'd cave at the lightest pressure.

If she didn't love the person she had sex with, if they didn't make her *orgasm*, they could at least show some appreciation, Séverine decided. She resolved to sleep only with men who were grateful, who expected nothing, who would devote their attention entirely to her.

Séverine was far away from that time and world, yet she still wanted to blow up Julien Laporte's house. He'd treated her like she was a footnote when she was the whole story. She was the one men were supposed to reminisce about twenty years later. Antoine Carsenti would stare into the ocean while his wife chased after their children, remembering the syrupy taste of her tongue, the sand grinding into his back, the shocking warmth of the first girl he ever had.

She was a better person than Julien, more important, and with more potential. She wanted to remind him of that, and to show him that his disregard for her was a symptom of his own insignificance. Pilar had wisely suggested that the world would right this injustice eventually, but Séverine did not want to leave it up to the whims of the universe. She wanted to enact it herself, and she wanted him to know it was her.

8. Contact

Everything was arranged. Tomorrow, Séverine would call her parents from a pay phone in Peruccia, some village an hour away.

She woke early that morning after a restless night spent dreaming of the next day, both excited and anxious. Again and again, she went over what she'd say to her parents. In her best version, she was eloquent like she was in the communiqué, and her parents would understand how grown-up and serious she'd become. They couldn't admit it, but they'd feel a little proud. In her worst version, she babbled incoherently at them; convinced she was being manipulated, they'd make things even more difficult for the group.

Bruno was up, too, drinking coffee. A pair of knockoff Ray-Ban aviators and a green baseball cap sat on the kitchen table.

"I know it's not very sophisticated, but you should try to stay low-profile," he said.

Séverine put on the hat and glasses and looked in the mirror by the front door. There was no disguising this gros pif; it literally preceded her wherever she went. If none of this had happened to her, she'd be preparing for her nose job in a couple weeks. She wondered if she could convince the guys to let her use some of the ransom money to go through with it, then sadly realized it wouldn't be Dr. Gaillard in Neuilly-sur-Seine performing the procedure, but a mafia doctor in some dirty apartment.

"You think this is good enough?" she asked.

"The spot I picked is discreet," Bruno said. He gave her a suspicious look, and she immediately understood that this phone call was her first test. It was a test for herself, too; she didn't want to break down, overwhelmed with homesickness, upon hearing her parents' voices. She wanted to see this bombing through.

In this middling disguise, she climbed into the 4x4 and left the bergerie in a more dignified way than she'd arrived. Merely sitting in the front seat and clicking her seat belt into place gave her a jolt of excitement, made her feel normal in a way that was now exotic. She was a girl in the passenger seat of a car, and here was her friend in the driver's seat, feeding a cassette into the tape deck before they began their little road trip.

The car rolled slowly down the drive, and Bruno turned up the volume on the stereo. The music was melancholy, which Séverine did not find appropriate for her first real excursion off the property.

"What is this?" she asked.

"Radiohead," Bruno said, and began singing along to the lyrics in a baby babble that approximated English.

"It sucks," she said. "Don't you have anything else? Ace of Base?"

"*Your* taste sucks," Bruno said, although he pressed stop. "Look in the center console."

Séverine dug through a mess of cassettes before pulling out the one she wanted, pushing it in the deck, and fast-forwarding to the second song.

Bruno groaned when Dolores O'Riordan's voice came in after the swell of guitars and cymbals. "This is girl stuff," he complained.

"No it's not," Séverine protested, then felt self-conscious. "You don't like 'Dreams'?"

Bruno shrugged and turned it up. The 4x4 rollicked down the dirt road, rattling loudly, and Séverine extended her arm out the window, letting her hand bob up and down on the wind. It was like an American movie: the handsome but inflexible guy and the girl who'd loosen him up. If she was doing this properly, he would take his eyes off the road to see her long hair streaming and think: *She's beautiful.*

The tires hit pavement, and everything became smooth and quiet. Séverine turned down the music.

"How come you never told me you lived in Paris?" she asked.

"Who told you that? Tittu? You're like two old ladies." He sighed. "It was a weird time in my life."

"But you don't just quit Sciences Po," Séverine said. "I mean, if you'd stayed, maybe *you'd* be the prefect one day."

Bruno made the sign of the horns, as if Séverine had just cursed him. "Believe it or not, I couldn't wait to get out of Corsica—I never felt like I fit in. All the serious intellectuals and people of influence seemed to be on the continent, and Corsica was some backwater. So when I got into this top school, it was like winning the lottery. But it was *not* what I thought." He laughed spitefully. "My classmates were from these old, wealthy, connected families; my parents are teachers. I didn't even realize I had an accent till I got made fun of for it. Suddenly I felt *very* Corsican, and middle-class, and different on this whole new level. I wanted to fly under the radar, but no one let me forget I wasn't one of them.

"Then my aunt put me in touch with her neighbor's kid who was studying film at Paris III—this guy Nico. And he introduced me to Matteu, and we had this little gang of Corsicans in Paris. Matteu was the one who turned me on to all these radical ideas. I'd always thought the island was so small potatoes, and I wanted to do something *important*—but Matteu was about doing something important in Corsica. We'd stay out all night talking and drinking, and we got super close. We just understood each other."

"So why'd you leave?" Séverine asked.

"We all did. The first generation of I Fratelli fought to get the university in Corte reopened after it had been shut down for two hundred years, so why not honor that? And at the same time do something concrete to help the island."

"But knowing the right people is everything!" Séverine lamented. "You could have changed things from the inside."

"I would have become another mealymouthed functionary," he said. "The most obvious path isn't necessarily the best one. Like you—you'll reach more people as our spokesperson than you ever would have as an actor."

"You think so?" she asked, although she didn't see why she couldn't still be an actress in the future, like Jane.

"One hundred percent. Actors are vectors for other people's ideas. But you have your own ideas, and you can transmit them effectively. Not everyone can do that."

"Thanks," she said, and felt her face warm—his compliment made her bashful, which in turn made him bashful, and he changed the subject.

"As for the plan," he said, "the pay phone is outside a pizza place. It's off the beaten path for tourists, but you never know. What's gonna happen is, you'll stay in the car while I call. Once I get through, you'll have three minutes to talk."

"That's it?" Séverine exclaimed. "Why three minutes? Does it have something to do with the call being traced?"

After a brief hesitation, Bruno said, "Yes."

"No it doesn't, you just made up that number."

"It's three minutes, okay, Séverine?"

She slumped in her seat. He could be such a buzzkill.

He placed his hand on top of her hat and wiggled her head, a conciliatory gesture. Séverine imagined that having a brother was like this: fighting, then playing around again without officially making up, a cycle of resentment and tenderness, a shared experience singular to the two of you.

When they passed the small green road sign that indicated they were entering Peruccia, Séverine began to bounce her legs with anxious anticipation. Another minute and they were in town, driving by homes in shades of salmon, beige, and tawny stucco, set in the face of the hills. An old mammona sat on her front porch, knees spread under her cotton housedress, hands folded over her belly, watching the empty street. She was the first woman Séverine had seen in a month; funny, she hadn't really missed the company of women. It went without saying she missed Hélène and Pilar, but she'd missed them a long time.

Bruno pulled in front of a building with a Heineken sign hanging over the door; a few meters from the entrance stood an old, beat-up pay phone.

No cars navigated the narrow, curving street, no one was walking into the pizzeria for lunch; the only movement came from a few trees whose leaves lazed in the breeze. "Where is everyone?" Séverine asked.

"Honestly, this village probably never recovered from so many men dying during the First World War; then people left to find work—you know the story," Bruno said. "Maybe some families come for a few weeks in the summer. Enough for there to be a pizza place."

He checked his watch. "It's time. Stay here till I call you over." He got out of the car, picked up the receiver, and fed some change into the pay phone. He was talking to someone. Séverine slipped her hand into the door handle, ready to be summoned, but Bruno yammered on. If it was her parents on the other end of the line, she hoped he was being polite. Sick of waiting, she opened the door and hovered behind Bruno, who was speaking in low tones.

"Monsieur, I'm not the one you want to talk to about this," Bruno murmured. "It's your daughter." At this, she snatched the phone.

"—we're willing to move Casanova to Borgo—"

"Papa?" Séverine said in a little girl's voice.

"Séverine?" her father responded. She'd never heard him so rattled, and it was devastating; she felt both relieved and guilty, and she began to cry.

"I'm here. I can't believe I'm finally talking to you, I've missed you so much."

Bruno moved in front of her and put a hand on her shoulder, turning her towards the wall as he kept an eye on the street.

"I'm going to ask you some yes or no questions," her dad said, recovering a steely calm. "Do you know where you are?"

"Is Mom there?" she asked. "Put her on."

There was some clacking and rustling as her mother took the phone.

"Séverine, are you okay?" she cried.

"Yes," Séverine said in English, and the tears started all over. "Can Papa hear me?" She switched back to French.

"I can hear you," her father replied. She imagined their cheeks pressed together and the receiver touching both their ears.

"Are you hurt? Have they done anything to you?" Her mother's voice broke at this last question.

"No, not at all!" She made the effort to steady herself. "No, they've actually been great," she said, glancing at Bruno.

"I know you can't say much because he's still there, but any clue, it doesn't matter how cryptic it may seem, we can use it," her father said.

"Papa, listen," Séverine started, thinking back to the speech she'd rehearsed. "You know how you say the right choice is usually the hard choice?"

"Yes?" he said, already lost.

"I can help these guys," she said. "What they're fighting for isn't wrong. I just—there are a lot of problems in Corsica, and we've done a terrible job trying to fix them—'we' meaning the French; well, also you specifically. I'm not saying it's totally your fault, but I've learned about incremental change, and I know that's your policy, and that doesn't seem to be working. Anyway, why not give independence a shot? And like, if I have an opportunity to help, I should," she rambled. It was worse than she'd envisioned her worst-case scenario.

"Have you been drugged?" her mother asked, hysterical.

"No! And I'm not making stuff up because someone's listening," Séverine contended, getting frustrated. "I've been reading a lot and having really interesting, *intellectual* conversations with one of the guys, and it's opened my eyes to like, colonialism and capitalism, and I don't want to be a part of that anymore. What I'm saying is that I want to fight against it . . . actually."

Their silence manifested as a buzz.

"I don't understand," her mom said.

"I've joined Soffiu di Libertà," she replied, finally finding clarity.

She could hear low, indistinguishable tones coming from her mother as she whispered into her father's ear.

"What?" she asked, annoyed.

"This guy you've been talking with. You have a little crush on him? Is he the one with you now?" her mom asked in English.

She'd managed to catch Séverine off guard. "Mom, seriously? That's so condescending. You don't think I'm smart enough to get this stuff, do you? Well, guess what: I read Lenin and I totally understood it."

"Séverine, I think it's great you want to help," her father interrupted before they could devolve into an old argument. "We can do a volunteer trip this summer to Senegal, Cambodia, wherever."

"No, be straight with her, Paul," her mom said, her tone harsh. "You'll go to prison, Séverine. And Papa won't be able to help you."

"I don't care!" Séverine cried. "It just feels like I'm supposed to do this, like everything happened for a reason."

"Look, I was just saying to . . . that man with you—that I think we're going to be able to get Casanova to Borgo," her dad said.

She felt a pang of excitement, then everything she'd felt so certain about suddenly felt less certain. "He needs to be released, not transferred," she said.

"It's a first step—a sign of good faith," he explained. "It's touchy; I went to President Schneider, over Jonnart's head. But his approval ratings are low; he lost a lot of sway when the conservatives took Parliament. We have to go about this very carefully."

She cast a guilty look at Bruno, who was watching the street. If her dad made it happen and fulfilled the demands of her release, would she forget the whole thing and go home? It seemed too late for that; she was on a whole other train, an express route to the place she really belonged.

"Séverine, please, if you're being coerced in any way, I want you to say, 'You don't understand,'" her mother cut in, now on the brink of tears.

"You're not listening," Séverine said. "I've joined Soffiu di Libertà. We sent out a press release. It'll be in the news tomorrow."

"Séverine," her mother murmured, in awe.

"We should go," Bruno interrupted.

"I'll call you again soon," Séverine said, gently, like a parent. "This is a good thing. I honestly think I'm becoming a better person—someone who thinks about other people, like you always said I should."

"Wait—" her father interjected. "I bought a mobile phone no one knows about. He has the number; call me there."

"Okay. I love you. Bye," she whispered.

"Séverine, don't hang up—" he tried, but she placed the phone back in its hook while her parents' voices streamed from the receiver, thin and distant.

"Come on," Bruno said gently, his arm around her shoulder as he guided her into the car.

Séverine cried silently on their way out of Peruccia, angling away from Bruno, who didn't try to impose. It was too much: their suffocating love, the familiar frustration. She missed them terribly and felt so misunderstood by them. When they were well out of town, Bruno pulled into the parking area of a designated vista point and turned off the engine. He sat with his hands in his lap, staring blankly at the splendor of the maquis through the windshield.

"I just want to say that I'm sorry," he said. "For everything—the trunk, the closet, that night. That we took you out of your whole life. But at the same time, I'm not sorry, because I'm glad you're with us. When you said this was how it was supposed to work out, that seemed true to me, too."

He dragged his thumb across her left cheek, then her right, wiping away the tears in a way that was both carelessly rough and tender. It stirred something within her that she recognized as deep and real and dangerous.

When they turned onto the dirt road that led to the bergerie, Séverine felt a bittersweet relief: she was home now.

9. The First Bomb

Monday morning, Petru and Tittu drove to Calvi to figure out their entry and exit plan from the Laporte property and to plant a rental car.

"Seems simple enough," Tittu said when they returned. They'd brought back patisserie and were eating around the kitchen table. "There's a cemetery two properties down; we can enter there. Once we cross through, there's an empty lot, then the house."

"Most of the cameras are at the front of the property, and the two out back face into the yard. Once we get over the wall, we can shoot those two cameras out, then we have free range," Petru said.

"I'll take care of that," Tittu volunteered.

"We wanna place the bomb at the weakest part of the foundation," Petru said. "It looks like the property starts sloping down towards the cliffs around the back patio, so that's pretty straightforward."

"And what do we do?" Séverine asked, thumbing towards Bruno.

"Lookouts," Petru said. "Bruno will take the front, you take the wall that divides the property from the empty lot."

"But that's so boring!" Séverine exclaimed.

"Everyone's role is important," Bruno said like a grade school teacher. "Operation plans are Petru's forte; if he says we'll best serve as lookouts, there's a reason for it."

Séverine pouted. She hadn't just wanted to build the bomb; she'd wanted to throw it through the window, too.

"Cheer up," Petru said. "I have something for you." He rifled through a bag of unpacked groceries and produced a newspaper.

There she was on the front page, in color—a flash of sun-lacquered hair, face lifted towards the source of all that yellow light, skin glowing. It was exactly as she'd imagined.

"We went three places," Tittu explained. "The guy at the petrol station said his whole stack was gone before lunch. People are buying them like they'll be worth something one day."

They all examined the photo in thoughtful, reverent silence. She could sense something complex emanating from each of them: awe, uneasiness, yearning, and a uniform awareness that everything was about to change again.

"So I'm like, a celebrity?" she asked with unconvincing sarcasm.

"Come on, Laetitia Casta," Petru said. "We have work to do."

⌒

Things were not quite so exciting in the shed, watching Petru strip wires from a plastic alarm clock. It was a warm afternoon, the kind that induces drowsiness.

"This is an SCR: silicon controlled rectifier," he said, holding up a small black tab with three long silver prongs. "This amplifies the electric current from the timer so enough energy reaches the blasting cap."

"Okay," Séverine sighed, chin in hands.

"You're not watching," Petru said.

"I learn more from doing than watching," Séverine said.

"You know what happens when a bomb-maker lets their apprentice do electrical on their fourth day of training?" Petru asked, bringing two closed fists together. "You, me, Tittu in the vegetable patch, the house, all the wine, *pkrrfff.*" He fanned his fingers out and made them rain down. "Look, evidence of early mishaps." He pointed to a long, mottled scar on his left forearm and smaller purple nicks on his hands.

"Bullshit, those are from cooking," she said, and he raised an eyebrow as if to be mysterious.

He then took a Tupperware container from the shelf and opened it to show her what looked like a block of orange cheddar cheese. "Semtex. Worth more than gold."

"How'd you get it?" Séverine asked with due reverence.

"Stole it from I Fratelli on my way out."

"They don't care the three of you defected?" Séverine asked.

"They take us even less seriously than we do them," Petru said. "For now, at least. You might change that."

"But like, do they know your identities?"

"Considering our main demand was Matteu's release, probably."

"So I Fratelli knows you and Bruno and Tittu kidnapped me?" Séverine asked. Her father worked closely with the Partitu di a Corsica Unificatu, or PCU. These politicians had surely gone to her father's office with baskets of brocciu and lonzu, expressing their horror and vowing to do everything in their power to help find the prefect's daughter, just say the word.

"What pieces of shit," she said aloud.

"Anyway, the anode—"

"What was the first thing you blew up?" she interrupted.

He sighed, exasperated. "Some condos in Porto-Vecchio."

"How'd you feel?"

He stared thoughtfully at the wall. "Capable. Part of something bigger than myself," he said, and resumed his task.

"Do you have to be good at science to do this?" she asked.

"What does that even mean, 'good at science'? Just pay attention," he said.

But she couldn't. She was thinking of all the people in France and Corsica buying newspapers, loitering in their vestibules or perched on their café stools as they examined her photo, the image demanding standstill attention. She was thinking of righteous orange flames. She was thinking of seeing the sea again.

⁓

Tuesday morning, after they'd completed their exercise regimen and eaten breakfast, Bruno asked Petru, "She'll need a crash course in weapons training before tomorrow, yeah?"

"You want to give her a gun?" Petru scoffed.

"How else do we expect her to look out?"

"She can *look out* and call, 'Hey, guys, look out!' if need be."

"You don't trust me, Petru?" Séverine asked ironically.

"Not particularly, no."

"Either she's part of our cell or she's not," Tittu said. "It can't be halfway."

Begrudgingly, Petru went to Séverine's room and came back with the exact handgun she'd held up to the mirror the time they'd left her home alone.

"Beretta 92F, light and compact," Tittu noted. "Good call."

She held out her hand to take the gun, but Petru slapped it away.

"Safety first," he said.

The four of them trekked into the maquis, past the old bomb-making shed, into an open space where two paper targets, spotted with bullet holes, were nailed to trees. Petru spent the first half hour explaining how the gun functioned, its parts and rules for handling it. Next, she watched the three of them shoot, instructed to pay attention to their stance and technique. Petru was evidently military-trained, and Tittu must have spent every nostalgia-gilded autumn of his childhood hunting boar and small game. Their movements were unselfconscious, ingrained, devoid of apprehension. When the gun recoiled, their hands jerked with a placid acceptance of how the weapon could and could not be controlled. Bruno, although a good marksman, had a performative swagger, as if he were still fascinated by being a man who shot guns.

"All right, your turn," Petru finally said. He stood behind her, kicking between her boots to widen her stance, angling her hips with his big hands, lifting her arms ever so gently by the triceps, his breath on her ear as he crouched to get a sense of her sight line.

"Are the front and rear sights aligned? The black box is centered inside the notch?"

"Yes," she said.

"Both eyes open. Hold it tighter."

"Your arms and wrists are granite," Tittu added.

"Focus on the front sight, not the target. Now squeeze the trigger, slowly."

A sick thought bubbled from the depths of her mucky brain: she could turn this gun on Petru and Tittu and Bruno; she could shoot them in quick succession before they even registered what was happening, then drive the 4x4 back to Ajaccio (okay, she didn't technically know how to drive, but she could figure it out). But the daydream burst just as soon as it formed. She squeezed the trigger, the gun twitched, a raucous crack reverberated from where she stood, and in the outermost circle of the target, a hole appeared.

"Not bad. At least you hit," Bruno said.

She emptied the rest of the chamber. A gun had always seemed frightening and mysterious—occult—but in fact, its rules were intelligible and practical; it involved none of the alchemy required in romance or manipulation. She'd practice and master the technicalities of this instrument, and it would become as ordinary as a hair dryer.

The last thing to do was write the communiqué that would accompany the Laporte bombing. They'd mail it to *Corse Matin* and France 3 on the thirteenth so that it would arrive the morning of the fifteenth, right after the holiday.

Bruno admitted that Petru had a point; it would get out that Séverine knew the Laportes, and so the attack had to be very deliberately contextualized. Then there was the question of demands.

"This is the first thing Soffiu di Libertà's doing that's not just about Matteu," Séverine observed.

"In a way," Bruno said evasively. It was curious: the idea of her bombing Julien's house for revenge was so distasteful, but the fact that Soffiu di Libertà had been wreaking havoc for an equally personal reason hadn't occurred to them, or else they didn't want to admit it.

Bruno produced a typewritten copy of Soffiu di Libertà's manifesto. "We can just go point by point and explain how this aligns with our goals."

What a snooze! It was hard to make anyone outside Corsica care about what was happening here. The reasons for resistance were legitimate, but they seemed so regional and irrelevant to non-Corsicans. According to Bruno, I Fratelli had never successfully connected itself to other struggles the way the IRA had collaborated with revolutionary organizations in the Middle East and South Africa, so if Soffiu di Libertà wanted to distinguish itself, if it wanted anyone outside Corsica to pay attention and eventually lend support, it needed to do just that.

"You were saying before that Laporte planes were involved in a bunch of different military operations, right? Always on the wrong side of oppression?" Séverine asked.

"Always," Bruno confirmed.

"What if we dedicate this attack to the victims of those conflicts, to stand with everyone around the world who's suffered because of Laporte weapons?" Séverine ventured. "If we act like we care about them, maybe they'll care about us."

"Bombing the Laporte villa as an act of solidarity with other liberation movements."

"Sure," Séverine agreed. He always managed to take whatever she said and make it sound smart. She loved that about him.

After dinner, Bruno laid out the next day's plan: Petru and Séverine would drive together, with the bomb, to the Mr. Bricolage in L'Île Rousse, where they'd switch cars. Tittu and Bruno would go on the motorcycle directly to Nico's—

"Nico—who's that again?" Séverine interrupted.

"A necessary evil," Petru said under his breath.

"'Necessary' is generous," Tittu added.

Bruno shot them an irritated look. "I told you about him—he's the filmmaker I was friends with in Paris. The guy who introduced me to Matteu. He's letting us stay with him in Calvi."

"Is he part of the cell?" Séverine asked shrilly. She didn't like the idea that there were other comrades they hadn't told her about.

"Not officially," Bruno said.

Petru and Tittu exchanged looks. "His uncle is Fanfan Bartoli," Petru clarified.

Séverine laughed, incredulous. "Nico's uncle is the head of I Fratelli?"

"He's not a crony; he wants a new order like we do," Bruno said.

"What's your problem with him?" she asked the other two.

"He's got a particular personality," Bruno explained. "Maybe he's not for everybody, but he is a comrade."

"He's a wannabe," Petru stated.

"What about his documentary following the environmentalist group fighting development along the coast?" Bruno said. "He got them a lot of attention."

"You'll see," Tittu said to Séverine.

⌣

The next morning, Petru packed the bomb in a small cardboard box, which he placed inside a paper grocery bag, which he nestled in the trunk alongside another grocery bag that held bagged lunches he'd prepared the night before. Reluctantly, Séverine dug through the bag of clothing from Bruno's sister and put on a white-and-black-striped baby tee with a black denim skirt.

Petru knocked on the doorframe as she packed her overnight bag. "We're leaving in fifteen."

"Okay," she said.

He came inside the room. "I realized there's a wig you could wear. As a disguise," he said carefully, as if he might change his mind. He opened the closet and removed a skirt hanger that clamped a plastic bag full of dark curls.

"Maybe you should tie your hair up," Petru said.

When she'd done so, Petru stretched a nylon wig cap over his fanned-out fingers and expertly maneuvered it onto her head, tucking in stray hairs with gruff care. He stepped aside so she could examine herself in the mirror. She'd begged her parents for a perm in collège and they'd refused—*Thank God*, she now thought to herself. The short brown curls framing her face made her look both prepubescent and middle-aged. She was about to say something self-deprecating, when she realized this must be Petru's aunt's chemotherapy wig and shut her mouth.

"It's not your style, but maybe that's a good thing," Petru said.

Even with the nose, Séverine looked completely different. Like a good girl who obeyed her parents and was afraid of boys. She tugged at the curls. If she brushed them out, she could make it cuter.

"What kind of cancer did your aunt have?" Séverine asked, self-consciously touching the back of the wig.

"Breast."

"When did she pass?"

"Last September."

Séverine nodded and said, "Thanks, Petru." It was the most intimate gift anyone had ever given her.

—————

"Where's the Beretta?" Bruno asked as Séverine and Petru were about to walk out the door.

"In my bag," she said, patting at a straw tote she'd found in her closet.

"No no no," Bruno said, darting off to his room. He returned with a black leather holster, from a bygone era but of excellent craftsmanship.

"You'll have easier access this way."

So many gifts in one day.

"Here, I'll show you how to use it," Tittu offered. He bent to unbuckle and remove her belt, which slipped through the loops of her jeans with an intimacy equal to his hands skimming her waist.

"You just slide it on like this," he showed her, then rethreaded the holster through her jeans, turning her by the hips with a bold proprietorship. She looked at the other two, smiling stiffly as if to say, *What's gotten into him?* But the way they watched his hands, they understood everything.

———

For a while, Petru and Séverine rode in silence as the car twisted down the mountain. It was a welcome change to sit with their own thoughts; collective living meant constantly talking. Then Petru spoke.

"Tittu has a crush on you," he said, eyes on the road.

Séverine was startled. "Oh. You think?"

He shot her a stern look.

"Maybe," she acknowledged.

"Don't encourage him."

"I'm not," Séverine said defensively. She wondered if Tittu had dared tell him about the two times they kissed.

"It's not good for the cell."

"Nothing's going on between us!" She turned towards the passenger-side window, pouting.

Petru entered the big, anonymous Mr. Bricolage parking lot, backing into a space so Séverine could slip into the passenger seat of the waiting rental car, exposed for only a moment before they continued on their way.

Suddenly the sea rose before them, hovering halfway up the sky and so still, as if collected at the bottom of a glass. It had been

Séverine's one comfort since she'd arrived in Corsica, and here it was, a friend who never changed.

The road weaved inland then skimmed the Bay of Calvi, shaped like a bite mark taken out of the island. She could smell the sea and feel the sticky heat of the coast—if only she could convince Petru to let her go to the beach!—but buildings lining the side of the road obscured it from view. More than a metaphor, it was precisely what they were fighting against: a few individuals enjoying what belonged to the people.

They began to climb into the hills. Terra-cotta roofs peeked over stone privacy walls, greenery spilled from whatever lush paradise those walls protected. Dozens of homes towered in various stages of construction.

"It's like Whac-A-Mole," Petru noted. "One vacation villa's bombed, another goes up across the street."

"Do you ever get discouraged?" Séverine asked.

"Me? No. I understand it's a long game," Petru said. "But other guys do. They start thinking it's pointless to fight. It's better they quit; the worst are the ones who lose their fire but stick around to collect a paycheck."

"Like Fanfan," Séverine ventured.

"Like Fanfan," Petru agreed.

"What did your aunt think of your . . . hobby?" she asked.

"She didn't approve," Petru said. "Her ex-husband was I Fratelli back in the day, and she hated it then, too. She just—she was scared I'd end up in prison without any second chances."

"For good reason."

"Not me. I'll go down fighting first."

Séverine remembered that first night at the bergerie, a lifetime ago, Petru pressing the gun to her chest and saying, *I'm not going back.* She didn't often think about those masked men being her comrades, but occasionally some word or movement flattened the present onto the past, superimposing memory and new reality like paired carbon copies. Whenever this happened, it gave her a chilly thrill. She knew that that violence, albeit bridled, still bucked inside them.

"What landed you in prison in the first place?" she asked. She wanted to hear his version.

Petru didn't take his eyes from the road. "I was mixed up with some not-great people when I was younger. We'd break into places at night and steal stuff. And one time the owner of this electronics store came down from his apartment with a golf club, and I just wailed on him. I don't know, everyone was watching me, and it felt like I had something to prove. Dumb boy stuff. I guess the guy wasn't in great shape to begin with, and I nearly did him in. So they carted me off to the juvie in Fleury-Mérogis."

"I didn't know they had a juvie there," Séverine said.

"There's a designated 'minors quarters' within the prison, but really everyone's all mixed up together."

"That sounds dangerous."

"No shit," Petru said. "I was there three years, and it was the fucking worst. They treated us like animals, and it was boring, and there were rats. So when I had my first parole hearing, I told them I'd sign up for the Foreign Legion, and they let me go. That was a different kind of shit show. The guys who end up there are total maniacs: crooks, runaways, literal psychopaths. But I was a maniac, too, I guess. It was good for me, honestly. As you can see, I'm re-formed now," he added with a sly smile.

You like me, she thought with self-satisfaction as she smiled back.

⌒

Nico's apartment complex, near-Soviet in its austerity, was located on the side of a hill a bit out of town and tucked away from the road.

Séverine found her comrades inside, lounging on a secondhand sofa, smoking cigarettes and watching the Tour de France on a large TV. It was strange to see them in a different house, looking like normal boys doing normal boy things.

An unfamiliar guy sat in a papasan chair, staring at her intently. He had wavy, chin-length hair, tanned feet, hangdog eyes, and wore long shorts with an oversized T-shirt. He was nothing like she'd pictured from Bruno's description; he looked like a burnout. The idea of him being a militant was a joke.

"It's crazy you're here in my apartment right now," Nico said, hoisting himself out of his chair.

"It's me," Séverine said breezily, taking in the nappy beige carpeting, the floor-to-ceiling bookshelves filled with VHS tapes, and the framed movie posters of American indies.

He gripped her upper arms and enthusiastically kissed her on each cheek. "You could change the whole game. I mean, the front cover of *The Guardian*!"

Séverine perked up. "You have a copy?"

"Do I have a copy," Nico said with fake offense. He went to the kitchen and reappeared with a small stack of newspapers, which he dropped onto the dining room table with a performative thud and fanned before her.

"*Séverine. Séverine. Séverine. Séverine,*" he said, pointing at each appearance of her name.

She drew the tips of her fingers along the newsprint with reverence. On each front page, her own image, the headlines bold with her name! The newspaper on top was today's: July 14, 1993. Down the page was an insert of Jonnart sitting before a cluster of microphones, mouth open, one finger raised. It just wasn't right for a man of his age to have such a full head of thick, silver hair; it made him too assertive. "'Séverine Guimard is a fugitive, not a victim.'" What an asshole. She hated him. He'd probably love for the police to shoot her dead; that way, no one would ever know what he'd done to her. At the same time, he'd assumed she'd keep his secret, and he was right, and she hated herself for it.

"What are the geezers in I Fratelli saying?" Bruno asked.

"You know, groups splinter off now and then, but not much comes of it," Nico said. "They think it's a lot of noise, not a lot of action."

"Yet," Séverine cut in.

"Listen to her!" Nico clapped his hands, delighted. "Can I ask—how did the switch happen?"

"What switch?"

"From this"—he pointed at a picture of her at a benefit gala with her parents—"to this." Then, pushing that paper aside, he pointed at her photo with the Kalashnikov.

She bristled. "Didn't you listen to the communiqué?" Her impulse to be a little mean felt Darwinian, as if the effort required to be kind would be a negation of the natural order.

"Of course," Nico said quickly, almost apologetically. "You say something like, 'I knew there was injustice, but it seemed so far away.' But for us, the injustice was right there. I was a little kid when Montedison was dumping chemicals off the coast, and I remember the dead fish on the beaches. No Corsican alive remembers a time when there wasn't mass unemployment." Nico nudged Bruno. "So what exactly did the professor say to open your eyes?"

There was something suggestive underneath this stupid comment, something that reminded Séverine of when her mother had asked, *You have a little crush on him?*, and it made her rigid with irritation. She glared at Nico for a moment, and although he was taller, she tilted her head and squinted her eyes so that it was like she was looking down on him.

"Oh, I don't believe a word of what I said. I'm only doing all this 'cause I wanna fuck him."

Nico laughed while Bruno looked at the carpet, discomposed. Séverine did not notice Tittu's brows knit together.

"What *I'm* wondering is," she continued, "if you're so moved by all this *injustice*, why aren't *you* the one blowing up the Laporte house?"

"He's aiding and abetting a crime as we speak," Bruno cut in. "You think the courts wouldn't prosecute him because he didn't plant the bomb himself?"

"She's not wrong!" Nico exclaimed. "What can I say, I'm an observer, not a doer. I'm better behind the camera. But you—" He extended his arms in her direction as if to say, *Behold*, and turned to Bruno. "You need to start filming her communiqués."

"She already acts like she's in a movie 24/7," Petru complained. "Don't encourage her."

"I'm serious!" Nico said. "The media's usually our worst enemy, but she's got what it takes to make it work for us. I'll send you home with my camcorder. It's not complicated."

He's got vision, Séverine thought, but he was otherwise a total joke—whatever Bruno liked about him came from a nostalgic, irrational place. She understood why this put Petru and Tittu on edge.

For the rest of the afternoon, the five of them ate frozen pizza alsacienne and chain-smoked while watching *Coucou c'est nous!* reruns; it had been a month since Séverine last sat in front of a TV, and the dissociation felt palliative. As the room grew darker, they began to hear groups of people tromping past the apartment, festive and drunk.

"Making sure they get a good seat for the fireworks," Nico said, peeking through the blinds. He checked his watch. "It's already 21:30."

"I'll go now," Tittu said, picking up his helmet from the floor and pulling it over his head. He was supposed to drive past the Laporte villa on his bike to verify no one was home; after twenty minutes, he was back. "Empty," he confirmed. "Should we move out?"

"Ten more minutes," Petru said. He sat very still on the couch, staring at the TV while his cigarette burned listlessly between his fingers, but Séverine could tell he wasn't watching; it was as if he were meditating.

Then the waiting was over. At 22:00 Petru said, "Let's go," stubbing his cigarette into a full ashtray.

"I'd say good luck, but that's bad luck, isn't it?" Nico asked, clapping Bruno and Tittu on the back.

She put on her wig and walked outside. The street was empty; everyone had made their way downtown to celebrate. Petru and Tittu got in the back seats of the rental car; just as Séverine was about to get in the passenger seat, Bruno asked, "Can I talk to you over there?"

Arms crossed, she followed him to the other side of the parking lot, out of the light of the apartment building. She knew he was unhappy with her. She also knew as long as he was mad at her, she wouldn't be able to focus on anything else, the bomb included.

"Nico's sticking his neck out for us, and you're being a bitch for no reason," he said.

"A bitch—really?" Séverine asked, already hot.

"A bitch!" Bruno confirmed.

"Tittu and Petru are right," Séverine said. "There's something off about him."

"Well, he thinks you're the Second Coming."

"What's that supposed to mean?"

"*Séverine's revolutionizing the revolution, Séverine's a big, big star,*" he mocked.

"You sound like a jealous prick," she said, aware that jealousy could be rooted in either resentment towards Séverine or possessiveness of her. He hesitated, as if the source of that feeling was unknown even to him.

"Nico's good people," Bruno said, composing himself. "When we met, I was lonely and depressed, and so stressed about school, but he brought me out of my bubble. He introduced me to guys who literally changed my life. So in a way *he* changed my life. Maybe even saved it."

"All right, I'll be nice," she relented.

As they got in the rental car and drove away, she wondered if he detected some truth in her sarcastic remark about wanting to sleep with him, and if he'd detected that truth in himself, too.

They rolled past the villa; it was just as Séverine remembered. White stucco facade lit from below, a frosted glass door flanked by white columns, the architecture both Mediterranean and modern. Gaudy magenta bougainvilleas cascaded over the wrought iron gate, grazing the street below. Inside were seven bedrooms plus a number of other rooms filled with unused furniture, an excess of balconies, and a lima bean–shaped pool.

The villa so reflected its owners, Séverine thought. The Laportes were not new money, but because Madame Laporte's family had amassed its wealth on a tiny island in the Indian Ocean, so far from French society, she exuded the desperation of new money. When Séverine and her mother had visited last August, she had darted around the house pointing out every detail, and they had oohed and aahed so politely that their failure to match Madame Laporte's enthusiasm bordered on impolite.

Bruno parked across from the cemetery, a dense village of white granite mausoleums crested with crucifixes like weather vanes.

"I'll see you in twenty minutes," he said, squeezing her wrist in encouragement, and energy and ability surged within her. All was forgiven. She could do anything as long as Bruno believed she could.

Petru, Tittu, and Séverine exited the car and slunk through the stone-paved, cypress-lined alleys towards the Laporte villa. It was such a perfect summer night. On the one hand, Séverine felt a degree of melancholy thinking of the festivities below, even if that excitement was ordinary and comparatively wholesome. On the other hand, the excitement she felt in the darkness of the cemetery among her comrades was razor-sharp, momentous. There was no way she was going to stand around in an empty lot while Tittu and Petru had all the fun.

Tittu, bringing up the rear, suddenly grabbed Séverine's hand and gave her a little yank backwards while Petru continued on unaware.

"Are you into Bruno?" he asked. Even in the dark, she could hear emotion in his voice, but it was not the time or place for emotion.

"Are you insane?" she whispered, and wrested her arm from his grip.

"Move it," Petru reprimanded, and Séverine jogged ahead, leaving Tittu to catch up.

They pulled on their ski masks before climbing over the cemetery wall and stalking through the empty lot. When they reached the taller, smoother Laporte wall, Tittu first gave Petru a leg up, then Petru straddled the wall and hauled Tittu up by the wrists.

"Please please please let me come with you," Séverine begged, tugging on Petru's pant leg.

"Absolutely not," Petru said. "We need you to cover this area. Everyone has their job."

"Please, Petru. This was my idea, and it's my first bombing, and it won't feel real unless I do it myself," she said.

He took this in, nodded curtly, and pulled her up onto the wall. Even that was thrilling. She paused to look over the town, its droplets of orange light bleeding into the black bay, which elongated and distorted their glow. With a little squeal, she jumped down into the Laportes' backyard.

Tittu drew his pistol and pointed it at the camera above the sliding glass door, but Séverine put a hand on his arm.

"What if we left them running?" she whispered, thinking of Nico telling Bruno: *You need to start filming her.* She pulled off her mask. "This way they'll play the footage on TV and know without a doubt who did it."

"That puts us at risk," Tittu said, motioning to Petru.

"Not if you keep your masks on," Séverine replied. "How often does the news show the explosion itself? Never—just the rubble. But the explosion is the most impressive part."

Petru was mulling it over.

"All that glass," Séverine goaded. "It'll look crazy."

"All right, fine," Petru relented. "But no more improvising. We need to get a move on."

They left Tittu to patrol the perimeter, and Séverine loped after Petru towards the western side of the house. She felt the same restless thrill as she had on summer nights playing Kick the Can with her American cousins, darting between cars and trees, listening for the sneaker slaps of the other kids prowling the neighborhood. Those nights, she hadn't wished to be a grown-up like she usually did.

No one was home, but it was still unnerving to creep alongside all that glass. Recessed lighting, although dimmed to its lowest, warmest glow, made the interior perfectly visible. She thought of her own kitchen viewed from her own pool with a pang of homesickness.

They turned the corner of the house, then Petru knelt, took a hand hoe from his belt, and began hacking at the grass. They'd bury the bomb so the blast was directed towards the house; it was called "tamping." If they merely laid the bomb against the wall, the undirected energy would do a lot less damage. Sweating, Petru looked up at her.

"You're not trying to jump in and do this part, though," he said.

"'Cause you're doing such a good job." Séverine smiled.

The digging took an eternity; it was so quiet that the silence yielded to a hidden layer of sound, magnifying noises that Séverine couldn't distinguish as real or imagined. But then she remembered the gun on her belt, authoritative in its presence alone. Every girl should have a gun, Séverine thought.

"Light," Petru instructed, handing her a pen flashlight that Séverine held steady. His hands worked quickly and deliberately as he connected the detonator to the bomb. When it was done, he exhaled and hooked a finger at Séverine. She crouched beside him, and he held out the egg timer, connected to the neat brick of plastic-wrapped ANFO by three thin coated wires.

"Thirty minutes," he said.

She took the little plastic egg, warm and sticky from Petru's hands, and twisted it, the serrated plastic grinding earsplittingly loud. When she let go of the top half of the egg, it began ticking maniacally. The ticking grew more and more muffled as they shoveled the dirt around the bomb. Once it was buried, Petru patted the soil like a farmer willing a seed to sprout.

"Is someone there?"

Before he even turned the corner, beer in hand, wearing a white polo and khaki shorts, tanner and blonder and less acned from the sun, Séverine knew it was Julien. And before Julien knew what was happening, before he could cry out, Petru had tackled him to the ground, and his beer bottle shattered on the flagstone, and Tittu came running with his gun drawn.

Séverine took a moment to observe Julien in this completely subordinate position, with Petru digging his knee into his back and wrenching his arms behind him. A smear of blood spread from his nose onto his chin, and his face reddened as he strained pointlessly against Petru's weight, jerking like a fish on a line. She felt a surge of tenderness for him, this character from her past. It was good to see him! This last month made her old life seem like a too-vivid dream, but here was a flesh-and-blood person who confirmed it had been real.

"Help!" he called, his voice hoarse.

"Shut up, dummy, it's me," Séverine said warmly. As he turned his head, she crouched beside him and kissed his available cheek with enthusiasm.

"Séverine?" he asked with a disbelieving laugh.

"Pick him up," Séverine instructed, and Petru pulled him to his feet.

It had been a year since she'd last seen him, and Julien had grown more manlike: broader in the shoulders, razor bumps along his squarer jawline. It was strange to notice the changes; it meant their lives were no longer so intertwined, for better or for worse. The hate she harbored towards him unexpectedly felt like the other side of a long-standing affection.

She used the collar of his white polo to wipe the blood from his nose. "Why aren't you at the Dorbons' party?" she asked.

"I was. I'm going to Club Manège for the DJ Clams set later."

"That's stupid, why wouldn't you go straight to the club after the fireworks? You get the best view from the yacht."

"I don't give a shit about the fireworks," Julien said. "And I needed to pick up some party favors."

"Like, macarons?" she asked, confused.

"Like ecstasy," he said, as if this should be obvious. He looked between the masked men. "You let them both fuck you?"

Now she remembered why she'd loathed him forever; he was such a pig. Matter-of-factly, she plunged her hands into his back pockets, then front pockets, sliding her palms against his thighs. He twitched, and she gave a knowing smirk. From Julien's front left pocket, she produced a small tin of breath mints that contained a baggie of six yellow pastilles stamped with alien heads.

"What's it like?" she asked.

"It's called 'ecstasy,' isn't it?"

"You're so rude. I'm just asking," she said.

"It makes you want to fuck anything on two legs. You certainly don't need it," Julien said.

She slipped the tin into her pocket. "I forgot to mention, I'm here to bomb your ugly house. We have about twenty-six minutes till it blows, so we should probably get going."

"You're not serious."

"You wanna wait around and see?"

His eyes widened. "You crazy bitch!"

"I'm not blowing you up, too," Séverine replied. "You're lucky we ran into each other."

"We need to go, now," Petru demanded.

So with Tittu's gun pressed against his back, Soffiu di Libertà led Julien out of his family compound. Like a circus act repeating their routine, they propelled and pulled each other back over the wall, gun always trained on Julien.

A few meters from the cemetery entrance, Petru said, "This is far enough."

"Don't leave me in here," Julien whined as Petru zip-tied his wrists to the ornamental gate of a mausoleum. "Why *my* house? What did I ever do to you? We were always cool."

He was being serious, she realized. The thought of explaining his crime to him suddenly seemed degrading. *She* knew it was personal, but if *he* knew, he regained some traction. He could then paint her as obsessive, desperate, over-the-top. And maybe she was! But she could not allow him to claim that power over her, to once again shape the public narrative about a private affair.

"It's not personal, Jules," Séverine said, leaning to kiss him on each helpless cheek. "It was actually so nice seeing you. Tell your mom I say hi."

The three of them ran out of the cemetery and into the idling car. No one spoke as Bruno drove at a restrained forty-five kilometers an hour down the hill. The clock read 22:57. He turned onto the main thoroughfare, among taxis, people drinking on their balconies, and a few latecomers hurrying towards the quai. As they turned off the main road onto Nico's street, they heard the explosion. Their heads swiveled behind them, in the direction of the terrible crack, just as a bloom of acid-green light burst and faded in the rear windshield, and then another in pink, and another in silvery white. Bruno parked in front of the apartment as Nico came out to meet them, and they stood around the car watching the show. The squawking, pre-recorded dramatics of "La Marseillaise" didn't make it up the hill from the Citadel—none of the patriotism, none of the propaganda— only the violent rending of nighttime by dazzling lights and opaque clouds of smoke accumulating above the sea.

Then there was a new explosion, profoundly deep, hostile, and earthly; reflexively, Séverine clung to Tittu. She felt stupid for ever mistaking the fireworks for the bomb. A fiercer and swifter cloud, like smoke from the nostrils of an angry dragon, blackened the navy sky. Then she remembered this was her doing, and exhilaration burst forth from her fear. Grinning, she turned to her comrades, and they hugged her, kissed her, ruffled her hair. She'd been initiated. She could never go back; she knew it, and they knew it, too.

As the finale commenced, the fireworks seemed to explode all at once, an unartful barrage of light and sound that ended as abruptly as it began. Their ears rang, and the smell of the smokes intermingled, one acrid, the other like a campfire. Then the wail of a police siren rose from the town center, and the spectators filed inside.

Nico took five Pietras from the fridge and festively opened them one by one. Before they'd even had a chance to cheers, Petru said, "I was right about the Laporte kid. You had a thing with him."

"Can you just drop it?" Séverine snapped, glancing at Bruno for his reaction, but he was focused on downing his beer. Determined to change the subject, she declared, "Let's get drunk!"

Nico clapped his hands and turned on the radio.

"Coming at you live from Club Manège—" the DJ announced.

"I guess Julien's not making it tonight," Séverine said smugly. "Oh!" She fished the mints tin out of her pocket and shook it like a maraca. "But we shouldn't let his fun go to waste."

"No way." Nico laughed, taking the tin and emptying the yellow tablets into his palm. "It's not easy to get this stuff here."

"What is it?" Bruno asked.

"Ecstasy," Séverine said with the same condescending tone Julien had used. "I don't want to do it *alone*."

Petru shook his head no.

"I'm down," Nico piped up, but she ignored him.

"Me too," Tittu said, then looked at Bruno for consent.

Bruno shrugged. "It's your brain."

"Bruno?" she asked, offering him the tin.

"I'm good," Bruno said.

"Oh come on, it'll be fun," she cajoled, Julien's description of its effects echoing in her head.

"I'm having fun," Bruno said, unruffled.

"No use peer pressuring him," Nico said to Séverine. "Believe me, I've tried."

So Séverine, Tittu, and Nico each swallowed a pill with a mouthful of beer, laughing nervously afterwards, anticipating the imminent high.

"How long does it take to kick in?" Séverine asked.

"Maybe an hour? You'll know," Nico said, dancing a little.

Although Petru and Bruno didn't take any E, they drank plenty of beer—a long row of empty Pietra bottles edged the length of the kitchen counter, and the mood finally lightened.

"Petru was like a rugby tackler the way he took down Julien! He didn't even make it one step before Petru was on top of him," Séverine said.

"And Tittu flying around the corner like James Bond with his gun out." Petru laughed.

"I want to be in on the action next time," Bruno complained, which caught Séverine off guard; she couldn't imagine him doing what Petru or Tittu or even she had done. Hearing Nico call Bruno *the professor*, she realized that was exactly how she thought of him, too.

"What *is* next, children?" Nico asked.

The four of them looked at each other, unsure whether to share that they had absolutely no idea. "We have a few things in mind," Bruno said.

Just then, "What Is Love" came on the radio, all raw synthetic energy, and it slammed Séverine with euphoria and longing.

"This is my *song*!" she cried, jumping to her feet and dancing like the vampire girls in the music video, all swinging arms and hair.

"You know, I was listening to this cassette when you kidnapped me. Isn't that crazy? And crazy how different everything is? Life really is unpredictable," she yammered. It filled her with emotion to know that a few kilometers away, a club full of people was dancing to her song, and the blessed radio waves connected her to them.

Nico made a sound like he'd forgotten something and went into his bedroom. He returned with a camcorder held up to his face.

"No no no no no," Bruno protested, jumping up to block the camera and upsetting a beer left on the carpet.

"Yes yes yes yes yes," Nico replied, maneuvering around him.

Séverine let the men argue; she was too involved in the music to care.

"He said no," Petru said. When he laid a giant hand on the camcorder and gently pressed it away from Nico's face, it carried a more palpable threat.

"Think: we're in your apartment. This is self-incriminating," Bruno said.

"It's a question of history, man. It must be documented," Nico said.

"It's just for fun," Séverine interjected as she bounced on her toes. "None of you know how to have any fun."

Nico looked warily at Petru and Bruno, then raised the viewfinder back to his eye. It was as if someone had yelled "Action!" Séverine was acting both on impulse and by lightning-quick calculations— she really wanted to dance, and she knew it would translate beautifully on camera.

"Are you feeling it?" Nico asked mischievously.

She inhaled like she was taking a huge gulp of cold water. "I think so," she said. The song ended, and Séverine collapsed to the floor, legs folded to one side. She took a flirtatious sip of beer, eyes fixed on the camera, communing with it.

"You just set off your first bomb," Nico began. "What was that like?"

"The most fun I've had in ages!" she exclaimed, smiling radiantly.

Nico stood over her, and she felt like she was filming the opening to a porno. She wished someone else was behind the camera; he was like a cloud obstructing the sun of her high. She felt her experience spoiling, but a more rational part of her brain allowed him to hover above her, to point the camera like a dick she was about to open her mouth for, only because she knew that the camera, the man, the eventual viewer, were completely in her thrall.

The quick, relentless beat and chanting vocals of "Darla Dirla-dada" by G. O. Culture came on the radio, and the apartment began to feel very small and bright. Séverine's body buzzed with electricity that was too noisy, too loud here. She wanted to transport through the radio to the club, she needed to be surrounded by people, to feel her shoes stick to the floor, to absorb the happy, free energy of so many beautiful people.

"Let's go to Club Manège," she pleaded, ignoring the camera.

"She's definitely feeling it," Petru snorted.

"I'm serious," she said. "I'll put on the wig, no one will recognize me; it's one in the morning, everyone will be wasted already."

"I'll take you on the bike," Tittu said. He'd been sitting on the floor, silently running his hands along the carpet, but now he jumped up and fetched his helmet.

"No, this is crazy," Bruno said.

"Come on, man, she's right; no one will recognize her; no one would expect her to ever be there," Nico said. "Don't you think you owe her after—you know, keeping her captive in the middle of nowhere?"

"I need to feel free," Séverine agreed, crawling over to Bruno and placing her hands on his knees. "I just want to dance. Don't you trust me now? I'm with you guys for real, don't you see that?" Her eyes shone with beseeching tears. "Just this one time, I promise."

"It's not about trust, it's about safety," Bruno said.

But she wasn't asking permission. There was no question that she was going; the idea had been articulated and had its own independent gravity that was pulling her out of the apartment. As Tittu and Nico tried to convince Bruno and Petru it would be fine, she leapt up and skipped to the dining area, where she unceremoniously tore off her black guerrilla clothes and put on the skirt and baby tee she'd worn earlier.

"Stop, I'm serious," Bruno said, getting angry, as she arranged the wig on her head.

"I'll call a cab and meet you there," Nico called as Séverine took Tittu's hand and led him out the door.

"Wait!" she heard Bruno yell, knowing he'd never come outside and make a scene.

Tittu handed her the helmet, and she straddled the back of the seat with little grace.

"I'm impressed," she said. "I didn't think you had it in you."

In reply, he smirked and turned over the engine; when he accelerated down the road, she screamed and cemented herself to his back, although she fully trusted his driving. Oh, Tittu. Forced into this sustained embrace, she rested her cheek against his knobby spine and let herself appreciate his taut thinness, the way he smelled of fresh dirt, a clean smell. As it turned out, she could care for a man without sleeping with him—a revelation! She loved Tittu. She loved all of them. Wasn't life funny? Wasn't it marvelous!

Fifteen minutes later, they pulled into the sand parking lot of Club Manège, cramming into a packed row of motorcycles and scooters. Music pulsed from the direction of the ocean. Séverine felt no fear approaching the door; the cashier and bouncer gave them a cursory glance as they collected the entry fees and stamped their hands. They were in, and it was as if Séverine had passed through a wormhole, back into the dimension she'd occupied before she was kidnapped.

They entered by the main bar; below, directly on the sand, were the DJ booth and dance floor. Everything was awash in marine-blue lights, making the dancers' skin look alien, making the sea look chemically enhanced. And there were people everywhere: normal, unassuming people, thinking about nothing but getting drunk, getting laid, having a good time. People dancing, laughing, clinking glasses of slushy neon liquor, hiking up their skirts and kicking seafoam at each other.

"Don't cry," Tittu said, taking her face between his hands.

"No, it's incredible. I'm so happy," she said. "Get me a mojito?"

As he jostled his way to the bar, Séverine descended to the beach. It was amazing that just a few kilometers away, a bomb had decimated someone's home, and here everyone—tourists, Corsicans—danced like nothing had happened. She was too high to decide if that made it Sodom or utopia.

The DJ put on "Sing Hallelujah" by Dr. Alban, and the music moved through her, pianos jangling her eardrums and synths running along her nervous system and the bass overpowering the rhythm of her heart. She kicked off her shoes and danced. Multicolored lights swept over her skin, and the sand beneath her feet felt smooth and cool as silk. She was dancing alone, but she didn't feel alone—she'd never felt less alone, or safer.

"She's here," she heard Petru say, and when she opened her eyes, she saw his big, dependable body in front of her, frowning, and the other three walking towards her. They'd changed out of their black clothes and looked like any other group of single guys out for the night. Séverine jumped and clapped, overjoyed to see them.

"What'd I tell you?" she yelled over the music. "Aren't you glad we came?"

She could tell that Nico and Tittu were as fully in the throes of the drug as she was—Nico was dancing with total, ridiculous abandon, his long hair swinging in his face, and Tittu was staring seriously at his feet and bobbing his head. She felt both pleasantly separate and completely synced with them. Bruno and Petru found two low chairs by the water where they could nurse their beers and cigarettes and watch Séverine, Tittu, and Nico with irritated protectiveness. They loved and indulged her like her papa did, but she was their equal. Maybe that's what true love with a man was like. As she was roaming through these lovely cotton candy thoughts, she felt Nico wind his arm around her waist from behind.

The fact of something unwanted happening was like a pea under the many feather beds of her bliss. She reached for Tittu with a panicked look; he immediately understood and took her hands, gently pulling her out of Nico's grasp. Nico didn't resist, and Séverine found herself in Tittu's arms, enveloped.

"Tittu," she yelled over the music, pulling away with his hands in hers. "I love you."

"Me too," he exhaled.

"And I loved bombing that house with you."

"Me too!" he said, and bent towards her, but she placed a hand firmly on his chest.

"—so I think it's better if we're friends and comrades only."

His tooth-grinding grin faltered. "Oh," he said.

"Because we have a higher purpose, Tittu. We're gonna change the world."

"But you just said you love me," he said, rolling this idea around his addled brain.

"Right! You gave me that purpose," she explained. "So it's a pure love. Purer than boyfriend-girlfriend love, purer even than family love."

This penetrated. He looked at her tenderly, and she took his other hand. Because his serotonin was gushing like an open fire hydrant, what could have been perceived as a rejection was flushed downstream, forgotten in the radiance of her smile, her touch, her wanting to dance with him, and they jumped and swung arms like kids.

Séverine glanced towards the other two men; Petru was talking to Bruno as his eyes scanned the crowd, and Bruno was watching her with a funny look, protective but also confused, slightly agonized. Another pure thought flowed from her powerful brain: *He wants me.*

10. *Escalation*

Séverine woke up in a bed—Nico's, she quickly realized—alone. The sheets felt greasy and smelled unwashed. She had no idea what time it was; the room was blessedly dark. They'd gone to sleep well into the morning, in full daylight.

She felt fine; just stiff and very, very thirsty. In fact, a mild exhilaration, a sense of limitless possibility, persisted. After she dressed, she found the four men sitting around the TV snacking on too-soft brioches from a plastic bag.

"Good morning," she said breezily.

"It's two in the afternoon," Petru replied. Bruno didn't so much as look her way.

Nico put down the spliff he was rolling, grabbed the newspaper sitting on the coffee table, and handed it to her. "Delivered as you slept the deep sleep of the innocent."

And there it was: a picture of the Laporte villa, not demolished, but badly gashed by the bomb, looking like something left over from wartime, shiny white decadence recognizable along the fringes, but the core of it ash. The headline read, "Séverine Guimard Bombs Laporte Villa in Calvi." For the first time, she felt like she'd accomplished something. This must be how her dad felt when some policy of his was enacted, or how her mother felt getting a collection published: self-assured, fulfilled, useful.

She pictured the coast guard pulling up beside the yacht, pointing landward to the pillar of evil smoke, and Madame Laporte collapsing into her husband's arms. She imagined the gendarmes finding Julien in the cemetery. And later, when the communiqué had been played and the news relayed, Madame Laporte ranting, "Séverine Guimard did this!"

Petru had been flat-out wrong; Séverine felt very much relieved of the resentment weighing on her this last year. She felt a pure, Christian joy, a sense of justice that went beyond petty revenge— like she'd put the world back in order.

"That was a good bomb, Petru," she said.

He grunted without looking at her; so he was still mad. Bruno, too, kept his eyes on the TV, although she could tell he wasn't watching.

"There's one other thing," Nico said, and he pushed in a tape that was resting in the VHS player. The opening sequence of the France 3 Corse morning news appeared on the screen.

"I set it to record before we went to bed," Nico said.

"You think of everything!" Séverine cried and turned to Bruno with a mean little smile, but he continued to ignore her.

Nico fast-forwarded the tape until the photo of Séverine in the immortelles appeared floating beside the newscaster's head, then he pressed play as it cut to a reporter standing in front of the cracked egg of the Laporte house.

"—when the bomb detonated just shy of 23:00 last night. No one was harmed, but the damage to the home is catastrophic. France 3 received a recording earlier this morning in which Séverine Guimard claims responsibility for the bombing in the name of Soffiu di Libertà, the group that kidnapped her only one month ago. A security tape confirms Guimard and two associates carried out the bombing."

Grainy black-and-white footage showed Séverine and her comrades climbing over the wall; then it cut to her and Petru, masked, burying the bomb, then leading Julien away; then it cut to the explosion, a nonsensical, tremoring image, then static. It was as disorienting and cinematic as Séverine had hoped it would be.

"We now go to Mélanie Sozzi, who is with Claude Laporte." Monsieur Laporte appeared, tan arms folded over a crisp white Oxford with the sleeves rolled up. He was a compact man with deep-set eyes, and he exuded an intimidating hardness that had always turned off Séverine and her mother, who were used to the warmth and loquaciousness of Paul Guimard.

Séverine heard her own voice as a clip from her communiqué played: "The Laporte family profits off the death of oppressed people throughout the world. They used those blood-soaked profits to build the tackiest villa in Corsica. But they're not welcome here; and if they try to rebuild, we'll blow up that house, too."

As Monsieur Laporte listened, he remained expressionless.

"Monsieur Laporte, are you surprised to hear Séverine Guimard has taken responsibility for the bombing?"

"No," he said, quietly and firmly, in the manner of a disappointed parent. "She's undisciplined, attention-seeking, sheltered . . . I respect Paul and Bonnie Guimard, but they raised a child who thinks she can do whatever she wants without consequence."

"Yet the prefect and his wife are convinced she's being coerced," the newscaster said.

Monsieur Laporte was shaking his head before she'd finished speaking. "She was looking for adventure, and she found it. But she needs to know this is not a game. She will be tracked down and the consequences will be very, very real."

She hated the scolding, fatherly tone of his voice, as if her parents had failed so miserably at raising her that someone else needed to step in. As if Julien was such a prize!

"Where's that camera of yours?" Séverine asked. Nico grabbed it from the coffee table where he'd left it the night before and directed her into the dining room, where she stood against the blank wall.

"Short and sweet is good, more clippable for TV," he advised before pressing record.

"I just wanted to say that Monsieur Laporte is one hundred percent right. The consequences of our actions are very, very real. Maybe this is the first time he's felt that. But it won't be the last. U futuru avà!"

Nico hit the stop button. "Awesome. I'll copy this onto a new tape and send it to France 3."

Séverine turned to her comrades. "Any thoughts? Or is Soffiu di Libertà just me now?"

"It does seem more and more like the Séverine show, now that you mention it," Bruno snapped.

"Are you seriously still mad about the club?" Séverine asked.

"Yes, I'm still mad!" Bruno exploded. "You endangered every single person here, and for what? So you could get high and go dancing?"

"Bruno, lay off; it was fine," Tittu cut in.

"Oh, you, of course!" Bruno cried, turning on Tittu. "Boy, does she know how to work you. And you just follow her around like a starving puppy, as if she's gonna throw you a scrap."

Tittu's chin tucked as if Bruno had hit him there, and Bruno whipped back towards Séverine.

"How are you supposed to be part of this cell when you only think about what *you* want, when you're always manipulating everyone into helping you get it? You don't give a shit about anyone besides yourself."

"Nothing happened!" she cried, insulted. After pulling off the Laporte bombing, he *still* didn't take her seriously.

"You don't know that. The repercussions could be developing as we speak."

"Oh my God, I'm sorry!" she shouted, not sounding sorry at all. "You know what I think this is about? You're mad we had fun! You don't think we're doing revolution unless everyone is bored out of their minds! Maybe that's how it is at the bergerie, but once we leave, you don't have that power anymore." This last part she spoke deliberately, knowing it would get under his skin.

Indeed, Bruno shut up; she'd hit a nerve.

"Enough," Petru said with paternal authority.

There was no hanging around after that; they packed quickly, tensely. Before Séverine got into the 4x4, Nico handed her the camcorder, housed safely in a nylon carrying case.

"You're right, Bruno's too serious. He's always been that way," he whispered conspiratorially, his breath sweet from the brioche. "But if there's anyone who can lighten him up, it's you. Make him understand it'll be good for the cause."

She thought of what Bruno had said about Nico bringing him out of his bubble; it seemed that Nico was passing her the torch. Flattered, she gave him a hearty kiss goodbye on each cheek.

Driving back through town to the highway, the streets were filled with people walking to the beach with their straw hats and sunburned shoulders, umbrellas tucked under their arms. A bomb had decimated the home of one of France's most powerful businessmen, and not even twenty-four hours later, all was back to normal. It was like it had never happened. In the too-bright light of day, it depressed Séverine, like her big accomplishment was actually quite insignificant.

"Things shouldn't be so calm. The whole island should feel in chaos," Séverine said.

"It's causing enough chaos for the Laporte family; wasn't that what you wanted?" Petru asked with an edge of reproach.

Yes, but clearly it wasn't enough. Maybe an act of solidarity with international liberation movements (Bruno's words) was too lofty and impractical for now. It didn't mean anything to these tourists beyond an exciting little anecdote for them to tell their coworkers.

She remembered that strange year—she was about ten—when a Hezbollah-affiliated extremist group carried off a dozen bombings throughout Paris. Not symbolic attacks, but ones aimed at civilians shopping for records, eating lunch, commuting. A bunch of people had been killed. Séverine recalled an atmosphere of vague and irresolute fear, her parents not wanting to scare her but behaving cautiously, avoiding crowded places and the metro.

When they got back to the bergerie, the guys went straight to bed. Séverine was tired, too, but still overstimulated. She went out back to smoke, and as she watched the trees sway in the herb-fragrant breeze and tiny gnats dance in the sunlight, she thought, *This sucks.* What a fucking buzzkill to be back at the bergerie—imprisoned again.

It made no sense to try and stoke revolution from an isolated speck of maquis. According to Fanon, any massive change required mass participation. They should be mired among other people. Fuck the country. Fuck being holed up here with a bunch of books. She wasn't Bruno, she wasn't the Sorbonne girlfriend, and she wasn't Bonnie Guimard; she was a performer and a doer. She and Bruno were the yang and the yin; they could push the movement for independence further than ever if he let her use her special knowledge and talent. They could make each other better, too.

Petru emerged from the bedroom to start dinner, then the other two followed, sitting at the table with Coca-Colas for a hit of caffeine. Séverine entered the kitchen quietly. She knew, against her will, that she had to apologize.

After taking her own bottle of Coke from the fridge, she sat primly at the table. She set her jaw and said, "I'm sorry if I *endangered* anyone last night. I was being impulsive, and I should have been more . . . considerate."

Tittu added, "I'm sorry, too. I got caught up."

"Look, I get it," Bruno said. "You're both young, and you wanna do the things young people do. But this life is a sacrifice. If you're not up for it, it's okay, but tell us before you get in too deep."

"I'm up for it!" Tittu avowed, but Séverine's neck grew hot.

"Up for what? Sitting around for weeks, then setting off *one* bomb that everyone immediately forgets about?"

"It was *your* idea!" Bruno exclaimed.

"It's a start," Tittu said, cutting off any finger-pointing. "We'll plan something else."

"We have to do something that forces people to pay attention," Séverine said. "Not just the villa owners, not just Jonnart, but normal people. Tourists. They should be scared to come here."

"We're not gonna build public support if we terrorize the public," Bruno said.

"I'm not saying we should target like, daycares. I'm talking about hotels, Jet Ski rentals—tourist stuff."

"Tourist stuff is the whole economy," Petru said. "So that'll piss people off, too."

"You're terrorists and you're concerned about pissing people off?" Séverine exclaimed.

"This is the time of year when Corsicans make money," Bruno explained. "Bombing some pinzutu's mansion is one thing but messing with our people's livelihood is another."

"You yourself said Corsicans want freedom but are afraid to play dirty. That's where we come in," Séverine said, losing patience. "I Fratelli and all the other splinter groups have been doing the same old routine for what, twenty years? And has there been a revolution? Is Corsica independent?"

"But you act without thinking!" Bruno exploded. "You don't listen, you do whatever you want, there's not a proper ideology behind your proposals."

"And you act like it's so hard to change anything, like it has to be debated and strategized for years and years." Her tone cooled dangerously. "Sometimes it seems like you blew your whole load when you kidnapped me, and now you can't *act* at all."

Bruno was tongue-tied with rage and humiliation. Before he could reply, Tittu said, "We're all listening—what is it you want to do exactly?"

Séverine did her best to compose herself and explained, "We need to be blowing something up every single day. Send the tourists running home, spook the developers and speculators. Ruin the whole summer! Make people all over the world say, 'What the hell's going on in Corsica?' Because once they know about the unemployment and the housing crisis and the pollution and destruction of the coast, Jonnart and the rest of the government will look like the villains they are."

"What if we're up-front about it in our communication?" Tittu ventured. "If we say, 'We know this will sting at first. But it won't last, and it'll be worth it in the end.'"

The men took this in for a few moments. Then Petru said, "With our explosive stores, we could set off a midsize bomb every day for a week, then we'd be done."

"How do we get more?" Séverine asked.

"Our options are nicely asking I Fratelli"—Petru raised an eyebrow, obviously a no—"going to L'Anguille Noire"—the mafia, another no—"or Baptiste Kadiri."

"Why does that name sound familiar?" Séverine asked.

"As in, José Kadiri," Bruno said. "Leader of Novi Patriotti. They're brothers. I hate this idea even more than Séverine's."

"Kadiri—that's not Corsican?"

"Their dad's Moroccan," Tittu said with a hint of disapproval.

This came as a surprise to Séverine; while plenty of Arabs lived and worked in Corsica, mostly as farm labor, they seemed to comprise an entirely separate society. She'd never heard of any becoming nationalists. She had, however, heard nationalists decry Arab immigration as a threat to the already-vulnerable Corsican culture.

"Yeah, but their mom is an Agostini," Petru clarified. "That family is OG I Fratelli, from when they were still reputable."

"What are the chances Baptiste Kadiri tells us to get screwed?" Séverine asked. "Does Novi Patriotti see us as competition? Or comrades?"

Petru and Tittu gave Bruno an anticipatory look, and Bruno scratched the back of his head self-consciously.

"Unclear," he said. "Some context is that Matteu and I actually tried to join Novi Patriotti."

"And what, they turned you down?" Séverine joked.

"More or less," Bruno admitted.

"Oh," Séverine said, embarrassed. "Why?"

"It's beurs only," Tittu cut in. "They were always complaining about I Fratelli treating them unfairly, so they started their own thing."

"To be fair, some of the guys did give them a rough time," Petru said. "Anyway, if we're willing to pay a premium, I think they'll help us out. I have a feeling they're hard up for cash, and that's why we haven't seen any action from them in a while."

"Can you set it up?" Séverine asked. Petru nodded.

"In the meantime, why not set off the rest of our explosives at once?" she suggested. "Kick off the new campaign with a spectacle."

"So a nuit bleue. Multiple bombs in one night. We're not reinventing the wheel," Bruno said.

"If I'm the one doing it, it's automatically different," Séverine sniffed.

Bruno laughed unkindly. "I've never heard anything so arrogant in my life!"

"You know I'm right, though," Séverine said. "As long as people keep seeing my face connected to our actions, they'll talk about it. The movement has been uninspiring for a long time now. It needs a facelift. A woman's touch."

"Fuck it. What do I know? All hail Séverine," Bruno muttered, and his unsheathed hostility pierced Séverine like a dagger.

"We're talking weeks of organization," Petru said, and trailed a finger down the calendar tacked to the wall by the telephone. July was almost over.

"Like two weeks?" Séverine asked.

"Everything's gotta go so fast with you," Petru said. "It makes our work more dangerous."

"There's six, seven weeks of summer left," she replied. "We can't wait."

"A weekday would probably be best; people expect things to be quiet. The night of the twenty-eighth? Or I guess technically the twenty-ninth," Tittu proposed.

"The twenty-ninth is my birthday," Séverine said quietly, remembering the plans she, Hélène, and Pilar had to do karaoke at an Irish pub in Ajaccio. A part of her longed to still be that girl, but a stronger part of her was anchored to these men, this mission; strange, strange.

"Anyway, the twenty-ninth is perfect," she said. "The best gift ever."

"Ajaccio seems like the obvious target," Bruno muttered, neither wanting to endorse the plan nor be left out of it.

"I don't wanna go back there. Let's do Bastia," she replied. She wanted physical distance from that old plan, from her old life.

"But Ajaccio is the tourism hub," Petru said.

"What if we split up?" Tittu suggested. "If we set off half the bombs in Ajaccio and the other half in Bastia?"

"That would make it look like we have a multiregional coalition." Bruno nodded.

"But there aren't two of me," Petru said.

"Aren't you training her?" Tittu asked.

Petru huffed. "She's not ready."

"But in two weeks?" Séverine grinned.

⌒

Those next two weeks were spent sweating in the workshop with Petru. It was tedious work, but methodical. There was a lot of back-and-forth about which businesses to target, which would inspire the least ire in Corsicans while still impacting tourism. They decided to leave alone Corsican-owned small businesses; the web of interrelated people made Séverine's head spin: I Fratelli connections, mafia connections, this friend's godfather, that sister-in-law's mother. It seemed safest and most ideologically sound to go after foreign-owned enterprises and larger-scale companies owned by Corsicans they saw as traitors. They ended up assembling four bombs. In Ajaccio, they'd hit the casino and a currency exchange on the Rue Cardinal Fesch, a shop-choked pedestrian alley in the center of town; in Bastia, both bombs would target Corsica Mare Ferries. The smaller one would be planted at the terminal, and a big one—so big they sacrificed three additional bombs—was meant for the *Corsica Regina*.

The *Corsica Regina* was a 146-meter-long ferry, privately operated by Corsica Mare Ferries under the Panamanian flag, which conveniently excused the company from having to adhere to French labor laws. Currently, it sailed between Corsica and Sardinia, but the French government was allowing them to begin service between Toulon and Bastia, officially ending the state's monopoly on ferry travel to and from Corsica. Séverine knew this because Chantal Cipriani, in the class below her, who *stole* the role of Hélène when they performed *La guerre de Troie n'aura pas lieu* last year, was of the same Ciprianis who owned Corsica Mare Ferries. When the agreement had been negotiated, Chantal came into school the next day wearing the tackiest Chanel backpack, a celebratory gift from her papa.

Better not to mention Chantal, though, and no need; when Séverine suggested the *Corsica Regina*, they heard "privatization" and saw visions of labor violations, hordes of pinzuti sailing in on cheap tickets, and the foreign interests that would build sprawling, cheap resorts to accommodate them. Séverine asked if she could be responsible for that bomb, and after the requisite bickering, her request was approved.

⁓

Each comrade would plant their own bomb. It wasn't overly complicated, but Petru emphasized the stress of the scenario and how it could cause even a pro to fuck up. He made them practice with a flashlight bulb standing in for the detonator, over and over again:

set the timer, connect the wire from the timer with the wire from the "detonator" with a twist of the wrist. Done. It was imperative that the motions become second nature, that they could do them unthinkingly in the midst of panic.

It was agreed upon that Bruno and Séverine should go to Bastia and Tittu and Petru to Ajaccio. Bruno had access to a safe house there, and it was better to keep Séverine out of Ajaccio, where her parents lived. Séverine also suspected that Petru didn't trust her alone with Tittu, although the precaution was unnecessary. Things had managed to go back to normal with Tittu since their conversation at Club Manège, and she was relieved that their friendship had been salvaged before they crossed the point of no return.

The thought of being alone with Bruno was both nerve-racking and exciting, even though he was still very unhappy with her. The feeling was mutual! He was so inflexible, so pompous, so humorless. If she could only focus on that irritation, she might distract herself from the unseemly fixation at the root of it.

11. *Jouissance*

E arly Thursday morning, before they drove off in opposite directions, Petru and Séverine packed up the bombs. Without warning, he grabbed Séverine's wrists, and she flinched, some instinctive
fear flaring up.

"Trust these," Petru said, giving her wrists a little shake, unaware
of how he'd frightened her. "And don't seek out distractions."

"Why would I seek distractions?" Séverine huffed.

"To entertain yourself." Then he let go of her and said, "Otherwise, I have full confidence in you."

She knew he'd only say it if he meant it. And if he meant it, it was
as good as true. She could do this.

The four of them kissed goodbye, aware of but unwilling to give
voice to all that could go wrong.

The drive to Bastia cut through some brutally jagged mountains,
and as Bruno and Séverine ascended in their little rented Renault

Clio, the landscape took on a Swiss aspect: a rushing river could be heard below, down a terrifying slope with no guardrail, and the air was fresh and cool, the highest peaks on the island dusted with snow.

Neither Bruno nor Séverine initiated conversation; it was like they were playing a game of chicken. Relenting first would be akin to apology, which neither was willing to make—so the ride was silent, tense, longing for a concession neither would give.

Then they descended out of the mountains into Bastia. The sea was different up here than in Ajaccio or Calvi: more functional, less romantic. The docked ferries loomed larger and shone newer than any building in the city. They looked like the transport of invading armies.

They parked on the street and walked to the apartment where they were staying, located down an alleyway too narrow for cars to pass through. It was a lovely town with cobblestone streets, leafy trees, small plazas lined with benches, very old and very young people. Séverine wore her disguise, soaking up the few minutes she could pretend she was just like the people walking dogs and riding bikes with tennis rackets strapped to their backs. But no—she was a person about to plant a bomb.

The apartment building was old, its vestibule drafty as a country church. *"Courage,"* Bruno said, leading the way up the smooth-worn wooden stairs. Six floors later, panting, they reached the last landing. Bruno unlocked the door to a large, airy apartment: white walls with a few tasteful framed prints, a huge bookshelf, a futon and flat-weave rug in earth tones, a blond-wood dining room table beneath a large paper lantern, and a split-level galley kitchen.

"Whose place is this? It's way nicer than Nico's," Séverine said.

"Mine," Bruno replied.

"No, really," Séverine said.

He plucked a framed photo from the bookshelf and brought it to her. The time stamp on the corner read 25 April 1984. There was Bruno, younger and with longer hair; he would have been her age, actually. He was standing in front of a stone house with a huge pink mimosa tree alongside three normal-looking people who were unquestionably his parents and sister. They were sunburned and grinning, while Bruno smiled closemouthed. Even here beside his family, he looked apart. No wonder he'd gone off to Sciences Po—in Paris, he'd have the freedom to be different, to be solemn and pale and studious. The singularity of purpose required to return to the island must have been enormous.

"Our family home in Fozzano. My mom was born in that house, literally," he said, tapping the photo.

"You care about this sort of thing?" she asked, handing back the photo. "Having a nice apartment, making sure everything is just so?"

"I'm not going to pretend I don't appreciate comfort," Bruno said. "It's something everyone deserves, no?"

She shouldn't be surprised; he did like nice clothes and being well-groomed. But he had the politician's flair for painting a tall tale of who he was and where he came from—*just a simple boy from the wilds of Fozzano.*

"I'm going to run down to the grocery," Bruno said. "Madame Buffa would not be pleased to know I've been home for more than ten minutes without saying hello."

The full impact of their being in Bruno's apartment hit her. "Our safe house—on this night of all nights—is *your apartment?*"

"I'm a schoolteacher," Bruno said. "I don't work summers. I travel. It would look weird to my neighbors if I wasn't popping in and out."

Something occurred to her: "And it's normal for them to see you bring random girls home."

He shrugged with a self-satisfied, boyish smile.

Once Bruno left, Séverine took the liberty of poking around the other rooms. The bathroom was clean enough. Inside the mirrored medicine cabinet was a tube of toothpaste methodically folded, a pebbled leather manicure kit—and a bottle of Cerruti 1881.

In the bedroom, the mattress was on the floor but the bed was meticulously made. A large poster from a Rodolphe Bresdin exhibition at the Musée d'Orsay depicting two ominous black trees and a moth hung on the wall beside a carved wood armoire that, though doubtless a hand-me-down from his family, fit the room perfectly. He didn't own much, but what he did was studied and tasteful.

Bruno returned with cherry tomatoes, pepper-encrusted saucisson sec, sheep's milk cheese, olives, a baguette, and wild strawberries. He cheerfully pulled out knives and glasses and linen napkins, back in his element, and Séverine imagined him kissing the grocer as she warmly pestered him about where he'd been all summer. He arranged the food on his white plates with blue rims, and they sat at the table beneath the paper lantern. On the chair at the head of the table sat an authoritative and silent guest: an Etam bag that held one pair of new pajamas and one staggeringly potent bomb. Six kilos of ANFO boosted by a generous helping of Semtex, all nestled inside a Gallimard edition of *Les roses de pline.*

The plan was for Séverine to carry it to the ferry terminal, a fifteen-minute walk, board the ship at 14:15, deposit it inside the toilet tank of a ladies' room on the ship's first passenger deck, then disembark. It would take six and a half hours for the ferry to get to Savona, Italy, and the bomb was timed via Casio watch to explode at three in the morning, well after the ferry docked, the passengers went ashore, and the crew finished cleaning and making any repairs. The great risk, as always, was priming the bomb and pulling the pin on the timer. She and Petru had reviewed the procedure and practiced innumerable times at the bergerie, but once she finished lunch, she went through it once more with her doctored flashlight bulb. They'd practiced it so consistently, it took on its own rhythm. Push, twist, drop. Push, twist, drop.

"Are you nervous?" Séverine asked.

"I think I can handle throwing a pack of cigarettes in the trash," he said dryly. His bomb, concealed inside an empty pack of Lucky Strikes—small but powerful, consisting solely of Semtex—would be discarded inside the terminal after Séverine had boarded the ferry.

He went over to a CD tower in the living room, chose Dire Straits' *Encores* EP, and inserted it into the stereo system. As he cleared plates, Séverine wrapped up the leftover saucisson and cheese and placed them in the fridge. It was like they were cleaning after hosting friends for lunch, except it was only the two of them, and they weren't really friends.

"Will you ever like me again?" she asked, standing at the threshold of the kitchen.

He looked up from the sink with surprise.

"What are you talking about?"

"You're different around me now. Quiet."

He turned off the faucet, shamefaced. "Look, I had this idea of how everything would work out. We'd get the money from your parents, Matteu would go free, we'd send you home. You were supposed to be a blip in the whole story. But something I never anticipated is happening, and it feels totally out of my control."

"You think *I* have control?" she asked.

"Completely," he said. "You make things happen at this exponential rate, in ways that never occurred to me. It's unsettling. And a little humiliating."

She heard his admiration beneath the humiliation and wondered if this would make him a bolder or more reticent lover. She didn't know why she was being such a coward; she was normally the kind of girl who just went in for the kiss! But it was different with him, and he'd made her different.

"It's 13:30," Bruno said, looking over her shoulder at a big wall clock like the ones they had in school. "You should get ready."

Séverine did as she was told, changing into her "vacation" outfit, a red wrap dress from that unfortunate bag of hand-me-downs. She tucked her hair under the wig cap, pulled the wig onto her head, and placed a straw hat on top of that. Then she attached a new leg holster to her thigh, slipped the gun in place, and did some experimental gymnastics—twirling at high speeds, touching her toes, cancan kicks—in front of the mirror to see if it revealed itself.

As she slung the strap of her duffle over her head and grabbed the Etam bag, she felt enlivened, like she was indeed about to depart on vacation to Italy, leaving behind a whirlwind love affair. According to the carte d'identité that Bruno had doctored, she was Dominique Martin of Troyes, age twenty. This was a role, she thought. She couldn't half-ass it; she must be convincing. And so she method acted herself out of the apartment, ignoring the bomb hiding beneath the pajamas, feeling only excited and a little sad to kiss Bruno goodbye and board the ferry.

They began their walk to the terminal in the Place Saint-Nicolas, Bastia's main plaza, a long and wide rectangle of reddish concrete. To Séverine's right was the sea, where huge yellow and white ferries waited solemnly along the quai like war elephants. To her left was a row of lush trees and overlapping white umbrellas, where people were eating ice cream in shallow coupes and waiting for their train or ferry.

They continued along the quai, four blocks up to the Corsica Mare Ferries terminal. The Savona ferry was leaving soon, and a ferry from Livorno had just arrived, so it was buzzing with people. They hurried by Bruno and Séverine, concerned only with their luggage, their children, locating their tickets. Across the terminal, cars crept into the backside of the ferry. They queued up to board along with everyone else—so many people, hundreds of people on their way to Italy to go shopping, for work, to say goodbye to a dying relative; people who, over the next twenty-four hours, might even make love in an unfamiliar apartment. So many events no one could anticipate, and one of them was waiting in the bottom of Séverine's bag. Tomorrow they would tell their friends and neighbors that they'd been on that ship only hours before the bomb went off—it would become part of their personal mythology. Maybe this was power: creating moments of history that normal people could attach themselves to, feel part of.

At 14:15, forty-five minutes before the ferry sailed, they moved towards the entrance of the ship, where an employee in a neon-orange vest was checking everyone's papers. Séverine became nervous. He might detect her papers were fake, ask her to please step aside and call for his supervisor on his walkie-talkie while eyeing her with accusation. She wouldn't just stand there and let them take her away; she'd have to run, or brandish the Beretta holstered around her upper thigh. She felt Bruno grope for her hand, then thread his fingers between hers. She looked at him, bewildered, and he gave her a casual smile and squeezed her hand, as if it were only natural that he should grant this small intimacy to a fling before she exited his life forever.

"Ticket?" the man in the orange vest droned.

Séverine held out her ticket and carte d'identité. He looked at her papers, then said, "Sunglasses off, please."

She complied, exposing this cursed beak, and tried to maintain an impassive expression. She felt the gun heavy at her thigh, begging to be torn from its Velcro.

"Are you traveling with her?" the man asked Bruno, absentmindedly returning Séverine's papers. It was crazy how it never occurred to people that they may come into contact with something or someone extraordinary.

"No," he said as Séverine placed her sunglasses back on her face.

"Then it's time for goodbyes," the man said, waving them to the side.

"I'm sad to leave you," Séverine said to Bruno, and he looked at her suspiciously. "For Savona," she clarified.

"Oh right," he said clumsily. "Savona."

"Bye," Séverine said in a small voice.

"Bye," he replied.

She rose up on her toes and draped her arms around his neck, then lifted her face towards his mouth. He didn't flinch; he was actually going to let her kiss him! But at the last moment, he turned his head slightly and they caught each other on the sides of their mouths. Her throat burned with embarrassment as she lowered onto her heels.

She was going to walk into that ferry, go straight to the bathroom, and bawl her eyes out. But as she turned to walk through the huge doorway, Bruno grabbed her arm, pulled her back, and kissed her on the mouth. It wasn't the passionate, desperate kiss of her daydreams; it was gentle, lips scarcely parted, a concession. She had never imagined he was capable of such softness. After a few suspended moments, he pulled away, too disconcerted to look at her.

Séverine boarded in a daze, taking the escalator up to the first passenger deck, right in the middle of the ship. According to a handy brochure Petru had procured from the tourism office, on this deck you'd find a revolving bar, an arcade, an Italian-style cafeteria, and multiple lounge areas with overstuffed chairs that faced floor-to-ceiling windows. It was crowded with kids running up and down the hallways, couples exploring, seniors settling in with their paperback thrillers.

Distracted, Séverine got in line with all the women waiting for the bathroom. She checked her watch: thirty-five minutes till the ferry left. That snapped her back to reality, to her purpose.

She inched into the ladies' room, which was chaotic with faucets surging and hand dryers roaring and toilets flushing and mothers wrangling their children. She dared to consider the possibility of the bomb going off early, of it exploding while this mammona with strawberry-colored hair was washing her hands, and this toddler peeked out from beneath a stall, and this elegant, obviously Italian woman brushed her hair in front of the mirror. The bomb was impersonal when it destroyed property, but if it hurt someone innocent . . . The only solution was to make no mistakes.

Or—there was another solution. She considered Bruno's mistrustful look when she'd said, "I'm sad to leave you." She could chuck the Etam bag overboard, call her parents from the ship's pay phone, and settle in for the ride to Savona. When the gendarmes collected her, she could tearfully explain that she'd been coerced into saying and doing all that crazy stuff—the justification was so plain. And then she could be free again, like the people around her. Free to go on a trip to Italy, to shop for pajamas at Etam, to have an espresso in a café with some boy. But she didn't want to do that with *some boy*, she wanted it with Bruno, and he had communicated an opening to her just now. If she sailed off to Savona, she would never have the chance to kiss him, for real this time, not as Bruno and Dominique from Troyes, but as Bruno and Séverine.

"Mademoiselle," the lady behind her pointed to an open stall. Séverine went in, removed her sunglasses, and locked the door.

She went to place the bag on top of the toilet tank, then froze. There was no tank. There was only a silver lever to flush the toilet; all the necessary parts of a tank would be under the floor. What an absolute idiot she was! She tried not to panic and looked around the stall, searching for something that wasn't there. *Stupid, stupid connasse!* she kept saying to herself. Then she noticed the steel tampon receptacle mounted to her left. Séverine wedged the bag between the toilet and the wall and took out the book. It would probably fit. God, it was so hot; she was actually sweating! She tore off her hat and wig.

Now it was just a question of—what was it? Pinch, twist . . . something? She dabbed her hairline with toilet paper then threw it in the bowl. She could not fuck this up. Jonnart and Monsieur Laporte insisted she was nothing but a spoiled, delusional rich girl, and she would not prove them right. Let any of the others fuck it up—she would not.

Séverine wiped down the toilet seat, removed the book from the bag, then sat and placed the bomb on her lap. First, she set the alarm to three in the morning, then twined the two wires around each other until they were snug. That was it. Petru said to now treat it like the ticking bomb it was. With a little inward plea to whichever god might be listening, she began to ease the deceptively heavy book through the receptacle slot. Yet it would not slip in; the mouth of the receptacle wasn't wide enough. She tried to pry open the little door, but it was locked. In a flash of inspiration, she slipped off one of the bobby pins that secured her wig cap and bent it open. She'd never picked a lock before, but people did it all the time in movies. She pushed the pin into the lock and wiggled it around, but nothing happened. This was the practical sort of skill Petru should have taught her weeks ago!

She usually felt like she was in a movie, like some omnipotent, voiceless director was watching her, prompting her to tilt her head a certain way, to deliver a line with a certain gesture or tone. It had always been reassuring; perhaps this was her personal relationship with God. But in this moment, the director's silence felt like abandonment.

"Mesdames, messieurs," a voice crackled through the ship's loudspeakers. "We apologize for the delay; we will be raising anchor in five minutes. Thank you for your patience."

Séverine looked at her watch; it was 15:01! They were already supposed to have left the dock, and she was about to be trapped on this ferry. She had to get the fuck off this boat. Bruno was waiting. Forgoing delicacy, she pushed the book through the slot with all her might, bending the pages, and jammed that sucker into the tampon receptacle. With a troubling clang, the bomb disappeared and hit the bottom of the can. Séverine froze for a moment, waiting for any number of terrible things to happen—but they didn't. The normal restroom whirs and flushes carried on.

She took a breath to compose herself, to return to her role. With a rallying nod, she flushed the toilet, put her wig back on, collected the shopping bag, and opened the stall. The woman next in line angled past her with total indifference, but she was still afraid to look in the mirror, afraid she'd see everyone else staring at her, knowing who she was and what she'd just done. When she did look, what she saw was just another young woman in a long line of women preoccupied only with themselves. The shopping bag hiked up her forearm, Séverine quickly washed her hands, fascinated to see how they trembled.

It was 15:06. As she hurried through the halls of the deck, people kept streaming towards her with their luggage and their kids running loose like wild dogs. So much noise: babies crying and engines thrumming and arcade games singsonging and smooth jazz blaring from the loudspeakers. Séverine clambered down the escalator to the gangway, where a crew of ferry workers in their identical orange vests were gathered.

"How do I get off?" She hurled her question into the group without direction, and they stopped talking and turned; their eyes on her felt like an accusation. Instinctually, her hand shot to her outer thigh.

"Miss your boyfriend?" It was the man who'd checked her papers, wearing a knowing little smile. That smile brought her hand off her thigh and made her own strained facial muscles melt into a relieved grin. She was in role again; she'd only needed someone else to play along. Instead of replying, she released a breathy, self-conscious laugh.

"You're cutting it close; hurry," the man said, and he led her jogging down the long, now-empty concrete hallway until they reached a big metal door that made a big metal sound as he swung it open, and the afternoon light gushed in.

"Thank you," Séverine exhaled, and dashed into the terminal.

She scanned frantically for Bruno and spotted him coming towards her with an anxious expression. At the sight of him, she laughed with relief and threw her arms around him.

"What happened?"

"There are no tanks on public toilets," she said.

Tensely, he asked, "Where is it then?"

"It's fine, I improvised," she said. "And you?"

"No issues. But let's get out of here."

They left the terminal along with everyone who'd just arrived from Livorno. When Séverine glanced behind her, the ferry was chugging away from the dock.

"We should take a circuitous route just in case," he said. "Honestly, I need a minute to chill out, too."

They walked into the town, weaving through the narrow streets. At first, they didn't speak, but after a few blocks, when it became clear no one was following them and their nerves had settled, Bruno began pointing out landmarks of his personal history: the one bar in the world he'd gotten himself banned from, the home of his Corsu teacher where he attended lessons every other Thursday. A church bell pealed four solemn times as Bruno and Séverine approached a yellow building with a sign that read *Collège Simon Vinciguerra* over the gate.

"This is where I teach," Bruno said.

Séverine could imagine Bruno walking up to the schoolyard every day, a group of girls behind the gate calling out his name, flirting. She felt jealous of these nonexistent girls, and at the same time had a vague, instinctive knowing that she possessed something they lacked, that she straddled some important line between their fresh, intoxicating, untouchable girlhood and the ripeness of womanhood, and that this straddling would not last very long but was perhaps now at its most potent.

"You aren't thinking of going back this fall, are you?" Séverine asked, dumbfounded.

"I was." Bruno looked at the building, taking it in. "But maybe that's delusional. I don't know how long we can keep doing this until we'll have to go underground."

"Wasn't that part of your plan with Matteu?" she asked.

"Abstractly," he admitted. "I don't know, a part of me hasn't caught up with the fact that things are really happening and I'm not just talking about it. Anyway, we had a vision, but it wasn't this."

"I have a vision," Séverine offered.

"It goes without saying." Bruno laughed tartly.

They walked back to the apartment in contemplative silence. Séverine vibrated with a sense of what Bruno needed from her; now to give him a sense of what she needed from him.

⌣

They'd arranged for Petru to call Bruno at a tabac downstairs at 21:00. It was now 17:00. In the meantime, they had to write and film her communiqué. They decided not to specify how many bombs they'd planted, or their locations, in case any of them failed to explode, and explained Soffiu di Libertà's rationale: disempowering foreign business interests and forcibly opening opportunities for Corsicans to regulate their own tourism industry and their own economy. They banged it out in less than an hour without too much squabbling; that part felt routine. But this was the first time they'd record it on film, and Séverine felt something like stage fright as she applied her eyeliner in the bathroom mirror. She'd never acted on camera before, only in school auditoriums, and part of her was afraid she'd be bad at the thing she was so resolute to do. Actors must have chemistry with the camera, but that was a matter of divine bequest— either the camera loved you or it didn't.

Ideally, this dynamic was improved by a good director, but Séverine didn't know what to expect from Bruno. However, once he was behind the camera and Séverine in front of it, the energy shifted. They usually sat beside each other, or if he faced her, he was bent over some book; now he was forced to look at her, engage not on an intellectual level but a physical one. He took it seriously; when he told her to lower her chin or repeat a line with more conspiratorial intimacy, she trusted that he wanted her to look and sound her best. And there was a twisted thrill in obeying what he dictated she do with her body without touching her. She could give him control. Their roles were clear. It was freeing.

When they finished, it was time for Bruno to take Petru's call. He packed up the VHS and left Séverine alone again. While she waited, she sipped a beer and distractedly watched TV, thinking about their kiss. Everything hinged on how she played the rest of the night. She must recognize her moment and pounce; she might not have another opportunity to be alone with Bruno. Luckily, acting on a whim was her great strength. She did manage to plant the bomb on the ferry, after all.

"So far, so good," Bruno said when he returned. "No incidents on their end. For the rest, we'll know in . . . five and a half hours."

"Cool. You want a beer?"

"This calls for liquor," Bruno corrected. He went into the kitchen and returned with a bottle of bison grass vodka and two glasses of ice.

They sat in the living room, Bruno in an armchair and Séverine on the couch, quietly, slowly, steadily sipping their vodka. They didn't speak much; the waiting burdened them.

"We need to lighten up," Séverine announced, springing out of her seat. She took the liberty of browsing Bruno's record collection and putting on *Au cœur de la nuit* by Téléphone.

Bruno nodded along, finger-drumming against his leg. "It says something that you chose this one instead of *Dure Limite*," he said.

"What?"

"That you have taste."

The compliment made her warm. "Yet 'Cendrillon' is one of my karaoke songs."

"Of course you do karaoke," he said dismissively.

"I *love* karaoke," Séverine said. "My girlfriends and I were supposed to go for my birthday tomorrow, remember?"

Bruno turned sheepish. "Oh, that's right."

"Did you get me anything?" she teased.

"As a matter of fact," he said, and went to the kitchen. He came back with a Kinder egg, which he presented to her in the palm of his hand.

She picked it up as gently as if it were Fabergé. "Thank you," she said, so touched she felt awkward. "How did you celebrate your eighteenth birthday?"

He considered for a few seconds, then said, "I have absolutely no idea. Dinner with my family, probably."

"Your life sounds pretty lame before I came around," Séverine said.

"I guess it was," Bruno replied.

The minutes ticked by. It was such a long time to wait between when they planted the bombs and when they actually exploded, both dull and nerve-racking. Without meaning to, they fell asleep on opposite ends of the couch.

A cracking boom split through the apartment, startling them awake. For a few moments they were frozen in tense half recline, staring at each other with alarm and anticipation, unsure if it was really a bomb that had shaken them conscious. Then they heard neighbors' windows opening, groggy and aggravated voices. Bruno stood and went into his bedroom, which faced north to the ferry terminal, and Séverine followed. He opened the window and poked out his head, one of dozens craning their necks into the night. In the distance, heavy masses of smoke moved ponderously heavenward, while below, filmier clouds passed through the greasy orange light of the streetlamps. The noxious smell pervaded the room.

"We shouldn't breathe this in," Bruno said, shutting the window. Séverine went back to the living room and turned on France 3 Corse. It took twenty minutes for the "Breaking News" chyron to finally flash on screen, and there was the casino in Ajaccio, squat and sprawling, its butter-yellow facade electrified by purple lights that trimmed the parapet like neon icing. That was a photo of the casino before; the screen switched to a live broadcast that showed an outpouring of smoke issuing from the center of the building like from a steam locomotive. What was left of the facade was illuminated only by the intense white lights of the news crews. "Le Casino d'Ajaccio has suffered severe damage," a newscaster said, stating the obvious. When the camera cut back to the studio, the newscaster said reports were coming in of another bombing in Ajaccio, and more information would be provided as the story developed.

"What about the ferry?" Séverine asked.

"That news has to make its way from Italy," Bruno said. "Give it time."

As he predicted, fifteen minutes later, a newscaster declared that a bomb had exploded on the *Corsica Regina* while docked in Savona, noting they were not yet sure of any injuries.

Séverine and Bruno gave each other tempered smiles. Without a word, Bruno went to the fridge and dug around till he found a bottle of champagne. In the living room, he draped a napkin over the cork and popped it with a flourish, like a waiter at a fancy restaurant.

"Happy birthday, Séverine," he said, and they clinked glasses. Then he moseyed to the stereo, where he put on a record of an old disco song, "Où sont les femmes" by Patrick Juvet.

"Oh no," Séverine groaned.

"What? This song is a classic," Bruno said. He was doing a little dance with his elbows tucked in and fists clenched, trying to embarrass her, and it was working. "You're not gonna dance?" Bruno asked. "I thought you were the dancing queen."

Séverine demurred but rose from the couch and began to swish with her drink in hand. The chugging bass line and tinselly drums and weirdly plaintive falsetto reactivated the alcohol in her blood-stream, and her movement became looser, less self-conscious. Bruno, too, was no longer joke-dancing. It was so hard for men to truly be free. Even now, there was an unconscious stiffness about him, a fear of being sensual. She wished he'd done the E that night at Nico's, if only to see him let go.

She wondered what Bruno was thinking as they danced privately, together. She wanted him to want her, to move towards her and touch her while her eyes were closed, but maybe that was expecting too much; maybe he needed this first initiation into vulnerability. Beneath the pretentiousness and pontificating there was something shy about him; he might be the type of guy who needed the girl to make the first move. Séverine opened her eyes and he was still there, dancing so inwardly, and she felt a tremendous amount of love to-wards him, a love with texture and depth, not just that sexual ache but also sisterly tenderness, an understanding that he was imperfect and that was entirely appropriate.

Then the stylus lifted, and the record demanded to be flipped, and Bruno switched it out for some bossa nova, and the moment passed. He lounged on the couch and Séverine spread across the rug.

The champagne bottle was finished in no time; then they re-turned to the hard stuff. Instead of talking about independence or postcolonial theory like they always did, they talked about movies, their childhoods, Paris, restaurants, their travels. As the night wore on, as they got drunker and drunker, Séverine waited for him to slip off the couch onto the floor and kiss her. She was staring at him, but he was looking everywhere else. Then he closed his eyes and began murmuring his replies, slipping away from her into sleep.

"Wake up," she demanded, poking him with her foot. He grabbed her foot, shook it, then rolled onto his side. If he was going to be lazy, she'd have to make it happen herself, as usual.

She got up to use the bathroom and brushed her teeth, washed her face, reapplied deodorant. As she sat on the toilet, she held her chin in her hands, elbows resting on her thighs, eyes unfocusing on the small, hexagonal floor tiles. She was drunk, but she knew what she wanted and felt capable of doing it. Séverine flushed, washed her hands, and examined herself in the mirror—What a relief to be beautiful. How could he not agree she was beautiful?—and shut off the light. She was surprised to find that Bruno was no longer on the couch; the apartment was dark save for a soft glow coming through the crack under the bedroom door. Without hesitation, she entered.

Bruno was lying on the mattress, hands wrapped around a big glass of water and staring at the wall, either lost in thought or very, very drunk. The only light came from an industrial-looking lamp, like something from an architect's desk, sitting on a low nightstand. It created a chiaroscuro effect in which everything was black except the sparkling glass, Bruno's golden hands and golden arms, his glowing white T-shirt, his golden face. When Séverine came in, he looked at her without surprise, like he'd been waiting for her. His face was placid but betrayed some lowlight of distress and uncertainty. She sat on the mattress facing him with reproachful expectancy. He sighed and reached out to touch her arm, then aborted the motion and replaced his hand on the water glass.

"What?" Séverine admonished.

He parted his lips, but no words came, no bossiness, no know-it-all-ism. If anything, he looked like he wanted to be told what to do. And so Séverine leaned in slowly, concealing the desperation she felt, until her lips just touched his. That was as far as she was willing to go; she demanded reciprocation. For a second, they remained that way; then she heard him set the water on the floor, and he slid his fingers into her hair.

It was a kiss like a sigh. His hands glided down her neck, over her shoulders, down her back. There was so much confidence in his touch; perhaps she hadn't read him correctly at all. Instead of letting it throw her, she told herself she could finally let go, she could let this more experienced man lead her. He guided her on top of him and lifted her shirt over her head, revealing the white lace bralette from the night she was kidnapped. It was soft and delicate, even chaste. When Bruno saw it, he recoiled, covering his face with his hands.

"You're so young," he said in a muffled, self-loathing wail.

"No I'm not," Séverine replied, annoyed, dragging his hands away from his eyes.

"You're a lycéen."

"What are you talking about? If you hadn't kidnapped me, I'd be on my way to university."

"It's wrong, the whole thing is wrong," he said with the same conviction he used when talking about revolution.

"*Now* you have a conscience?" Séverine pressed her hands against his shoulders, forcing him flat on his back. Her hair slipped over her shoulder and unfurled around his face. "Enough."

Her physical need flared with a heat like anger. She was done playing games. He very seriously evaluated her expression, then drew her down towards him, allowing himself to be overcome by the same brainless need. He flipped her onto her back and yanked down her jeans with a new certainty that thrilled and unnerved her. On his knees, he contemplated her body.

"You know you're very beautiful," he said.

"I still like being told," she replied.

He lay beside her and they kissed and undressed, and though it was not the first time they'd touched, a new, essential aspect of him was being revealed to her. She felt like she was understanding him better as he touched her so conscientiously and responded to her touch. Yes, she'd placed her hand on his arm before, but she'd never felt the muscles shift and enlarge as he repositioned her with seemingly no effort; she'd never had time to appreciate how smooth his skin was, or notice the divot of his smallpox vaccine scar. All this dark hair across his chest and down his stomach was astounding: he was a man, really! And she could still have him.

Bruno sidled all the way down the bed, making Séverine feel exposed, in too-close proximity, while at the same time she was taut with anticipation of some unprecedented event. When he touched his tongue to her, the sensation was so discrete it was nearly unbearable. He then slipped his fingers inside her, and at this, she felt a combination of intensities: one specific, the other wide. Her head fell back onto the pillow, and she let it roil and build until finally, it crested. Her voice broke out, a legitimate cry of anxiety and wonder and delight at something so astounding that had been concealed inside her all this time, waiting for someone to release it.

He brushed her hair away from her face, kissing her temples. She luxuriated in the dry warmth of his hands and the rippling inside her that was slowly, slowly receding. She opened her eyes to see his face above hers, and it struck her that the last time she'd looked up at him this way was that strange, faraway night when he'd meant to kill her. As had happened before, the image of Bruno above her flattened over the image of Bruno holding the gun to her head. And as before, Séverine felt a bitterness tinged with a sense of conquest, as well as an equal sense this was in fact the most disarmed she'd ever been, and if he still wanted to kill her, now was the time.

But she felt a deeper and more primeval power in that defenselessness. She *wanted* to submit to his touch whether it be gentle or ruthless, to the pure instinct of their desire for each other, which opened her in a way that was both terrifying and exciting; and she understood that she'd only experience real pleasure, the kind that is bound up in love and also transcends it, by fingering that trigger.

The moment he entered her, she couldn't help but think, *Number six*. A number that implied experience and expertise. Up until now, sex had always felt fine but nondescript. Boys liked it, and they liked her for providing it, and that seemed to be the point. But this sensation was different: the closeness of him, his pressure, and his surrender of control to the innate grip of her body extended and transformed her orgasm into something sentimental and rosy-edged. He didn't last long; as he drew nearer, she held his face between her hands and forced him to look at her. She felt an unruly, overwhelming tenderness for him as he came. She loved the low waver in his voice, his unguarded expression, his man's body. He lowered his full mass onto her, face in her hair, and caught his breath; she loved the weight of him, his dense sweat smell mingled with his faded cologne.

After his breathing steadied, Bruno lifted his head to look at Séverine, to push her hair back from her face and kiss her softly.

"Was it nice for you?" he asked.

"Very," she said. "Was it nice for you?" she asked a bit nervously, as she was the novice.

"Extremely nice," he replied, kissing her again.

The room began to reveal itself as bleary dawn light leaked through the window slats.

"What are we gonna do?" he asked.

"What do you mean?"

"Come on—Petru will not approve, Tittu is in love with you," he said.

"And you—are you in love with me?"

She asked this question like a schoolgirl bullying her teacher, and like a teacher, he paid her schoolgirl silliness no mind.

12. *New Order*

Séverine woke feeling shaky and flimsy, her first near-hangover; it was also the first time she'd spent the whole night with a guy, and both events seemed like milestones. Bruno slept heavily, his mouth slightly parted like a child's. She woke him with kisses down his neck, along the curve of his waist and the fin of his hip. By the time she'd reached the lower part of his stomach, his fingers were entangled in her hair.

After, she slipped out of bed and pulled a white collared shirt from his closet. As she buttoned it up, she felt overwhelmingly glamorous and grown-up. She crept to the bathroom to brush her teeth and apply a little mascara. Then she went to the kitchen, put on some coffee, and made eggs in a nest, the one breakfast dish her mother had taught her to cook. Bruno meandered over to the television, but Séverine stopped him. "If you watch the news, you're only going to want to talk about the news," she said.

They sat at the table and ate quietly as the wind caressed the window sheers. Séverine felt a radiant sense of peace. How magical to do the most basic things in the afterglow of good sex.

Once the toast and eggs were eaten and the coffee drunk, Bruno picked up the remote and asked, "Ready?"

"Ready," Séverine said, and collected the plates.

She heard the reporter as she was rinsing the dishes: "The victim killed by shrapnel from the explosion in Savona early this morning has been identified as thirty-nine-year-old Laura Brunner of Bern, Switzerland."

She rushed into the living room, and on the TV was the photo of a blond woman with slim, tan arms wrapped around a little tow-headed boy.

"The ferry bomb?" Séverine asked, her stomach dropping, thinking of the women in the bathroom with a sense of dread.

Bruno blanched and nodded, but Séverine was more confused than anything. The bomb went off in Savona, not mid-crossing, which meant the women were safe—she'd done her job. No one should have been on the ferry at three in the morning.

Was Bruno looking at her differently? She snatched the remote and shut off the TV just as they began to play her communiqué, as if it were a soap opera and not reality, a reality she'd created; as if by turning off the TV, she could undo it, or at the very least pretend it didn't happen.

"She was a mother," Bruno said quietly.

Séverine thought of her own mother, then swept the image from her mind. She thought of the blond woman bleeding on the cobblestone and swept that away, too. She thought of a little boy asking for his mother and his father having to explain again. Unfamiliar, unwelcome emotions roiled inside her, ones she wouldn't name for fear they'd surface—for now, they were still contained beneath the ice of her shock.

They stared at each other for an unnatural amount of time as Séverine tried to figure out how Bruno felt, and how he thought she should feel. Did he want her to fall to pieces, show the depth of her sensitivity? Or did he like her hard, the unrepentant revolutionary who considered violence a cleansing force like Fanon had said?

She swallowed down the horror and guilt that were threatening to come up like bile. It was a freak accident—it wasn't like Séverine had personally targeted the woman. She'd planted the bomb without intending to hurt anyone, but some shard of metal had flown from the ship—not the bomb itself—and hit this woman. By some absurd, minute chance, it had killed her.

And if she was Swiss, she must have been in Savona on vacation. There was something deeply upper-middle-class about the photo they'd shown on TV: the woman's thinness, tanness, the whiteness of her teeth. Séverine didn't need to feel as guilty as if she'd been some poor cleaning lady just doing her job.

Séverine didn't want to feel guilty at all, and neither did Bruno, she knew. The idea of guilt struck her as deeply unrevolutionary, actually. The guilt she'd initially felt might be nothing more than an ingrained bourgeois reaction. The more she thought about it, the less implicated she felt. The death of this random woman was remote from Séverine, Bruno, the ideology behind the attack, everything. It had barely anything to do with her.

"You're not freaked out?" Bruno asked. "This doesn't upset you?"

"What was a *mother* doing in the port at three in the morning?" she asked in reply.

"Does it matter?"

"Obviously—she's dead because of it," Séverine said. She slid her hands around his waist, under his shirt, and pressed her head to his chest. "Don't get hung up. Last night was a success."

"I don't know, this feels fucked up," Bruno said, not touching her.

She lifted her head to look at him coldly. "Okay, what do you want to do about it?"

"What do you mean?"

"You want to turn yourself in? You want to call this whole thing off? You want to forget about independence?"

Bruno shook his head, dazed. She could tell he wasn't allowing himself to go through the same justifications she'd gone through, that he was tempted to hold onto guilt as some proof of his goodness.

"It was an accident," Séverine said. "A freak accident."

Bruno's headshaking turned into nodding. An accident. In that moment, she understood something else essential about Bruno: as long as she assured him of his virtuousness and correctness, he'd believe it.

They packed and locked up the apartment and walked quickly to the car, heads down. Southbound traffic was horrible, everyone on edge and fleeing to the quiet interior for the weekend, which only intensified Séverine's headache and nausea. However, her mind was not on the impact of the attacks, but whether Bruno had only submitted to her because they were outside the bergerie. He must not find the resolve to resist her back among the boys. She felt a kind of spiritual hangover, too, although she wouldn't name its source.

Shortly after they turned onto the dirt path to the bergerie, Tittu's motorcycle came roaring behind them. When they got out of the car, Séverine saw that Petru and Tittu looked as conscience-stricken as Bruno had. She would have to snap them out of it, too.

Before they could say anything, she stated, "We did everything possible to avoid casualties, and we did. The bomb could have gone off while the ferry was in the middle of the sea with everyone on it—*that* would have been a disaster. But this? All things considered, we did okay."

"Damn, when did you become the coldest of us all?" Petru said, only partly joking.

"I'm not trying to be a bitch, but we are gearing up for revolution, no? We're all on the same page about what that means, right?"

No one dared disagree, and she knew with relief they wouldn't talk about the Swiss woman anymore. At the same time, Séverine realized she hadn't really considered her own question. She hadn't witnessed the woman's death, and it hadn't happened by her own hand—could she do it for real, under more personal circumstances? Maybe she could take that responsibility if her comrades needed her to—if it would bring Bruno closer to the future he envisioned.

"Petru, it's time to get in touch with the Novi Patriotti guy," Séverine said. "What do we do, call and place an order?"

"No, it's not like getting a pizza delivered," Petru said. "I'll have to go down to Bonifacio and show face."

"Ooh, I've never been to Bonifacio," Séverine chirped.

"Correct me if I'm wrong, but you just claimed responsibility for the bombing of a five-hundred-million-franc ship, which resulted in a casualty," Bruno said. "It might not be the best time for you to go sightseeing."

It was semi-flirtatious, not combative, and Séverine responded with a knowing smile. "Dominique Martin will go, then. I have a feeling they'll want to meet me in the flesh."

⌣

Séverine and Tittu were in the garden picking vegetables while Petru prepared dinner and Bruno unpacked, setting everything straight in the house. As Tittu told her all about how things went down in

Ajaccio, Séverine looked towards the bergerie, sensing Bruno's aloneness and everyone else's busyness.

"No lie, I won 150 francs on the slot machine," Tittu was saying. "That's when I stopped being nervous; it felt like a sign."

"Totally!" Séverine interrupted. "I'll be right back. Bathroom."

She made her way to the house, depositing her basket of tomatoes on the kitchen counter before going to the guys' bedroom.

She lingered in the doorway, watching as Bruno kneeled to place the folded laundry in the bureau. He gave her a polite smile and continued his task. She wandered to the stack of books and ran her finger down the spines as if they were Bruno's own vertebrae, crouching as she went, and when she landed on *Les damnés de la terre*, towards the bottom, she pulled it from the pile.

"What's that?" he asked, suddenly over her shoulder, and wrestled the book from her. "So, you're sentimental."

She shrugged, a little mortified. He took a pen from the dresser and scribbled inside the front cover.

"Me too," he said, smacking her arm with the book before handing it back to her.

With a total lack of self-possession, she flipped to the first page and read the inscription: *To my darling serpent, that we take back our paradise.*

Without giving him a chance to object, she pushed the door closed and kissed him, unzipping his jeans and steering him to the floor. He planted a booted foot against the doorjamb. It was over quickly; she just wanted to claim him again, to make sure what had happened in Bastia was real.

"You're reckless," Bruno whispered, his nose grazing hers. The sounds of steaks sizzling and Petru's metal spoon scraping against the pan bled into the room.

"You're worse. You should know better," she replied.

The door banged against Bruno's boot, opening a fraction. Séverine twisted around, and in the moment before the door ricocheted shut, she saw a sliver of Tittu's face, the mouth frozen open. She rolled off Bruno with the gracelessness of the guilty.

"Shit," Bruno cursed as Tittu's boots clunked towards the kitchen and through the back door.

"Maybe he didn't see," Séverine said unconvincingly, sidling up to Bruno and kissing the side of his face.

"Don't." He stood brusquely, leaving Séverine on the floor like a cast-off doll.

⁓

Séverine was the last to enter the kitchen, head high, having resolved not to slink around guiltily. Who she slept with was up to her. Bruno, on the other hand, seemed abashed, focused on cutting his steak into small pieces.

Petru placed his plate at the table and sat with a heavy exhalation. Tittu, who was trembling with vexation, glanced at Petru, urging him on, and Petru took a deep breath.

"What's going on between you two?" he asked. "You're—you're sleeping with each other?"

Bruno blew air through his lips, the beginning of a denial, but Séverine cut him off.

"So what if we are? It's nobody's business."

"Yeah, it is," Petru said, mocking her haughtiness. "There are only four of us. So if two are fooling around, that changes the whole dynamic."

Tittu was slumped in his chair with his arms crossed protectively, staring at the edge of the table; Séverine wondered if he was fighting an explosion of anger or tears. She felt her first shadow of regret—

this progression in her relationship with Bruno would come at the expense of her relationships with Tittu and Petru, she realized. There had been a question in the air that enlivened all four of them, and now that it had been answered, the harmless flirtations—the fun and games—were over.

"It was only once—well—one day," Bruno explained, flustered.

"You should know better," Petru said, and it was this echoing of Séverine's words that fully chastened Bruno.

"We'll stop," he mumbled. "I'm saying it's not too late to stop."

Séverine's throat burned and her stomach dropped. Bruno would not look her way. She didn't understand why he wouldn't stand up for the special connection they shared. *Or was it not special for him?* she thought, feeling embarrassingly naive. If that was the case, she was going to give it right back to him, let him see how it felt to be dismissed like that.

"We got caught up in all the excitement, but it won't happen again, I swear," Séverine said. "Total mistake."

Bruno gave her a quizzical look.

"We're good then?" Petru asked. The other three nodded. Petru shook his head and cut into his steak. "You let a high school girl into your cell, you get high school drama."

That night, Séverine lay in bed, waiting for Bruno. Thirty minutes had passed since they'd all said good night. She'd played a risky hand with her comment at dinner, but she knew he'd come. She hoped he would.

Just as she was drifting off, the door creaked open, and Séverine sensed a presence beside her. The night was so impossibly black. Without words, Bruno removed his clothing and slid into bed behind her, hiking up her nightgown and pushing himself inside. She couldn't help but cry out. At this, he clamped a hand over her mouth, and for the second time, she experienced a queer déjà vu: Bruno, fused with the surrounding darkness, his arm coiled around her waist, constricting her breath, and that invisible force that had seized her from her bike coiled around her waist, knocking the wind out of her. Then, she'd bitten him, but now she came.

13. *Alliances*

All four cell members would make the two-and-a-half-hour drive down to the southernmost tip of the island to demonstrate their seriousness to José. A few empty bags of chestnut flour packed with fifty thousand francs would help their cause. Tittu and Séverine sat in the back seat, Petru drove, and Bruno navigated. Tittu looked out the window the whole ride, his back to her. He was not *not* talking to Bruno, but he was decidedly not talking to Séverine. In his mind, she was a conniver, attention whore, and tease; Bruno's betrayal, however, was forgivable because of the masculine need. If Tittu was going to be an asshole, she didn't want to talk to him anyway.

Reaching between the seat belt and headrest, Séverine tapped Petru's shoulder. "Have you dealt directly with this Baptiste before?"

"I used to see him around, but I wouldn't say I dealt with him," Petru said. "He's all right. It's José we have to worry about."

"I hate to say it, but we should probably be a little deferential," Bruno explained. "Make it clear we're not trying to step on anyone's toes. They're doing their thing and we'll do ours."

"Hold on, I'm gonna stop for petrol," Petru said, and pulled into an Esso station. He went inside to pay the cashier and returned with a newspaper and pack of cigarettes, looking grim. He slid back into the car and passed the paper to Bruno.

"What is it?" Séverine asked, leaning into the front seat. Over Bruno's shoulder, she read the headline: "Paul Guimard Ousted as Prefect." She tore the paper from his hands but was too stunned to read the article. It couldn't be true! He was doing such a good job, all of the power players on the island liked him; he had so many plans! The prefecture was supposed to pave his way into a cabinet position, then one day, the presidency. What would happen to him now, his brilliant career?

"Will they still transfer Matteu to Borgo?" Tittu asked.

"Doubtful," Petru said.

"Give me your télécarte," Séverine demanded to no one in particular. She had to talk to her papa.

Bruno fished his card out of his pocket, and with her sunglasses secured on her nose, she strode to the pay phone and called the number her father had given Bruno.

"It's me," Séverine said when he picked up.

"Séverine, what have you done?" He took a ragged breath; he was fighting tears, she realized with alarm.

"If you're referring to the Swiss lady, I didn't *do* anything; it was an accident," she said irritably. "Anyway, what's going on, you got fired?"

"A woman is dead, Séverine, and that doesn't make you think you should stop?"

He was being so annoying. "I'm not talking about that, I'm trying to talk about *you*. What's gonna happen to you now?"

"It's the same conversation, Sév!" he exploded. "This is serious—someone innocent died, a foreigner, a mother. The Ministry of the Interior doesn't think it's appropriate that I keep my role when my daughter is—is—"

A terrorist, a murderer? Whatever it was, he couldn't say it.

"The Ministry of the Interior—you mean Jonnart's behind this?"

"Of course, he's in charge of the prefectures," her father said.

"Of course," she repeated, burning with anger. "What about moving Matteu to Borgo?"

"Forget it. They're replacing me with Vincent Pignon. They're announcing it at noon."

"Who?"

"The prefect of the Pyrénées-Atlantiques. The guy who pushed the Basque separatists into Spain. He'll be very, very tough on the nationalists." He lowered his voice. "The most we can do at this point is get you out of the country, then join you somewhere. The States, Australia, wherever. It's all set up, just tell me where you are."

"I can't leave," she said, vexed. "I'm sorry you got fired because of me, but I'm like, changing the world."

"This is the only way I can still help you," her father said. "When they find you, they'll charge you with murder, attempted murder, conspiracy—anything that might stick. They'll make an example of you, and you'll go to prison for the rest of your life. Do you understand what I'm saying?"

She did not understand. She'd never considered that her papa's status, her mother's wealth, her own charm couldn't protect her. For the first time, she felt a little scared. It was unnerving to hear the fear in her papa's voice. And guilt, which had previously been hazy and vague, began to solidify. "I'm not quitting," she maintained, more weakly than she'd meant to.

She felt Petru's hand on her shoulder. He jerked a thumb towards the car.

"I'll call when I can," she said, and hung up, unable to bear his anguish any longer.

When she got back in the car, she began to cry quiet, shameful tears. "It's over for Matteu," she said, but really, she was thinking of her papa. "Jonnart's replacing him with some guy—Vincent Picard?"

"Vincent Pignon?" the three men asked in unison.

"Yeah, you know him?"

"He's that bastard who crushed the Basque movement," Petru said. "He had the cops plant weapons on innocent people, just threw civilians in jail left and right."

The men mulled this over, an edge to their silence. Séverine dried her tears. Her dad's firing was a terrible consequence of her actions, and her sole recourse was to hit harder than before. Moving doggedly towards independence was the only way to make it right. Petru was wrong about revenge, Séverine decided once and for all; she'd find a way to make Jonnart pay.

⁓

Bonifacio was perched high on a peninsular cliff, surveying the Mediterranean. The village was beautiful but foreboding with its steep, winding streets and panoramic sea views. Its relationship to the sea that surrounded it on three sides had a fixated, anxiety-ridden quality. Indeed, it had functioned as a citadel for a thousand years, from which Corsicans watched their conquerors come by sea. Now it was primarily a tourist destination—slightly off the beaten path, quieter and quainter than Ajaccio or Porto-Vecchio.

They drove the car up the narrow cobblestone streets to the very peak of the town, where Chez Martine was situated on a little plaza with pétanque courts, very busy at this time of evening. A low wall hemmed in the plaza, beyond which loomed high cliffs illuminated by the sun's last rays, radiating an intense, holy yellow, and below, the bay in shadow, gloomy as the underworld.

"Keep it professional," Bruno said before they exited the car, shooting Séverine a pointed look.

Chez Martine was ill-lit, with terra-cotta floors, whitewashed stucco walls, and exposed beam ceilings. There were shelves of knick-knacks and mismatched furniture with large, dusty jugs of dried lavender that had probably sat there for decades, but the effect was homey.

Petru leaned over the bar, where a waiter was catching espresso in a little cup, and asked, "Where's José?" The waiter placed the cup on a saucer and strode past Petru to place it on the table of a man sitting alone in the front corner of the restaurant, half indoors, half outdoors.

They'd entirely missed him when they'd walked in, and he dropped a cube of sugar into his coffee with a theatricality that indicated his awareness of them. His eyes were very large and dark, and he had a hawkish nose that rivaled Séverine's. His long, black hair was tied in a ponytail that fell over a black dress shirt with the sleeves rolled up. He looked more Arab than Corsican, and as serious as Bruno had warned, like he would have no patience for Séverine.

Bruno offered a hand and said, "Bruno Pieri. We've met a couple times."

"I remember you and Matteu. You're the one who dropped out of Sciences Po," José said as he took his hand, but this was a dig. He pointed a finger at Petru, "And you were on the bomb squad."

Séverine asked, "What about me?"

José studied her, his face placid. "Pretty good disguise. You've kept busy, Pieri. Sit." He waved to the waiter and held up four fingers.

"What should I call you?" José asked.

"Dominique Martin," she replied, extending her hand à l'améri-
caine.

"José Kadiri," he said, shaking her hand once, firmly. "What
brings you all the way down here?" His tone was not exactly welcoming. Séverine sensed that deference was not the way to go; this
was a man who respected people like him: blunt and rigid.

"We'd like to place an order with your brother," Bruno said.

"He doesn't take orders from just anybody."

"That's why I came," Séverine said. "To show you who you'd be
dealing with."

"Take off the glasses," he instructed.

She hesitated.

"You're among friends."

Séverine realized there were other eyes on them and had been
since they'd pulled up—a man playing pétanque out front who kept
looking their way between throws; another eating lasagna at a table
by the bar, glancing at them over his newspaper; the waiter as he
wiped down tables—they were surrounded by Novi Patriotti, and
not all of them, as Tittu had asserted, were Maghrebian.

Straightening in her chair and moving deliberately, as if it were
her own idea, Séverine removed her sunglasses. José scrutinized her,
and the scrutiny itself seemed like the test. Something about him unsettled her; he radiated a single-mindedness that gave his militance
a more severe edge.

"You approve?" Séverine asked curtly.

"You've been bold, I'll give you that," he said.

"More so than Novi Patriotti," she replied, putting her sunglasses
back on.

Bruno winced, but José snorted, taking it on the chin as she knew he would. "I run a business," he said. "I'm not in the habit of scaring off customers during peak season."

"Sure, but the situation is changing: my father was fired—"

"I know," José interrupted.

"But do you know they're replacing him with—what's his name?" Séverine turned to Bruno.

"Vincent Pignon," Bruno replied.

"Right, him."

José looked unsettled. "Where'd you hear this?"

She grabbed Bruno's wrist to glance at his watch and said, "They're holding a press conference in ten minutes; see for yourself."

José motioned for the waiter to turn a TV over the bar to channel 3, where a bird-watching documentary was playing. "As for this order with my brother: What are you in the market for?" he asked.

Petru produced a list from his pocket and slid it over the table.

José examined it and nodded. "Baptiste!" he called to one of the pétanque players outside. Mid-throw, he dropped the heavy silver boule into the sand and sauntered their way. He possessed the same physical characteristics as José but looked wholly unserious with his loose gait and striped drawstring pants and floppy hair that kept falling in his eyes. Anyone would have taken José for the arms dealer, not Baptiste.

"You called?"

"Prospective clients," José said.

Baptiste took in the group, his eyes lingering on Séverine. He flashed her the practiced grin of a hospitality worker and shameless flirt. José handed him the sheet of paper.

"Big plans, huh?" Baptiste said. "When do you need it by?"

"ASAP," Petru said. "How much?"

Baptiste considered a moment, took a pen out of his back pocket, scribbled on the backside of Petru's list, and set it on the table among the empty espresso cups. They craned their necks to see the figure: one hundred thousand francs.

"This is highway robbery," Petru objected.

"And you're radioactive," Baptiste explained without defensiveness. "A very nice-looking Swiss lady is dead because of you. We need to offset our risk."

Petru raised one hand, yielding. He'd seen it coming anyway.

"Give me a week," Baptiste said. "We'll take a fifty percent deposit and the rest at delivery. I'm assuming you didn't come empty-handed?"

Petru tapped the grocery bag with his foot, and Baptiste called over the waiter.

"Delivery for the kitchen," he said, and the waiter collected the bag.

Séverine was impressed by the efficiency of their organization: they had procedures, designated roles. They were somehow able to operate in plain sight, which meant they must have some structure that protected them. By comparison, Soffiu di Libertà was downright chaotic. She understood why Novi Patriotti had rejected Bruno's membership application; he was an intellectual, not a foot soldier. But he was lucky, which might be more important in the long run. Ideally, an organization had both: dreamers and doers, luck and military precision.

The TV above the bar flashed red: "Breaking News." Who should appear next but Monsieur Jonnart, with his perfectly cut suit and voluminous silver hair, standing in front of a podium. The chyron below read, "Vincent Pignon appointed new prefect of Corsica."

"Look," Séverine said, pointing. Pignon stood behind the minister, his small mouth pursed, a slight weasel of a man. He cut an especially unsettling figure beside Jonnart, who was all glowing white teeth and vitality. Pignon, on the other hand, gave the impression of a shadow, the torturer, the one willing to get his hands dirty.

"Turn it up," José called out.

"Law and order," Jonnart was saying. "Too many lives are stolen in the name of these silly games. We say, 'Enough.' The people of Corsica say, '*Enough.*'"

He paused for applause.

"Monsieur Pignon has extensive experience rooting out extremism, and I am confident that expertise will bring a long-awaited peace to Corsica."

"Call Lydia," José instructed Baptiste. "We need to be sure the after-school program is ironclad, legally."

As Séverine watched Baptiste go behind the bar, she had the queasy feeling that the more extreme the government's response, the less they could rely on instinct alone. They'd need support from people who excelled where they didn't; they'd need collaborators.

"We want to set off a bomb every day for as long as we can go. Scare off the tourists, scare off the pinzuti developers, make Jonnart pay attention to our demands, and get the Corsican people behind us," Séverine announced. "We could set off even more, across the whole island, if Novi Patriotti helped us."

Petru leaned back in his chair, massaging the bridge of his nose like an exasperated parent. Bruno sat there stiffly, doing his best to seem like he was in on Séverine's idea. And Tittu looked back and forth among the other three, trying to parse if he'd missed something.

"What are you proposing, that we join forces?" Baptiste asked with a laugh. José was poker-faced.

"Why not?" Séverine said. "Look how nervous we made the government after one nuit bleue! They made a whole regime change! Imagine if the bombing was relentless."

Bruno cleared his throat. "Jonnart's trying to make it look like he's got everything under control, but if we wreak enough havoc, it'll be obvious he has no control over us. And when the colonizer shows weakness, that's when the people realize they can fight for independence and win."

He knew what she was getting at. There was that special connection again; he must feel it, too.

"Look, I'm not some petit bourgeois who only cares about my bottom line," José said. "But Novi Patriotti is focused on what's best for the Corsican people. I don't see how it's possible to terrorize the tourists and foreign enterprises without terrorizing normal Corsicans, too."

"Unless the target is already unpopular, people aren't a fan of bombings," Baptiste added. "And our strategy for independence is to make it a popular venture."

Suddenly, there were two Séverines in the room: one at the table, one on the TV. They were replaying a clip from her last communiqué. She was radiant in the evening light as she spoke and gestured passionately; everyone's eyes drifted to the screen involuntarily.

"Sometimes you have to drag people into the future," Séverine said, watching herself. "Maybe they're scared, but that can also be harnessed. Look at me."

There was a flash of excitement in José's eyes. "Say you manage to drum up popular support and you reach the moment where it's time to do something with all that power—what next?" he asked. He was speaking to Séverine. Bruno didn't even try to jump in; he, too, wanted to hear what she had to say.

In her mind, she was at the head of a crowd of thousands of kids her age dressed in black jeans and T-shirts like her, marching to the Palais Lantivy in Ajaccio—or, no, the Hôtel de Matignon in Paris itself—armed to the teeth, and all the trembling ministers, including Jonnart, threw themselves to their knees upon seeing Séverine and her army. Okay, maybe her vision looked a lot like the Women's

March on Versailles. She tried to remember what Fanon wrote about the post-revolutionary period.

"Turn it over to the Corsican people," she finally said. "I'm not trying to be your next queen or anything. I'm just trying to help however I can."

José let out a curt laugh, then yielded. "If we go along with this, we're not flying under Soffiu di Libertà's banner," he said.

"It's not about that," Bruno jumped in. "We're not I Fratelli; we don't care about dumb shit like who the government negotiates with. We're not trying to absorb you. Our cells have different strengths, and we should be able to individually operate according to those strengths—"

"—but there are ways we can be more influential together," Séverine finished, and smiled at Bruno. He had wanted to be part of Novi Patriotti, and she was giving him an even better version of that.

"Not everyone will be happy about this," Baptiste said to José; the way he said it, it was clear he was talking about one important person. But José brushed it off.

They all shook hands and arranged to pick up their shipment that Friday. Séverine was thrilled; she knew what she'd just negotiated was a major step forward for the group, but she sensed Tittu and Petru simmering. A big argument was coming.

Once they began driving out of town, Petru was the first to let his frustration loose. "What was that back there? We never talked about an alliance."

"They went for it, so who cares! You know this is going to make our impact much, much bigger," Séverine said.

"I'm not against it," Petru continued, "but you can't propose something that'll affect all of us without discussing it first. I mean, there are very legit reasons to be wary about this. It compromises our security. It's the type of thing that might get I Fratelli's hackles up. It'll definitely get Jonnart's hackles up."

"We're only four people," Bruno said evenhandedly. "Some cooperation between our groups will be necessary for a revolution, no?"

"Why aren't *you* more pissed, Bruno?" Tittu exploded. "She made us look stupid in front of them. That's the second time Novi Patriotti comes away thinking you're a joke."

He hit his target; Bruno sat back in his seat, chastened.

Then Tittu turned his sights on Séverine, muttering, "We may be four, but we were better off as three."

That was it. "Pull over," Séverine demanded.

Petru did as instructed, and Séverine took Tittu by the wrist and dragged him into the maquis at the side of the road like a mother dragging her child to be spanked.

"Whatever you have to say, say it," she commanded.

At first he waffled, rocking from foot to foot, then with effort asked, "Why him?"

She felt a twinge of guilt; the question was genuine and vulnerable.

"I don't know," she said. "I can't control it."

"But you could control yourself when it was me," Tittu said.

She shrugged extravagantly, arms wide.

"Fucking Bruno is the only thing you *can't* control, huh?" Tittu continued, working himself up again. "Everything else you do is so manipulative and self-interested. It's bullshit what you did back there. That's a decision that affects all of us. But you only care about how anything affects *you*, what *you* wanna do and how *you* feel. Sometimes I think you don't give a shit about any of us, or any of this; all you care about is being on TV."

She felt the white-hot insult of someone exposing you to yourself, and it rendered her speechless. "That's not true," was all she could muster. She did care about the men, and she did care about the cause. She cared about them so much, the prospect of losing Tittu's friendship was physically painful; he didn't understand how it was just as essential to her as Bruno's attention.

"I love you," she swore. "Just in a different way."

"What is that supposed to mean?"

Her instinct was to be just suggestive enough that his ego would be soothed and his devotion would remain intact. But that was the exact type of manipulation Tittu was talking about. If she wanted to keep him, she needed to be real.

"You're like, my best friend," she said. "Maybe my only real friend ever. I'm sorry, please don't be mad at me."

Tittu rolled his eyes, but she knew she'd softened him. "You don't realize your actions have consequences," he said.

"Yes, I do," Séverine protested. It would be truer to say that the consequences didn't matter as much as the consummation of her fleeting desires; suppressing them would be like crushing a butterfly, senselessly cruel.

"You said it yourself that night at the club: we have a higher purpose," Tittu began. "I hate the idea of working with Novi Patriotti, but I know it'll make us level up." His tone became bossy in the way Bruno's often was. "This means it's more important than ever that we trust each other. You have to promise you'll stop." Despite his effort to be imposing, his chin trembled. She didn't *want* to hurt him.

"I promise," she lied.

That night, Séverine was woken by a hand stroking her shoulder, along her rib cage, her waist, her behind, between her legs. She let him touch her without stirring, although she knew that he knew she was awake. When she couldn't take it anymore, she turned, her arms outstretched. He undressed her with a ruthlessness that both excited and startled her; when he came, it was like an exertion of his authority. After the glow of mutual orgasm faded, Séverine sat up and collected her nightgown from the floor, feeling conflicted. His lack of restraint was unnerving and exhilarating, but she couldn't parse what it meant or which emotion it reflected. There was tenderness, but also resentment, the wish to humble her.

"What the fuck was that?" she asked.

"Passion," Bruno said, pulling her towards him. But there was something phony in his voice.

"Are you mad at me or something?"

"Why would I be mad? It seems like you're the one who's mad." He kissed her forehead, her temples, and she relaxed in his arms.

"You're different when we're all together," she said. "You act like you don't care about me."

"Well, I can't tell them the truth, can I?"

"What is the truth?"

"That I can't resist you," he said, and bit her neck.

Often enough, he didn't try. Over the next week, as they waited for Baptiste's shipment, the comrades fell into their old routine—drills, reading, planning—while Bruno and Séverine started a new one: meeting in her room every night. Soon, they took other opportunities, too, sneaking into each other's showers post–morning exercise, or while they were supposed to be discussing *An Essay on Liberation* by Marcuse in the shed. They started creeping into the maquis at night so there was no risk of Petru and Tittu hearing them through the thin walls, luxuriating in the secluded wilderness, the night that seemed unruled by time.

However, there were other occasions he did too good a job concealing the truth: when he challenged her in front of the others, or didn't hesitate to shoot down an idea or point out some error she'd made in an especially withering way. Tittu and Petru seemed to accept that Séverine and Bruno's fling was indeed a fluke, and things went more or less back to normal among them, which meant Bruno treated her with the same half-patronizing, half-bemused attitude he always had. It wracked her with uncertainty, a feeling she was not accustomed to. When they were having sex, things seemed so sure between them; he focused on her as if she were the only thing in the world worth paying attention to. But when they were around the others, he was infuriatingly professional towards her. Séverine worried she misunderstood his fervor, that she was on some unfamiliar sexual terrain that she was confusing with love.

14. *Disorderly Conduct*

The first bomb went off Monday, August 9, at the Sperone clubhouse, orchestrated by Novi Patriotti; the next day, at the Bastia Airport Europcar, Petru's handiwork. The press was bewildered by the haphazardness of the attacks—they were happening across the island, striking not only old standbys like foreign banks and police stations but places that had never before been targeted, *quotidian* places: a bar in Calvi where the Foreign Legion liked to drink (Petru again, assisted by Séverine), a fleet of Jet Skis in Propriano (Novi Patriotti), a currency exchange bureau in Bastia (Bruno and Tittu). Splashiness was sacrificed for constancy. Sometimes the target was annihilated, as in the case of the Jet Skis, where charred plastic was found all the way in the gallery of the famed Propriano lighthouse, and sometimes it was merely put out of commission for a few weeks, like U Scimarellu, an Italian-owned café in the center of Ajaccio.

In response to these initial attacks, the Corsican Assembly imposed a 22:00 curfew that was promptly rescinded after the tourism industry bigwigs flew into an uproar. How dare leadership set a curfew during the summer, especially as they were trying to reassure tourists the island was still safe! But something must be done to deter future attacks. A right-winger from the French National Assembly proposed the curfew only extend to Corsicans, not tourists; the fuss this created, without being implemented, was incredible. Séverine latched on.

"You've always known what the French regime thinks about Corsicans, but now they're saying it out loud: you're all criminals!" she ranted in a communiqué filmed with Nico's camcorder. "This is the point of our revolutionary campaign: to tear off the masks, to lay bare the injustice, and make a change. But we can't do it alone— every Corsican needs to stand up for themselves. We know you want peace, but as long as you're subjects of the French colonial government, they'll treat you like the savages they think you are!"

I Fratelli did its best to ride Soffiu di Libertà's wave, wanting to give the impression they still controlled the independence movement. They began claiming attacks, a couple of which they may actually have carried out. But their campaign seemed quaint beside Soffiu di Libertà's; the latter dominated the airwaves, whereas I Fratelli's main source of propaganda was *A Paghjella*, the island's independent press, which was written single-handedly by an infamous curmudgeon called Saveriu and read like the private diary of a madman.

Meanwhile, Jonnart and Pignon held their own press conferences calling for law and order: businesses with suspected ties to terrorism would lose their licenses to operate; homes of suspected terrorists would be randomly searched for illegal guns and explosives; a dozen major companies with rumored ties to I Fratelli would be audited; the Patrimonio guitar festival would be canceled because of a supposed bomb threat, which was a lie and petty punishment. Funnily enough, this was what really rankled residents. Most Corsicans didn't concern themselves with the cops-and-robbers games of the militants and gendarmes, but canceling the guitar festival? That was personal. People began to grumble, not about Soffiu di Libertà but Pignon.

Then the Ministry of the Interior announced the creation of a new police squad called the Peloton anti-terroriste—PAT for short— an "elite platoon of gendarmes specially trained in domestic counter-terrorism operations," an ominously vague description. One of the first things the PAT did was set up checkpoints across the island to make random car stops all night. A few days into their campaign, Tittu and Bruno were stopped on the way home from planting a bomb in L'Île Rousse; by a holy stroke of luck they weren't stopped on their way *to* L'Île Rousse, with the bomb in Bruno's backpack. After that, it was decided that Séverine shouldn't actively participate in the attacks for the time being. Instead, her sole job would be propaganda: every day's bomb came with an accompanying dispatch from Séverine. She agreed, with mixed feelings; she knew this was how she could best contribute to the cause, but it seemed like every time she got a taste of freedom, every time she dipped her toe into civilization again, the men shut her back up in the bergerie.

If she was going to commit entirely to propaganda, she decided she needed a real studio setup. The homemade nature of Nico's camcorder gave every video a crazed, fringe look; upping the production value would lend them legitimacy.

"We have to bring in Nico," Séverine said.

"Here?" Tittu asked.

"Where else?"

"That'll put him in a tough position," Bruno said.

"What about us?" Petru cut in. "We've managed to keep our location secret this whole time. We bring in outsiders, the less likely it'll stay that way."

"We can trust Nico," Bruno asserted.

So Bruno went to Calvi, and over beers, asked Nico if he'd lend his services. Nico laid out his conditions: a new Arriflex 35 III—a film camera, completely impractical, "what Tarantino used for *Reservoir Dogs*"—and ten thousand francs a week. Tittu and Petru balked.

"This isn't a *job*," Tittu said. "Either he's committed to the revolution or he's not."

"It's to cover expenses and offset lost wages," Bruno explained. "He won't be able to freelance if he's producing five videos a week."

"Freelance?" Tittu laughed. "Everyone knows he leeches off his parents."

"We have the cash—who cares?" Séverine said.

Now, after physical training, Bruno and Séverine spent the rest of the morning in the immortelle patch, writing communiqués. Lying on her stomach with the legal pad in front of her, Séverine would say, "How does this sound: For three hundred years, the occupation government has made millions of francs off Corsican land and labor, and they have the nerve to tell you you're too lazy and stupid to support yourselves without their so-called welfare," all the while aware that Bruno's hand was sliding her skirt over her ass, tugging her underwear aside, touching her distractedly.

"Go on," he'd urge when she faltered, and she'd read aloud in little gasps until she no longer recognized the meaning of what she was saying.

In the afternoon, Nico came to shoot the communiqués. These videos—which Nico painstakingly edited overnight and dropped in mailboxes all around the island—aired every evening on France's major networks and were impossible to ignore. It was impossible not to watch them, in all their unseemly Rohmerian-ism—the saturated colors of the maquis, the motes spiraling in the sunlight, the gold aureole around Séverine's hair, the gauzy quality of film—and more important, it was impossible not to listen. Séverine spoke to the camera with an intimacy that viewers, no matter their stance, found jarring. Even the most hard-line Jacobins, right-wingers, and anti-separatists tuned in every night because Séverine was irresistible. She was objectively and inexplicably attractive to those observing her from the other side of the screen, their eyes drawn to her face, that nose that should be so overwhelming, her innocently full lips as they spilled forth such nasty ideas.

In turn, I Fratelli began releasing their own video communiqués, but they were plagued by the privilege and burden of anonymity. Everyone may have known Fanfan was head honcho, but he could never be their official spokesperson. Instead, they filmed ten hooded I Fratelli men seated behind a table talking over each other, which made *them* look like the amateur organization.

Séverine began to feel an evolution like the one Bruno had described to her at the beginning of their time together; through shooting these communiqués she felt she was becoming more herself. There was a satisfying ease in doing what you'd been made to do; it was a sanctified feeling. Séverine felt infused by the light, divinely capable, and she knew she and her viewers were in a symbiotic relationship, that they longed for her light and she longed to shine it upon them.

Something in the men also changed with every attack they carried out. They'd get home late, jangly with adrenaline, laughing manically once they crossed the threshold of the bergerie, like they were on some exhilarating, nerve-racking drug, and come down with a shot of acquavita on the patio as the sun came up. It imbued each of them with an unsubtle virility, especially Bruno—who felt more and more like the guerrilla he'd always wanted to be—and the fact that

Séverine stayed home put his maleness in special relief. But Bruno continued to reserve some of himself from her, and it was making her infuriatingly insecure.

"Is this what it's like with the other girls?" she asked one night in the maquis, after they'd finished. He was lying on his back, face marbled with moonlight filtered through branches, and she was perpendicular on her stomach, ankles crossed in the air and wrists resting against his rib cage while she fussed with his chest hair.

"The mechanics are more or less the same," he said lightheartedly.

"I mean, does it feel different with me?"

He propped himself on an elbow and kissed her but didn't answer. He refused to indulge her the way she most wanted, and she was beginning to resent him for it. At the same time, it made her pander to him sexually because sex was supposed to clinch love. He already revered her mind and spirit, and veneration of the body was supposed to be the final component of this trinity that cohered into love. She didn't get why he wouldn't just admit it, or what more she could do to coax it out of him.

⁓

The second Sunday of their campaign, Nico hauled not only the camera equipment out of his car, but a huge gift basket of cheese, saucisson, cookies, jams, and olive oil, all wrapped up in cellophane and tied with a gaudy red bow.

"What's all this?" Séverine asked.

"A peace offering from my uncle."

The five of them assembled around the kitchen table, the gift basket in the middle like an enormous nesting bird.

Nico began with a long, dramatic sigh. "First, remember that I'm just the messenger. I'm not endorsing any of this."

"Spit it out," Petru said.

"Fanfan would like to arrange a meeting," Nico said. "He's concerned about the effect your campaign has had on the island's small-business owners. He says they've come to him all upset, and he'd like to discuss it with you."

"That's rich, considering he's probably bleeding most of them dry with his revolutionary tax," Tittu mumbled.

"Wait, wait—" Séverine interrupted. "Why did Fanfan send you? Does he know you're shooting our communiqués?"

"The work speaks for itself," Nico joked, but no one laughed. Turning more serious, he said, "He figured this was Bruno's cell because of the demand to release Matteu. And he knows me and Bruno are pals."

Right, Séverine remembered bitterly. I Fratelli always knew who was behind her kidnapping and didn't dare get involved.

"Back to the point—Fanfan's just going to tell us to stop our bombing campaign," Bruno said. "And he must know we'll say no. So why bother meeting?"

"Like I said, I'm just the messenger," Nico repeated, raising his hands.

"He sees us as a threat to his authority now," Tittu said darkly. "People are talking about Soffiu di Libertà, not I Fratelli, and he's thinking about how that's gonna affect his reputation."

"And income," Petru added.

"Tell him thanks but no thanks," Séverine said, pushing the basket towards Nico.

"Okay, but you have to keep the basket," Nico said, horrified. "That would really cause a civil war, returning the basket."

⌒

As August ran on and the daily attacks continued, the state made good on their threats. Yet it was normal Corsican citizens who most felt the effects: who were stopped and searched on their way to the market, who found themselves face-to-face with a gendarme holding an order for the closure of their business, who had their homes torn apart. At best, they had to replace ripped-up floorboards; worse was when the PAT found an unregistered rifle that had been in the family since the Second World War, carting away the man of the house for a few days of questioning.

Reports of this came through Nico, who, by virtue of being a Bartoli, had his own apartment searched. Luckily, the PAT didn't think to shake out the videos from the sleeves of *Nikita* or *Rosemary's Baby*, which contained copies of the tapes he mailed to the networks each day.

"After it happened, my old Gaullist neighbor stood at my door and said, 'We need law and order, but it's a disgrace what they're doing to us.' To *us*! Before now, I'd always been some hashish-smoking scoundrel."

Attacks began replicating exponentially, many of which couldn't be attributed to the organized militias. Some actually targeted the militias themselves, including a drive-by in which an I Fratelli chef de secteur caught a bullet in the shoulder. Rumors circulated that Pignon had hired L'Anguille Noire to execute these attacks, just like the Italian government was known to collaborate with the mafia. It wasn't that far-fetched; the Corsican mafia, who was in bed with the real estate developers, would love nothing more than to wipe out the guerrilla element.

Then there were the attacks that seemed too spontaneous and nonprofessional to be guerrilla-led. Nothing spectacular—a brick through the window of the gendarmerie in Corte, a PAT tank set on fire—but it was happening. The people were taking up the fight, little by little.

15. *Defiance*

On the morning of August 26, two and a half weeks into the campaign, the phone rang in the kitchen. The comrades had just finished their morning training and were eating breakfast. When the bell pierced the bright, gentle air, they stiffened. The phone never, ever rang.

"Don't pick it up," Séverine said, but it was already ringing, irreversible, and whatever awaited them would have to be confronted one way or another.

Petru stood and took the receiver off the hook. His shoulders lowered. "It's Nico."

He passed the phone to Bruno, who listened for a few moments, then said, "Seriously? That's horrible. I'm so sorry, Nico. How old was he? Shit."

"What is it?" Séverine asked, but Bruno ignored her.

"We understand, you should be with your family today. Don't sweat it."

"What happened?" Séverine demanded.

"Nico's cousin was killed in a fire. The circumstances are a little suspicious."

Séverine wrested the phone from him. She always liked to hear drama straight from the source. "So your cousin died?"

"Yes, Fabien. He was killed in that fire on the Rue Cardinal Fesch," Nico said.

"What fire? You know we don't have TV up here."

"A whole row of shops burned down, where all those tourist traps are. My family owns a gelato shop there. I guess Fabien was crashing in the office after a night out. We all used to do that when we had to work in the morning," he said wistfully.

"Gruesome. So you can't come today?"

"There's something else," Nico continued. "The guy who owns the shop across the way said he saw Fabien go in around three in the morning, alone—what *he* was doing there in the middle of the night, God knows—but then around four, he saw flashlights inside the gelateria—"

"So someone broke in? You think it was murder?" At this, the men leaned forward.

"You keep interrupting!" Nico scolded. "What I'm trying to tell you is that we found a two-way radio in the alley out back, the kind the PAT uses."

A sick feeling of excitement coursed through Séverine as her comrades reacted with astonishment. They'd been provided a martyr—with concrete proof the PAT had killed him, that Pignon was organizing barbouze attacks against innocent citizens. The courts would have to investigate; people would riot in the streets! They only needed to transmit the image properly. This would be the final push that normal Corsicans needed to turn completely against Pignon, Jonnart, the whole state. They'd support whatever Soffiu di Libertà did if it was in this kid's name.

"You think the PAT killed him on purpose?" she asked Nico.

"The office is on the second floor, so I doubt they knew he was there. But all the same: he's dead," Nico said quietly.

"I met Fabien a couple times around Corte," Tittu murmured. "He was kind of a prick, but—damn."

"What's the news reporting?" Petru asked into the receiver.

"Arson, but they're blaming the militants," Nico said.

"Where's this walkie-talkie?" Séverine asked.

"At Fanfan's olive farm. I'm calling you from a pay phone in town, but I'm about to head over there."

"You know where Fanfan's olive farm is?" Séverine asked the men.

"Yeah?" Bruno replied hesitantly.

"Great. We'll see you there, Nico," Séverine said.

As she hung up the phone, she could hear him, tinny and distant, saying, "Séverine, no—"

"We should go over and pay our respects," Séverine said. She sensed she shouldn't tell them her plan with the walkie-talkie yet; it would be a whole argument, as always. But like the partnership with Novi Patriotti, she knew it was the right thing to do, and she knew they didn't have time to mull it over for days; they had to act now. They'd be mad afterwards, but they never stayed mad forever.

"By now, they've probably figured out I took some souvenirs with me before defecting," Petru said. "I doubt anyone there wants my respects."

"You don't have to come, but I do think it's worth going in a spirit of solidarity," Bruno said.

"What about her?" Petru asked, pointing his fork at Séverine. "The whole family will be there, and a bunch of I Fratelli guys. That's a big security risk."

"Is it?" Séverine asked resentfully. "Apparently they've known since day one that you guys kidnapped me, and no one was very eager to share that information with the authorities."

"We have our differences with I Fratelli, but I do think this is an opportunity to come together in good faith," Bruno said. "Plus it counts as us accommodating Fanfan's request. Maybe he's even ready to talk about collaborating."

"Will it be a real Corsican wake, with the women dancing around the corpse and singing the vengeance song and scratching their faces?" Séverine asked brightly.

"You may be surprised to learn it's 1993 in Évisa, not 1893," Petru replied.

It was an hour-and-a-half drive northeast to Évisa, yet another small town hacked out of the maquis. They listened to *Achtung Baby*, one of the only albums they could all agree on, and the mood was strangely thoughtful, as if they sensed another change was at hand, another intensification.

As they drove through the town center, Séverine noticed a group of lycéens, probably fourteen or fifteen years old, hanging in front of a closed-up auto shop, smoking and passing around a poison-green bottle of crème de menthe. They were three girls and a boy, dressed in black jeans, black T-shirts, and combat boots, and all four, including the boy, who possessed a feminine slightness and languidness, were wearing lots of black eyeliner. They looked like her little teen army. They were her fans!

"They'll want your autograph," Tittu remarked dryly.

"You think so? Should we pull over?" Séverine asked earnestly, causing Petru to accelerate as he turned off the main road. But it meant something, she knew—she couldn't quite explain it, and the guys wouldn't get it anyway. It was like the miniskirts of Mai '68 and the Black Panthers' leather jackets. It was how you could tell the cause was seeping into the culture.

They approached a small hand-painted sign for L'Alivettu Bartoli and turned in the direction the arrow pointed. After a few kilometers, they emerged from the chaos of the maquis into an olive grove. Ahead stood a modest stucco home, its front lawn crowded with 4x4s, the sight of which caused a flicker of apprehension in Séverine. They looked so military, so commanding.

"Respectful," Bruno reiterated before they got out of the car.

When they approached the porch, they found a small group of women sitting in lawn chairs, smoking.

"Can I help you?" one woman at the center of their group asked frostily. Her expression was neutral, as if she didn't recognize Séverine, unlike the other women, whose eyebrows lifted and hands paused bringing their cigarettes to their lips when they realized who she was. The woman who'd spoken exuded the tempered authority of a president's wife, so Séverine assumed she must be Fanfan's.

It had been well over a month since she'd been in a woman's presence, let alone five or six. She never felt as confident around women as she did men. Men were predictable; their buttons were all the same, whereas women differed vastly. It was fruitless to try to strategically charm other women because they saw right through the bullshit. You could only be yourself and hope they were your kind of girls, but for Séverine, they were rarely ever her kind of girls.

She drummed up her courage and announced, "We're here to pay our respects."

"If you wanna pay your respects, hand over whatever you're packing," Fanfan's wife said, pulling a Tupperware container from under her chair that was already full of guns; they obeyed.

Her sangfroid threw Séverine; *she* was normally the cool customer making other people anxious.

Inside, a crowd of both men and women had gathered, picking from plates of food, talking loudly: the whole Bartoli clan. At first, they didn't notice Séverine come in, and as she stood dumbly in the doorway, she was struck with something like stage fright. She hadn't been around this many bodies since Club Manège and felt completely overwhelmed. Up in the bergerie, doing nothing but filming the communiqués, she was untouchable, but in this moment, she was regular old Séverine Guimard in a roomful of people she didn't know. She felt Bruno's hand on her shoulder, and he gently guided her through the door. His touch brought her back. She wasn't alone; he was with her, and so were Petru and Tittu. She had come for a reason, and she must follow through—she must play her role. She gathered herself and strode onstage.

As people noticed Séverine weaving through the crowd, quiet followed her like a wave flattening as it moves towards the shore. In the kitchen, about a dozen men, including Nico, sat at a large table. When one recognized Séverine, his silent astonishment circulated through the room. Chatter ceased as every person there took her in, looking like she did in the communiqués, in her uniform of black T-shirt tucked into black jeans, with that golden, tousled hair and Cleopatra eyes. This gave her the last boost of confidence she needed.

Nico glanced nervously at an old guy seated at the center of the table who Séverine immediately recognized as Fanfan. His thin lips and shiny head were those of an old man, but the large blue eyes scanning her face were sharp. For being an infamous showboat, he exuded cool gravitas.

Séverine clasped her hands and stared at Nico, who stammered,

"Ziu, you remember my friend Bruno Pieri. And that's Tittu, and Petru, and Séverine Guimard."

Séverine held out her hand to Fanfan. "It's about time we met," she said as he shook it. "I'm just sorry it's under these circumstances."

Beside Fanfan sat a man who looked absolutely wrecked—this must be the father. And in the middle of the table where a flower arrangement might normally go was the two-way radio, emitting a hot, dangerous energy.

"I'm sorry for your loss," she said to Fabien's father, who nodded blankly. He seemed to hardly register her intrusion.

Fanfan crossed his arms and leaned back in his chair.

"I wanted to pay my respects," Séverine said; then she couldn't help but give Bruno a brief, contrite glance. "And to offer my help."

"Your help?"

"The people need to know that Pignon killed Fabien." She cast a lingering glance at the radio. May as well go for it now, she thought. "I'd like to take the radio back with me and use it in my next communiqué."

As expected, she sensed her comrades tense.

Fanfan let out a derisive laugh. "Let me remind you, you're not the first radical on this island. I was there at the beginning, and we had the full support of the Corsican people. We weren't threatening their safety and livelihoods. You detonate a bomb every night?" He shrugged. "Back in the day, it would've been a dozen. In '85, we did some real damage to the Palais de Justice—in Paris. Twenty years I've been doing this. I've dedicated my life to the fight for independence. The people trust and respect me because they know this and because I'm one of them. You, mademoiselle, cannot say the same. You're making enemies on all sides—with the state, your fellow continentals, practically everyone here in Corsica."

Séverine was unmoved by his warning. Just like her, Fanfan was playing a role for the people in the room. No one would admit the fight for independence was secondary to accruing power and wealth. They were all pretending to be dedicated body and soul to the struggle, and maintaining the charade was essential to the operation. This was the level she had to meet him at—flattery was his predictable button.

"You blazed the trail, I'm not trying to downplay that," Séverine said. "But movements go through phases, and the fact is, we're in a phase where my communiqués are getting a lot of attention. No offense, but I Fratelli's just don't have the same reach. I'm not your enemy; I mean, we're working towards the same thing, right? Independence, like you said. So why not cooperate with each other? You're good at a lot of stuff, but I'm good at getting the message out."

"The answer is no, mademoiselle," Fanfan maintained.

"Séverine," Bruno whispered, and put his hand on her shoulder again; this time was a warning, but she was not yet deterred. "I apologize if we disturbed you," he said, looking around the table. "That was not our intention. We just wanted to say we're very sorry about Fabien and that we'll do whatever we can to help avenge him."

The father was sitting immobile during this whole conversation, staring at a bare spot on the table—haggard, red-eyed, and numb.

"Monsieur," Séverine said gently, shaking off Bruno's hand. The man looked up at her. His attention was acute and feverish and unsettled her far more than Fanfan's. "People have to know that the PAT killed Fabien before Pignon leads everyone to believe this was just another blood feud. He's going to try and pit us against each other, but in this case, it doesn't matter who gets credit for what. What's important is that Pignon pays for what he did to Fabien, and you know no one can get the word out better than me."

The men around the table exchanged conflicted looks.

The father continued to stare at Séverine without replying, and she made a concerted effort to meet his gaze. She tried to convey, through her expression, an authenticity and trustworthiness that Fanfan no longer could.

"Give her the thing," the father said.

"Charles," Fanfan murmured.

"I'm not arguing!" the father shouted. "She's right. What matters most is taking that bastard Pignon down. He killed my son, Fanfan; he needs to hang, and the press makes a fuss over whatever she says."

Fanfan didn't dare contradict him, and Séverine nodded professionally. "Do you have a picture of Fabien I can use?" she asked.

"Nico, get the folder from Mélanie," Fanfan instructed, and Nico scrambled from his seat. Fanfan laced his hands on the table and glowered as he tried to figure out how to salvage some leverage.

Séverine's comrades stood with new swagger instead of their initial nervous rigidity. She'd still get an earful, but it would be half-hearted. They were too impressed that she'd pulled this off.

She shuffled through the photos Nico handed her: Oh! The kid had been hot. Dark hair, short on the sides and curly on top, tan, with a wide, symmetrical smile. There was a photo of him with his siblings in front of a Christmas tree, another of him shirtless at the beach, lying on his side, skin flawless. She could tell he was cocky and arrogant and probably slept with everyone. She imagined all the girls that would be at his funeral, sobbing like a harem of widows.

Séverine tucked the folder under her arm. "Thank you. And thank *you*." She directed this last one to Fanfan, to give the false impression he'd given his blessing. That would be the narrative now, when the reality was that she'd humbled him in his own home. This was her peace offering to him, and her own life insurance. Then she snatched the two-way radio from the table and Soffiu di Libertà left through the front door, the kitchen humid with Fanfan's silent anger.

They set right to making the communiqué. This video had none of the casual glamour or camaraderie of her other videos, partly because they couldn't wait for Nico to film it, but more so because of its static, seething quality. They tacked a pink sheet against the kitchen wall and dragged the table in front of it. Séverine sat like a newscaster with the walkie-talkie in front of her as she revealed the truth behind Fabien Bartoli's death at the hands of the French state. Her voice and expression were steel. When she signed off with "U futuru avà," it sounded, more than ever, like a command.

"This is a bomb," Petru said, hefting the weight of the videocassette in his hand. "I hate to admit it, but she's right; people are gonna riot when they see this."

"And we'll be there to guide them," Bruno said, eyes shining.

That night was different, the closest Bruno had come to expressing something real to Séverine. They were the only two people in the world, the only two who'd ever been in the world, and when they came together, with starlight reflected and spinning in their night-blackened eyes, Séverine felt a wild, frightening energy conjured between them, something with its own will. Maybe it was that sentience that possessed Séverine, that made her recklessly say, "I love you."

He kissed her and nestled closer but didn't reply. She lay there for a few moments, waiting. And then he began to softly snore. Burning with irritation and embarrassment, she tore herself from his sleep-heavy arm and sat up naked in the grass.

"What is it?" he mumbled.

"Seriously?"

He lifted himself onto his forearm and rubbed one eye with infuriating innocence. "Come here," he said.

"Why won't you say it?" As soon as she asked, she realized the simple, humiliating answer. She wouldn't give him a chance to confirm it out loud.

"Do you only fuck me because I'm the closest available hole?" she snarled. "Because you're too busy to see the slut from the rental agency?"

"Don't be disgusting," Bruno reproached her. "Why does everything have to be so literal? Can't you tell how I feel by the way I touch you, how I look at you?"

"If—if you're trying to say you *show* me you love me, why can't you say it, too?" she asked sulkily.

Bruno closed his eyes and massaged the space between his eyebrows as if he were very tired. "Sometimes . . . I feel like I still don't really know you. The real you. What's Séverine and what's . . . *Séverine.*" He made an arc with his hand as if he were envisioning her name on a marquee. "Sometimes it feels like you're never not performing."

"This isn't real enough for you?" she asked, gesturing to her nakedness.

"That's not what I'm talking about," he said. "I mean—it's not always clear what's behind the performance."

Boiling with anger, in a low voice she asked, "Are you saying you don't think I'm committed to the cause?"

"I don't know what appeals to you more: the revolution or the attention."

She slapped him across the face. The icy crack of it was unnatural amid the softness of the night. His expression steeled, but he didn't flinch.

"You think I was faking it today?" she hissed. "When I walked into Fanfan's house and convinced them to give us the radio, while you were standing there scratching your balls? Everything I say in the videos, you think I make that up for attention?"

"No," he said. His voice was taut and controlled. "But don't lie to yourself. Your motivations shift."

"What more can I possibly do?" She began to cry just as reflexively as she'd hit him. How awful to feel this way because you loved someone and only wanted them to love you back.

"Don't cry," he said, wrapping his arms around her and kissing her wet face. "I'll be patient with you if you'll be patient with me."

She let Bruno cradle her. She let him find her mouth, and she opened it for him. She let him once again assert his conditional, reluctant, and apparently unspeakable love for her. And as she let this happen, she considered how she would prove herself to him.

16. *Fallout*

The video aired the next morning, on Friday, August 27. Shortly after, hundreds of Corsicans marched to the gendarmeries in Ajaccio, Bastia, Porto-Vecchio, Corte, and Sartène and set them on fire. Another crowd stormed a PAT training camp near Calvi, and the troops shot back, killing a twenty-year-old student. Dozens more were hospitalized. Hearing Nico describe the footage in detail was no less astounding to the comrades than seeing it themselves.

Flights were canceled into Corsica and airports filled with panicked tourists clambering to get out as quickly as possible. When they failed to get on a flight, they chose to sleep in the airport rather than risk going back into the towns; the newspapers the men brought back to the bergerie showed pictures of the terminals looking like refugee camps with everyone spread out on the floor. In a solemn press conference, Jonnart, sounding older and grimmer, announced he was flying to Corsica that Monday to personally assemble a task force to investigate Fabien Bartoli's death and put an end to the unrest.

The trouble was not limited to the island: on the continent, the one million Corsicans who'd left their homeland heard tell of Fabien Bartoli's murder, and it plucked a string deep in their hearts. In Marseille, the city with the largest concentration of Corsican expatriates, the news reported police cars burning and protesters filling the streets. Makeshift bombs exploded at the Palais de Justice, two Gendarmerie nationale buildings, and Baumettes Prison, destroying the grotesque sculptures representing the seven deadly sins that decorated the outer walls. It was as if there was an army of sleeper cells on the continent this whole time, Bruno noted with awe.

Here was Séverine at the top of some mountain, speaking to a camera for five minutes, and consequently, down below, fire, blood, smoke, ash. She was missing out on all the excitement! And she wasn't the only one who thought so; the next day *A Paghjella* ran an article asking, "Is Séverine Guimard sending her Corsican drones to do her dirty work, putting themselves in danger as she hides away like some monstrous queen bee?" A more reputable journalist from *Libération* wrote, "It's disturbing that predictable patterns of colonization have reproduced themselves between Séverine Guimard and the people of the island she is purportedly (and not literally) fighting for." She took the criticism personally; this wasn't her choice. She would have done anything to get out of the bergerie again, to participate in the chaos.

"I need to get back out there," Séverine said to her comrades, tossing the paper onto a stack of newspapers that Tittu used to smother weeds. "I have to participate same as you guys if people are gonna take me seriously."

"It's risky enough for us to go out every night, let alone with you," Tittu said.

"I need to at least make an appearance so they stop painting me as a figurehead," Séverine said.

"What do you have in mind?" Bruno asked.

She knew Tittu was right, that it was a risk for her to leave right now. The island was swarming with PAT officers, traffic stops, police patrolling the city roads. If she were to leave, it would have to be for a really good reason, a special occasion.

"It's not every day Bernard Jonnart pays us a visit," she said.

It made sense to reattempt the failed car bombing from the last time Jonnart was in town; Soffiu di Libertà knew the hotel he stayed at, which suite he took, which limousine service he used, what the shape of his days would be like. All there was to do was pick a date and liaise with the Kadiris, see to what extent they wanted to be involved. They set a meeting for the next evening, a Saturday, at Chez Martine after closing.

Séverine and Tittu went together on his motorcycle, and Petru and Bruno followed in the 4x4. Tittu drove like such a speed freak, the cars they passed mutated into mere streaks of light. But he exerted complete control; when he sped around a blind corner, slanted so close to the road that Séverine could skim the concrete with the tips of her fingers like a surfer skimming a wave, she leaned with him, totally trusting.

Séverine and Tittu waited for Petru and Bruno at the pétanque court, reclined against the stone wall facing the sea. Séverine noticed someone had left a glossy magazine on the ledge nearby. She held it up in the low light and squinted; it was a copy of *Paris Match*. The headline read: "Séverinemania!" On the cover, a group of four girls posed in front of a boarded-up shop with the security grate pulled down to prevent looting. All four were dressed like Séverine in her videos: black T-shirt, black Levi's 512s, combat boots, heavy eyeliner, hair loose and tousled. Their fists were raised, but they were looking at the camera with little smiles, giving the readers of *Paris Match* precisely the shock they wanted.

These weren't Corsican girls; they were French. Normal French girls raising their fists in support of Corsican liberation. Girls who wanted to be like Séverine, who would readily do what she told them! Everyone read *Paris Match*—the right, the left, women, men, people with fancy office jobs and their housekeepers—so everyone must be talking about her. Everyone must be watching her communiqués. She felt both a sense of wonder and inevitability; she couldn't believe it had happened—she was a bona fide celebrity! And at the same time, she'd always known it would. All these people were primed and ready for an explosion, and they expected Séverine to light the match.

"Oh no," Tittu said, snatching the magazine. "I hoped you wouldn't see this. Your head's already big enough."

She stuck out her tongue and snatched it back. "It's too dark to read anyway," she said, slipping the magazine into her bag.

As they watched the pétanque games from the shadows, Tittu produced a pack of cigarettes from his back pocket and asked, "You want?"

"Sure," she said.

He stuck two in his mouth and lit them. Then he took her chin between his thumb and forefinger, using his thumb to pull down her lower lip, and inserted the cigarette. It was more playful than seductive but exhibited a new, previously unthinkable confidence.

"You're different," she said.

"How?" he asked cannily, like he already knew but wanted the pleasure of hearing her say it.

"A man."

They sized each other up, smirking, a shared joke. She'd never felt this way in a friendship before, not even with Pilar or Hélène—this ease and comfort, the freedom to be her unmodified self, and the ability to appreciate someone else that way.

Just then, the 4x4 pulled up, and together the four of them entered the restaurant. They found not only Baptiste and José at the table in the front corner, but a third person, a woman.

"We have bad news," José began. "Matteu was attacked by another inmate."

"Stabbed," Baptiste clarified. "Eight times!"

"But the press is reporting he's alive," José quickly added. He turned to Séverine. "And your dad's been arrested."

Séverine stiffened. "For what?" she asked at the same time the men demanded to know what happened to Matteu. José explained that Paul Guimard had been accused of misappropriating public funds to pay Séverine's ransom, which was ludicrous—everyone knew her mom came from money. And although the prison claimed that Matteu's attack was standard drama, people were suspicious.

"So Matteu's alive, but is he gonna recover?" Tittu asked, furious. "Is he gonna die tomorrow, or will he be like, all fucked up for the rest of his life, or what?"

"Jonnart just made this personal," Bruno said in a hot, angry whisper. For the first time, Petru did not say, *We don't do vendettas.* He, too, was ready for revenge.

Jonnart was brazenly targeting their loved ones now. It didn't matter that the accusations against her papa were untrue, and Jonnart knew it—Paul Guimard would be stained forever. He'd never be elected president with this hanging over him. If he was a neoliberal and an incrementalist, he was still the best among them; he still cared about people over cheap power and profit. This was what he was born to do, his life's work. It was unjustifiable what Jonnart had done—to her papa, to Matteu, to her. She could kill him. She would kill him.

"I'm really sorry about Matteu," the woman said. "I knew him a little from APT"—Amnistia Per Tutti, an organization that provided aid to political prisoners and their families—"and he was a good guy."

"Sorry, who are you?" Séverine asked the woman.

"Oh, that's Lydia. Our sister," Baptiste explained.

Once Baptiste said it, it was obvious she was a Kadiri: the same large, dark eyes, narrow face, and a finer, more feminine version of her brothers' nose. On José these features were grim and intimidating, but on the sister they were arresting. Lydia looked up at Séverine with bemused curiosity, but she wasn't in awe of Séverine like everyone else, which annoyed her. Yes, Lydia was beautiful, but it had been coaxed out and accentuated with a practiced hand. It wasn't spontaneous beauty like her own, Séverine thought with a sniff.

"I've heard about you," Bruno said to Lydia. "You're the lawyer who got Yves Pacchini's charge dropped after that incident at the oil refinery." There was an admiration and respect in his voice that made Séverine's hackles go up.

"That's me," she said with an air of boredom. She was wearing a short black skirt, pale yellow tank top, and unfussy woven sandals, like someone who didn't think about clothes. She was sitting sideways in her chair with her legs crossed: gorgeous, long, thin legs, with perfect knees—Séverine had never even realized a knee could be perfect—and a silver anklet, which was maddeningly sexy. Something about the severity of her face made the whole package with the legs even more alluring. She made Séverine feel young, and for the first time not in a good way—underdeveloped.

"What's your involvement with Novi Patriotti?" Bruno asked.

"Officially? None. But I'm here."

Bruno mulled this over with a little smile; it was a riddle for him to figure out. *She* was a riddle for him to figure out. Séverine realized with dread that she herself must seem less mysterious to him now. Well, there was plenty she could still do to surprise him.

"I'm assuming you want to plan something big for Jonnart's visit, considering recent developments," José started.

"We've had the plan figured out for a while, but if we can get our hands on more Semtex—" As Petru explained what he needed, Bruno turned to Lydia.

"Wait, are you behind the after-school program in Les Jardins de l'Empereur? Because I wanted to set up something similar in Bastia—"

"That's right, they told me you're a teacher. You should talk to my friend Claire, she's been running the program—"

Séverine watched Bruno rearrange himself as they spoke, first leaning back in his chair, then leaning forward with his chin on his fist. His curiosity towards the woman was palpable and infuriating. There was only one thing that truly got his attention. The anger planted inside her when she'd heard of her father's arrest was fertilized by her resentment towards Bruno, and it grew into a hybrid anger, thick and fibrous as a root.

"I'm going to kill Jonnart," she announced. Everyone stopped speaking and turned to look at her.

"Forget the car bomb," she continued, loosening as she warmed to the spotlight. "I want to be the one to pull the trigger. I want him to know it's me."

"You're going to kill Jonnart," Bruno repeated, as if he'd misheard. Petru cleared his throat but said nothing; he never dissented in mixed company.

Lydia was shaking her head. "The public doesn't approve of assassinations. All the support you've managed to drum up will vanish like that." She snapped her fingers.

Séverine fished the *Paris Match* from her bag and tossed it in the center of the table. "They'll approve."

"I'm telling you, an assassination can only hurt our cause," Lydia said. "Which would be devastating when it seems like we can actually harness this energy for change."

"That's what he said about the bombings," Séverine said, flicking her chin at José. "If the reason behind the assassination is legit, people will get behind it."

"People do want blood spilled for Fabien's blood," Tittu ventured.

Séverine fanned her hands as if to say *Thank youuu.* "Killing Jonnart makes sense. There's a direct line of cause and effect."

"And there will be a direct line of cause and effect when the state uses this to justify reversing every single gain we've made towards autonomy," Lydia pronounced.

"I'm not interested in autonomy. I'm fighting for Corsica's independence," Séverine snapped. Now Bruno's focus beamed squarely upon her. "The protests have given the people a taste of their own power, but this—this would be a call to revolution." As she spoke, she became more convinced of her rightness.

"I'm not against the idea," José said. "We've discussed political assassinations before. We made a list, and Jonnart was on there."

"I'm with you, Séverine. Fuck Jonnart!" Baptiste exclaimed. "But what happens after you get rid of him? You'll hide in the maquis the rest of your life like the bandits of yore? You're not a lay-low kind of girl."

"He's right," Petru said. "Soffiu di Libertà as we know it would be over."

Séverine looked at the *Paris Match* on the table and thought of all those people in France who'd pulled off their own bombing campaigns, Corsicans who wanted to fight for their homeland in whatever capacity they could. But there were so many other people in France with a reason to fight: all the poor minorities ghettoized in the banlieues; the former colonial subjects who were denied jobs because of their surnames; the students who would graduate in the worst unemployment crisis in 150 years; and maybe even normal, restless girls like the ones on the magazine cover, who needed less convincing than their parents would like to think.

"What if we went to the continent? Marseille, maybe. Or Paris." As soon as Séverine said it, this whole impossible fantasy unfurled in her mind: the four of them living in the old home she grew up in, taking breakfast in the garden with its high walls covered in ivy; a mix of guys and girls scattered about the sitting room's burgundy Persian rug and the big, beige, American-style couch, planning new attacks. No matter that the Guimards' furniture was all in storage, that their house had been let to some Austrian businessman and his family.

"Why would we go to the continent to liberate Corsica?" Tittu asked.

"To bring the fight to the enemy's doorstep," she said matter-of-factly.

Bruno cleared his throat and finally spoke. "I see what she's getting at. The worst IRA bombings haven't happened in Belfast, they've been in London. And the ETA? Madrid, Barcelona."

"People in France want to get involved," Séverine added. "We just need to recruit them."

"How many Corsicans live on the continent?" Baptiste asked.

"Over a million," Petru grumbled.

"They're already rioting on their own, but imagine if we organized them off the energy of a truly radical act," Bruno appealed to Lydia.

"And not just Corsicans," Séverine said. "There are plenty of other people who want France to burn. We can form the coalitions Fanon talked about. We could start the fourth revolution."

Everyone was quiet for a moment, engrossed in their own personal fantasies of a new world. It had never felt closer, less theoretical, more within their grasp. They just had to reach.

"So you'd go to the continent to recruit an army and lead attacks there, and Novi Patriotti would stay in Corsica to develop the people's war?" José asked.

"Sure," Séverine said, and José nodded solemnly.

"I understand your rationale, and I agree in theory," Lydia said. "But the people haven't been properly primed for protracted conflict, and this government won't capitulate. Clearly, this is moving forward whether I like it or not, but for the record, it's a terrible idea."

"Then don't be involved," José said snippily—like a brother, not a general.

Séverine expected Bruno to start propounding on foco theory—how the conditions for revolution didn't need to be perfect as long as there was a vanguard to lead the charge and show common people the way—but he was strangely quiet, in his own head.

In a distant voice, Tittu said, "I've never left Corsica."

"You won't," Petru muttered under his breath. Séverine seemed to be the only one who heard.

"I'd say this calls for a drink," Baptiste announced, heading to the bar.

Bruno turned to Séverine and asked in a low voice, "Can I talk to you?"

She nodded, and they rose from the table. He led her into the dim toilet in the back of the restaurant and locked the door.

"You're serious about killing Jonnart," he said.

"Yes," she replied.

Without another word, he pulled down her underwear and lifted her onto the sink. He was looking at her differently. Something had changed, some dam had succumbed to the liquid pressure of true feeling. Clutching him, she felt a warm, inner heat melt around her, the molten core of his love that couldn't be articulated. She understood that her declaration of violence was the aphrodisiac. The Séverine of his fantasies was becoming real; not a spoiled, cosmopolitan rich girl playing revolutionary, but a guerrilla with cold, killer instincts, a woman who was principle above emotion, who perhaps was the person he didn't quite have it in him to be. She would be it for him, she resolved.

"Say it now," she instructed.

"I love you," he sighed over her shoulder.

She leaned back so he was forced to look at her. "Again."

"I love you." His gaze was intense, nearly deranged.

"Again."

They returned to find everyone smoking and drinking tiny glasses of clear acquavita, the mood lighter. Lydia gave Séverine a small, amused smile and raised her eyebrow.

"All good?" Petru asked. His tone was falsely calm, like a parent who's saving a scolding for after company has left.

"All good," Séverine replied breezily and took her seat beside Tittu, who poured her a glass, oblivious.

"Jonnart's going back to Paris on Saturday," José said. "I think the time to do it is Friday night. That gives us six days."

"Friday night it is," she agreed, and her stomach flipped in excitement the way it used to when she was bored in class, anticipating the weekend. She raised her glass and said, "To the fourth revolution." Petru tossed his down without clinking, without making eye contact.

"Petru," Séverine tsked, "that's bad sex for seven years."

"If only I'd be so lucky," he replied.

⁓

Everyone slept as Petru, chain-smoking, drove them home. It was very late when they got back to the bergerie, but Petru said, "In the kitchen."

He poured himself a glass of rum and placed the bottle on the table with a thud that made the liquor slosh over. "I don't agree to this," he said.

Séverine sighed dramatically and poured her own glass although she knew it would take her from buzzed to drunk. There was always someone pushing back, someone who needed convincing. It was exhausting. She had been right every time, yet they still questioned her judgment.

"We've talked before about political assassinations diminishing the authority of the state," Bruno said calmly.

"We've *talked*," Petru said.

"That's what we do; we talk and then we act," Séverine said.

"Not always," Petru said. "Sometimes we leave it at talk."

"What are you afraid of?" Tittu asked.

Petru folded one arm over his belly and held the elbow of his other arm, rubbing the stubble on his cheek. "I just have a feeling that if we do this, the whole thing implodes. Everything we've built. Us."

"That's what your sixth sense is telling you?" Séverine asked meanly.

Petru shook his head. "For a woman, you have no intuition. You're like a bull, mindless."

"Oh, you don't like how things have turned out?" Séverine asked, her voice rising. "You wanted to play bandits, but it's gotten too real?"

"The foundation is rotten," Petru replied. "This whole time, it's been personal for you—personal vendetta, personal fame." He gripped the edge of the table and leaned towards her. "To you, this is all fun and games. Even if you do manage to kill Jonnart, what will happen to you? Nothing! Daddy will come to your rescue, he'll hire a big-time lawyer to say you were brainwashed, that what you really need is rest, not punishment, and everyone will say, 'Oh, poor Séverine, captured by those Corsican savages, she was only doing what she needed to survive,' and you'll go about your merry way, back to your old life! But they'll put *us* away forever." Now he leaned back in his chair, hands on his lap, as if resigned to it. "Actually, no—that's best-case scenario. They'll kill us. If you think we're making it to the continent, you're out of your goddamn minds."

Séverine was fuming. She felt betrayed by this speech, and also dejected. She needed Petru on her side. If he loved her, he'd support her. But he did love her—maybe she'd made a mistake trying to convince him on the political level.

"You're right, it's personal with Jonnart," she began. "He—did something to me." As she spoke, she wondered how to take it back or downplay it; she had never told anyone, and it was so gross. She didn't want anyone, least of all Bruno, to see her that way.

Bruno knitted his eyebrows. "What?" he asked.

She took a large gulp of the warm rum and winced; better to be drunk for this. "Two Christmases ago, at a party—it was at some haute fonctionnaire's house. Jonnart was minister of the economy at the time. I hadn't even noticed him noticing me." Why did she say that? She *had* noticed, and it had thrilled her. "But as I was coming out of the bathroom, he was waiting, and sort of blocked the doorway—actually, he pushed me back inside. And he lifted me on the sink and lifted up my dress and—" She shook her head and scrunched her nose. She wanted them to understand what she was getting at so she didn't have to say it, but they were listening too intently.

"He kissed me and—touched me," she finally said.

"Touched you," Tittu repeated.

"He took me by surprise; it all happened so fast. But then he unbuckled his belt, and I realized what he wanted and shoved him away. He laughed, like it was this funny misunderstanding, so I think I laughed, too. He didn't try to stop me from leaving the bathroom or anything. He didn't tell me not to tell my dad."

It was so unpalatable to say aloud. She could not tell them the things Jonnart murmured in her ear, how his hot, vodka-scented breath condensed on her skin, and most shamefully, how he was somehow saying the exact thing she wanted to hear, having the exact reaction she'd hoped for by wearing that dress, those heels, experimenting with her brand-new femininity. She wouldn't say that her body had betrayed her, that he'd noticed, and that was what made him feel he had permission to unbuckle. And she didn't admit that, despite her revulsion and bewilderment, a part of her was curious, wanted to know what a man like Jonnart actually wanted to do to her, if it was like the movies, if it was better to take an older lover as your first as some people said, if he could teach her something invaluable about herself and the world even if she found him disgusting.

Bruno was looking at her with a mix of pity and helplessness, which mortified her. This sort of thing wasn't supposed to happen to her; she wasn't supposed to be the type of girl who allowed it. She was supposed to be above victimhood. But apparently she wasn't, and *that* was the element that debased her. Weakness resided inside her, or else it had when she was younger and less experienced, and she needed to amend the record.

"I know what he did wasn't that bad. I know girls who've had it way worse—"

"Stop," Petru said, looking into his glass. "You're right. He deserves to die." But there was no conviction in his voice; he'd given in to the fate he'd foreseen since her kidnapping. Maybe he was touched by the primeval forces of the island after all, Séverine thought. Maybe he was a kind of oracle, and maybe they were hurtling towards a cliff's edge on a train whose brakes she herself had dismantled.

17. *Plotting*

T he Kadiris proved themselves indispensable in helping to plan Soffiu di Libertà's big finale. Baptiste arranged their passage from Propriano to Nice for Saturday morning, on a cruiser boat with a part-time charter captain, part-time smuggler named Vincent ("Nice guy, real patriot," he assured them). José knew a receptionist who worked the evening shift at the Marbella who confirmed that, since Monday and generally every time Jonnart stayed at the Marbella, he held early business dinners in the hotel's restaurant, then around 20:00 retired to the Scopa di Mare suite, which had its own private beach entrance on the ground floor. Séverine imagined Jonnart wrapping himself in a terry-cloth robe and bringing a glass of cognac out on the patio, surveying the sea, thinking how nothing happened in this country without his knowledge and approval. She imagined shooting him from the beach, his confusion when the first bullet hit, his understanding as the second and third and fourth and fifth and sixth bullets followed.

Planning his death made everything vivid and desperate. After Séverine told them about the incident, Bruno wisely didn't try to comfort her or ask more questions. But he did pursue her with new intensity, either because he'd admitted his love, or because the disconcerting combination of her vulnerability and ruthlessness had deepened it. They'd venture out to the maquis after dinner and make it a dozen feet into the forest before she'd feel his hand sliding around her throat, ostensibly gentle. He kissed her this way, suspended, like he was holding her over a ledge and might release her at any moment.

She felt herself becoming more unrestrained, surrendering to his feigned threat of violence and the real threat of violence that permeated their days and the air of the island itself. All parts of her were overstimulated, yet she sought more intensity both within and outside sex, and her desire for Bruno converged with her desire to exterminate Jonnart.

If Soffiu di Libertà hadn't exposed the PAT's involvement in Fabien Bartoli's death, the stabbing of Matteu may have looked merely suspicious; now, it was considered a government conspiracy, no question. The riots multiplied. Over the last three days, they'd become a self-sustaining organism. Every day more citizens were beaten and rounded up by the PAT, and each name on the news demanded vengeance. It was happening in Corsica, it was happening in France. It was happening to Corsican construction workers in Marseille, and Arab and African immigrant kids in the Parisian banlieues, and university students in Lyon. Séverine knew they weren't all taking to the streets for the sake of Corsica. Everyone had their own bone to pick—police brutality, unemployment, institutional racism in schools and public housing—and here was an opportunity to pick it. The dynamite was stacked, all she had to do was light the wick. They called Nico for one last communiqué.

They hadn't seen or heard from him since the scene at Fanfan's, but to his credit, he showed up at the bergerie the day before Séverine was to kill Jonnart. All week, Petru had been leading their training in precision firing, ammo conservation, identifying cover, and changing position as frequently as possible. When Nico arrived they were in the maquis, where Séverine was unloading her clip into a burlap dummy, metallic blooms of sound exploding one after the other, bullet after bullet tearing into the grass stuffing.

Nico stood behind them, serious and edgy, like he was watching a firing squad. Petru noticed him first.

"Nico," he said.

Séverine smiled over her shoulder, still pointing the gun at the dummy. She knew she'd have to use the full force of her charms to loosen him up again. She put the safety on, holstered the gun, and flounced around him, draping her arms around his neck from behind, cheek pressed against his long hair. "Oh, don't be mad, Nico," she murmured. "It all worked out in the end, no? Fanfan must realize that."

"He's gonna make you pay for embarrassing him," Nico said testily as he rubbed Séverine's forearms, which made her skin crawl.

"How would he know how to find us?" Tittu asked, his face stony.

"In bocca chjosa ùn c'entre mosche," Petru warned. *Flies don't enter a closed mouth.*

"He would never," Séverine said, her voice falsely bright. "Besides, we won't even be in Corsica after this week."

Nico looked genuinely surprised. "What do you mean?"

"We're going to the continent. To harness everything that's happening there, to organize the rioters," Séverine said.

"Seriously? To the continent? That's very bold. I get your thinking, though," Nico said, brain churning as he caught up. "It's short notice, but I guess I can meet you there. Did you make contact with the guys who are still in Paris?"

"Oh, Nico, no; you can't come with us," Séverine said with a touch of condescension.

He looked genuinely crestfallen, and Séverine felt bad for once.

"It wouldn't be safe, Nico," Bruno said quickly. "Like you said, think how Fanfan would react."

"He doesn't have to know; I'll tell everyone I got a job or something."

"No, he'd find out eventually and you'd be screwed," Bruno said. "I wish it didn't have to be this way."

"But if I don't go, who will film the communiqués?" Nico asked.

"You can't throw a stone in France without hitting a filmmaker," Séverine said, and then added, "I mean, whoever it is won't be as good as you, but . . ."

Nico sat on a rock, knees splayed, looking dazed. "That's it, you're leaving? Not even any fireworks at the end?"

Séverine, Tittu, and Petru all shot Bruno a warning look that said, *Keep your mouth shut.*

Nico noticed. "You won't even tell me that much," he said bitterly.

"As soon as we get set up and find a safe house, we'll figure out how to get you up there," Bruno said. "We don't want to be hasty. This way is safer for all of us."

Nico, ever obliging, nodded.

The men left to attend to their tasks while Séverine and Nico shot the communiqué, in which Séverine encouraged everyone to keep expressing their long-simmering anger, to tell the state that they weren't going to sit and take it anymore, that the people were the ones in power, and they'd be flexing that power from now on. She said there were many accounts to balance, and that auditing had begun; she alluded to paradigm shifts that would become clear very soon . . .

As Nico packed up his equipment, he asked, "Is it an assassination?"

"Don't ask questions you don't wanna know the answers to," she said.

He dropped the camera case with an unsettling thud. "Why do you all treat me like I'm a chump?" he asked.

She'd never seen him look so injured, and the directness of his question destabilized her. "What do you mean?" she asked innocently.

"I've helped you guys a lot, no?" Nico said. "I've contributed just as much as anyone else in the group—definitely more than Tittu! I mean, half of the Séverine effect is the video production."

"You think people are rioting in the streets because of the *video production*?" Séverine asked, her temperature rising. "You think anyone can do what I do so long as *you're* behind the camera?"

"That's not what I mean—"

But he'd pissed her off, and she was no longer feeling sympathetic nor prudent. "You know why everyone treats you like a chump? Because you *are* a chump, Nico. No one wants to be stuck underground with you, not even Bruno."

Nico pressed his lips together and slung the camera bag over his shoulder. His expression wavered between anger and woundedness, and it made her falter. Maybe she'd been imprudent in her harshness, but it was too late now. He'd done a good job with the communiqués, but Nico wasn't one of them; he was a one-foot-in, one-foot-out kind of guy who craved the contact high of their militance. But they'd reached a point where they didn't have room for poseurs.

"I certainly wouldn't want to make anyone feel stuck with me," he said, and started off towards his car. Without turning, he added, "Good luck with your revolution."

That night, the Kadiris traveled up to the bergerie to deliver the second getaway vehicle. "Shit, you're really in the middle of nowhere," Baptiste observed as he dismounted the powerful new 250cc scooter, unregistered, that Soffiu di Libertà had given them cash to buy. After killing Jonnart, they would return to the bergerie, gather their supplies, and make their way to Propriano. If they were pursued, there were places a two-wheeler could access that a car could not; they would just have to shake their tails. If necessary, they would camp in the maquis as other outlaws had for centuries.

"What happens once you get to Nice?" Lydia asked. She was wearing a black spaghetti strap dress over a white T-shirt, her hair coiled up in a claw clip, a few loose strands framing her bare face. It was beginning to occur to Séverine that there was a sensuality beyond the obvious, and that its lack of obviousness could make it even more potent than Séverine's kind.

"One of my old comrades from Paris lives in Nice now, and he agreed to take us in," Bruno said.

"I guess you're never on your own when you have five million francs," Baptiste said. "Or rather, 4.94 million. Vincent wants sixty thousand for his trouble."

Séverine didn't venture to correct him and reveal they had two hundred thousand less than he guessed. Anyway, it was a fair price.

"And," José said. "You'll need to leave some capital with us before you leave."

"How much?" Séverine asked.

"Two and a half million should do."

Séverine laughed in his face. "You can have a million to start. That's more than enough to buy some plastic explosives and pencils, or whatever you need for 'mass education.'"

The brothers exchanged a look, then nodded in assent.

"You came all the way up here; you want a beer?" Petru asked.

"Hey," Lydia said, tugging the sleeve of Tittu's shirt. "You got any more of those peaches you sent home with my brothers last time?"

Posture straightening with pride, Tittu said, "Tons, this season's been a good one. I'll go grab you some."

He went off to the orchard, the men carried their drinks to the back patio, and Lydia stopped Séverine in the kitchen.

"You're sleeping with the good-looking one, right? Bruno?" she asked as she sat at the table and lit a cigarette.

Séverine was taken aback, then defensive. "That's right." She remained standing.

Thoughtfully, Lydia tapped a bottle cap against the table. "Did he force himself on you?"

"What? No," Séverine said, appalled.

"I'm thirty-one, an old hag compared to you," Lydia said. "But I know how men are."

"So do I," Séverine replied frostily.

"The 'intellectuals' are the worst ones," Lydia continued. "They'll read fifty pages of Fourier, cheat on you on the basis of 'praxis,' then accuse you of being bourgeoise if you object."

"It's not like that," Séverine said.

"Not yet," Lydia warned.

Séverine pulled out a chair and sat. The conversation was moving towards something more personal, she could tell.

As if on cue, Lydia said, "This whole time, I've been trying to figure out why you're doing all this; why you'd join their cell and devote yourself to our independence, which absolutely no one outside of Corsica cares about. At first, I thought, 'They must be coercing her.' But my brothers met you and swore you were in it for real. I had to see for myself, which is why I crashed the other night. And it was so obvious: you have a thing with that guy Bruno. So then I thought, Stockholm syndrome? But you've gone way beyond that. The only other option I can think of is, are you trying to incite revolution to impress a guy?"

It took a moment for Séverine, agitated as she was, to get her wits about her, but when she did, she replied as calmly as she could, "When people like you ask why I'm fighting, it kinda makes it sound like you don't take your own cause seriously. I see injustice and I'm trying to do something about it—isn't that how it should be?"

Okay, yes, she was also doing it for love, but so what? As if that wasn't as legitimate a reason as trying out some theory you read in a book! Her willingness to learn, her performances, her ideas, her legitimate zeal for the cause all sprang from her love for Bruno, to prove that she loved what he loved, which would always be the only way in with him. Each act of virtuous violence was dedicated to him. Her comrades and this woman in front of her might be in it for love of country, but that was a faceless love. Even if it was earnest and deeply felt, it couldn't have the potency of her precise, mortal love. That's why she was the better revolutionary. But she couldn't say this to Lydia, so cool and self-possessed and *rational*.

"It *is* how it should be, but people don't usually care unless something affects them personally. I don't know, maybe Bruno is just a *really* good teacher," Lydia said as she stubbed out her cigarette in an ashtray on the table. "But I can tell your education has been one-sided: the bombs, the bullets, the blood of the enemy flowing through the streets. There's a lot more to revolution."

"Like?"

"Providing for your people outside of state structures. Programs that connect children with their culture and language, that free us from dependency on French welfare. Taking care of our elderly and sick and, unpopular opinion, immigrants. Watching each other's children. Using our land to feed our own people."

"I'm for all that," Séverine said as she thought, *Yawn!*

"You never mention that sort of thing in your videos. It's all fire and brimstone. You're kind of a doomsday cult." Lydia laughed, but Séverine did not. "Anyway, the point is that guns aren't the only weapon. So is softness. Care."

"Tell that to José."

"I do, all the time! And I'd like to think it makes a difference." She gave Séverine a sentimental look. "You're young. You probably don't have a ton of experience, but believe me, an intense sexual affair—it can make you do crazy things. And once it's over, you're left in the wreckage like, *What the fuck just happened?* Except in your case, you're about to kill a high-ranking minister."

"Correct," Séverine said stonily. "And talking about kids and old people won't get me to call it off."

"I'm not trying to," Lydia replied. "I do hope once you get to the continent, you'll recruit more women. Maybe they'll provide some balance and perspective."

She got up from the table, signaling the lecture was over. But Séverine had to clear up one point.

"It's not just a sex thing," she said. "Bruno and I are in love." At that exact moment, Tittu barged into the kitchen with a basket of peaches, the door smacking noisily behind him. He froze, then turned on his heel and left, then turned again and came back in, the screen door slapping each time. Jaw set and ears burning red, he placed the basket on the table and strode outside without saying a word to the women.

"Shit," Séverine whispered, and lowered her head into her hand.

"What, he didn't know?" Lydia asked, bringing a peach to her nose. "God, men are dense."

Tittu waited until the Kadiris left, which wasn't long after he'd burst into the kitchen; Lydia had seen to that. The four of them were sitting on the patio, insects clamoring around the light of the wall sconce. The minute he heard their car rattle away down the path, he said, "You're still fucking each other, aren't you?"

Bruno stiffened in his chair and looked between Tittu and Séverine, awaiting her cue.

"Yes," Séverine said; resurrecting the lie was futile. Petru let out a loud sigh and started rolling a cigarette.

"Did you know?" Tittu asked Petru.

"I suspected," Petru said.

"You, too, admit it," Tittu commanded Bruno, but he said nothing, only stared at his hands in his lap.

"She's not ashamed—why are you?" Tittu cried, losing his cool. "Because you're weak, and you know it."

Even Séverine was stunned silent.

In his teacher's voice, calm and assured, Bruno replied. "It just happened between me and Séverine. And if it had happened to you, you wouldn't have stopped either."

Tittu's anger acquired a note of anguish. "Are you like—in love with each other?"

Séverine and Tittu looked at Bruno with equal expectancy. "Yes," he said.

Tittu stood, his chair screeching horribly against the stone.

"Tittu, wait," Séverine cried and grabbed his hand, but he wrenched it away.

"It's dangerous for us to go into tomorrow like this," Bruno said. "We have to talk."

"Will you please just leave me alone?" Tittu begged, and in the bulb of the patio light, before he bolted inside, Séverine saw tears wavering in his eyes.

"Petru," Bruno began, and Petru held up his huge hand.

"You fucked up," Petru said. "But Tittu's a soldier. He'll do what he's gotta do."

"And after?" Séverine asked.

"The four of us have been stuck together for a while," Petru said. "We're about to have a change of scenery, some fresh blood hopefully. But in the meantime, lay low, okay? Give him space."

"And you? What are you thinking?" Bruno asked.

"I'm thinking I'm pissed," Petru said. "I think you're two selfish assholes. But I've never been in love, so what do I know." He stood and took one last, fierce pull on his cigarette, burning it to the quick. "I'm going to bed. You may recall, we have a big day tomorrow."

Then it was just Bruno and Séverine, uneasy, knowing they should choose propriety and go separately to bed, but instead they ventured into the maquis. It would be the last time they'd get to lie on this land together. They approached each other sheepishly, Tittu and Petru's disapproval thick between them; but their discomfort gave way to the desperation of *last time*, the apocalyptic quality of it, and as Séverine watched the stars buzz and vibrate, she had a vision of them plummeting to earth, turning fiery and immense as they struck the ground around her and Bruno, and the two of them carrying on, heedless. Then he flipped her onto her stomach, and her mind careened back into the dirt.

As always, Bruno refused to sleep in the bed with Séverine. Morning crept up after a restless night. She felt as if she were in the wings of a theater, about to walk onstage in the starring role. She knew the lines, she knew the blocking, she'd rehearsed so often it had become second nature. The only thing was to put one foot in front of the other and let the show unfold. They packed for the continent (plus supplies to hide out in the maquis for a few days, just in case) and split the ransom money among their four rucksacks. Petru made eggs and toast, but the food went untouched.

No one wanted to be the first to speak, but the longer they were silent, the heavier the pit in Séverine's stomach became. She wouldn't be able to perform in this state. In a manic burst, she pleaded, "Tittu, don't be mad."

Tittu was smoking and brooding, staring at the tablecloth, and his piano fingers trembled. "I'm not mad," he said.

Séverine opened her mouth to plead with him, but he continued. "I just thought joining the cell would mean I didn't feel alone. I thought we'd be like a family, but better, because we chose each other. But that was stupid, I guess."

"That's not true," Séverine said.

"We *are* a family," Bruno said. "Soffiu di Libertà doesn't exist without you."

"Don't patronize him," Petru snapped.

"I'm not," Bruno replied, taken aback.

"You don't get it because you have each other," Petru said.

It was true. Séverine and Bruno were enjoying a more complete experience of life within the cell. There was an imbalance, and Séverine couldn't put it right for all of them.

They shut up the bergerie, as if vacation was finished and they'd be returning to the city. There was in fact a slight chill in the air that presaged fall. It was September. Summer was over, and it was shocking; Séverine had somehow believed those months would go on forever and ever, and the fact that autumn was upon them gave her a sense of uneasiness. When they closed the door of the bergerie, it was with palpable melancholy. They'd be back in a few hours, but only to leave again, and in a hurry. This was the real goodbye to the house that had protected them so well.

Bruno patted one of the facade's large, misshapen stones. "It's a good house, Petru," he said.

"It is," Petru sighed. "The only thing my family didn't fuck up."

"Not the only thing," Séverine said, and took his hand. He was too bashful to look at her but squeezed it back.

"No, but Petru's a distant second," Tittu said, and the four of them couldn't help but share a smile.

⁓

She rode on the big new scooter with Petru, and Bruno hopped on the back of Tittu's motorcycle. She was hunched over, holding Petru around the waist, her skirt billowing in the wind. The Beretta, silencer attached, was nestled inside her straw tote. The sun was setting vividly, spreading lurid pinkness everywhere. She was in a bad mood—about Tittu, about Nico's tantrum, about Lydia's lecture. As they approached the center of town, she coaxed her anger into something more productive. She would not linger like a movie villain, waxing poetic about why it was time for Jonnart to die. Her anger would be so white-hot that she could shoot him before he even opened his mouth. He would see her and know.

Porticcio was an ugly, impractical town, developed only to give tourists staying at the luxury beach resorts somewhere to buy sunscreen—squat, faceless buildings with identical little balconies, everything quick and cheap-looking. About ten minutes from the hotel, in the center of town, Petru cut the engine, and Séverine hopped off.

The idea was that Séverine as Dominique would meet Bruno at the port and they'd take a cab to the hotel, as if they were dining at the restaurant. According to José's concierge friend, after dinner

Jonnart's personal bodyguard, who hovered over him all day, decamped to a room beside Jonnart's suite; the hallway would be empty and Jonnart alone. As long as Bruno and Séverine dressed the part, they could waltz into the hotel unchecked, and she could enter Jonnart's suite via his private beach, which was walled off from the main one by nothing more than landscaping. It essentially functioned as a back entrance into his room.

Exiting was a different story; the driveway of approximately two hundred meters that branched off Porticcio's main artery and led to the hotel was the only way in or out, so it was crucial they escape before the police blocked off the road. Luckily, the gendarmerie was a full twelve-minute drive from the town center to the hotel; the hotel's seclusion, the source of its appeal, could also be used to its disadvantage. This was where Tittu and Petru came in; they'd linger in town until 20:10, then head to the hotel on their vehicles and simply collect Bruno and Séverine out front in the same spot the taxis used. With only one surface exit, there was no room for error. If anything went awry, the sole backup plan was to shoot their way out.

Petru checked his watch. "It's 19:02. I'll see you in front of the hotel in one hour and twenty-eight minutes."

Séverine kissed him on each cheek, and as she pulled away, he gripped her shoulder, making her wince.

"It's not nice, bringing someone to the edge," he said. "I couldn't cross the line. I didn't want to. I know your situation is different, but still." He held her gaze. "If you can't cross the line either, it's okay. You won't be failing us. We can just pick up our plan same as before. Okay?"

"Okay," she whispered unthinkingly, wanting only to get out of his painful grasp.

Unnerved, she walked briskly towards the port they'd just passed and spotted Bruno waiting for her. He was dressed in a navy polo shirt and chinos, looking very yuppie, like the son of a local developer. He'd fit right in with the hotel clientele. Séverine was in Dominique drag, wearing a blue and white gingham halter dress from United Colors of Benetton that Bruno had bought her expressly for this occasion. The style was more precious than she'd have chosen for herself, but the thrill of the gift lay in being interpreted by Bruno. Even if it wasn't quite right, she was delighted that he'd wandered through the store, touching the clothes, consulting with the salesgirl, thinking about what Séverine might like, the kind of dress he wanted to see her in.

Bruno flagged a taxi, and the driver looked Séverine up and down as they clambered inside the cab.

"You're from Paris," he observed. "Couldn't get a flight out?"

"I fell in love with a local," she said, taking Bruno's hand in hers.

"See," the driver said. "Love makes you do crazy things. But you'll be fine at the Marbella as long as you stay in bed." He chuckled to himself.

They turned at the large, gilded sign for the Hotel Marbella and started down the driveway. It seemed to keep going and going, and Séverine prayed for it to end now, or now, or now. Finally, the sprawling, faux-rustic building with its whitewashed exterior and wooden beams came into view. She'd been here a few times with her parents and had always found it classy, a little sexy, with continental sensibilities. She led Bruno through the lobby, across the glossy marble floors, and past the vases of purple and white orchids flanking the reception desk. The air smelled of salt and jasmine and rosemary— of Corsica the fantasy.

As the hostess led them to the bar, Séverine surveyed the dining room. It appeared to be filled with the last wealthy foreigners on the island. On the other side of the dining room, diagonal from the bar, two suited men stood in front of closed double doors, as expected. That, she knew, was the private dining room, where she herself had dined before.

They ordered glasses of wine and 150-franc seafood dishes, neither of which they touched. It struck Séverine that this was their first time sharing a meal in public, of getting to pretend they were normal. Bruno swirled his wine absentmindedly while watching the sun sink below the horizon. It was a cloudless evening, and the sunset's colors were diffuse and underwhelming.

"Isn't this nice?" he asked, and took a big, edgy gulp.

"What's wrong?" Séverine asked.

He laughed, but it was jittery. "You're cool as a cucumber, aren't you?"

"I've imagined it so many times, it's like I already know how it's gonna go."

"Tittu's right," Bruno said. "I'm weak."

"That's not true."

"You said it yourself, after the Laporte bombing. I'm happiest with my books, and when it comes to *doing* any of the things I've read about—" Flustered, he whipped the cloth napkin from his lap and wiped his forehead.

She rested her hand on his leg. "We've gotten this far because you're good at what you do, and I'm good at what I do." As she said it, she encountered a whole new chamber of her love for him, a place unconnected to sex. "You're not weak. You're here, aren't you?"

She felt his muscles relax, and he nodded. They kissed, his lips tasting of wine from another, more tranquil life.

At 20:00 on the dot, the doors to the private room opened, and a crowd of men in suits streamed out. It was impossible to miss Jonnart, not only by his silver hair but his mere presence, so dazzling compared to the men around him. She recognized three others, too—former colleagues of her father's—plus Pignon. She'd never seen him in person, but he was as he appeared on TV: a rodent. Despite her loathing, she felt no desire to end his life. That feeling was reserved for Jonnart.

She waited another ten minutes, imagining him alone in his room, removing his suit jacket, fixing himself a drink. Then she stood.

"If you're not back in fifteen minutes, I'm coming for you," Bruno said, restating the plan. She nodded and they kissed again, a kiss too deep and long for the occasion of a girl going out to cool her feet in the sea.

When Séverine lived with her parents in Ajaccio, she'd gone to the beach every day, even during the chilly, wet winters, trying to amass enough pleasure in the feeling of her feet in the sand and the feeble lap of the sea to convince herself to not run away. Now, as the water slipped around her feet, she felt like that girl again, then remembered that she was *someone* now, more than a girl: a girl with a man, and a movement behind her, and a gun in her bag.

She arrived at a huge hedge of purple bougainvillea, a privacy screen between the hotel's main beach and the Scopa di Mare room's private one, which was further buttressed by a jetty of black rocks. She removed her wedges and stepped into the warm water, wading deeper until it lapped over her knees. At this point, she removed the wig and tucked it into her bag, shaking out her hair—she wanted Jonnart to recognize her—and crawled over the rocks into the "private" part of the sea. The beach in front of her was a little manicured square, peaceful as a postcard in the fading lavender light. Séverine resented that this most perfect slice of coastline should belong to the hotel, which pimped it out to people like Jonnart.

She tramped towards the shore, trying to avoid a floating mat of brown seaweed; once she sloshed out of the water onto the sand, she looked up, and there was Jonnart leaning over his balcony, watching her with curiosity—he hadn't put two and two together yet. They were only a few meters apart. Her heart leapt in her chest; she thrust her hand in her bag, pulled out the gun, flicked off the safety, and pointed it at him, all with a depressing gracelessness.

When he saw the gun, he raised his hands in the air.

"Well hello to you, too," he said. In the three seconds that elapsed between recognizing her and uttering his first words, he'd decided on his strategy—affability and insouciance.

Barefoot, Séverine climbed the steps that connected the balcony to the beach, gun trained on him although her hands shook with adrenaline. His arch, controlled smile revolted Séverine at the same time she was drawn to it, which was his whole shtick. He didn't pretend to be anything other than a slimy politician, knowing people would be attracted to his crude brand of power and magnetism. She'd forgotten the quality of his attention, how it was impossible not to be flattered by it. Resisting him, upholding her hatred, was the harder path.

"I didn't recognize you out of uniform," Jonnart said. "I like this getup better. Can I get you something? Sparkling water? Juice? They stock every sort of nonsense in these suites."

She shook her head no.

"Well, I was in the middle of making myself a drink. Do you mind?"

Without waiting for an answer, he backed into the room, hands still up. He wasn't wearing a robe as she'd imagined but faded navy slacks and a white shirt, collar unbuttoned, sleeves rolled up. No shoes, no wedding ring. He'd taken on a healthy glow in the five days he'd been in Corsica, which seemed distasteful under the circumstances. Séverine followed apprehensively, lingering in the sliding glass doorway before entering the dimly lit, air-conditioned suite.

He moved to the minibar, then slowly lowered his hands and poured the already-uncorked cognac into a snifter. She watched him like both predator and prey. She could sense that he was sensing her just as keenly, but he was more experienced at concealing it.

"Can I sit?" he asked. She flicked the gun towards an overstuffed chair in the corner of the room, beside the sliding glass door, and he settled in as directed.

"So what can I help you with, Mademoiselle Guimard?" Jonnart sighed. Séverine couldn't tell if he was genuinely tired—tired of her, tired of the Corsican Problem, tired of being the one who had to clean up the mess, upon whom so many people relied for peace and security—or if he was being ironic.

"Why accuse my dad of stealing money for my ransom?" she found herself asking. "You know that's a lie."

He crossed his legs and jostled one elegant foot as he considered her question. "Being a politician means making tough decisions for the benefit of the republic," he said. "Your father was not capable of making those hard decisions—not after your kidnapping, and not before it either. He wants so badly to be liked. Really, he should have been an actor."

"What was he supposed to do, not pay my ransom?"

"Precisely."

"And releasing Matteu so I could go home would've also hurt the republic?" She was going against her better judgment, but she couldn't help it; she wanted to know.

"We don't negotiate with terrorists," he said self-righteously.

"It was one guy," Séverine continued. "All you had to do was let him go. I mean, you know my dad, you—you know me." She paused. "They almost killed me."

"And yet, here you are! Look how resourceful you've become." He leaned forward in his chair and spread his arms, taking her in, but the movement was too fast, and Séverine flinched, raising the gun back to eye level. It wasn't an assertive reaction but a fearful one, and he perceived the difference. With self-possession, he dropped the grin and nodded in concession, carefully placing his hands—one still holding the snifter—on the arms of the chair.

"But it's not just about politics, is it?" she asked, steadying herself. "It's like you wanted me to stay kidnapped—like something about me gets to you."

"You think this is personal?" Jonnart asked with a note of delight. "Darling, you're fomenting rebellion. You're inciting violence, destruction of private and government property; people have died! You've created absolute chaos throughout the country. Of course I'm coming after you. I'm trying to maintain order."

"No—" Séverine continued, flustered. "At that Christmas party, when you followed me into the bathroom—" She couldn't finish the sentence. Why was she even asking this? She already knew the answer: everyone and everything was there for him to play with. Even now, he was playing with her.

Jonnart took a drink of cognac and squinted at her. It appeared she'd actually thrown him for a loop. Maybe, she thought with mortal embarrassment, he didn't remember. Finally, he said, "I'm quite good at reading cues, and you seemed interested. Like you were taking your new woman's body for a test drive. Looking for attention."

He was in a small way correct, but he'd completely missed the mark in the way that mattered most. Julien hadn't understood his crime either. For the first time, Séverine recognized Jonnart as a mere man, someone who perversely believed in his own good character, that he'd generously shepherded her into womanhood. She wondered if she could forgive this transgression as she had Julien's, and found herself considering Petru's offer.

Then Jonnart frowned and swirled the glass, considering his own words. "Is that what this whole circus is about, 'U futuru avà' and all that?" His voice dripped with condescension. "You've been try-ing to get my attention again?"

Any possibility of grace evaporated. Of course he thought this was about him; for all his talk of responsibility to a greater good, he didn't truly believe there were stakes higher than his own. He didn't care about the people he was appointed to serve—if they could feed themselves, if their children were killed by police, if pollution gave them cancer—and so couldn't conceive of Séverine caring about anything beyond herself and some perceived slight. That was why he'd pushed her into that bathroom, too; he'd assumed Séverine's general curiosity was directed specifically at him. In his mind, there was no consciousness *not* directed at him, inviting him to take what he wanted. But he'd made a miscalculation; she harbored no grati-tude or forgiveness, only unalloyed hatred.

Someone knocked at the door. Séverine froze, and Jonnart gave her a hard but impassive look, as if to say he did not care what she did and went to the door. The clock over the minibar ticked: 20:25. They were supposed to meet Petru and Tittu out front in five min-utes; she knew who was on the other side.

"Jean-Marc?" Jonnart asked as he opened it, and Bruno burst through with his gun drawn, pushing him back into the room. He surveyed Séverine, making sure she was okay, but he looked ab-solutely unhinged. The gun visibly trembled in his hands, a line of sweat had collected across his hairline, his jaw twitched from being clenched so hard. Séverine and Jonnart had been dancing the same choreography, playing characters in the same film, but Bruno injected a sense of inelegant reality that discomposed ev-eryone.

They hesitated just long enough for Jonnart to hurl his snifter at Séverine; it streaked past her head and exploded against the opposite wall, the cognac splattering her face.

She frantically wiped her stinging eyes with the hem of her skirt, and when she opened them again, she saw Bruno standing alone in the room, bewildered, the gun limp in his hand. This was not his arena—he'd told her as much fifteen minutes ago. Really, it wasn't the arena of any of her comrades—only she could take the dare, only she could alchemize the anger. Only she could fire the shot, and this would be her ultimate gift to them.

Jonnart had bolted into the hall and was banging on the neighboring door, a whole suite's length away, but when he caught sight of Séverine with her pistol raised, he turned, and like a parent at the end of his rope said, "Enough of these games!" He cast a snide glance back towards the suite. "I'm sure your dithering boyfriend is sufficiently impressed. Now put the gun down."

Instead, Séverine pulled the trigger. The silencer produced a quiet, furious buzzing, like a hornet, and Jonnart released a strange, shrill howl, an uncontrolled sound she never imagined him capable of. He gripped his left shoulder where blood was seeping through his shirt, his expression one of shock. Equally shocked, Séverine lowered the gun. She'd done it; she'd shot him. But it wasn't the single, clean shot she'd imagined, and now he was running down the long hallway towards the lobby, yelling for help.

As she pursued him, people poked their heads from their rooms, but once they saw Séverine with the gun, they slammed their doors. There was commotion behind her as Jonnart's bodyguard scrambled out of his own room, and she glanced back to see him in a towel with wet hair. Before the guard could fully register the situation, Bruno was shooting from the doorway of Jonnart's room. Those shots sounded so much louder in the hotel than in the maquis, as if the noise alone could bring the walls down around them. But Séverine processed the scene with detachment; she'd finally accessed some mechanical, masculine sense of cutting through the world as thoughtlessly as a shark in pursuit of her target.

No longer debonair and self-possessed, Jonnart crossed into the lobby, frantic as any hunted animal. She shortened the distance between them to the length of a tennis court. To her left was the restaurant, separated from the lobby by huge panes of glass; to her right was the hotel entrance; and before her were floor-to-ceiling views of the mountains and sea. When she fired again, the bullet missed and shattered one of these windows, which cascaded to the floor with operatic grandiosity, causing diners to scream and run towards the beach. But the noise only reached Séverine's ears as dull, senseless sound. Right away, she discharged a third time, and this one hit her target in the ribs, judging from the axis upon which his body pivoted, where his hands clutched. Then, somehow, he was up again, heading for the front doors. The sound of shots continued from a distance, but she didn't turn back. Séverine was focused on one thing.

She followed Jonnart past the concierge huddled in a corner and through the front doors into the vivid blue twilight, where she spotted him limping across the vast, circular driveway as bellhops and people waiting for taxis watched, mouths open, useless. He fell to the ground; a man rushed to assist him, and Séverine screamed, "Get away from him!" The man saw Séverine dashing towards him in her little gingham dress with gun in hand and did as he was told. Jonnart turned; she was now standing over him. His crisp white shirt was soaked with dark blood. With her bare foot, she nudged Jonnart onto his back, and he yielded. He was weak, and she was strong, and if she was strong, the people were strong. Bruno was strong. She unloaded one more shot, and it hit him in the chest;

a small spray of blood splattered her skirt with the force of an accusation.

The sight of that blood, his life, issuing from him made Séverine sick in a way she'd never felt before: an entwined physical and spiritual nausea. Jonnart's gaze detached and his arms, which had been curled into his torso, fell to the cobblestone. She had released him from his body and the earth, and she felt a heaviness settle into her very marrow, aware that she'd performed powerful magic that now marked her, a mark she'd bear forever.

Séverine turned away from the body and vomited onto the driveway. It cleared her mind, unpopped her ears. So much screaming; she had to leave. There was a plan for this. She wiped her mouth with the back of the hand that held the gun, and Tittu and Petru came racing down the main driveway. The only person who was not in position was Bruno—then she remembered the gunshots she'd heard, and with pure dread, spun back towards the hotel. Before she could get there, Tittu and his bike screeched in front of her, cutting her off. He flipped up his visor.

"Where's Bruno?" he barked.

"I don't know, he was in the room. I have to go back—" Two more gunshots echoed from inside the hotel.

"Go with Petru, now," he said firmly.

Séverine hesitated. She hadn't envisioned it happening this way, and no decision felt like the right one. People were beginning to cautiously move from their hiding places; one of them would be making their way towards a phone.

"Séverine, go. I'll find him," Tittu said, gently this time. Like he talked to her in the garden. Her gentle friend.

She nodded and walked past Jonnart's body to where Petru was waiting, helmet obscuring his face and scooter chuttering like a horse ready to gallop. If she could just get on the scooter, he would take care of everything. Wordlessly, he passed her a full-face helmet and a black windbreaker that she zipped up to her neck, and she wrapped her arms around him. He revved off down the driveway, and the distance between Séverine and Bruno grew and grew and grew.

18. *S'enfuir*

Séverine and Petru were approaching the end of the long drive- way when a police cruiser rounded the corner, whipping past the scooter, both vehicles going too quickly to fully register each other. Then the scooter turned onto the main road, speeding north. To reach the bergerie, they'd have to cross two well-trafficked roads; Séverine prayed they weren't already blockaded. As they sped around the roundabout that intersected the highway, three police cars en- tered simultaneously, sirens screaming. But the cops exited south towards the Marbella, and Séverine shuddered with both relief and anxiety.

She should have gone back for Bruno herself. Her chest ached, but she was too tense to cry; she just clung to Petru, waiting for this to all be over. But that hope felt hollow. What she'd done was mo- mentous, would precipitate a transfer of power. Pulling the trigger might have been the last action under Séverine's total control; the scale of its effects was beyond comprehension. This was not how she'd imagined feeling. Things were not playing out how she'd imagined at all.

They went around the airport and cut over to the T20 without issue. Up in the maquis, it was eerily quiet, as if nothing had happened. Cars zoomed by lazily, unaware of the hell unleashed down south. Thirty minutes later, they pulled up to the bergerie.

Petru strode into the sitting room, plugged in the TV, and turned it on; it emitted an otherworldly light in the shadowy room.

"It works?" Séverine asked with utter astonishment.

"So we lied, a thousand apologies," Petru said impatiently as he fussed with the antennae. Static was replaced by a picture that Séverine's brain struggled to decipher. Slowly, she understood she was watching an aerial feed of the T20, irradiated by helicopter searchlights, in which a squadron of flashing cop cars trailed a motorcycle—Tittu's motorcycle, with Bruno on back. The newscaster's narration came to her as if she were behind glass, warped and distant.

"—Minister Jonnart's bodyguard was wounded in the shoot-out, and one of the suspects is said to be wounded as well. Accomplices are now heading north; please be advised that the T20 is closed from the Ajaccio airport to Effrico, where police are expecting to head them off."

"It can't be that bad," Petru said. "Look, they're both upright and holding on fine." Séverine was so grateful for Petru's usual pessimism; it made his current optimism as good as true.

They watched as the motorcycle approached the blockade at an undaunted speed. Right before colliding head-on with the row of cars and steel barricades, Tittu swerved right, cutting through the maquis and popping out on the T20 a few meters away. The cars that had been following them at 130 kilometers an hour slammed on their brakes, skidding into the blockade, and the motorcycle rushed along the narrow highway up into the maquis, followed only by the helicopter.

Petru and Séverine cried out in relief, but it was momentary—the horrible reality of what they were watching settled in.

"Where can they go with that helicopter trailing them?" Séverine asked.

"At some point, they'll have to jump off the bike and find cover in the maquis," Petru said.

"So we wait," Séverine said with an obstinate belief that everything was on track, that she'd have her comrades back by the end of the night.

The feed switched to a second aerial of the Marbella. Even from that height, the floodlights revealed a stain on the pinkish flagstones of the circular drive. "Monsieur Jonnart was pronounced dead on arrival at La Miséricorde, suffering from gunshot wounds to his abdomen and chest," the reporter said. "Eyewitnesses have identified Séverine Guimard as the shooter."

"What happened?" Petru asked warily.

She couldn't say Bruno had frozen; she couldn't betray him like that. "He came to the room like he was supposed to, and then Jonnart like, attacked him and ran out. After that, I don't know." She began to cry. "I fucked up, didn't I? I took too long, and now—"

"Tittu's Evel Knievel on that bike," Petru said, his tone scolding. "No one can catch him on those mountain roads, I promise you."

The two of them sat on the sunken sofa, watching the helicopter follow Tittu and Bruno like some insidious hawk. They'd turned off the T20 and gotten quite far up into the mountains, moving northeast, farther and farther away from the bergerie. The road grew narrower and more jagged, causing the motorcycle to disappear and reappear from sight as it took each hairpin turn.

"Where are they going?" Séverine asked.

Petru didn't respond; they both knew they should have abandoned the road ages ago. Neither acknowledged that Bruno was no longer so upright; it looked as if Tittu's back was bearing most of his weight. The circle of unnatural light beaming from the helicopter must have been blindingly bright for Tittu; he couldn't drive this way all night.

For thirty minutes, they watched in silence; the video feed migrated to a corner of the screen as reporters prattled on about this unprecedented assassination and predicted reactions.

Tittu turned onto a one-lane road that went right up the Monte Rotondo, one of the highest peaks in Corsica. Switch after switch, the bike flicked in and out of the spotlight. And then it did not reappear. The helicopter circled, searching for its prey.

"It looks like we've lost sight of the suspects," the newscaster said evenly.

Neither Petru nor Séverine spoke as they searched the screen. There was no need to fear, Séverine assured herself; they'd taken advantage of the crooked road and ditched the motorcycle and run into the maquis, as they should have before. It was a long trek over the mountain, but they could make it overnight. She would never let Bruno out of her sight again. They'd leave Corsica, they'd get married, they'd have beautiful children, they'd go somewhere no one could find them. Fuck the revolution. She just wanted her man.

"Madonna," Petru exhaled, and Séverine was stirred out of her fantasy by the sight of smoke snaking from the trees.

"They threw the bike over the mountain to make it look like they crashed, right?" she asked.

"Probably," Petru said distantly. The anxiety of watching the motorcycle be pursued had a hot, white hopefulness to it, but now that hope was occluded by a heavy black cloud.

Perhaps ten minutes passed. Séverine babbled theories of their disappearance, asking over and over for Petru's assurance and receiving none; he was large and silent as a menhir. They watched as a second helicopter appeared, from which some special unit of police or medics rappelled into the chasm.

Then a stretcher floated towards the helicopter like a web-snared insect being dragged up to a spider's mouth. From his navy shirt, Séverine knew it was Bruno. A chyron blazed white across the screen: "Motorcyclist dead. Second suspect injured." Her brain spluttered: Who was dead? Who was injured? Who was that on the TV? Who was missing? Dead? It made no sense. Where was Tittu? She felt dumb again, as dumb as she'd felt before Bruno came into her life. And impotent. She didn't understand; everything had always worked out.

"It can't be true," Séverine said.

They watched as the pompiers hauled a long red bag up the side of the mountain.

"Tittu," Petru murmured.

A pang of horrible clarity shot through Séverine. They were saying that Tittu was dead, inside that bag. Tittu dead, Bruno injured but alive. If this was indeed Tittu in the bag, dead, Séverine would never see him again. Their last interaction would be him telling her to leave with Petru, that he'd find Bruno—a sacrifice he didn't owe her and that she didn't deserve. She could never earn his forgiveness.

"Is this my fault?" she whispered to Petru, who was also watching the red bag, blankly.

"We knew this was a possibility," he replied, not looking at her. She felt no relief; she would never feel relief.

Séverine thought of Tittu's family—the ill mother, the sister who dreamed of making a life on the continent—watching this on their TV in their final moments of ignorance; or else experiencing a strange knowing that it was their own flesh in that bag.

This helplessness was incomprehensible to Séverine—it must be a failure of action. "We have to get Bruno from the hospital before they send him to prison," she exhorted.

"Séverine, there's nothing we can do," Petru said.

"What about once we get to the continent?" Séverine ventured. "We can do a jailbreak."

"If you get caught, you're going to prison for the rest of your life. Do you understand?" Petru said as if talking to a child. "You're not waltzing up to Fresnes with a machine gun and demanding Bruno's release. You're underground, for real."

Underground, in hiding—yes, that was the plan—but Bruno was supposed to be with her, too. The loss of control made her reel; there must be some way to rewind. But there was no rewinding, just as there had been no rewinding when she was kidnapped. Even then, she'd felt some agency, some crumb of faith in her abilities. Now, she felt utterly helpless. How would she see Bruno again?

On TV, the helicopter flew away with Bruno and Tittu inside, and as it went, it was like the vital force of the island did, too. The whole place suddenly felt desolate to Séverine, inhospitable, like the hunk of cold granite it was.

She clambered for Petru on the couch, and he took her in his arms like a child.

"Do you hate me?" she sobbed.

"I can't," he said, pressing her closer to him. "You're all I have left."

⌒

The TV stayed on, depicting new riots on the island and continent. The newscasters seemed unwilling to specify whether it was in support of what Séverine had done or in protest; either way, Séverine hardly took notice. Around 23:00, Petru went to the kitchen. She heard the rotary phone spinning as he dialed a number—it wasn't a long conversation—then the spit of eggs frying.

A familiar voice brought her attention back to the TV. "I cannot express how devastated my wife and I are to hear of Monsieur Jonnart's death." It was her father, looking haggard, his voice thin. He was at the prefecture in Ajaccio, in the same room where he used to hold press conferences; there was something both correct and humiliating about that.

"I worked closely with Monsieur Jonnart for many years, and he was devoted to his family and country. This is a terrible, terrible loss." He spread some papers on the podium, face downturned.

"It's been reported that Séverine was involved in the shooting. I would like to remind everyone that my daughter is also a victim; she was kidnapped by terrorists and coerced into participating in their deplorable activities. This is not who she is. I am confident that once the investigation of Monsieur Jonnart's murder concludes, my daughter will be exonerated. President Schneider has ordered an exhaustive manhunt for Séverine, and I say—good. It should have been ordered three months ago. Thank you."

He didn't believe what he was saying, she knew, but it was a fine performance. Séverine felt a shred of shame at causing her father to be the kind of lying politician he hated. She wanted so badly to talk to him, to ask his advice, and at the same time, she had no idea how she'd ever face him again.

Petru set a plate of fried eggs in front of her and said, "Eat. We might have to abandon the car on our way to Propriano and do the rest on foot. José says there are checkpoints set up everywhere."

"You mean we're still going to Nice?" Séverine asked. The idea of going without Bruno and Tittu seemed vulgar and futile.

"Yes, we're still going," Petru said, his face tightening. "This was *your* plan!"

"But nothing has gone according to plan!" Séverine cried.

"Not nothing—Jonnart's dead," Petru said coldly. "You had a reason for that—remember launching the fourth revolution?" He suddenly became very angry, his voice thundering. "Why did we just go through all this? Why kill Jonnart? Why's Tittu in a body bag, why's Bruno being helivaced off the island? For what reason, if we're not gonna keep fighting for Corsica?"

"I don't give a shit about Corsica!" she screamed.

Petru went quiet. "You mean that?"

Tears streamed down her face. She shook her head. She had no idea if she meant it or not. She didn't know what to think without the illuminating force of Bruno. She could barely remember what function *Séverine* served, let alone what Jonnart's death was supposed to accomplish.

Petru sat beside her. "You're allowed to be sad. Just not right now. José says people don't know what to think. Some are taking action, but not everyone—a lot of people are nervous about the government reprisal. They need direction and reassurance."

She nodded and wiped her face with the backs of her hands. A communiqué was the one way she might reach Bruno, let him know that she was not giving up, that she'd wait for him. She went into the kitchen, took the pen and legal pad from the junk drawer, and sat at the table. She'd never written a communiqué without Bruno, and she struggled. It didn't sound as elegant as what the public was used to, but it would have to do. Having Petru behind the camcorder Nico had lent them was strange; the natural order of their cell was disrupted, and she could not fathom what it would take to create a new one.

"Six hours ago, Bernard Jonnart was executed for his crimes against the people, which include the murder of Fabien Bartoli; imprisoning our citizens in violation of international law; the use of torture; and persecution against an ethnic collectivity," she said, still wearing the bloodstained dress and Petru's enormous black windbreaker. Her eyes weren't lined in their signature black cat-eye. She hadn't even glanced in the mirror before sitting in front of the camera. She probably looked demented, but she didn't care. She didn't want to perform, she wanted to be real.

"I know the state will come down on us harder than ever, but that's because they're beginning to get how powerful we are. The thing is, they still have no idea. I was one person who did this, but imagine what we can do when we join together.

"If I can execute Jonnart—who, let's be clear, would have had me killed if he'd been able to find me—you can stand up for yourselves, too. Maybe last week while you were protesting, a cop broke your jaw. Make him pay for that. Maybe the PAT destroyed your mammona's house while they looked for guns they knew weren't there. Make them pay for that, too. For too long, we've allowed our oppressors to do whatever they want to us, but we don't have to take it anymore.

"This movement isn't about me, or even just Corsica. It's about everyone who has been screwed over by the ruling class. But they only have that power because we let them. So stop letting them! And when they threaten to come after you, you can come back with the whole movement behind you. The movement is your friends, neighbors, family, and everyone else who's fed up just like you are.

"I'm not a bad person, and neither are you. If someone's hurting the people you love, and you hurt that person back, that's an act of love. It's not destructive if you're trying to make a better world. I'll never give up on that dream, and I know you won't either. Especially now—we're so close to building a new, better Corsica and France. And once we do it, the rest of the world will know they can, too. U futuru avà."

Petru encouraged Séverine to sleep, and Séverine agreed to try. She went into her room and sat dumbly on the bed, staring at the shadows of trees on the wall. She unzipped her jacket and threw it to the floor, feeling like a doll sitting on a doll bed in a dollhouse. She pressed her finger to the bit of Jonnart's blood on her skirt; it transferred, adhering to the swirls of her fingerprint. He was gone, and she'd done it: here was the proof. Here was what still connected her to Bruno; a blood oath sworn with someone else's blood. The quiet took on a hum. Everything was so peaceful, and it felt undeserved, inconsistent. She removed the Beretta from her bag—an impartial killer, a dog trained to fight—unscrewed the silencer, and set it on the nightstand. Numbly, she lay on the bed and closed her eyes.

She woke to the rattling of a car coming up the driveway. Bruno! The dawn light had a pale, underdone quality. The rattling was so loud, louder than the 4x4 alone, and she remembered that Bruno hadn't taken the 4x4. She remembered the stretcher. A surge of adrenaline propelled Séverine to her feet just as Petru burst through the door.

"It's the PAT," he said with military dispassion. He squatted and yanked the black case out from under the bed. "We have to get out before they surround us. Put your boots on."

Sleep-disoriented, she managed to obey. Then she ran to the sitting room and pulled back the yellow curtain: a caravan of black-and-white 4x4s streaked into the front yard. They were faster than her; everything was happening so fast.

"Séverine!" Petru bellowed, and she ran back into the bedroom.

"How did they find us?" she asked.

"Doesn't matter, they're here," Petru replied as he slung the Kalashnikov strap over his head. "Take the Beretta."

"We need our stuff!" She ran first into the kitchen to grab the addressed envelope with the video she'd just recorded, then into the guys' room, where the rucksacks were. They had split the cash among the four rucksacks, and Séverine realized she'd be abandoning over a million francs in Tittu's and Bruno's bags. Feeling like a grave robber, she dumped theirs on the floor and shoveled packets of money into the other two. Car doors slammed, she heard men's voices.

Petru appeared in the doorway; he was dripping in sweat although the morning was unseasonably cool.

"Put it in your bag. Hurry," she told him, handing him a bundle, which he dropped to the ground. She looked up and scowled; without the money they were as good as dead.

"Forget it—we have to go, now," he said.

Some man was saying something on a bullhorn. They heard the glass of the sitting room window crash and something thud on the carpet.

Petru trampled across the remaining bills to wrench open the bedroom window and toss out their packs. He grabbed Séverine's arm and practically flung her through the window as thick, evil tear gas flooded into the bedroom. Her skirt caught and tore on a nail in the windowsill. Petru clambered through, coughing and hacking.

They lugged the rucksacks over their shoulders—the cash added five kilos at least—and sprinted into the maquis. Uniformed officers flooded into the backyard with their FAMAS rifles pressed against their body armor. When they spotted Petru and Séverine crossing into the tree line, they raised their barrels in one synchronous motion. If it weren't for the tree cover, Petru and Séverine would have been mowed down immediately.

As the raucous discord of bullets continued, they pushed deeper into the maquis, past the now-seeded immortelle patch. It was cool and foggy, and Séverine lost sight of Petru as he ran ahead of her; she felt the burden of the extra weight, but he did not. She looked over her shoulder and saw blurry silhouettes becoming sharper; the PAT had penetrated the maquis and were gaining on her, unencumbered.

Petru turned and became aware of how far behind Séverine was lagging. He threw off his rucksack, cocked the Kalashnikov, and shouted, "Keep going!" as he ran towards then past her, shooting into the throng of cops. They took cover behind the trees and returned fire. The sound was cacophonous, desecrating this quiet space. Séverine dropped her own pack and doubled back, but as she reached Petru, he thrust out an elbow to block her. It caught her right in the chest, and she landed on her ass.

"Go!" he hollered as he reloaded.

"I'm not leaving you," she said, positioning herself behind a tree and shooting blindly; the dawn mist was so thick, it was impossible to properly aim, or even know which direction the enemy's bullets were coming from.

"Séverine, go!" Petru repeated. He turned to look at her. He was sweating, and his eyes had a fervent, ecstatic brightness, like Joan of Arc willing the fire to engulf her. It scared Séverine. An ancient side of humanity had been awakened in Petru, and she knew she must respect it; it was a holy force. A bullet exploded a chunk off the tree he was hiding behind, only a few inches above his head, and he broke eye contact with her to shoot back. He was one against dozens. Séverine knew how this would go down, and so did Petru.

Mindlessly, she obeyed, turning away from Petru, grabbing her pack, and running into the dense, gray maquis with an acquiescence that was perhaps the other side of the coin of Petru's zeal.

There was commotion behind her—they'd overtaken Petru, she knew with a stomach-turning feeling. But she pressed on. Running down a hill, running up a hill, scrambling over a rock, splashing through a creek. She couldn't see four feet ahead of her, and all the time, her pursuers following. She felt a runner's high, her breathing labored but even, her head clear and empty, the pack bumping against her back in a consistent rhythm. It might have been five minutes or thirty or thirty thousand that she'd been running through this forest. She could do this forever, this physical action that warded off thinking.

Séverine ran until she almost tripped into a wide stream that blocked her way; she reeled with déjà vu. This stream. This maquis. Cursed, cursed. But it wasn't the time to be superstitious. She waded into the bracing water up to her rib cage, and her veins throbbed with the full pressure of her blood. The current strengthened towards the center of the stream, just as it had before, but this time Séverine pushed on. She slipped and spun a ways downstream, her hands and legs scraping on little jagged stones until she was able to dig her boots into the mud and latch onto a large, algae-covered rock. She caught her breath, then forged onward. When she scrabbled onto the other side of the stream, she lay with her face in the grass for one moment, grateful for this frantic heartbeat and breath.

Not far was a huge slab of granite jutting up from the ground, and she crawled behind it, panting and sore, and waited. Nothing but the twittering of oblivious birds. And yet the calm seemed like a trick.

The sun began to color the fog a goldish green. It was officially morning. Tittu was dead. Petru had to be dead. Bruno would live, she knew instinctively, but he was lost to her. She wanted to die but also refused to. And remaining in this maquis, teeth chattering with fear and cold, was a sort of death that she couldn't stand any longer.

Séverine lifted herself out from behind the rock, looking all around, through the trees, on the other side of the bank, up above. No one.

She moved deeper into the woods, to a spot that was thickly covered with trees and began to rise at a steep incline. There she changed into dry clothes: khaki shorts, an Oktoberfest sweatshirt from Petru's aunt, and a khaki sun hat. The idea was to pass as a hiker. The wig was in her straw tote back at the bergerie; one more fuckup to add to the list.

She picked through the pack to make sure everything was undamaged. The francs were sopping but intact in their little bundles; everything else had been stored in plastic: tent, sleeping bag, groundsheet, clothes, first aid kit, flashlight, packaged food and utensils, water bladder and purification tablets, Swiss Army knife, Ziploc bag with two boxes of 9mm ammo (a thousand rounds each), and another Ziploc with her fake carte d'identité, map, compass, her annotated copy of *Les damnés de la terre*, matches, cigarettes, and a waterproof watch, which she strapped on her wrist. It read 07:23.

The PAT must have come just after 06:00, and it couldn't have been more than fifteen minutes from the time she woke up to fleeing into the maquis—it was hard to wrap her mind around. But she had to think ahead: if she was to get to Propriano by 11:00, when the charter was scheduled to leave, she'd have to hitchhike or—ridiculous as it sounded—call a taxi. Either way, she needed to get to civilization.

She buried the bloodstained dress, filled her water bladder in the stream, shrugged on her pack, and began walking southeast. In her mind, she saw Petru's thick finger dragging along the map, from the stream to the T20 to Terraperta. Sure enough, after about twenty minutes, she reached the road. She didn't have it in her to laugh, let alone imagine the alternate trajectory of the last couple months if she'd only forded the stream the first time she'd wandered into this maquis.

She marched on, staying just deep enough in the woods that she could follow the road without walking on it. Few cars passed, and anyway, Séverine couldn't work up the courage to jump out and thumb a ride. For the first time in a long while, she felt vulnerable.

She wished to be all physicality, nothing but automatic electrical pulses—but against her will, Séverine's brain stirred up images she'd rather ignore: Bruno on the stretcher, Bruno in his navy polo, Bruno standing with his mouth slightly open in Jonnart's hotel room. The lifeless red bag. Petru unloading the Kalashnikov into the swarm of PAT officers. She couldn't even let herself pray for the miracle of his aliveness. How the fuck did the police know where to find them? It required the utmost concentration for her despair to remain un-spilled, and in the silence of the maquis, it was beginning to slosh over.

She reached Terraperta at 08:45. There was nothing to do but emerge from the woods and stroll into town. As she wandered into the village, she felt like a ghost in a ghost town—no one was sitting on their porch, no one working in their garden or shopping at the market. The only sign that the town had ever been inhabited was someone's laundry on the line, white linens whipping in the wind like flags of surrender.

When she came to the post office, Séverine dropped the enve-lope with the videotape into a mailbox, then made her way to the pay phone. She flipped through the phone book and found the number for Chez Martine. But once she poised her finger over the first but-ton, she hesitated. Say she went to Nice. The guy who was supposed to shelter them was Bruno's friend; she had no idea how to get a hold of him. If she could somehow make her way to Paris, Pilar would surely take her in (Hélène was a maybe—she was such a priss about getting in trouble), but she couldn't realistically hide in her friends' parents' apartments. Novi Patriotti would put her in contact with sympathizers on the continent, but she didn't want to fight without her comrades, without their fantasy to live up to and inhabit; she didn't want the violence without the refuge and release of Bruno— without their love for each other, if a word so insipid could describe whatever the four of them experienced together.

What was the promise she'd made to Bruno, exactly? What did she still need to do to honor their commitment, to avenge him and Petru and Tittu? It would never be enough, and she couldn't do it without them anyway. She wasn't like Petru, though, prepared for martyrdom. She was meant to be alive, and any version of her continuing the fight ended with her dead, she knew now. Let Novi Patriotti lead the charge; she'd delivered them an uprising like a cat with a still-alive mouse in its mouth. Let them finish it off however they wanted.

She dialed her father's mobile.

"Séverine?" he asked uneasily.

"It's me," she said.

He released a sob of relief and anguish. She heard her mother in the background asking, "Is she okay?" in a weak, weepy voice that she'd never imagined her mother could produce.

"I wanna go with you and Mom to Australia or wherever. Please don't make me talk about the rest."

Composing himself, he said, "We can't go anywhere right now; we're being monitored. A car has been parked outside of the house since last night. We can't leave the country while I'm under investigation— not while Pignon is being held hostage."

"What are you talking about?"

"Haven't you heard?" It was her mother, wrangling the phone away. "A mob stormed Lantivy and took Pignon. Eight people are dead. The PAT officers are beginning to desert. Schneider's sending the army down."

Séverine didn't respond; the news washed over her. It strangely meant nothing to her.

"We can't leave, but there are people who'll help you get to the States."

"The States?"

"One, you're an American citizen, so the US won't extradite you," her mother said. "You won't have that same protection anywhere else. Two, you speak the language. You'll have the same comforts you've had your whole life. We can get money to you there; we already have a reason to go. We want you to be able to live as freely as possible."

"You think I deserve that? After what I've done?" Séverine asked tearfully, thinking not of Jonnart but her comrades.

"You were kidnapped, Séverine. You were forced to do things you'd never, ever do otherwise," her mother said slowly and vehemently, as if she were trying to reprogram her, impressing upon her the statement Séverine could fall back on if she ever needed to.

Her parents explained their plan, the one that had been set up for weeks, if not months. All the players were in place, waiting to ferry her to Sardinia, then a long list of other locales that led west. She half listened, her brain ticking like a cooling engine. No more thinking. She'd follow their instructions like the obedient child she'd never managed to be.

⌒

While Séverine waited at the edge of the maquis for her ride, she took out *Les damnés de la terre*. The sentimental object was imbued with the holiness of a relic—a remnant of Bruno. As she flipped through, she realized Bruno had replied to her notes; she'd had no idea. Where, next to Fanon's description of the sensation of revenge, she'd written *Sounds like love*, Bruno had written *Not normal love, but being in love with Séverine, yes*. She found herself crying with abandon, unafraid of letting her sobs echo through the woods, which had absorbed sobs of equal anguish: so many dead lovers, dead sons in the history of this island. Séverine's grief may not have been new in the scope of history, but it was new to her.

An hour later, a car pulled up to the designated mile marker. Black, perfectly discreet, just like its driver: a man of indefinable age with indefinable characteristics. He wasn't chatty either. He pulled a hidden tab behind the back seat, which popped out to reveal a slim compartment between the seat and trunk that Séverine was to crawl into. It seemed to have been constructed with the express purpose of hiding people.

As he helped her into the compartment, she felt his professionalism waver, as if he wanted to tear his hand away. She dared herself to meet his gaze, and he looked at the floor. It wasn't the fascination she was used to, but some curdled version that made her stomach turn, that made her afraid of herself and what she'd done. He shut her into the compartment, and she remembered entering the interior of the island like this, cramped in the trunk of some rental car. She guessed it was only right she leave the same way.

⁓

When they arrived, the driver popped open the compartment and pulled Séverine out of the car. There was the sea in front of her, gray and hazy as the still-foggy sky, and rows and rows of boats. There was a freshness in the air, a slate-blue quality that stripped the sand and sun of its summer goldenness. She realized the dock was right beside the paillote where she'd seduced Antoine Carsenti that whole lifetime ago, and laughed aloud. The tables and chairs were stacked, the umbrellas closed like dormant flowers.

Another man came from the pier, took Séverine's bag, and led her to the boat. She turned to thank the driver, but he'd already pulled away. Walking down the dock, she felt like she was meeting Charon to ferry her off to hell. The boat he led her to was a modest yacht; the stern read *Onore di capitanu*. They boarded, winding down the tight spiral staircase into the gently rocking cabin. Blond wood, long upholstered benches with overstuffed pillows. The captain continued to the cockpit in the bow of the boat, where a short bench faced all the myriad controls and buttons and lights.

In these close quarters, she got a better look at him. He was radiating something odd, respect without reverence: the respect one has for a viper in a glass case.

"Thank you for what you're doing for me," Séverine said. Her voice came out differently than it had in a long time, like a teenage girl's.

"It's not charity," he said, his tone perfunctory. "You'll have to lie down in here." He popped open the bench. "You can come up after we leave port, but if we run into any patrol boats, you'll have to go back in."

Séverine maneuvered herself into the compartment. He shut her in, and the seat squeaked as he sat on it. Then the boat rumbled to life, vibrating beneath her. The last twenty-four hours had been so excruciating, so cataclysmic, that she was suspicious when ten minutes later, the captain told her she could come up. But naturally her parents would arrange her escape to go like clockwork. The best that money could buy.

When she climbed out and positioned herself on the bench, she saw only open sea. The fog had been burned off by the sun, which hovered right above them, bright and white, an exploding star. Its blazing light trailed along the surface of the waves, glinting with both menace and optimism—that of a renewed earth after the flood. Oh, Bruno, he in the air and she on the water. She sent out a prayer, fierce and quiet as a flame, that they would find each other; their love was buried alive in this land, and she swore one day to exhume it.

"Where's the island?" she asked the captain.

"Behind us. We're heading east-southeast," he replied.

Séverine had envisioned herself watching the island fade away, but she wouldn't have that bittersweet pleasure. Instead, she faced nothing but sea, vast and unknown.

Los Angeles

2013

1. *Good Behavior*

Tara Lane had gotten it into her head that she could surf the wave of popularity from *A Life Like Any Other* out of soaps and straight to the A-list, which meant Ramona Frisch was frantically scheduling auditions for a replacement when she received an even more frantic call from her daughter.

"Ricky dumped me. The day before yesterday," Petra blurted tearfully. "I know you hated him, and I know I'm moving back home tomorrow, but can you come downtown this afternoon? Everyone's busy with finals, and I just need—some—support—"

Petra was a freshman in USC's Interdisciplinary Major Program, pursuing a very sensible degree in "Grassroots Activism in the Age of Neoliberalism." Ramona had planned on working through lunch but agreed to drive down. Petra said she was scheduled for dinner prep at the soup kitchen and suggested Ramona join her there before her shift; Ramona laughed and said to meet her at the restaurant inside the L'Adresse Hotel.

She knew most mothers would love to be the first person their daughter called for advice and comfort, but it concerned Ramona. Petra should have friends she'd rather talk about boys with. Ramona had tried to raise Petra to be independent, and in many ways she was. But for some reason, she continued to cling to her mother at a time when most kids couldn't stand their parents, and Ramona feared the reason was her own unconscious failure.

Traffic was light, and Ramona arrived early. She smiled suspiciously when the hot young host gave her the up-down eyes. He was at most thirty, a child when the *60 Minutes* special on Séverine Guimard and the Summer of Terror aired. The unrest had only occupied the back pages of the world news section in the US, as anything that happened outside this country was a curiosity, irrelevant.

For peace of mind, the Cuban nose job had been well worth the $1,700 and weeks of suffering during which she'd eaten nothing but mashed yuca (every time she swallowed, it felt like the pressure would push her eyes from their sockets). Still, Ramona would never forget peeling off the nasal cast and upon seeing her new, unremarkable nose—the cartilage thin and straight as a finger, the nose she'd always dreamed of—bursting into hysterical tears. But perhaps her paranoia was irrelevant; Ramona understood with relief and regret that the older she got, the less chance there was of anyone recognizing something in her thinning mouth or slackening jawline that they'd seen on TV twenty years earlier.

"Let me clear these for you," the host said, collecting the newspapers some guest had left after finishing their breakfast.

"Can I keep this one?" Ramona asked, putting her hand on a copy of *Le Monde*. "I'll practice my French while I wait."

Just as she began scanning headlines—"Le Sénat adopte l'article qui ouvre le mariage aux homosexuels"—Petra hurtled through the door. She was always rushing, always looking harried. With her hair unbrushed and blown about, her hazel eyes wide and panicky, she brought the impression of a cold blast of wind into the restaurant. She plunked into the seat opposite Ramona and let her ratty canvas tote slump off the chairback, onto the floor. She was wearing black jeans, black nurse clogs, and a faded black T-shirt under a man's denim jacket. Ramona's only daughter could be so pretty, but she considered all that grooming a waste of time. Lucky for both of them, she had not inherited the original nose.

Right away, Petra started to cry, unashamed to carry on as the waiter brought her water glass.

"I'm so sorry, sweetie," Ramona said, doing her best impression of empathy. What she really wanted to say was that Petra was better off, that she'd realize it sooner than felt possible now; that she could use the indignity of being dumped as motivation to remold herself, to be more outgoing and fun and a tiny bit stupid in a refreshing, forgivable way. But she'd given some version of this speech dozens of times, and Petra never wanted to hear it.

"It was awful, and doing it the last day of the semester was so calculated," Petra replied, dragging her napkin across her nose.

Ramona had hated Ricky from the moment she shook his hand outside some consciously hip downtown restaurant last October, only blocks from City Hall, which Petra had "occupied" on weekends during the fall of her senior year of high school. He was originally from New York, and his cliché comments about LA's vapidity, the pleasure he took in his own obnoxiousness—Ramona found it all abhorrent.

The thing was, she'd gotten what she'd wished for. USC was not an obvious fit for Petra, but Ramona had hoped she might reinvent herself, loosen up, get a hot, dumb, fratty boyfriend. She hadn't expected her to find the one militant on campus. She certainly didn't want Petra to loosen up the way Ramona had been loose at that age.

But she completely understood why Petra gravitated towards him: having Ricky for a boyfriend gave Petra a sense of herself she liked. He was brash, confident, and uncompromising in his beliefs. Cautious, earnest Petra, meanwhile, was still searching for her purpose—she volunteered for the Fight for $15 campaign, a community garden in South Central, and at the soup kitchen; she was also a member of Students for Justice in Palestine and had recently completed Narcan training. Ramona knew, when you can't *be* a certain way, sleeping with someone who *is* is the next best thing, but it was essential Petra eventually unearth those qualities in herself.

"Are we ready to order?" the waiter asked.

Ramona pushed her gold bracelet watch down on her wrist and snuck a glance. She needed to be back in Burbank in an hour and a half at the latest. They ordered, Ramona asking for her food to go and grimacing in apology at Petra.

"It's been so crazy at work," she explained. Ramona thought of all the headshots she'd pored over the last week, all the lukewarm screen tests, and sent out a prayer that one of these actresses would be right. But she hadn't been summoned to talk about her own problems. She reached across the table and placed a hand on her daughter's arm. "Are you okay?" she asked as gently as she could.

Petra let the floodgates loose, ranting about the signs she'd missed, her suspicion he was cheating, while Ramona nodded along, thinking her own thoughts. At only nineteen, her daughter was so busy and thoughtful, determined to solve the world's problems. She'd been this way since she was a toddler, instinctually collecting litter off the sidewalk. Then, it was cute (if disconcerting that such interests could be genetic), but as an adult, Petra ran the risk of becoming rigid, a woman who'd one day stop listening to music or watching art films and would only read books of nonfiction that dealt explicitly with her work.

That said, there were worse alternatives—just ask Bonnie Guimard. Over Christmas, Ramona had caught Petra reading a biography of Celia Sánchez, and she'd blanched then let out a queer laugh, startling Petra. The thought of her daughter as a guerrilla fighter was horrifying and absurd; she was both dangerously close to and laughably far from following in her mother's footsteps. Petra talked a big game about rejecting capitalism and bringing down neoliberal institutions, but she would never try the methods Soffiu di Libertà did.

Or would she? an irrational voice asked. No, not this one, Ramona told herself with motherly knowing. In high school, Petra came home at midnight every weekend even though Ramona had never set a curfew. She still had a habit of texting Ramona throughout the day to let her know where she was; it seemed less a safety measure than to provide Ramona reassurance she didn't need. At heart, her daughter was a rule-follower, and any change she effected would be the slow kind, the kind Lydia had advocated for all those years ago. Petra was patient and steady and sensible. Ramona didn't need to worry about her the way *her* mother had.

The food came, and Petra asked the waiter, "Actually, could I get a to-go box, too?" She turned to Ramona. "Sorry, I just remembered they asked me to come early to help with the Facebook page."

"Go, go," Ramona sighed, and Petra ran off while Ramona waited for the server to bring the check. She returned to *Le Monde* with partial attention, flipping to the bottom half of the paper: a review of a new poetry collection by Houellebecq, a summary of yesterday's quarterfinals game between PSG and Barcelona, and "Bruno Pieri libéré."

Ramona's heartbeat accelerated and her limbs trembled with a pure shot of adrenaline. Her senses felt blown out, like she'd narrowly stepped out of the way of a roaring train, but no one else in the café seemed affected. She was alone with this revelation. Carefully, as if the words in the article might cause her literal harm, she read that Bruno's thirty-year sentence had been reduced for good behavior and expressing remorse.

"'Let me remind you that M. Pieri took no one's life,' a representative from his legal team commented. 'Twenty years served is more than appropriate for the conviction. We are very happy with the judge's decision.'" A summary followed of the events of that summer—what they called "L'été de terreur." Then, "When asked how he planned to spend his newfound freedom, M. Pieri said, 'Continuing the peaceful fight for Corsican autonomy, taking long walks around my ancestral village, and eating a lot of coppa.'" *Autonomy*. There was no photo.

"Take your time," the waiter said as he placed the check on top of the article. Ramona gave a weak, spacey smile. Bruno was out. She felt slightly exhilarated and enormously afraid. She was being irrational; he didn't so much as know her name or where she lived. Why did she think he'd want to hurt her anyway? He'd loved her! He'd loved her—that's exactly why he'd want to hurt her. He'd loved her and she'd fled, abandoning the cause. She'd fled and never tried contacting him. Not to say she hadn't wanted to. The ache she'd felt for that man—she'd cried so much those first days in Sardinia that it had become a security risk, the hotel manager knocking on her door to relay her neighbors' complaints.

Actually, she'd written Bruno many, many letters: incoherent letters that declared love and fidelity; that dared to rehash lingering, petty resentments; that blamed him in hysterical, incendiary language; and letters that were pure smut. Any time she developed photos of Petra, she considered mailing him the doubles without comment, knowing he'd recognize the shape of his mouth, her dark hair and olive skin as his own. Instead, for many years, Ramona had talked to Bruno inwardly, as if he were God. She'd think, *Bruno, your little girl took her first steps today. It only took fifteen months. She's like you, so cautious, nothing like me who barrels towards everything.* Sometimes those conversations turned to actual prayers that he would hear her, that he'd feel her love suffuse him in his cell all those thousands of miles away. But time healed the wound of his absence no matter how intent she was on scratching it open, to maintain the connection. Eventually, she felt as grateful for that healing as she'd been desperate for the wound to stay fresh.

The waiter came to the table and tactfully retreated, noticing no credit card had been placed in the tray. Ramona was running late.

"Sorry," she mumbled, pushing aside the newspaper. She handed him a hundred-dollar bill and hurried out of the restaurant to resume her real life.

That day was a bust; news of Bruno's release was feeling like a bad omen. As she was trying to work, moments Ramona hadn't thought about in years appeared in disorienting flashes. The grainy Sardinian yogurt she ate each morning, drizzled with honey; the yellow walls and pink and red tile of her Havana hotel; the soldiers at her door saying if she wanted asylum, she'd have to accept a work assignment in one of the resorts; how she'd burst into tears upon seeing the lawyer her mother's friend sent to Tijuana, an unknown face that felt familiar because it was only two degrees separated from her mom.

That was when she received her new passport with its falsified stamps, her new identity. The first Ramona Patience Frisch was born January 14, 1973—adding two and a half years to Séverine's age—and died two days later. This fact repulsed her. At first, assuming this identity felt like wearing a coat of someone else's skin.

But she was now accustomed to doing distasteful things. It had been essential that she get to the US before the baby was born so there would be no complicated questions of its citizenship. They'd cut it close, but Ramona rode across the border in a hired car and made her way to the women's shelter in the Santa Ynez Valley at thirty-nine weeks pregnant.

The shelter was a commune, mostly off-grid, a forgotten relic of the radical seventies, which is what made it safer than being set up alone in an apartment in some city. Ramona gave birth there—terrified to be assisted by midwives instead of doctors, terrified by the unmitigated pain and unsterilized nature of a home birth, and yet somehow she did it—and stayed four years. Four years of sweeping, stacking firewood, mending clothes, cooking, tending to chickens, washing the dishes and diapers of eight women and their children, plus a rotating cast of refugees.

Initially, she confused and frustrated the women of the shelter with her airs, her ineptitude and aversion to their lifestyle. The women were not always friendly with her, nor she with them. But they understood that if she'd ended up there it was because she'd survived some nightmare, maybe like the one they'd survived, so they tolerated Ramona. It was obvious when someone told only half their story, but the women never pried for more details.

It was also one of the saddest parts of life underground, that there was no one to talk to about what had happened. So far from Corsica, knowing no one, having adopted a new identity, Ramona sometimes wondered if any of it had really happened. But there was one souvenir she'd brought with her.

As soon as she got home, Ramona went directly to the safe in her walk-in closet. She keyed in the code and removed a folder containing her and Petra's essential documents; some jewelry a married studio exec had given her years ago (yellow gold and emerald cut, proof of how out of his depth he was, how excruciatingly boring the sex the one time she'd capitulated); and a copy of her will. Underneath this pile lay Bruno's edition of *Les damnés de la terre.*

She left the jewelry and papers strewn across the beige-pink carpet of the closet and padded towards the window beside her bed, opening the front cover of the slightly dry-rotted book in the golden-hour light. The spine made a peevish cracking sound. She hadn't touched it since she'd first put it in the safe twelve years before, when they moved into this house. A signature, in blue ballpoint pen, greeted her: *Bruno Pieri.* She shivered with some entrenched memory of the hand that had written that name. As she flipped each page, she read Bruno's notes and her notes in response, and it was like being in conversation with him again.

Some of them were humorless rebuttals (*Territorial collectivity = limited control over crucial gov't orgs i.e. justice system*), but also questions posed back to her (*Might lycéens identify the colonizer with the parent? Metaphorical patricide?*), as well as his own jokes and flirtations (adding to a stick man's penis so it dragged on the ground; below Séverine's *My ransom* ☺ writing *Not worth it* ☹).

Like a fool, when she read his profession of love, she felt the same girlish flutters as the first time. But she also felt re-familiarized with Séverine, recognizing parts of her—a tone, a way of wrapping her head around new information—that still resided within Ramona.

The first blow to Séverine the persona was when her nose was shattered. The second was giving birth. Third was the humbling experience of the women's shelter. Early on, she'd had an argument with the council about procuring eyeliner, and one woman had quipped, "Don't worry about looking pretty for us, honey." In that moment, Ramona had the unsettling realization that everything she'd ever done, any choice she'd ever made, was in consideration of men. Without an audience of even one man, who was she?

It was reflexive to shed Séverine's worst vanities at the shelter, but in LA, Séverine needed to be fully repressed. For the safety of her little family, she had to become Ramona Frisch. Luckily, it didn't require much effort: Séverine primarily spoke French, Ramona only spoke English; Séverine had family and friends, Ramona was effectively an orphan; Séverine had a big schnoz to compensate for, Ramona had an unexceptional nose, a conventional beauty. To be sure, there were elements of Séverine that were impossible to exorcise, and it would have been misguided to try—her charm and sociability, her way with men.

Thanks to these qualities, Ramona, upon arriving in Los Angeles with the last $7,000 of her ransom, arranged for the super of their building to babysit Petra one night a week and quickly began making the right kind of friends—like Amy Diehl, whom she met in line for the bathroom at The Cherry. Over the manic thump of the music, Ramona recounted the Official Story: She was born in Sedalia, Missouri, to religious fanatics who'd thrown her out when she got pregnant at twenty. Petra's father was a sweet, simple man who was four years older than Ramona, someone she'd loved from a distance as a child. He'd gone off to Bosnia with the army as part of a humanitarian relief operation and was killed in a car accident. Petra hadn't even been born yet. With no family and no boyfriend, Ramona took a Greyhound west, and the rest was history.

Through Amy, Ramona landed her first job as a production assistant—Amy's father was executive producer of *Hotel Rondelle*, a soap opera that had aired on NBC for two decades. Although she had no experience or education in the field, Ramona quickly worked her way up and around the network's soaps division; there was always some superior who took a shine to her, who sympathized with her story and wanted to help this young single mother make her way in the world. After a few years, one of the senior producers at *A Life*

Like Any Other recommended her to Bunny Davis, CSA, when her longtime assistant was poached by CBS.

At first, it was painful being in such close proximity to the actors. Other women's good looks and charisma felt like a personal affront. Ramona would find herself silently fuming during auditions, knowing that she was better, that *she could have made it*. After one particularly exasperating audition, Bunny took Ramona aside and said, "This business might be full of egos, but our little corner of it is not. You wanna act the big shot, go right ahead, but you won't be working for me."

In that moment, Ramona understood she needed to bury the old dream once and for all. She devoted herself to work, gradually building a life for her daughter that approximated the one she'd enjoyed growing up. Now she found other women's beauty creatively stimulating, as if it could be innovated and advanced through her own special talent for making actors feel reassured and paid the attention they deserved.

Over time, she'd begun to think of Séverine as the id, suppressed by the ego of the tempered, adult Ramona. However, as she sat on her bed reacquainting herself with Séverine's mind, she encountered a more sophisticated person than she'd remembered. She was only a little younger than Petra when she'd written these words. She knew Petra considered her hopelessly bourgeoise, and likely Séverine would have, too. After all, she'd abandoned Séverine's project. She'd abandoned most of her hard principles with zero guilt. Throughout Petra's childhood, Ramona did consider how Bruno, so much more dogmatic, would want his daughter raised, but she always came back to the same conclusion: he wasn't there.

Honestly, he may as well have been that imaginary Midwestern boy killed overseas for all the influence he exerted on Ramona's parenting, and perhaps it was better that way. More likely than not, arguing over how to raise their child would have ruined their relationship; together, they might have damaged Petra worse than Ramona had alone. She closed the book and tossed it with contrived indifference onto her nightstand. Life would continue as it had for the last twenty years, without Bruno.

2. Homecoming

I t was move-out day, and Petra was packed and ready to go at 3:00 p.m., when her mother was supposed to come collect her and all her stuff in the Prius. However, a lengthy message from Ramona popped up, a terse apology that work was too crazy to leave, she was sending a car, and she'd made reservations at Triton's that night. As usual, Petra was both annoyed at being ditched and pleased by the thought of getting a nice dinner out of her mom in compensation. When Ramona deemed an event important—like work obligations or birthdays—she came with bells on. But anything deemed *un*important? There was a fifty-fifty chance of her making an appearance, and she'd later compensate with fancy dinners or concert tickets, activities she herself enjoyed. Petra enjoyed these outings, too, but wished her mother understood that it would mean more to show up the times she'd rather be elsewhere.

A young, stocky Armenian guy showed up in Ramona's stead and efficiently loaded everything into the town car. Petra slid into the back, across the AC-cooled leather seats, feeling like a spoiled brat. On campus, among so many ostentatious displays of wealth, it was uncomfortable to feel on the "wrong side" of these class confrontations.

The car wound up Laurel Canyon, and the light softened and greened through the tree canopy. Petra felt so much tenderness towards this place that would always be home. That was part of why she'd ended up at USC; she couldn't imagine not being able to return whenever she wanted. And she couldn't imagine leaving her mom all alone up here.

They climbed farther up the canyon and turned down the familiar potholed driveway. The property was unruly with old trees and bushes and overgrown tangles of flowers, and nestled among this leafy mess was Petra's childhood home: an oversized storybook cottage with false towers, mismatched windows, ivy blanketing the roof, and an air of aristocratic dilapidation. It was so weird. Even though it had delighted her as a child (what little girl wouldn't want to live somewhere so magical?), she couldn't understand why her mother bought it; Ramona was the most meticulously styled woman Petra knew. It seemed to imply some arrested development of her psychology, like she wanted to forever be a teenage Sleeping Beauty hiding in the fairies' cottage. Still, Petra loved the house. It was a safe haven, a place meant only for Petra and Ramona, as if protected by some charm.

"I drive all the bosses from the studio," the driver said with a slight accent as he pulled Petra's suitcases from the trunk. "They live in big glass houses worth ten, fifteen million. But this one is my favorite. It's like a Disney movie."

"Thanks," she replied, a little embarrassed. She opened the front door, and the driver came in with the first suitcase.

"Very nice, very classy," he said, nodding in approval at the walnut floors, the red and ivory Persian rug, the olive-green sideboard with a vase of white lilacs, the arched pass-throughs into the living room and kitchen, and the hand-carved balusters going up the stairs. As he bustled back and forth from the car, Petra found herself within his haze of tacky cologne, something manufactured to be erotic, and it was working. Everything about him radiated a fastidious masculinity and cleanliness—cleanliness, a foreign concept to Ricky. Ricky had been her first boyfriend, and she'd really thought she could be with him forever. Despite her mother's urging, she hadn't been interested in playing the field. Nevertheless, a familiar tingle ran up the backs of her legs.

After the driver brought in the last box, Petra timidly asked, "Do you want a drink?"

He grinned, more to himself than Petra. "I gotta get back," he said, offering a pressed-lip smile before he left. It was not unkind, but even that mortified her.

Petra showered, shaving her calves and underarms to avoid any pointed comments from her mother, then dug through her closet, but all the clothes reminded her of who she'd been in high school: shy, searching.

Even if Petra still didn't have her shit together, she wasn't that meek high schooler either—she was no longer a virgin; she'd survived her first breakup; next week she was going to start an internship at a tenants' rights organization in Boyle Heights. She was an adult, and she wanted to look like one, which inspired her to do something she never did: wander into her mother's room to raid her closet, thinking specifically of a black leather miniskirt from Zadig & Voltaire.

It had always been understood that Petra was not to root around her mom's bedroom; nothing was ever said, but Ramona's room was decidedly *her* space. To be fair, that respect extended to Petra's room as well, so entering felt like a little transgression.

A late afternoon drowsiness permeated the bedroom, accentuated by the lingering scents of the expensive amber perfume bottled in some French countryside that Ramona spritzed on her neck every morning. Everything so tasteful but never dull: the linen window shades, the Qing dynasty elm wood armoire that housed the TV, the plush white bedding at the foot of the French cane bed, which matched the cane armchair reupholstered in Schumacher's powder-blue Woodland Leopard velvet. Petra hated that she knew what that was.

She meandered into the walk-in closet, turned on the light, and gasped at the documents and jewelry strewn across the floor. At first, she thought they'd been robbed, but as Petra gathered the objects and placed them back into the safe, she was relieved to find everything valuable was still there (in fact, there were pieces of jewelry she'd never seen before). Still, it was strange; Ramona was too neat to leave this mess.

Petra ran her fingers along her mother's clothes, mostly crisp white shirts and tailored trousers with some eclectic pieces in rich colors and textures thrown in, but she was too distracted to browse, questioning what Ramona had pulled from the safe. She wandered out of the closet. Even the bed was mussed—or rather, the one slim quadrant her mother slipped into every night. Petra tugged up the corner of the bedspread and noticed a strange book on the nightstand.

It was in French, which was normal enough; her mother had an embarrassing preoccupation with France, subscribing to a special French television package, saying words like "croissant" with an overblown accent, special-ordering French titles from an Iranian bookstore in Westwood. Petra found this fixation juvenile and parochial, like a Midwestern housewife who collected Eiffel Tower figurines and dreamed of her husband taking her to Paris.

What was strange was that the book was by Frantz Fanon. What in the world was her mother doing reading postcolonial theory? There was no person on earth more apolitical than Ramona Frisch; she cared about her job, clothes, house, a good meal, and not much else, to Petra's exasperation. She opened the book, so old and yellowed that she nearly split it in two, and found little notes written in French down the sides of the pages; whole passages were underlined and starred, some in her mother's distinctly loopy handwriting and some in the careless, unquestionably masculine handwriting of a second person. It looked like a conversation between her mother and this other person, but Petra could only decipher a few cognates: "révolution," "libération," "méthodes," "violence." Those were enough to confuse her further. She'd never heard her mother speak French in full sentences, and although she bought the books and watched the French news in bed at night, Petra had assumed it was some lukewarm attempt to learn the language, that the words washed over her. She had no idea her mother's French was this advanced.

She flipped to the first page and found an inscription: *Pour mon serpent chéri: que l'on reprenne notre paradis. Basgiu, Bruno.* She took her phone from her pocket and typed the sentence into Google Translate: "For my darling snake: let us take back our paradise." But it didn't translate "basgiu" or even suggest what language it was. She took a picture of the page. Below the inscription was written *juillet 1993*. This book, the notes inside it, predated Petra, but not by long.

She replaced the book on the nightstand as she found it. The quiet in the room felt unbearably heavy—haunted. Numbly, Petra went down the stairs and strode out the front door. She took a deep breath but felt no comfort nor sense of escape. Her old Volvo sat in the driveway; she grabbed the keys from the hook inside the entry-way, started the car, and rolled onto Laurel Canyon.

Climbing up the hill towards the Valley, she attained a tentative composure despite the wild thoughts spinning in her head. The book was not an innocent object; it was a portal, and one foot was already irredeemably over the threshold. July 1993. Petra was born May 9, 1994. The book, presumably exhumed from the safe where it had been hidden all this time, exuded a significance she could read without knowing the language.

For the first time in her life, Petra's anxious mind quieted. She knew everything was about to be different. It made her hyper-aware of the sun blazing upon her left arm, the sweat surfacing to her upper lip, the nervous tick of her heart. By contrast, the cars whizzing by and the people inside seemed less real. Their lives were invariable. But Petra now occupied an in-between state, and there was nothing to do but wait for whatever happened next.

When she returned home, she first went back to her mother's walk-in closet and redistributed the contents of the safe across the floor as she'd found them. Then she went to the kitchen to pour herself a glass of already-uncorked chardonnay and brought it to her bedroom, where she sat at the white wicker vanity from her girl-hood. She remembered applying her mother's mostly used-up lipstick in this mirror, wondering what she'd be like as a grown-up. The image of that child was superimposed over the image of who she was now, in her men's Oxford shirt with the sleeves rolled above her elbows. And it would keep evolving, but some part of her would remain all these other selves. She wondered what remained of her mother from when she'd written about revolution in the margins of that book.

Outside, gravel crunched beneath tires. The front door opened and there was a clatter of car keys, bags dumped on the floor, and heels kicked off. Her mother's arrival always seemed to animate the house in an agitated way, but today especially.

"Petra?" Ramona called.

"I'm getting dressed," Petra hollered back.

Ramona climbed the stairs and knocked on the frame of the open door. "Sorry about move-out day, my meeting went late. Still no decent replacements, so everyone's starting to panic." Although she was from some shit town in Missouri, Ramona emanated a lived-in, sophisticated Europeanness. Today, it took the form of a black silk shawl draped around her in some simultaneously effortless and complicated-looking way, Lanvin ballet flats, and gold stacking rings on clean and unpolished fingers.

"It's okay, the guy did basically everything," Petra said absently. She was nervous, as if trying to hide her knowledge of a crime. Ramona had lied about something to do with Petra's existence, and Petra needed to take care digging up the real story; her mother was not someone who tolerated accusations or caved easily. A small, compassionate part of Petra considered she might have her reasons. The women's shelter, of which Petra had watery memories—the smell of roasting carrots, her head pressed against an unfamiliar breast—suggested an escape from some violence, not wanting to be found. It was just so hard to imagine her mother a victim.

"Well, I'm glad you're home," Ramona said, and leaned down to embrace Petra. They didn't often touch like this. Quick cheek kisses hello and goodbye, yes, but these sustained moments of closeness were rare and felt somewhat awkward. It occurred to Petra that the lack of physical intimacy might extend from the absence of another kind of intimacy—everything she didn't know about her mother.

Ramona possessed some suppressed bit of wild soul that made Petra wonder what her mother had been like as a teenager, before she'd been born. It revealed itself every now and then when they were around other people—at her few friends' dinner parties, colleagues' weddings, the NBC holiday bash. Ramona liked being the center of attention, and she manipulated it subtly. She didn't hold court, but she asserted her presence through withholding, exuding mystery. And when she'd been drinking, she turned into a dancer and an indiscriminate flirt.

She must have been at least a little crazed to get pregnant at twenty, before sending her boyfriend off to war, his death. This not-oft-repeated story of Petra's provenance: so plainly and unglamorously laid out, yet so enigmatic. Petra had always had questions. For instance: Why were there no pictures of her father? *Too painful*, her mother said, eyes focused on whatever task she'd spontaneously set herself to in that moment. And her grandparents never expressed any interest in meeting her? *You don't get it, these people are basically in a cult.* From an early age, Petra had been trained to drop the subject; the more questions, the curter the answers, the more withdrawn her mother grew.

In high school, when past and present and future all felt like gaping holes, desperate for answers, Petra begged to see a family therapist, which her mother stonily agreed to. They didn't make it past session number two; Ramona repeated her same party lines: *High school sweetheart. Bosnia, accident. Evangelical parents disowned me when they found out I was pregnant. Left everything and went west.* Along with a new one: *I'm sorry it's not enough.*

Once Petra started college and read feminist theory and learned that hardship could be a currency, she began to settle into the unresolved, understanding it as an essential texture of her being. She appreciated the life Ramona had given her despite the challenges of single motherhood. The whole institution of dads was retrograde anyway; if she'd had one, she'd probably hate him. But finding this strange book kicked up the dust.

Ramona pulled away from their embrace. "Whatever you're think-ing about, I don't like it," she said. "We're leaving in ten."

⁓

They pulled up to the valet, beneath the famous green lights of the Triton's sign. The hostess led them through the restaurant—all wood paneling, scarlet leather upholstery, and dim light fixtures—to a round booth in the corner.

"I haven't been here since my graduation dinner," Petra said as she unfurled a crisp white napkin over her lap.

"It never changes; I guess that's the point," Ramona replied.

An ancient waiter tottered up to the table. "Drinks, ladies?" he asked.

Petra looked at Ramona, waiting for her cue. She knew if her mom ordered a cocktail, that meant she could order one, and the waiter would defer to Ramona's authority.

"A Manhattan, please. When in Rome."

"Same," Petra said, and the waiter nodded solicitously.

"So," Ramona said, smoothing the napkin on her lap. "This in-ternship starts Monday?"

"Yep," Petra said.

"I still think you should have given yourself more than a week-end off," Ramona said. "What exactly will you be doing?"

"I'm not sure. I think helping to build an education campaign for tenants who live in buildings that are being sold to real estate corpo-rations."

"That's good." She paused. "You said it's in Boyle Heights? Do they know you don't speak Spanish?"

"I speak enough," Petra huffed.

They fell silent. Ramona always seemed uncomfortable talking about Petra's work, and Petra had no interest in the petty dramas of Ramona's. It felt too early to bring up the book.

The waiter mercifully arrived with their drinks. "Have you had a chance to look at the menu?" he asked.

"No need," Ramona said. "Steamed clams and iceberg wedges to start, a half chicken for me and eight-ounce filet mignon, medium, for that one, and also some creamed spinach, mushrooms, and potatoes au gratin on the side. Please."

"Women who know what they want. Very good," the waiter said before leaving.

"Oh shit, I forgot you're a vegetarian now," Ramona said.

"It's okay. Traditions die hard in this place." The truth was, Petra had decided to abandon her newly adopted vegetarianism the moment her mother had said "Triton's."

They sucked down their drinks and ordered another round. What was the way in? Petra couldn't land on anything natural, and so she relied on the alcohol for courage—her usual MO.

"Your first heartbreak is always devastating," Ramona said out of the blue. "But you can do better. He was such a poseur."

Petra laughed spitefully. "A 'poseur'?"

"He identifies as an anarchist?"

"Anarcho-communist."

"And his methods are what, wearing a leather jacket and being rude to rich people?"

"They use property destruction as a symbol for our country's gross obsession with capital over people," Petra snapped.

"I understand. I'm just not convinced it's worth the bad optics," Ramona said as their food arrived along with two more Manhattans. "The problem is you can practically smell the BO and stale cigarettes through the TV. People like their violence a little more glamorized." She waved an arm towards the dining room's Hollywood crowd.

"If you're expecting social justice work to offer a life of glamour, you're bound to be disappointed," Petra said.

"I agree," Ramona said. "I just didn't like how dismissive he was of everything you do. How did he put it? 'Nonprofits are a capitalist scam interested foremost in lining their own pockets'?"

"I mean, he's not entirely wrong; some are better than others," Petra said, at the same time realizing she didn't have to defend him anymore. She'd begun to suspect that Ricky's rhetoric, although valid in theory, concealed the fact that he didn't want to do the work, that he preferred to berate everyone from the rarefied air of his pedestal. Maybe it was cringeworthy to intern for a nonprofit, but it made Petra feel useful.

"Let's not get into it," Ramona said. "Bon appétit."

Although Petra was a vegetarian for ethical reasons, there was no denying the singular surge of energy one got from a hunk of red meat, and combined with her buzz, it gave her a renewed lucidity. She knew which direction to push Ramona.

"What's 'more glamorized' violence look like?"

"The Black Panthers," Ramona replied without hesitation. "The Zapatistas in their ski masks and colorful dresses. Che Guevara with his beret. And he was so handsome. But you know what the bigger issue is?" She speared a booze-soaked cherry with the stirrer and prodded it in Petra's direction for emphasis. "No leadership. That's why Occupy fell off."

"Occupy wasn't a formal organization, it was a social movement." Petra had tried to explain this at least a dozen times. "And it recruited a lot of people who wouldn't normally participate in organizations. The whole ninety-nine percent thing resonated because it said, 'This includes you, you're one of us.' So even if legislation hasn't come out of it yet, people are aware of the issues, and that'll be reflected down the line."

"Maybe," Ramona said, using her teeth to slide the cherry off the stirrer. "But it's important to harness the energy when you have it;

you can't let it dissipate like the *movement* did because then your opponents will say you flubbed it, it was just a flash in the pan, nothing changed. That's why leadership—the right leadership—is essential."

"That's how democratic movements turn into authoritarian nightmares," Petra said.

"Not necessarily. None of your professors assigned 'The Tyranny of Structurelessness' by Jo Freeman? From the women's lib era?"

Petra gave her a strange look; she'd never heard her mother talk so much about politics or social movements, and certainly not feminist scholars. It was new territory, and it didn't seem benign. Here was the opening to ask about *The Wretched of the Earth*, but she was uneasy again.

"I know a couple things about radicalism," Ramona said, reading Petra's expression. "Remember that commune you were born in?"

"Wasn't it more of a shelter?" Petra asked, reaching towards the subject like one would a spooked horse.

"It was both," Ramona said. "We were basically self-sufficient. We grew our own food, shared housework, took care of each other's kids. We took care of each other."

"If it was so great, why'd we leave?" Petra asked.

Ramona tapped the stirrer against her glass. "I wanted you to have a different kind of life. There were a lot of women who'd escaped abusive relationships, so they didn't like to make contact with the outside. We had to be insular for safety. And I wanted you to be able move freely through the world. To be normal."

Petra realized her mother was drunk. The women's shelter was another subject she was normally evasive about, that she treated as if it had only occupied the slimmest insignificant sliver of their shared history. Petra was pretty drunk herself. This was the first time they'd ever been drunk together, and it occurred to Petra this might put them on more equal footing.

"Was my father abusive? Is that why you had to go to the shelter?" Petra asked.

Ramona's soft, open face turned sober. "Your father was not abusive. He didn't force me to do anything I wasn't willing and ready to do." She broke eye contact with Petra and dabbed her napkin against the corners of her mouth. "We didn't run from your father. He was already dead."

Petra nodded, feeling scolded. But she was only quieted, not convinced.

The waiter came with two slabs of green-and-pink spumoni, crowned in whipped cream and a maraschino cherry. "On the house," he announced.

"Thank you, but we're stuffed," Ramona replied tersely. She was always suspicious of unsolicited favors.

"Mom," Petra hissed, embarrassed, "we can have some spumoni."

"Fine, we can have some spumoni," Ramona said, annoyed.

Stiffly, with an air of rejection, the waiter placed the plate on the table, and Ramona softened.

"I forgot how beautiful this is. That was sweet, Walter, thank you," she said, eyes grazing his name tag.

"My pleasure," the waiter replied, not about to forgive her. But then his eyes caught hers, and he was drawn into the light and sensuality they emanated, and an absolving smile slipped out. Petra had seen this happen more times than she could count. Her mother had this effect on men when she wanted to. It was in her smile, one that began shy then turned mischievous as it unfurled. Her eyes did the same thing; they started large and dewy, then narrowed in a way that suggested Ramona was considering the man in front of her, perhaps indecently. Every time, it achieved the desired result: to appease or convince. It icked Petra out to watch her mother interact with men this way, and to watch how unfailingly it worked, yet she still sat in front of the mirror and tried to replicate the look to no avail. If it was innate, Ramona hadn't passed down the gene, and if it was learned, it was hard-earned. Petra, even at that young and supple age, did not have the effect on men that her mother did.

Appeased, the waiter tottered off; Petra, however, was not appeased.

"You always say it yourself—I'm *so* sensible," Petra said, raking the whipped cream from her spumoni. "I can handle the truth about my father."

Ramona set her elbows on the table and rested her chin atop her laced fingers, staring at her daughter as if listening deeply, but Petra recognized it as an intimidation tactic. After a moment, Ramona said, "You can ask me anything, but I'm not sure you'll find the answers satisfying. It was less complicated than you probably think."

It was always the same opaqueness, articulated like there was nothing else to say, no more to the story, as if Ramona had already divulged all to her daughter, and Petra's doubt was wearisome and childish. In the past, this strategy had worked to quiet Petra— maybe it had made her quieter and more lenient in other parts of her life, too—but in this moment, Petra understood it to be a diversion. A part of her resented the now obvious lie, but more so, the crack in her mother's composure seemed like a crack in a sealed tomb—a sign that a long-sought artifact might finally be exhumed.

The waiter returned with the check, flushed and grinning. He expected Ramona to be sweet like before, but she was not doing encores.

3. Confession

As Ramona began her nightly skincare routine, she puzzled over Petra's eerily relevant questions, as if Bruno's release from prison had precipitated some metaphysical release, a demand for contact. She contemplated the automatic vehemence of her denial that Petra's father had been abusive. Years ago, having heard the stories of so many battered women at the commune, she'd reconsidered her relationship with Bruno, now aware of their power and age imbalances; she reevaluated interactions that up until that point she'd revisited only sentimentally or with yearning. But she came out of that thought experiment indignant and jaded. A more simpleminded person might think their romance was fucked up—fine. Americans were so neurotic about sex, obsessed with an arbitrary and fetishized age of consent. The French knew about gray areas, whereas Americans insisted everything was black-and-white. No, even after all this time, Ramona continued to believe that what she had with Bruno was real. More than real—fated.

Perhaps this sense of fate is what made it impossible to be with another man long-term. When they'd first left the shelter, finding a rich husband was Ramona's Plan A. There had been candidates, but no one sustained her interest. There had been only one serious boyfriend, when she was in her mid-twenties: George, a big Greek guy, native New Yorker, middle-aged, with a taut, inflated belly that's sexy on a certain type of man. George was that kind of man: loud, rude, generous, dismissive of everyone but Ramona and, by extension, Petra. He owned a glass company, whatever that meant. Well, it meant he was loaded. He recognized right away Ramona had a past she was running from, even sensed the backstory was bullshit. They were sitting side by side at the Ginza Sushiko counter when he told her as much. She was too stunned to protest. "I don't care. That's your business," he'd said, using his fingers to eat a slice of sashimi. She'd never forget the chill that ran up her spine, a combination of fear and relief and attraction.

It had gotten him further than the rest, but when he suggested they get married, she faltered. She knew she'd feel obligated to share the secret as his wife. Although she trusted George, she sensed that telling one person meant releasing the secret more generally, calling the attention of some greater force, asking for trouble she wasn't ready for. She knew George just wanted to take care of her, that he'd never try to control her or enforce his own terms, but she couldn't say yes. He took it graciously; he bought them the house as a parting gift, put Ramona's name alone on the deed, and she accepted his generosity without argument. As a couple, they took and they gave matter-of-factly, uncynically. Maybe she'd been stupid not to marry him. She'd made lots of stupid decisions, but she'd learned to live with them all.

She crawled into bed and eyed the book, flagrant on her nightstand. *I need to be more careful,* she thought as she placed it inside the nightstand drawer, beside a very sleek and expensive vibrator and equally sleek and expensive vape pen. Ramona pulled from the vape, exhaled a large plume of smoke, and placed it back in the drawer. It was part of her nightly ritual: after completing her toilette, she'd get in bed, take a small dose of medical marijuana, turn on the TV, and flip through her subscription of French news channels.

Since she'd learned of Bruno's release the day before, she anticipated the sight of her young, unaltered face back on-screen with dread and, admittedly, a little excitement. It would be *that* photo, the one of her with the Kalashnikov among the immortelles. She watched and waited for the special segment on Séverine Guimard, for a news anchor to say, "Interest renews in the hunt for Séverine Guimard." Not that she truly believed she'd one day look up from her desk to see Interpol standing at her door with handcuffs at the ready—but she couldn't rule out the possibility entirely either.

Suddenly, it was happening: the French news anchor announced that Bruno Pieri had been released from prison after twenty years. The newspaper hadn't included a photo, but here he was on video, exiting the gates of the Centre pénitentiaire de Lannemezan, now arriving at the Ajaccio airport, which was packed with sympathizers welcoming him home, cheering, and he waved and placed his hand over his heart like the Queen of England. He was handsome as ever: dark hair flecked with silver, dignified lines around his eyes and mouth, as slim as he'd been at twenty-six. Ramona's stomach flipped. Why couldn't he be a gross old man? Why did this unwanted attraction have to stir within her like a magnet sensing its mate?

They cut to the weather report, and Ramona realized with a start that they hadn't shown her picture. They'd only mentioned Séverine Guimard to say she'd never been apprehended. About sixty seconds was spent on the story before they'd just moved on. France seemed eager to forget Bruno, too, to let him fade back into civilian life.

Ramona laughed at herself—was she actually disappointed? She took another, thoughtful hit of the vape.

She switched the channel to Turner Classic Movies, which reminded her of her father, who'd owned an impressive VHS collection. He loved old American movies; Ramona wondered if that was part of what had initially drawn him to her mother. She missed them. They met once a year: quick, devastating, inadequate encounters, a few hours in random hotels in random towns. Petra had accompanied Ramona on these visits until she turned three, the age her eyes suddenly became shrewd, when she'd quietly watch or listen to her mother interact with other people and would later ask too-astute questions. As time wore on, there was less a sense that they were being watched or followed, so the brevity and infrequency of her parents' visits became less about protecting Ramona and more about protecting Petra from the truth.

The last time had been January, at the Balboa Bay Resort in Newport Beach. Reunions were always organized by Nancy, the same lawyer who'd brought Ramona's forged papers down to Mexico. Over time, their meetings lost any overwrought emotion for the sake of both parties. They embraced, they attempted to explain their lives to each other. Papa was planning on teaching two more years at Nanterre, then he'd retire; the foundation of the Paris house needed replacing, so they were tempted to sell and move south to the Gironde; Mom was publishing a new poetry collection, and they'd be going to New York in September for the release, was there any chance they could meet? Ramona brought photos of Petra, who they cooed over but always with an undercurrent of unease; they'd never get over the fact that their daughter had been impregnated by her kidnapper.

These reunions, complicated to begin with, would become even more problematic as her parents entered old age. Yet the thought of her parents falling ill or dying without Ramona by their side seemed impossible. She was their only child, and she'd put them through hell; she at least wanted the opportunity to take care of them. There were many things she wanted that she couldn't have, and here she was, pressing the bruise. Better to let the drowsy, fuzzy warmness of the indica envelop her. The TV, set on a timer, would turn off after she fell asleep.

⁓

The morning after Triton's, Petra took the Volvo downtown to the central library. With the call number of *The Wretched of the Earth* jotted on a small square of paper, she wandered through the shelves until she came to the proper section, then the proper shelf, and there was the book, perfectly benign, but it felt like uncovering the Rosetta stone.

After checking out, Petra went outside to the gardens and sat on the ledge of a long, narrow pool in full sun. She skipped the preface, and the first chapter title practically struck her across the face: "Concerning Violence." Shamefully, she'd never actually read the book, but the content was familiar enough. After reading for twenty minutes, it became clear that the text itself was less important than the handwritten marginalia accompanying it, so she packed up and went home to examine her mother's copy in tandem.

The book was no longer bedside, nor in the safe. After a few harried minutes of searching, Petra found it inside the nightstand drawer. She winced at the chrome vibrator next to it. Her mother's love life was mysterious. Over the years, men came and went, men whom Petra was rarely introduced to, but she sensed their presence in things like vague Saturday night dinner obligations, or when Petra had a sleepover and her mother picked her up with her own overnight bag in the back seat. Not to say that Ramona was one of those mothers who prioritized her own personal life; even in her clubbing days, Ramona always came home in time for blueberry pancakes in bed the next morning, face washed but smelling of last night's perfume.

The only boyfriend Petra remembered was George. In fact, they'd moved into this house at the end of the George era; Petra often wondered how her mother had managed to buy it when she was just beginning her career in earnest. She wouldn't put it past Ramona to have negotiated some settlement with him despite never marrying.

There was something so cunning about her; men were a natural resource to be utilized, judiciously, for personal benefit, and women were to be emotionally self-sufficient. That was the lesson Petra was supposed to learn from her example, but she didn't buy it. For some reason, Ramona didn't want Petra to see her vulnerabilities, she thought with a hint of bitterness as she closed the nightstand drawer. But she knew her mother was often lonely and prone to melancholy, and although she'd never admit it, she needed Petra close by.

Petra spent the next few days before her internship lying on the chaise beside the pool, reading *The Wretched of the Earth* and trying to decipher the marginalia with the help of Google Translate. She sensed a flirtation between the interlocutors, and they talked quite a bit about someone named Séverine. At the very least, her mother had an impassioned intellectual relationship with this man, which frankly shocked her. Ramona had passed her GED and gotten an associate's from Santa Monica College when Petra was in elementary school, but she'd never gone on to a four-year college; academia held no interest. She wasn't dumb, but Petra thought of her mom as savvy rather than cerebral. In fact, they each possessed the smarts the other lacked, but rather than making them feel like a complete unit, they unintentionally made each other feel deficient, inferior. Until the other night, Petra had never heard Ramona express an informed opinion on politics or current events. The odd tirade at the restaurant was connected to this book, Petra knew.

It was Sunday evening, and Ramona was still at work; she'd gone in every single day since Petra moved back, coming home when it was already dark with dinner from the deli counter at Bristol Farms. As Petra was studying the book by the pool, the afternoon haze burned off, and the sun flexed its full, yellow power, weighing on her like a warm blanket, lulling her to sleep.

Ramona returned around seven with a rotisserie chicken and tortellini salad. Through the kitchen door, she spotted a foot hanging over one of the chaises. She took the little stone path to the pool and found Petra asleep in the bluing light.

It was then she noticed the books beside her daughter—first the English library copy, then *her* book—a clear and accusatory tableau. Stupid, stupid to have taken it from the safe! No wonder Petra had resurrected old questions the other night. Then her anger flared: What was she doing snooping in her room? Why was motherhood antithetical to privacy? She wanted to snatch back her book and dare Petra to ever say anything about it. No, the cat was out of the bag. Or maybe just its tail? Ramona resolved to say nothing—if Petra had questions, she'd need to confront Ramona directly. What could she even discern from the book? It was more or less in code, and there was nothing truly incriminating about it. Regardless, it was an omen: Ramona's tight control was loosening without her consent. At least she had time to prepare for the confrontation.

She'd often considered what might happen if Petra found out about her past, what she'd done and who she was. She knew Petra found her trite and myopic, and the smallest sliver of her wanted Petra to know that she was a person in her own right, someone who'd done things, who'd participated in history in a way that was significant.

Petra stirred, and Ramona backed away, removing her mules so they didn't click on the flagstone. She went back into the kitchen and turned on the porch light to wake her daughter; a few minutes later, Petra came in groggily, a towel draped over her arm to hide the books.

"What time is it?" she asked.

"Past seven," Ramona said. "Have you eaten?"

"No, but you go ahead. I'm going to shower," Petra replied, and walked purposefully to her room. Later that evening, when Ramona went to bed, the book was lying in the nightstand drawer at the exact angle she'd last seen it.

⁓

If Petra's home life was nebulous and strange, the internship would be concrete; but Petra immediately noticed she was the only non-Latinx person in the office, as did everyone else. The director of the center explained her first task: to update informational materials that were entirely in Spanish. Petra stammered that her grammar was a little rusty; was there something else she could do? After a half day of similar humiliations, the director gave her a sympathetic smile and told Petra she could go home. She knew she'd get a text later that night saying not to come back tomorrow. She just made it into the Volvo before she started crying, feeling like an absolute gringa idiot.

It was three in the afternoon and rush hour had already begun. Dejected, she exited the 101 and pulled into Le Poitevin, a restaurant famous for not carding among local high schoolers.

Two Manhattans and a plate of pâté in, Petra only felt worse. It wasn't enough to show up. She'd never admit it aloud, but she resented the tenants' rights organization's sense of community, built along cultural lines and shared hardship. Her whole life, Petra had felt unlocated in history, unaffiliated; her mom was a pilgrim who'd left everything behind, which made Petra the first threadlike root in a new family tree. She was just some ignorant white girl from the Hills—sheltered, disconnected, ineffective, and unsure how to be a force for good despite it.

"Another Manhattan?" the waiter asked in a thick French accent.

"Yes. No. Are you French?" Petra asked.

"It is a French restaurant," the waiter said dryly.

She was past the point of caring if this guy thought she was a drip. "What does 'basgiu' mean?" she asked.

"Huh? That is not a French word."

Petra pulled up the photo of the inscription on her phone and handed it to him. He accepted it with professional annoyance, but as he read, he gave a little laugh.

"'To my beloved snake, that we take back paradise.' Or maybe more like a toast: 'Here's to taking back paradise.' 'Basgiu,' that must be dialect. Catalan, or—no, I bet it is Corse." He smiled and nodded once.

"What's that?"

"You say 'Corsica' in English? My family used to go there on holiday. It's very beautiful. But when I was twelve years, terrorists killed some people there, and I do not go since. Anyway, *les corses* love pretending there gonna be revolution. They were close that time. But they are a very lazy people."

At this, he handed the phone back to Petra.

"You want the drink or no?"

"Just the check," Petra said distantly.

On her way back to Laurel Canyon, she ran into traffic. She fished her phone out of her bag and saw the expected text from the director of the tenants' rights group, but swiped it away without reading it. She Googled "Corsica." Mountainous Mediterranean island, territorial collectivity, whatever that meant, ruled by the Republic of Genoa, birthplace of Napoleon Bonaparte, blah blah. She scrolled through the sections on its history and geography, pictures of important buildings and climate data charts, down to "Politics." She skimmed the paragraph, unsure what she was looking for. Autonomy, nationalist organizations, pieds-noirs, protection for the Corsican language, the failed revolution of 1993.

The car behind gave an impatient honk and Petra inched forward, closing the insignificant space between the Volvo and car in front. As she skimmed the section about this failed revolution, her eye caught on a name: Bruno Pieri. Bruno, like the inscription. 1993. She tapped on the hyperlink to his page. The mug shot that came up beside the article was of a good-looking guy, despite the busted-up face. His expression was one of belligerence, grief, and resignation. He made Ricky look soft. She read the details of what earned him that mug shot:

> Bruno Pieri is a Corsican nationalist convicted in the assassination of Bernard Jonnart, former Minister of the Interior. He formed part of the militant group Soffiu di Libertà, led by Séverine Guimard, that was responsible for multiple devastating attacks during the summer of 1993.

Led by Séverine Guimard. Petra tapped on the hyperlink to her page.

More cars honked as a lump formed in Petra's throat, the sensation before vomiting. One long, apoplectic honk made Petra drop the phone between her feet. Hands slick and shaking, she pulled onto the shoulder. Her body understood what her brain could not yet process. She didn't want to, but she picked up the phone, and the screen brightened to show a picture of a young woman who looked very much like her mother holding a machine gun in a field of wild-flowers.

The photo was grainy, likely taken with a Polaroid. It was hard to distinguish the girl's features, except for a huge nose, which her mother certainly did not have; nor did she have this gold-inflected hair—as long as Petra could remember, Ramona was a mahogany brunette. But there was something in this girl's eyes that mirrored her mother's: defiance, a certain wielding of sex appeal, enormous self-confidence, the conviction she was right.

The Wikipedia article was only slightly longer than Bruno Pieri's. It read:

> Séverine Guimard (July 29, 1975) was a leading figure in the nationalist Corsican militant group Soffiu di Libertà, active from June 1993 to September 1993. She is allegedly responsible for the assassination of former Minister of the Interior Bernard Jonnart and has been missing since the day of the crime.
>
> Guimard is the daughter of French politician Paul Guimard, former prefect of Corsica, and the American poet and heiress Bonnie Holt. She was kidnapped on the night of June 6, 1993, by Soffiu di Libertà, who demanded a five-million-franc ransom and the release of an imprisoned nationalist in exchange for Guimard. After a month of failed negotiations, Guimard issued a statement declaring she had joined the group that kidnapped her, along with the infamous photo of her posing with a Kalashnikov AK-74.
>
> Under Guimard's influence, the group executed a series of terror attacks during the summer of 1993, known as "L'été de terreur," which climaxed with the storming of the Palais Lantivy in Ajaccio on September 4, 1993, and resulted in the death of eight civilians and three guards.
>
> According to multiple eyewitness accounts, Guimard was the shooter who assassinated Bernard Jonnart on Sep-

tember 3, 1993, at the Hotel Marbella in Porticcio, France. While all other members of the group were either killed or arrested, Guimard is still at large.

Nico Girardi, who filmed the popular communiqués disseminated by Soffiu di Libertà, directed the documentary *L'été de terreur* using original footage.

Murder, destruction, political plots, mass violence: the extremeness nearly calmed Petra, it was so wholly impossible her mother could ever be involved in something like that, let alone precipitate it.

There was another picture on the Wikipedia page, a school photo of a young woman smiling confidently, cannily even; the same kind of smile her mom had given the waiter at Triton's. Petra had never once seen a picture of her mother as a girl. But the nose . . . Ramona's nose had always appeared unnaturally straight, like it had been constructed by a fine craftsman but deficient artist. When Petra reached the age when classmates came back from summer vacation with new noses, Petra had asked her mother if she'd had a nose job; Ramona took offense, asking Petra if she thought she was that shallow. The answer was yes, so Petra had never relinquished that sneaking suspicion. Now, it was the nose that indicted her mother most of all. This proud, bold nose that announced itself first and foremost did not by any means fit the face of this girl, but at the same time it was the thing that drew all her other features into relief. Ramona Frisch, with her shaved-off, unassuming nose, was a very beautiful woman, yet not singularly so. Séverine Guimard was sexy and special and thrilling to look at. If she needed to hide, a nose job would be the only way to do it.

Petra sat in the running car, stomach churning, scrolling. There were only a few articles about Séverine Guimard in English, but when she switched to French Wiki, the entry quadrupled in size.

Suddenly, the phone began vibrating and "Mom" appeared at the top of the screen. Heart pounding, as if the person calling was dangerous, she hit "Accept."

"Are you okay?" Ramona asked.

"What do you mean?"

"I just passed you on Laurel Canyon. I honked and waved but you were transfixed by your phone."

"Oh. I got a text from the internship people saying not to come back tomorrow," Petra explained, amazed by her own quick thinking.

"Why, what happened? It was the Spanish thing, wasn't it?"

She refused to admit that her mom was right. "It was a budgetary issue."

"It's not like they were paying you," Ramona said, then backpedaled. "Sorry, we'll talk when you get home. I ordered Thai; can you go pick it up?"

Petra ended the call and hooked a left to head back towards Hollywood. She couldn't tell anyone. No one would believe her if she did, even though the photos were proof enough; people dismissed what seemed impossible because it was easier than mentally negotiating miracles. Was it possible Petra was doing the opposite, refusing to believe her provenance was so ordinary as to come from a small-town teen mom?

She collected the food distractedly, then muscle memory brought her safely home. Odd to unlock the front door and walk inside the foyer—banal memories coming into relief against this grand, absurd lie. Nothing seemed benign—not the quiet comfort of the house, the worn Persian rug, the framed photos, or the glow of the recessed lighting emanating from the kitchen, where Ramona was sitting at the island with a glass of white wine and some work she'd brought home.

"Oh good, thank you," Ramona said when Petra came in, putting her papers aside and going around the island to pull two plates from the cabinet. "I finally tied up this recasting fiasco, thank God."

As Ramona recapped the drama, Petra watched her mother's hands fish in the utensil drawer and tried to reconceive of them as hands that had held a gun, pulled a trigger on another person. It seemed so absurd, but her gut told her it was true.

"What?" Ramona asked, pausing with a tongful of pad thai hovering over her plate. Her pointed stare incapacitated Petra.

"What is it, Petra?" she asked more forcefully. Petra understood that her mother knew she knew something and was challenging her. It was always this way: she was perfectly transparent and her mother perfectly opaque; she knew nothing and her mother knew everything.

"Are you Séverine Guimard?" Petra asked with a calm curiosity, and for the first time, she saw her mother blanch. They watched each other with guileless, expectant expressions. Ramona had dreaded this moment Petra's whole life, and at the same time never allowed herself to actually envision it. But she felt less exposed than ventilated, like a shut-up, abandoned house whose doors and windows had been flung open, and now a person—her daughter—could enter.

"Not anymore," Ramona answered.

There was something dignified and resigned in her slightly slumped posture, the hands setting the tongs onto the plate like lowering a weapon. The woman in front of Petra was and was not her mother; that is, she'd lived an entire life before Petra had come into the picture. But that was true of every mother.

"Then my father?"

"Bruno Pieri," Ramona said. "But I never had a chance to tell him. I didn't even realize I was pregnant till I was out of Corsica."

"So he doesn't know about me."

"No."

Both women waited for the other to say more. Ramona realized that Petra had made the agonizing first step, and it was her turn to be forthcoming.

"What do you want to know?" she asked.

"Everything," Petra said.

So while she poured Petra a glass of wine and served their food as if it were any other takeout night, Ramona started with the basics: her name, date of birth, who her parents were.

"Have I ever met them?"

"A few times when you were little. You wouldn't remember."

"Does anyone else know who you really are?"

"Two people: Carol, a childhood friend of my mom's, and her ex-girlfriend, Nancy, who's a lawyer. My mom's—your grandmother's—whole family is in Pennsylvania, but it felt too dangerous to involve them. Nancy was connected to some Weather Underground stuff back in the seventies, so she knew how to get my papers in order and set us up in the women's shelter. But I haven't seen either of them in years."

"How'd you even get to the US?"

Their food grew cold as Ramona explained the long, wayward trip: all those anonymous people her parents paid to shelter her in Sardinia and across the Maghreb and below deck in the *Lady Jasmin* as it sailed from Tangier to Punta Caucedo; and once she found her way to the States after Cuba and Mexico, the women's sanctuary. They brought the half-drunk bottle of wine to the back patio, where they watched dead beetles and decaying leaves travel across the pool in the stream of the return jets while Ramona went through the kidnapping, that crazy summer, described Petru, Tittu, and Bruno.

"Petru—am I named for him?" Petra asked. This was a quiet

revolution—being named for someone meant a connection to that person, deeply meaningful, a sort of forced reincarnation.

"He gave his life for me, although I didn't deserve it." Ramona gave a bittersweet smile. "You're most like Bruno, though. Your seriousness, your commitment to social change. Who knew that was genetic."

"And you weren't—coerced in any way?" Petra asked carefully.

Ramona shook her head. "No," she insisted, but Petra was unconvinced; it was the insistence that made her suspicious. No matter what Ramona said, the facts were the facts: she'd been impregnated by her kidnapper when she was a teenager and he was in his midtwenties. He wasn't a good person, and Petra didn't need him to be, although she understood why her mother did.

"And you killed that man?" Petra asked.

"I did," Ramona said, a remark that turned into a forceful sigh. "And there was another woman, an accident. Honestly, I think about her more than Jonnart. Really, I think about her son. I tried looking him up once but couldn't tell if it was the right boy. As if him being okay would make her death more okay."

She picked up her glass, then lowered it. "It's strange. I had pushed it from my mind until one day we were at the beach—you were about four, I guess we'd just left the sanctuary—and it hit me that you were the same age as that little boy when his mom died. And I felt this huge sense of injustice on her behalf, that she never got more moments like you and I were having—you know, collecting seashells, splashing around. Making a nice memory. Then it sunk in that that was my doing. And the fact it was an accident, all the justifications I'd made, suddenly seemed like bullshit. Yes, there was a very specific chain of events that led to her death, but at the end of the day, it wouldn't have happened if it weren't for me. There was no reason for it, and it meant nothing politically. It was just this nihilistic act of violence." She raised the glass to her lips, murmuring into it, "But I've done a lot of rationalizing to stay sane."

"What about Jonnart, though?" Petra asked quietly.

Ramona scoffed. "Oh, him? He was a horrible man. And at that moment, it felt like him or us."

Carefully, Petra asked, "What was it like?"

Ramona swirled her glass, trying to reach back to that moment, one that neither haunted nor left her. Snippets of the event would replay in her mind at random, like a scratched DVD. These memories couldn't necessarily be trusted anymore; they had the same flat quality as a movie, too. She did her best to fall back into the memory, silent for a good minute or two.

"It was factual," she finally said, her eyes trained to some target in the middle distance. "I shot him once, right outside his room, then I shot him twice more. It wasn't as clean as it should have been. There was a lot of blood, and for some reason that shocked me. He didn't take me seriously. I don't think he thought I'd do it, but that's what pushed me over the edge, I guess. And in a way, it felt like the only option, like the whole world would change for the better once he was gone from it."

"I could never do that," Petra said, and began to cry.

Ramona laughed, went to Petra's chair, and wrapped her stiff body in her arms, leaning back against the chaise and pulling her daughter tight to her chest. "That's a good thing, honey. I was out of my mind! I was a dilettante, really. We didn't liberate the island or take down the government. Nothing changed for anyone but us, the people directly involved. And not in a good way."

"At least you tried, at least you put yourself on the line in a real way." Petra moaned. "I'm a total fake!"

"No you're not. There are a million different approaches to a million different problems," Ramona said. "There's so much I don't understand about your world. I'm old, I have a foreigner's mentality. I sold my soul long ago." As Ramona spoke these words, she felt oddly remorseless for all of it: Jonnart's death, Bruno's imprisonment, the transition she made back into the bourgeoisie. The only things she regretted were Tittu's and Petru's deaths, and that her protectiveness had alienated her from her daughter for so long. She realized that the closeness Petra sought wasn't a symptom of her immaturity or dependence but a hand outstretched in the dark; only, Petra hadn't known what Ramona really needed, and how could she? Ramona herself hadn't grasped how isolated she'd become within the shell of her secret. As it turned out, she'd needed a confessor. And maybe Petra only needed Ramona to grant her that intimacy.

Petra cried, and Ramona held her in the chaise till she eventually fell asleep, her daughter's exhalations smelling of whiskey. She felt a love for Petra, something physical and weighty and choking, a love tinged with ultimate responsibility and fear that she hadn't felt so literally since Petra was a baby.

This young woman in her arms was the evidence of her past life, the product of her obsession with Bruno, the bridge between both lives. But Petra hadn't asked for this legacy; of all the monumentally selfish acts Séverine had committed, the most egregious may have been birthing Petra from the underground, raising her entirely alone yet at a distance. If Ramona resented Petra for being a searcher, it was exactly the kind of person she'd unconsciously raised her to be: unanchored. It was how Séverine had felt that June of 1993, and look where she'd ended up. Only by the grace of God was Petra different.

When Ramona had thought about being discovered in any capacity, it hadn't looked like this. Her vision was dramatic, as dramatic as that summer had been. But the reality was oddly, blessedly quiet. Ramona had taken so many measures to protect Petra from the truth, but just like that, they were no longer necessary. And though they'd been necessary, they'd come at a cost, Ramona realized as she held her daughter. Now she'd have to do something radical to make up for it.

4. Scene of the Crime

Petra woke up to find herself in bed with a vague memory of being led upstairs, half-asleep and drunk. She was gripped by a strange fear that her mother had flown the coop. Without peeing or brushing her teeth, she ran down to the kitchen, but there was Ramona in her muslin robe and kilim slippers, adding some sautéed mushrooms and shallots to a pan of gently setting egg. Her mother was actually a good cook and had always done so with both pleasure and solemnity, a quiet, private ritual.

"That smells good," Petra said, her heart rate calming.

"I was thinking," Ramona began. "What if we went to Corsica?"

"Like, now?"

"Why not? You've been fired, I could take a few days off."

"To do what exactly?" Petra asked.

"Bruno just got out of prison," Ramona answered. "If you want to meet him."

"But you're a fugitive," Petra said.

"I'm Ramona Frisch. I have an American passport. We can fly to Italy to be safe and take the ferry."

Petra and Ramona met each other's eyes in a mutual dare. Ramona had figured she'd never, ever go back to Corsica, even if the statute of limitations had passed. But what was she protecting now? Petra was grown. She was good at her job, and it fulfilled her, but with streaming and social media, the industry was changing, and not to her liking. The house had always been too big, something she could neurotically maintain, her longest romance. There was no man. What oppressive stagnancy. She'd engineered life to be staid and safe, and it had come to weigh on her like a stone over a burial vault.

Then and there, they looked up exorbitant one-way airline tickets to Florence, train tickets to Livorno, and ferry tickets to Bastia. They were going in only three days.

"What about work?" Petra asked.

"After this last month, I've earned my PTO," Ramona said as she clicked "Process payment."

Ramona was driving to Barneys to treat herself to a new dress when the broadcaster on KCRW spoke of an outbreak of violence between Sunnis and Shiites in Iraq that had killed hundreds of people in the last few days. It was the first time Ramona was hearing about this; she was so disconnected from the world. She wondered what Séverine would think. She often did, as if Séverine were a separate person living parallel to Ramona, a once-close friend she'd fallen out of touch with.

Just as frequently, she wondered what Bruno would think of her. That was why she was on her way to Barneys: she wanted an outfit that would make her look as daring and youthful as she'd been at newly eighteen. She knew she'd been at her most beautiful that dis-tant summer. Beauty was also spirit externalized, and at that time in her life, she'd never been freer or more confident or more in love. That said, she sensed a new calm, a quiet self-possession that was so different from the manic energy and arrogance of her youth. She was satisfied with the woman she'd become. The idea of impressing Bruno of all people by showing up in some designer dress was ridic-ulous, Ramona realized, and made a U-turn towards home.

Was she already falling back into the old insecurities about his love for her? Why should he still love her? Why should she try to rekindle that in him, if only for vanity? What she really wanted was someone with whom she could remember Tittu and Petru; never talking about them gave them an extra veneer of death, and she wanted to resurrect them through memories shared with Bruno. This was all she'd ask of him—and that he'd be kind to their daughter.

On the drive home, Ramona replayed different scenarios of her reunion with Bruno. Each began with her and Petra pulling up in a rental car, getting out. Then, recognizing her, he'd rush to her and kiss her; or, recognizing her, he'd rush to her and wrap his hands around her throat for all the ways she'd ruined his life; or he wouldn't recognize her, or wouldn't believe it, because she was so fundamen-tally different from the girl he'd known; or he'd refuse to believe Petra was his daughter. Or perhaps the scenario would be so banal and anticlimactic that Ramona couldn't possibly envision it.

⌒

The overall mood in the house was more convivial than it had been in a long time; the women ate dinner together, dipped into the wine, watched dumb TV. Leisure was permissible in this interim period, and their shared understanding of that made them less tense and irritable, more forgiving.

Ramona even consented to watching Nico's documentary, which she'd avoided all these years. It was a strange and mortifying experience for both of them—Ramona's sexuality was all implication, but Séverine's was flagrant. The communiqués explicitly sought to seduce the viewer, and it was uncomfortable for Petra to be among the audience. For Ramona's part, she felt painfully aware of the reasons parents didn't share their youthful exploits with their children as she watched herself dancing in Nico's living room, rolling on ecstasy.

She also felt a twinge of loss: she really did have the "It" Factor; her professional eye recognized it right away. Maybe she could have developed her craft at Paris III, moved to LA, had an acting career. On the other hand, Ramona knew all too well how many actors with "It" still failed to launch—likely, she would still have ended up as a casting director for the soaps. So was that heady brush with stardom through violence worth it? What about the death, the repression, the life that came out of it? As soon as she formed the question, she understood its futility.

The documentary ended with Nico narrating over footage of a building that looked like it had been bombed, but as the camera slowly zoomed in, it became apparent that it was new construction. Meanwhile, Nico reflected on why the movement had failed: "We thought, in this digital age, that the revolution would indeed be televised. Our messiah would be a movie star. We could repurpose the methods used to sedate the people to awaken them—if the revolution seemed like a sexy good time, if we advertised it the way you would cigarettes, or vodka, or a new luxury sedan, then people would line up to join. But, just as you can't make a film with a big-name star alone, you can't start a revolution with one charismatic leader. You need the unglamorous film crew. You need the financial backers. And you need the unions, the coalitions that advocate for everyone involved. You need a set of agreed-upon principles. You need a clear vision. You need trust."

That was rich, after selling them out. No concrete evidence had ever come to light, but the proof was in Nico being able to make this documentary without being charged with conspiracy. That could only happen if he'd cooperated with the police. He'd gone on to direct other films, but nothing as successful as *L'été de terreur,* which was fitting—a curse for your first work to be your best known and most lauded, for the public to take no interest in your development. He was living out his sentence.

———

The night before the flight, suitcases packed, Ramona sat up in bed, the TV on but muted, flashing blue against her face. She felt entranced, controlled by an external force, like she was yet again swept into the current of destiny and abandoning many years' prudence. If the worst happened, if she were somehow identified and sent to prison, she'd still be the luckiest of all her comrades, without question. Perhaps it was time to pay the price for her actions. Yet she also found that line of thinking, the tyranny of karma, to be bullshit. Justice wasn't a real, divine force. If there existed a principle of balance, it was mysterious and roundabout. She didn't believe she deserved punishment for the death of Jonnart.

Down the hall, Petra was trying and failing to pack economically. That monumental feeling that everything would change persisted— grew wider and deeper, even—with Ramona's confession. She wondered what Bruno Pieri would think of her. She'd done a lot of reading up on Corsica and its issues, including dozens of newspaper articles Bruno Pieri had written from prison that she put through Google Translate, her new best friend. They gave her a better understanding of Corsica's very legitimate grievances and who Bruno might be. Brainy, sober, a bit didactic—quite like herself, Petra thought with excitement. She wanted him to recognize himself in her, to be impressed by her and want to know her, and in turn, she wanted the option to reject him. She couldn't shake the sliminess of her origin story. Her mother had either been semi-brainwashed or, more likely, needed to believe they'd been in love. Petra didn't *need* to believe anything; she would be shrewd for both of them.

The day of their flight was disconcertingly un-hectic; they were ready hours before the town car was due to pick them up. They both expected that some obstacle would present itself to unravel the plan. Yet there wasn't debilitating traffic, and TSA only lazily glanced at Ramona's passport. They bought magazines they perused until it was time to board, then the waiting was over.

Both women popped a Xanax, drank a glass of sauvignon blanc, and passed out. When they woke up, they were in Florence. There was no dallying there; straight on the train to Livorno, then breakfast near the ferry terminal, surrounded by their bags. Only once the ferry—a Corsica Mare ferry, no less—began chugging southeast were they able to relax. They spent the four-hour ride in chairs on the deck, drinking Coca-Cola and watching the water sweep by, drifting in and out of sleep. Ramona thought of Napoleon's famous line that he could smell Corsica before seeing it from his ship. She inhaled deeply, and although she couldn't detect the scent of the maquis, the salt of the Mediterranean hit her potently. She was not the landlocked American girl from her false backstory; she was the girl who'd floated in the sea dreaming of her glorious future.

They arrived at 7:00 p.m. in full daylight. As the ferry docked, Ramona surveyed Bastia from atop the deck with a sense of unreality. Everything was as she remembered it: the trees leaning in the warm wind, the creamy buildings, the elderly people sitting on benches watching everyone else go by. It was touching, like the town had waited for her, sleeping in suspension of time like the castle in *Sleeping Beauty*. What an idiotic, self-indulgent thing to think, she scolded herself; this is just how life was on islands, where time naturally passed more slowly.

Debarking down the gangplank, she experienced excruciating déjà-vu of the day of the nuit bleue, the moment she'd rushed off the ferry into Bruno's waiting arms, that prelude to their first night together. The intensity of the memory hit Ramona in its fullness; she hadn't felt that ache in so long, but being here reactivated the sensation automatically, and it made her queasy, mistrustful of herself.

Petra stared at her inscrutable mother and the land before her, feeling mystified and overwhelmed by both. She knew she was supposed to have a reaction but was paralyzed by the reality of her situation, that this place existed and she was here. Her mother, she sensed, *was* having a reaction, but it churned tightly inside her.

They approached a waiting cab, and Ramona crouched beside the passenger window to exchange words with the driver in French. Somehow, this caught Petra by surprise. Her mother's French seemed a bit fast and nervous but also instinctual. The driver certainly understood her, exiting the car to load their bags into the trunk.

In the back seat, Petra quietly asked, "Is it a good idea for you to speak French here? Shouldn't you pretend you're just American?"

Ramona shrugged with a smile. "I don't want to fight what's natural."

Their hotel was for business travelers, clean and sparse. As Petra showered, Ramona opened the French windows and leaned out the balcony. She'd forgotten that it stayed light until nine o'clock this time of year, how the summer days felt endless. Below, the street was filled with people on their way to dinner or on their way home from the market, others having a drink outside, all the tables and chairs facing into the street so everyone could see and be seen. This was what she was meant for: leisure, gourmandise, idle chatting among friends. So much had been sacrificed, maybe unnecessarily.

They went to dinner at the restaurant Ramona had observed from the balcony; now they were the people sitting facing the street, drinking little goblets of Corsican rosé and sharing a pizza.

"This is so nice," Petra said. She felt an oceanic surge of energy but resisted letting it crash outside her. This was her land. These were her people. She took them in scientifically, trying to identify something about them that was unknowingly inside her as well.

"It is nice," Ramona agreed. The sun was beginning to set, so she swapped her sunglasses for a pair of eyeglasses with a low prescription that she in fact needed, thick tortoiseshell frames that made her look like an actress playing a college professor. She waited for a flicker of recognition, but eyes passed over her as quickly as they passed over every other person sitting at the restaurant. It struck her again that her fear of being identified was completely egotistical. She was scarcely out of childhood then and now was another ordinary lady verging on forty. The more time elapsed, the more she became another bit of local lore.

After dinner they walked through town, turning down a narrow street, towards the ocean.

"To the left, the building with the really orange light—that's where Bruno lived while he was teaching. Don't linger, I'm just pointing it out."

Petra stared up at this building that seemed to be hundreds of years old, all its windows thrown open. "Is he there now?" she asked.

"No, he's in Fozzano. But there's more I want to show you first."

The next day, they rented a car and drove down to Ajaccio, taking the coastal route, turning onto the hill that led to the gated community where the Guimards had lived.

"Here," she gestured, stopping the car randomly, "is where I got kidnapped."

Petra examined the utterly normal-looking road for—she didn't know what. "You must have been terrified," she said, although it was difficult to imagine her mother ever being scared.

"Yes." Ramona forced herself to say more. "But I was also stupid and entitled, which helped. I didn't think I could ever really be hurt, and maybe that somehow protected me."

They continued up to the guardhouse, where Ramona leaned out the car, flashing one of her glittering smiles, and spoke to the guard in French. After a minute of back-and-forth, the gate rose, and they passed through.

"What did you say?"

"That I used to live here and wanted to show my daughter around. The truth."

When they reached the house, built with thick blocks of multi-hued granite, they didn't stop, but cruised by slowly.

"It doesn't even look dated. My parents had such good taste." She laughed bitterly. "'Had,' as if they're dead."

"Should we try and see them while we're here?" Petra asked.

Ramona shook her head, eyes trained on all the lush but neat landscaping. "One thing at a time."

That night, they ate head-on shrimp at what Ramona thought of as "Antoine's paillote," only it had been renovated for a more upscale crowd. As Ramona sipped her daiquiri, she felt weary with the walk down memory lane. It was saccharine and desperate. What was she trying to recapture, and for what purpose? For Petra, but she wasn't used to negotiating this new transparency with her daughter, what to share and what she should still withhold. The people around them seemed like extras, and the paillote with the ocean in front of it looked like a cheap movie set—the TV movie of the story of her life. If Ramona had returned to Corsica, it wasn't to experience that, but to find something real. That could only be done with Bruno.

"Mom," Petra said, as if reading her mind, "what are you waiting for?"

The next morning, they drove to Fozzano.

5. *Reunion*

From the balcony of the house, he could see the ocean. It was just a little prong, like the foot of a sewing machine, two slivers of blue the same hazy color as the sky. But it was enough to fill Bruno with a wondrous if tentative sense of peace. He'd been home a month now, and it all seemed fake—his release, his return to Corsica, seeing friends, eating in restaurants, moments of solitude like this one. It was 15:00, a glass of eau gazeuse sweated on the table beside him, the sun was making everything lazy and ponderous, and he was considering a nap.

He was ostensibly reading *The Red and the Black* by Stendhal. He'd read it in university but hadn't paid much attention, so when he spotted the paperback copy deteriorating on the shelf in his childhood room, he decided to give it another go. Naturally, he'd read a lot in prison—not just nonfiction but novels, which he'd previously avoided. When he was younger, reading seemed like a tool, and if it wasn't obviously useful, it wasn't worth his time. But he'd come to appreciate the exercise of surrendering to a book, passively absorbing it, recovering something significant days or weeks or months later, unexpectedly, like putting your hand in an old coat pocket to find something you'd forgotten you'd even lost. Coming back to Corsica after twenty years felt like that, too. More than anything, the suspicion persisted that there must be some catch.

Thirty years was the initial sentence; when he got out, he'd be fifty-six, he remembered thinking. His own father was only fifty-two at the time. When he'd dwelt on the number thirty, he felt he may as well die now. Yet he'd ended up setting himself to work among the prison community, which gave his days shape and purpose, made the time pass in a way that didn't seem wasteful. He'd advocated for dozens of prisoners, helping not only with paperwork but publicity via his biweekly column in *l'Humanité*. A few Corsican political prisoners with more minor offenses got their status of "détenu particulièrement signalé" revoked, meaning they no longer required special surveillance and could therefore be transferred to Borgo, the island's prison, and he liked to think he had a hand in that.

Conditions in Lannemezan were no better than expected, but because Bruno was considered a political prisoner, he was afforded a certain respect that meant he wasn't fucked with. Even the Corsican gangsters (who had no love for the nationalists) didn't pick on him, as he'd fiercely fought for the island they missed so much. Pretty much everyone else was poor, Arab, Black, Muslim, an immigrant or a child of immigrants, and they'd watched the events of that summer with vested interest; if they didn't feel the call to revolution, they at least felt recognized in Séverine's communiqués.

The instant he'd stepped foot in the canteen, Bruno was approached by I Fratelli guys; he prepared for a confrontation, but they were children of Mai '68, good leftists who'd been locked up long before their dreams of revolution could be perverted by the financial interests that had so enticed Fanfan. They took Bruno under their wing and showed him the ropes. Other political prisoners were held at Lannemezan, too: a few Basque nationalists who spoke their strange, sibilant, prehistoric language to each other; then the ones everyone called "the Lebanese," although that included a few Palestinians and one Armenian.

All the inmates, not only the political prisoners, had been eager to explain to Bruno why the uprisings failed. The "common criminals" gave him short, lucid explanations: It was too fast. The girl wasn't one of them. The I Fratelli guys and the Basques were sympathetic, but equally blunt: There wasn't a cohesive enough theory behind their violence. Revolution needed to be a religion, not a fan club. The Lebanese talked about their own failures, which were at a scale that was incomprehensible to Bruno: gaffes dealing with foreign intelligence agents; incorrect assumptions they made negotiating with the most powerful political figures of their time; their overestimation of how long a person could hold out under torture.

Elie El-Khoury, serving a life sentence for three assassinations in protest of Israel's occupation of Lebanon, was the most notorious of the political prisoners. He looked like a professor but radiated a quiet, unexcitable authority—the kind of man who'd been dangerous so long, he didn't need to prove it anymore. A couple years into their acquaintanceship, he began to share stories that floored and humbled Bruno, that threw into doubt so many of his decisions and motivations—that made him feel like a phony. El-Khoury talked about forming coalitions among different ethnic and religious groups, securing financial backing from foreign bodies, his militia's various departments and their functions. There was a pristine, passionless logic to it all that abashed Bruno. He realized just how much Soffiu di Libertà, born of panic and desperation, had been guided by emotion. The emotional intensity had remained personal despite their claims to the contrary; it had never cooled and hardened into a real ideology, which was the only way to sustain the struggle.

And Séverine was the high priestess of panic and desperation! Not because of her youth or femininity, but because of the circumstances under which she'd been initiated. Bruno had seen himself as the rational force of the cell, but that was delusional: when Matteu was sentenced, Bruno's reaction had been just as hysterical as the girl's when they kidnapped her. The assassination had been hysterical, too. Justified, but hysterical. None of them had been prepared for that step, or the next one, life underground. Petru was right: the whole thing, all their grand plans, had been doomed to disintegrate before they could set foot off the island. Bruno had accused Séverine of playing dress-up, but he had, too.

He felt tremendous guilt about the aftermath of that summer. As always, ordinary Corsicans were the ones who bore the brunt of government crackdowns. The island was in a state of siege for a year, the military taking over all police functions. A strict curfew was instated, the right to assemble was revoked, *A Paghjella* was shut down, and the military was allowed to enter any home without a warrant. It would take years for tourism to bounce back, which meant the island suffered its worst recession in decades; they were forced to accept more French welfare, exacerbating their dependency.

Foreign corporations, however, knew the tourists would eventually return, and took the opportunity to buy up land and break ground on resorts during that year when Corsicans were at their most cowed. But his people were stubborn and resilient. According to Matteu, there was a sense of defiant triumph—now everyone knew that Corsica had the power to threaten the republic's entire system. They set about repairing their torn-apart island "à nostra manera," the government and militants both be damned.

Matteu was there alongside the whole Pieri clan when Bruno first landed in Ajaccio. He certainly didn't have anything very flattering to say about Séverine, but Bruno suspected he was jealous that he'd missed being part of something historic.

Matteu wanted Bruno to run for office with the new party he'd founded: Ventu di Cambiamentu, "Wind of Change," an obvious play on Soffiu di Libertà, but autonomy, not independence, was the goal now. But Bruno wasn't so sure, even though this was a legitimate political party, allied with the Greens, no clandestine arm. Those days came to an end when I Fratelli and Novi Patriotti were forced to agree to a ceasefire after the storming of Lantivy; some said that defeat was what gave Fanfan a fatal stroke a few months later. Anyway, revolution was a young man's game. Not to say he didn't see the need for violence, but Bruno no longer saw the need for his part in it. All that righteous anger now seemed so solipsistic. He hadn't undergone a religious conversion, but it felt close. Maybe it was maturation.

From inside the house, the phone rang. They still had a rotary phone, and its ring was shrill. He didn't get up; it was likely Monica, and he didn't feel like seeing her tonight. She was his father's friend's daughter; he'd never given her much thought despite the fact that she was pretty and kind. But when he arrived at his parents' house in Bastia, Monica was there with a carton of peaches the next day. She was shockingly, refreshingly normal, so sweet and unassuming that it was like a salve.

Funny that he was turning down the chance to get laid when he'd been so desperate so long for a woman's touch. Nights in his cot, he'd remember what it had been like with Séverine, and it didn't give him a frisson so much as a sharp pain in his lower region, an ache that was existentially intense and had absolutely no occasion for release. The first time he and Monica had slept together, the thought assaulted him that the last woman he'd been with was Séverine. He remembered it perfectly: it was the night before they'd gone to Porticcio, out in the maquis behind the bergerie. The whole act had a sort of ritual feel to it, with Séverine in the grass, skin glowing in the moonlight and hair spread around the ground like a defiled nymph. Then he refocused to find this other woman beneath him, a woman in a bed, everything clean and expected and lacking fatality.

"You will never see Séverine again," Michel, his lawyer, had told him repeatedly. Michel had heard on good authority that Séverine had skipped town, that she was overseas and underground. If she was smart, which at the very least her parents were, she'd change identities and never come back. Best to write it off as one crazy fling during one crazy summer and do what he needed to get the least possible jail time. The government needed to punish somebody, and the only warm body they had was Bruno's; they'd have no problem sending him away for life, unless he pointed the finger at Séverine.

That word, "life," had scared him. Anyway, there were fifteen witnesses confirming that Séverine was the only one who'd discharged her gun—so he cooperated and got thirty years. He felt like such a rat afterwards; despite what everyone already knew, he wished he'd stated that he was the one who'd shot Jonnart. But maybe that was his bruised ego talking. Over time, he'd decided his inability to kill wasn't a fault. He was meant to put his energies into life, laying the groundwork for a better future for the next generation. His own children. It wasn't too late for him to start a family.

The phone's ringing cut short, but he got up anyway to make a snack. The house was shady inside, curtains drawn to keep it cool. It was the house where his mother had grown up, and her father before her, and where his family had often spent weekends with his grand-mother. Although some cosmetic updates were overdue, the house had good bones. Bruno was going to suggest to his mother that he stay there for a few months and spruce it up room by room. He wasn't ready to fully reenter society, to go back to Bastia and be expected to jump into the fray. He felt a pang of guilt taking time alone instead of throwing himself right into the work, but he knew it was necessary. He hadn't been truly alone in two decades.

People liked to talk to him as if they knew how things really went down. They meant well, but no one could understand what it had been like. The only people who did were dead. Not even Nico, that fucking snake, got it right with his "definitive documentary." And Séverine—who knew. In the early days of his sentence, he'd spent hours, entire days imagining where she was, if she was safe, who she was with, and later, what kind of life she'd slipped into, if she was even alive. He couldn't blame her for disappearing, abandoning the cause. She couldn't have single-handedly pulled off the rest of their plans; they'd needed each other to do the work. They were partners. Ah, well. Bruno had long ago resolved to push her out of his mind in order to move on with his life, but admittedly, he'd never fully succeeded.

He took his sandwich out to the balcony. If he settled with Monica, they'd live a quiet and content life of instant coffee in the mornings and interview shows at night. That was essentially what Bruno wanted; no more excitement for him. At the same time, he was wary of this thing that had fallen into his lap; he couldn't help but think there was a woman better suited for him out there—Corsican, educated, someone he could read the newspaper with. A woman who connected him to the world, who enlivened him and brought a sense of possibility within the quiet and content life.

A car passed every fifteen minutes or so. Things were slow in

Fozzano, and that's how Bruno liked it. A little Citroën hatchback approached tentatively, like the driver was looking for an address. It stopped in front of the house. He watched over his book, using it like a shield. He could make out the shadow of two people through the windows and figured they were lost. Cell service was spotty up here; if they asked for help, he'd oblige, but he wouldn't nose around.

Then the car doors opened, and two women got out. The passenger door faced him, so he noticed that woman first. She was in her early twenties, with the long, shapeless haircut girls that age always had. He would have assumed she was Corsican with her olive skin and dark hair, but the sneakers gave her away as a foreigner— American or Australian most likely, judging from her cut-off denim shorts. She looked up at the house, through the wrought iron of the balcony, noticed him watching her, and froze. He quickly turned back to his book. His heart was racing. It was her fright that frightened him, the way she'd looked at the house. What did they want? He peeked out into the street again, and now the driver was standing beside the girl, who was staring down the road like it was all she could do to avoid looking at Bruno.

The woman beside her was older but not quite middle-aged, wearing a loose white dress, staring directly at Bruno with a slight, ironic smile. The mouth, the smile. Bruno stood. She was wearing large sunglasses and a sun hat, so he couldn't see the color of her hair or eyes. The nose was not right, but so radically not right that it became a red flag. That mouth. He clutched the balcony railing.

The sight of this man on his balcony numbed Petra with fear. She didn't look like him, but she looked of him, and it was too much for her. Let her mother lead.

Ramona, for her part, felt a strange lack of surprise upon seeing this new Bruno; of course he'd be here practically waiting for them. He looked healthy in a vain way. She allowed herself to first analyze him behind the screen of her sunglasses, then smiled forthrightly and casually removed her glasses and hat, as she'd been practicing for days.

The woman swept an arm behind the girl like she was presenting her and twirled the girl's hair around her hand in a way that struck Bruno as nervous. The girl would not look up, but the woman was staring at him with warm, hazel eyes that refracted the light in a way Bruno knew intimately.

His expression changed from confusion to an overwhelming understanding.

He was dying; that was the only way to explain it. He was being shown what he wanted to see, his most private dream that he was supposed to have thrown in the fire. His knees buckled against the iron railing.

"You all right?" the woman asked in slightly accented French.

He caught himself and nodded, although he wasn't so sure.

"Invite us up," she said.

"Hold on." He took his water glass inside with him and refilled it from a bottle in the fridge, drinking the whole thing in one go. The act of going down the stairs to let in the two women seemed inappropriately ordinary; he'd have been less surprised if they'd levitated onto the balcony.

He opened the door and the bright light behind them obscured their features, giving him the irrational thought that they were otherworldly imposters. Yet he stepped aside, and they went up the stairs, Bruno following. When the girl passed, she wouldn't look at him, but he couldn't help but stare, her profile only a few inches from his. She had the same smooth hair and aquiline nose as his sister Chiara, and a shadow of her gracefulness. Like a thoroughbred colt, the girl hadn't yet come into her lithe elegance and was still gawky.

They stood in the space between the living room and kitchen, looking around. The house was clean, but Bruno self-consciously looked around as well, through their eyes. It didn't betray much about him; it was simply his family's home, with all his mother's touches. Perhaps that fact betrayed plenty, though. Then the three of them looked at each other, saying nothing. It was so quiet inside, but lively sounds of the outdoors—birds and insects and a few snippets of voices—came through the portes-fenêtres like a recording played in another room.

"You know who I am?" the woman asked, and Bruno nodded. "I go by Ramona now. Ramona Frisch. And this is your daughter, Petra."

He clasped his hand over his mouth, thoughtfully, and rubbed his stubbly beard, taking the girl in. She offered her hand apprehensively, and Bruno removed his from his face to hold it. Instead of shaking it, he examined it—a fine hand, a hand he could imagine as a child's hand and then a baby's hand, one that would have gripped his finger with its new, strong fingers. But this was a young woman's hand, smooth with clipped, unpolished nails, those of a serious and unostentatious person. He used his other hand to clasp her forearm and squeezed, as if verifying she was made of real flesh.

Petra let this happen with a degree of wonder, but nothing seemed strange; they were making it all up as they went. His hands were warm and dry and calloused. A man had never touched her in such a way; she was unaccustomed to men touching her unless for seduction, and that, barely. She felt both the comfort in his touch and her revulsion towards it in equal measure. When he took her chin between his fingers, however, she flinched.

He let go as if he'd touched something hot; he was mortified by her recoiling.

"Tu ressembles exactement à ma sœur. C'est dingue," he said by way of explanation. Petra turned to her mother.

"He says you look like his sister. I dunno. Never met her."

"Elle parle pas français?" Bruno asked Ramona with a tone of reproach.

"Non," she replied without remorse. "We're Americans, we live in Los Angeles. You didn't think to learn English in prison?"

Bruno gave her a dry look and turned to Petra. "I'm sorry, my English is not good."

"It's okay. I'm sorry," Petra said, flustered.

"Something to drink?" he asked.

"Water, please," Ramona said in French. "For Petra, too."

As he busied himself in the kitchen, Ramona sat on the couch, and Petra followed. Ramona was appalled with herself, her impulse to be aloof and semi-ironic. They hadn't even embraced. There was a neutrality and banality to the interaction thus far that disappointed her, although she knew she was the one setting the tone.

Bruno returned with water, glasses, and a bottle of chilled vodka on an old melamine tray. "I think this calls for something better than water," he said in French. "You'll translate for me?"

"When necessary," Ramona said. Really, could she not help herself?

With glasses raised, they waited for Bruno, who kept opening and closing his mouth, to say what he wanted to say. "I have a lot of questions. But I just want you to know—I never thought—" He felt tears rushing forth and took a choking breath to keep them at bay. "I'm very happy you came," he finally finished. Ramona translated, and they clinked glasses.

"Did you know you were pregnant?" was Bruno's first question.

"No. But let's wait to get into all that. Ask her about herself," Ramona replied.

So Bruno turned his attention to Petra, and in a disorderly combination of translated French and broken English, he sought to learn about his daughter. She talked about her studies, her participation in Occupy, the organizations she now volunteered with. It was undeniable: she was his, she was perhaps more purely of him than of Séverine. He thought how powerful blood was. It carried something more significant than the thrill of resemblance—the essence of history. Petra was derived from him and his father and grandfather, going all the way back to a time when their land was unconquered, and his yearning for that time was also embedded inside his daughter. There was no question she was his.

Ramona leaned back into the couch cushions, drinking compulsively while she translated, feeling like a medium passing messages between her daughter and this ghost from her past. They were getting along swimmingly. This was what had often aggravated her about Petra, after all—her Bruno-ness—how she was so serious, so hesitant when it came to being young and carefree.

Despite her vow to be cool and impartial, Petra blossomed in the light of Bruno's attention. She sensed that he'd wanted her long before today, that part of him believed his wanting, rather than a biological act of reproduction, had brought her into being. It was bothersome having Ramona as the go-between; Petra didn't fully trust her to translate correctly. Her mother was being strangely distant, as if she had no dog in this fight, like she and Bruno didn't have their own histories to lay out for each other. Whatever, that was her shit.

Petra and Bruno's chatting progressed out of interview mode into easier, more natural conversations: what it had been like at the Occupy encampment, the amnesty work Bruno did in prison, what prison was generally like, what prison seemed to be like in the US—issues, so many issues to address. He was surprised and impressed that she already knew so much about the island's struggles. He described the mutual aid organizations that now existed in every town, how he and her mother had collaborated with the woman who'd spear-headed this system, although that was considered an open secret.

"Lydia?" Ramona interrupted herself as she translated, and Bruno confirmed. "None of the Kadiris ever went to prison?"

"I didn't say that." Bruno wagged his finger playfully. "But I hear they're quite behaved now. Like me."

As they veered off into a digression Petra didn't understand, she allowed herself a fantasy. She'd sign up for French next semester. She'd return to this place and do her part—maybe even alongside her father. But she was so behind! If only she'd known about her parents, she could have started ages ago. She'd have a language, an origin, a generational wound that would have shaped her sense of self. She'd have a claim. Instead, she was a half-formed being who'd spend the rest of her life trying to fit into this mysterious culture, struggling to reconcile the person she'd been for nineteen years with the hugely disparate person she would have been if she'd grown up with this father.

Then, looking at her parents, recalling everything that had happened to them, she realized a life can be long—maybe spending the rest of hers getting to know this man and this country and figuring out how she fit in to both didn't put her at a disadvantage; maybe it was an endeavor that would enrich and be enriched by her ambition to change this broken world.

At this point, Bruno pulled out the old photo albums and motioned for Petra to scooch towards the middle of the couch beside her mother. Bruno sat on the other side of Petra. All three of them sitting together, like a family. Ramona felt a bit nauseated from the whiplash, how everything already seemed to be changing with such little effort. She stood.

"It's dinnertime. Do you have anything to eat? I can whip something up while you talk."

"There are some premade galettes in the fridge, and ham and eggs," Bruno said self-consciously. Without a word, Ramona went to the kitchen and began cooking. She wondered about the future, how Petra and Bruno could maintain a relationship. He couldn't produce a daughter out of thin air—there would be so much gossip. A story needed to be manufactured; perhaps it was better for her and Bruno to discuss this without Petra. Life had just become so much more complicated, but Ramona would welcome it. She'd been in stasis forever.

Meanwhile, Bruno flipped through the yellowed album that probably hadn't been dug out since the eighties.

"Attends, il y en a une que je veux te montrer," Bruno said. He came to an eight-by-ten portrait of a lovely teenager with long, feathered hair and powder-blue eye shadow. "My sister, Chiara. Your aunt," he said, aspirating the *a*.

It was the first time Petra had ever seen herself in another person, and she was overcome with emotion, shuddering with tears, utterly embarrassed. In an instant, all this complex and layered history had been revealed, involving new places and strange people she'd never met but whose blood coursed through her own veins, and it was satisfying, dizzying, and frightening.

"I'm sorry," she said, wiping her face with her fingers. Bruno wanted to rest his hand on her back, but instead he handed her a napkin.

"Like sisters, non?" he asked.

Petra nodded.

"She live in Poitiers. En France. Maybe one day you meet." He produced a phone from his pocket and opened the Facebook app. "Your . . . *cousins?*"

"Cousins, yeah. It's the same," Petra replied, examining the faces of this new extended family. She hadn't even considered the people who radiated out from a father, who she was also connected to. Her world had suddenly quadrupled in size.

They ate indoors to be discreet. Bruno brought a bottle of wine to the table while Ramona slid a fried egg onto an oozing galette.

"Ah, Sév, will you bring the wine key from the utensil drawer?" Bruno asked.

Ramona tensed with something between nostalgic pleasure and discomfort. No one had called her that for twenty years. She wasn't that person anymore; she should correct him. But no, it was useless. He would only ever know her as Séverine, and perhaps she would always be Séverine in this place, using this language. She would always be Séverine, period.

The alcohol helped them relax and be as normal as they could considering the circumstances. Still, Ramona was remote, and Bruno noticed it. This woman wasn't the Séverine he remembered. She had a darkness about her, not the wicked kind, but like a cool, dark cave teeming with secret life. His various reunion fantasies—picking her up without a word and taking her to his bed, mainly—went out the window. She was still beautiful, even with this uncanny nose, but she was completely closed, the cave sealed. No matter. None of his fantasies had involved her bringing a daughter to him; this gladly consumed his attention.

"Where are you staying?" he asked after their plates were cleared.

"In Ajaccio, by the Maison Bonaparte," Ramona replied.

"I'd invite you to stay, but—"

"I know. We have some logistics to figure out."

"I can meet you in Ajaccio tomorrow," he said.

"Okay," Ramona agreed. The sun had nearly set over the distant bay, and a riotous sunset was fading into moody, dusky pinks and blues. "We should get going before it gets dark. I'm not used to driving these roads. Let alone with a stick shift."

"Right, right," Bruno said.

Ramona translated for Petra, and they stood to leave. With a moment's awkwardness, Bruno opened his arms and Petra accepted his embrace. For the first time, Ramona and Bruno approached each other, kissing dryly on either cheek. She was back in his atmosphere, no longer smelling of Cerruti 1881 but of laundry detergent and a slight, sweet rankness—nervous sweat. Although she'd remembered the cologne more than anything (even buying a sample that she'd kept in her bedside table), it was the smell of his sweat that resurrected the memory of his body, the whole dizzying experience of him. She pulled away abruptly. Then they left him at the top of the stairs and drove back to Ajaccio.

It had gone well, they agreed. Petra gushed, in fact; she'd never imagined it would go so well, even if it was also weird. She began to ask the questions that Ramona had been turning over earlier: How to explain who she was? What about the rest of his family? Could anyone know the truth? When could she come back? Could she get EU citizenship?

"I don't know. We'll figure it out," was all Ramona could say. She was destabilized. The smell of him had reignited a pilot light inside her; it had appeared with a small whoosh, like magic.

By the time they returned to the hotel, it was 10:30 p.m. In silent agreement, they each showered and put on pajamas.

"I've never been so tired in my life," Petra murmured from her bed.

"It was a big day," Ramona said distractedly, sitting on the edge of her bed and massaging lotion into her arms with her back to Petra.

"I just want to say thank you," Petra said. "For bringing me here."

"C'est normal," Ramona replied.

"And for letting me know about you."

Guilt racked Ramona so strongly she had to force herself to turn to Petra, to allow her daughter to see whatever her face revealed.

"I'm sorry I didn't tell you sooner," she said.

Petra shrugged and smiled. "It's okay. I understand why."

Ramona had had to make so many decisions, decisions she wasn't equipped to make, and she knew so many of them had been ill-judged. But she'd always made a bad decision in perfectly good faith and with Petra at the forefront of her mind; it wasn't an excuse, and it could never make up for her failings, but it was her only defense. The fact that her daughter understood and forgave her was a grace she didn't deserve but was overwhelmingly grateful for. Ramona didn't possess that level of generosity, had no clue where Petra got it from. It was mystifying that your child could be part of you yet also so different, channeling spirit and knowledge that was totally unknown to you. A literal miracle.

"To bed," Ramona instructed, and Petra pulled up the covers with the contentment of a little kid full of birthday cake.

Not long after, Petra's soft snores rose from under her blanket. Ramona stood and removed her pajamas, pulling on black linen joggers and a charcoal tank top; she didn't bother with jewelry or makeup, except a little mascara. She left a note on the bedside table in case Petra woke up and gently closed the hotel door behind her.

⁓

Bruno was sitting on the couch with a glass of vodka and one hand on the place beside him where his daughter had sat. Petra, like Petru. As it should be; he'd have chosen the name himself. He was dazed, a bit drunk, basking in the energy the women had left in their wake. He ached at having missed Petra's childhood. He thought he'd be good with young children, the sort of dad a daughter calls for before her own mother. He would have liked to pick her up, feel her small arms around his neck, smell her wispy, baby-shampooed hair. Maybe he could spend some time in the US once his conditional liberation period was over.

But he felt a regret about Séverine. She'd changed; he still didn't know what she'd been through. It must have been difficult to be so young and so alone. It didn't appear that she'd married; there was no ring, no mention of a father figure who'd assumed Bruno's place. He wanted her to be the same girl he'd loved so desperately but knew that was impossible. Still, he wished he'd been able to see some glimpse of her, that she'd felt less like a stranger. He wondered what she'd thought of him.

There was a light knock at the door; at first, he didn't notice, but it continued. Fear gripped him; was it a neighbor come to say he'd seen those two women leave his house, and he knew who they were? Was it Monica making a surprise appearance? He descended and opened the door. It was Séverine.

"I know it's late," she said. "I just—I needed to see you without Petra. We have a lot to talk about."

"Of course," he said, his tone overly accommodating, and he let her in.

He held up the bottle of vodka. "You want the rest?"

"Please."

He poured her a glass, then busied himself lighting a scented candle on the coffee table. It always touched Ramona to see how single men conducted themselves within normally feminine domains—the scented candles, the generic-brand olive oil, how their towels were folded in their linen closets. But this house revealed nothing; it was so plainly his mother's realm, filled with eclectic knickknacks and loud, patterned textiles, lacking the urbane asceticism of Bruno's Bastia apartment.

"Where to start?" Bruno asked.

Ramona took a healthy gulp of vodka and set it on the coffee table. "I wanted to tell you about the baby. I wanted to get in contact with you. I just—"

"You don't have to explain any of that," he interrupted. "Has your life been very difficult?" he asked, not looking at her.

"Sometimes. But overall, we did okay. I think Petra's had a good life."

"I can tell. She's a great kid."

"Despite me." Ramona laughed nervously.

"No," Bruno said with an impatient smile; he'd have none of that. "I wish I'd been there to help."

"I'm sorry about that day," Ramona replied. The transition made sense to both of them.

"I am, too," Bruno replied. "We don't have to do this. Apologize to each other for things that happened so long ago. We're alive. We're here now."

They finally made eye contact, each smiling a little sadly. No one else in the world knew what they'd been through, and they had found each other again in this room. Ramona felt a flood of compassion for Bruno, as well as gratitude. She was overcome with an impulse to hold him to her breast, to nurture him, to be a better mother, and she moved towards him.

She had lost the woodenness of that afternoon and was looking at him with an unfamiliar expression but a potency Bruno knew well. Here was Séverine, finally. As she approached him tenderly, innocently, he moved with wolfish urgency. Ramona found herself enveloped, his face in her hair, he was searching for her neck and sighing, "Séverine, Séverine."

It wasn't what she expected or intended, but when his lips found her skin, it was like gas feeding the pilot light, and something inside her ignited. She didn't need convincing; she found her mouth turning towards his, and he offered it to her. She hadn't realized she was still capable of such desire. She let it quiet her brain and became a pure nerve.

He immediately sensed a maturity in her. His being older had been such an integral part of their relationship—a point of contention and eroticism—but he'd forgotten about it since she'd showed up on his doorstep. They were equals for the first time. Before, they used sex to enact and resolve power struggles, but now, they simply wanted closeness. Maybe their memories were diluted, but they felt new to each other; at the same time, their old love was a reassurance. Unlike the past, they went slowly. They appreciated the gravity of the re-encounter, the delicacy of exposing bodies that had aged. He led her to the bedroom by the hand.

After waiting so long, it seemed imperative to draw out the moment, which—they'd learned from their youths—must eventually end. So they moved languidly, touched with the simplest intentions: to feel each other's skin, to pay reverence to what remained the same, and to acquaint themselves with what had changed. Making love this way was a revelation to both of them: not plowing towards orgasm, no matter how selflessly, but letting pleasure accumulate as a byproduct of total presence and surrender.

How unoriginal that intimacy was the missing ingredient that, for the first time in years—decades!—made Ramona feel so open and Technicolor. Though the character of this intimacy was different from before. When they were young, she tried to assert herself through sex, fuck him into loving her as much as she thought he should. She'd gotten there eventually but as if by a spell, something that occluded his free will. Tonight, however, he showed the willingness to love her without her insistence. This change must have occurred in prison, while he was so deprived. But in that case, he was in love with a memory exaggerated by fantasy; that would be all too apparent down the road. Down the road! Ramona laughed aloud, and Bruno smiled roguishly at her, as if he thought she was saying, *How funny life is! How miraculous!* Why did men never understand how complicated everything really was? That flowering was a sign of imminent death.

A pitying love surged within her, and she pulled him closer, clinging. She sunk her teeth into his smooth shoulder and kissed along his collarbone. She loved him and always would. He had both ruined her life and made it extraordinary.

The room was moonless and humid. He moved with utter attention, if not intuiting the melancholy source of her love, recognizing its force and purity, which amplified his own. She experienced all this emotion and sensation as the light of a collapsed star rushing outward, expanding and brightening and condensing with color, not realizing her eyes were closed until Bruno told her, "Look at me." When she did, there was no metaphor, only Séverine and Bruno in the dark.

6. *U futuru*

Bruno made coffee and they sat in the unlit kitchen; night was already losing its potency and fading into the first traces of morning. It felt both natural and contrived to share this silent hour together.

"Want one?" Bruno asked as he opened a new pack of cigarettes.

"I don't smoke anymore," Ramona said. "I've completed my American evolution."

"No, that's good. I smoke more than ever," he said, lighting one. However, the bright ember intruded too much, so he took one long drag and extinguished it.

"Petra wants to come back to Corsica," Ramona said.

"Really?" Bruno asked, his voice going up a note.

"It's your call, obviously."

"I mean, I'd love her to, if you think it's okay."

"I don't, but it's not my choice."

They listened to the morning encroach: the baker's scooter buzzing down the hill, birds rousing.

"And you?" Bruno asked. "Will you come back?"

"*That* we could not explain," Ramona said. Then, defensively: "I have a whole life."

He looked hurt. "I know—" He shook his head and let out his own little laugh. "Am I an idiot?"

"Yes," she replied tenderly.

He became animated, like a teacher lecturing, the way he did when they used to argue. "Why not try, though? I thought I'd never see you again. Isn't it a sign?"

"It's a test," Ramona said. "You get either me or Petra, but you can't have both."

"But why?" he asked, getting loud.

"What, you're going to shack up with me in LA? An illegal immigrant?"

"We could go somewhere else entirely, the three of us."

"Be real," she snapped. Then more gently, "Petra is just starting her life, and it needs to be on her terms, not ours. Besides, you'd give up Corsica? Everything you still want to do here?"

He looked out the balcony doors. It was still too dark to see the land, but it was out there. It resided outside him in the same way he resided outside his mother—although the connection often felt incidental and irrational, although he often felt unbearably separate, the two were forever inextricable. He'd devoted himself to the betterment of this place because no matter what he felt for it or it felt for him, Corsica was home. He reached across the table for Séverine's hands.

"That doesn't mean we have to be alone like before," Ramona said, threading her fingers through his in a rush of panicky sentiment. "Sometimes I had this feeling that none of it ever happened, that you and Petru and Tittu never existed."

He stood from the table and went into the bedroom, returning with a set of keys that he placed in her hands. She examined them, confused.

"They're from Tittu's motorcycle," Bruno clarified.

"How?" she marveled.

"I have no idea. When I was released, they returned my personal effects—everything I had on me the day of the arrest. And somehow these ended up in the pile."

Tittu's keys that had soaked up the heat of his hands, hands she'd admired for their elegance and adeptness. Hands that had touched her. Some of his warmth must reside within the keys and be able to infuse her skin; she should be able to commune with him. But nothing. They were a jumble of lifeless metal. Ramona placed the keys on the table.

"I don't feel anything. Maybe something's wrong with me." She laughed derisively, and a tear spilled down her cheek, which she hastily wiped away.

"I don't either, truthfully," Bruno said, taking the keys and giving them a little toss. "I mean, they don't make me feel connected to him. Like when you see someone's corpse and it's not *them*. It's the same with their stuff—it only keeps some of the person's essence while they're alive."

She nodded and sat back in her seat. She was crying and didn't want him to see—some ingrained habit of needing to grieve alone.

"I feel so much guilt," she ventured. "Petru sacrificed himself, for what? So I could go back to being the petite bourgeoise he always thought I was? So I could make shitty TV shows?"

"I have the same thoughts. About Tittu," Bruno said. "He wanted you, I got you. He died, I lived. I don't know. It's unresolvable. I've accepted that I've gotta carry it around forever."

"It's funny," she mused. "You have to go on being you every day of your life; everyone will look at you and know who you are and what you've done. But not me. I guess that's pretty unfair."

"To whom?"

She made a short, concessional laugh.

"Yes, people got hurt because of me, and although I know it'll never tip the scales, I'll spend the rest of my life trying to make up for it," Bruno said. "But I'm not ashamed about trying to change something diseased about our world."

Ramona had always felt like fleeing proved the flimsiness of her convictions, and the lifestyle she'd cultivated afterwards only confirmed that. But once more, she allowed herself to be swept up into Bruno's certainty and passion. Maybe she'd been compromised from the start, but part of her had acted in good faith, and a very large part of her had acted out of love. Maybe she could be unashamed of those parts, too.

"Do you ever dream about them?" she asked.

"Yeah, but it's unfulfilling. We don't sit and talk or anything."

"I rarely dream about them anymore," Ramona said.

"Maybe that means they're at peace," Bruno proposed. "I used to go to sleep praying for a dream about you. An explicit one," he said, like a little boy testing his limits. "But I was rarely so lucky."

Ramona couldn't help but smile conspiratorially. "I had a few good ones."

Their smiles faded; it felt silly to be talking this way when they were finally in front of each other.

Bruno cleared his throat. "In general, I think we delude ourselves about sensing the dead around us."

"Petru would disagree with you," Ramona said.

"True," Bruno acknowledged. "But we're not like him, are we?"

"Maybe because we've been disconnected from this place too long," Ramona suggested. "Maybe we'd have felt their presence with our feet on the land."

Light was swilling out the darkness; they could distinguish each other's features more clearly in the tranquil gray.

"You're so adult now," Bruno teased.

Ramona smirked. "That doesn't turn you off?"

He shook his head, taking the joke. "Oh, Sév. What am I supposed to do? Go back to this sad little life I was making for myself? You're all I thought about for twenty straight years."

Ramona felt herself falter. But no, she didn't want to encumber herself with more lying and concealment and looking over her shoulder. What *did* she want? Companionship, sure. Dawn coffee with a great lover was nice, but spontaneous texts to meet for drinks after work would be nice, too. She still wanted lots of time at home, cooking and sleeping alone, and when she fancied, with another person. She wanted to be close to Petra again, like they'd been when she was a child, and to see her parents more often. She could never live without concealment, but she wanted to redirect it, expand the lie in a way that facilitated living more authentically.

"You've also grown up," she said. "I can tell you want boring. So, get yourself a boring woman. Let your life be boring so you can have your daughter."

A ray of pure, white sunlight cut through the east-facing balcony windows. They were no longer in the private liminal period of the early morning dark; it was incontrovertibly a new day.

"So this is it?" Bruno asked.

Ramona nodded even though she felt a crazed uncertainty. A voice inside was pounding at her chest, screaming that she was an idiot, this was her great love, fuck the rest! He stood from the table and pulled her by the upper arm, drawing her against him, reaching up the T-shirt of his she'd thrown on.

"Then let me give you a proper goodbye," he murmured.

She sighed in resignation and with renewed desire. Would he never leave her alone? Would she be held willingly captive in this house, too? She imagined Petra sitting in the hotel room, pissed off and a little anxious, like a parent waiting up for a delinquent kid. And like the delinquent kid she'd been and apparently still was, Ramona put Petra's worry out of her head and caved to Bruno as she'd always done.

Bruno reveled in encouraging their worst judgment. He'd been so good for so long. Like Ramona, he had the sense that any place they occupied together became a bergerie, a sanctum. There was work to do, relationships to tend to, lives to be reestablished, but the future could wait till tomorrow. They drew the curtains and returned to the bedroom, to their old habits.

⸻

At first, when Petra sat up in bed and called for Ramona with no response, she panicked, then spotted the note on the table. She'd spent the night with Bruno. They were *fucking*, which real parents don't do. It hit her that Ramona needed Bruno in some way that was beyond the reach of any other man, beyond Petra's reach even. Her mother wasn't self-sufficient at all—she'd been exiled from her object of desire.

Only now did Petra realize that if there *had* been any coercion, her parents had nonetheless cultivated some deranged relationship in which they'd been perfectly united in ideology and appetite. Bruno had made her different, blown open her world, and Séverine had done the same for him. No one could live up to that, or understand—least of all Petra. There was only one person who could, and Ramona had chosen to be with him, after that earth-shattering day, instead of with Petra in the hotel.

Yet Petra didn't feel abandoned; if anything she felt liberated, secure. For so long, Petra had wanted Ramona to take her seriously, to be honest and real with her. They'd spent all these years in a deadlock, tense and unmoving, but finally her mother had yielded. She'd allowed Petra to see her as a whole person—one who'd acted unhinged and was fallible and even needed some man—and in doing so, acknowledged Petra as a whole person, too. What did she need the reinforcement of her mother's attention for, then? That acknowledgment was more than enough.

She opened the windows to gauge the temperature and found it was a perfect sunny day.

"Raiponce, Raiponce, dénoue et lance vers moi tes cheveux!"

She looked down and saw two guys, a bit older than her, looking up from the street and laughing. They were making fun of her, she knew.

"No français," she called back.

"American girl!" they exclaimed, as if this only made it better. They consulted, then one of them translated, *"Raiponce, Raiponce,* throw us your hairs!"

Petra burst into a laugh and retreated from the window but felt an instant claustrophobia in the small, dim hotel room. So much of her life was spent shying away from laughter, retreating into classrooms, meeting rooms, offices. Petra had thought serious endeavors were undertaken only in small, dim rooms. But in this moment, she felt criminally shut away. Her parents were shut away now, too. It was probably the only way they knew how to be with each other.

The immensity of their undertaking suddenly hit her. They'd been fierce in their actions but had burned fast and hot. What was left of that mania? Petra, for one. But something more consequential must remain, too, no matter what her mother said about being a flash in the pan. The energy of their movement had been revelatory, even if Séverine and Bruno slunk out of sight. What they exposed—

connections among different kinds of people, a sense of power within the exploited, the value and limits of violence—must remain. It seemed that history was comprised of a series of overcorrections, and progress somehow inched along between those wild swings. Her parents had precipitated one of those swings firsthand, and that was not insignificant.

Petra wasn't audacious or impulsive like them, and while this initially seemed like an inadequacy, honestly, she didn't want to be. Maybe it was fine to make use of her extraordinary inheritance by being one of the ordinary people, someone who nudges progress forward between the wild swings—unconcealed, acting in the full light of day. And if she was going to allow herself that privilege, maybe she could also embrace a bit of Séverine's vitality. Maybe it was correct that devoting yourself to a cause required loving life, loving the people you were fighting for—not abstractly but literally. Being open to the whole kaleidoscope of experience, including distractions, indulgences, sensuality.

With manic energy, she got dressed and dashed down the spiral stairs to the cool, shaded lobby. She had no sense of where to go or what to do on this island, no plan for herself or Ramona or Bruno, at least not today. She knew only that she must heave open the doors and join the bright morning world.

"*Du calme, du calme, mademoiselle,*" the concierge reproached as Petra sped by the front desk, throwing an absent smile over her shoulder.

She'd left no note on the nightstand in their hotel room. Ramona would relish worrying about her this way; so rarely had Petra given her mother that opportunity.

Acknowledgments

Thank you to Chris Clemans for his vision, acumen, and tenacity. Thank you to Seema Mahanian for the brilliant care and attention she put into the editing of this book and for making artistic collaboration a pleasure. Thank you to James Roxburgh for the essential contributions he made to the editing process and to Shana Jones for her keen eye. Thank you to Roma Panganiban and Maya Petrillo-Fernandez for their invaluable input. Thank you to Pamela Dorman for her enthusiastic support and to the Viking team for bringing this book into existence.

Thank you to Jacob Albert, Nick Almeida, Christina Drill, Fatima Kola, Vincent Scarpa, and KC Sinclair for their profound insight on early drafts—the most generous expression of their friendship. Thank you to my cohorts at the University of Texas and the Stegner Fellowship.

Thank you to Jennifer Egan, Ben Fountain, Adam Johnson, Chang-rae Lee, Jim Magnuson, Lou Mathews, Elizabeth McCracken, and Elizabeth Tallent for their mentorship. Thank you to the staff of

UCLA Extension, the Michener Center for Writers, and the Stanford Creative Writing Program.

Thank you to the following friends and family for opening their homes or Rolodexes in service of this novel, for their patronage, or for introducing me to a subject that became integral to *The Bombshell*: Will Brewer, Nick and Kate Delacruz, Suzanne and Jim DePietro, Jim Gavin, Alexandre Joly, Stu Katz and Elaine Gavalas, Karan Mahajan, Andrew Morse, the Petaccio family, David Sanchez, J. Ryan Stradal, and Alex Weisler.

Thank you to Kim, Tom, and Hallie Farr for their unquestioning confidence that I could pull this off. Thank you to Carmen Petaccio for being a ruthless and perceptive critic, for making innumerable sacrifices for the benefit of this book and my writing life, and for embodying the kind of writer I wish to be: one whose craft is rooted in a vision of a more beautiful world, love for others, and a lust for life.